SECRETS IN THE HEATHER

Gwen Kirkwood titles available from
Severn House Large Print

Home to the Glen
Children of the Glens
A Tangled Web
Laird of Lochandee

SECRETS IN THE HEATHER

Gwen Kirkwood

Severn House Large Print
London & New York

This first large print edition published 2008
in Great Britain and the USA by
SEVERN HOUSE PUBLISHERS of
9-15 High Street, Sutton, Surrey, SM1 1DF.
First world regular print edition published 2007 by
Severn House Publishers, London and New York.

British Library Cataloguing in Publication Data

Kirkwood, Gwen
  Secrets in the heather. - Large print ed.
  1. Scotland - Social life and customs - Fiction 2. Domestic
  fiction 3. Large type books
  I. Title
  823.9'14[F]

  ISBN-13: 978-0-7278-7670-6

Printed and bound in Great Britain by
MPG Books Ltd, Bodmin, Cornwall.

Where the pools are bright and deep,
Where the grey trout lies asleep,
Up the river and over the lea,
That's the way for Billy and me.

Where the blackbird sings the latest,
Where the hawthorn blooms the sweetest,
Where the nestlings chirp and flee,
That's the way for Billy and me.

Where the mowers mow the cleanest,
Where the hay lies thick and greenest,
There to track the homeward bee,
That's the way for Billy and me.

Where the hazel bank is steepest,
Where the shadow falls the deepest,
Where the clustering nuts fall free,
That's the way for Billy and me.

Why the boys should drive away
Little sweet maidens from their play,
Or love to banter and fight so well,
That's the thing I never could tell.

But this I know, I love to play
Through the meadow, among the hay;
Up the water and over the lea,
That's the way for Billy and me.

A Boy's Song
James Hogg (The Ettrick Shepherd)

One

Thirteen-year-old Andrew Pringle found himself further up the glen than he had ever been on his own but he was eager to catch a glimpse of the vixen and her cubs. He knew he ought to keep well away from the old quarry but he was sure he had heard a whimper from an animal in distress. His blue eyes scanned the scrub and rough grass which had grown up in crevices since the quarry was last worked a dozen years ago. The sound came again. He thought it was below him and he stepped as near the edge as he dared. Loose stones and rocks immediately broke away, rolling and crashing over the jagged outcrops, some of them to land in the water which had gathered far below. Andrew shuddered, but the animal whimpered again. He had to investigate. He lay on his stomach and eased himself towards the edge of the quarry. He gasped when he realized he was on the edge of an overhang which could break away any minute. He moved back swiftly and as he did so the soft whine became more distinct, more urgent. It doesn't want me to leave, Andrew thought.

He walked further round the rim of the quarry until he judged the ground was firmer. Again he lay on his stomach and shifted forward. Almost directly beneath him was a narrow ledge. A scrubby sapling seemed to have sprouted from the bare rock but it was enough to prevent the animal from falling to its death. It was not a fox. It was a collie dog. Andrew's heart began to thump. His eyes searched the surrounding area. There was no path to the ledge, but there were several boulders interspersed with stunted bushes. He judged the ledge was not much more than twelve feet below him. He refused to let his mind dwell on the nothingness beyond.

Andrew was intelligent and he was not usually impulsive, but he knew the collie was pleading for help and his young heart couldn't resist. He eased himself over the edge. Slowly, testing each rock, each bush, he made his way down. He breathed a huge sigh of relief when he reached the ledge. The collie looked up at him with melting brown eyes. He dared not rest his own weight against the sapling and the ledge was narrower than he had realized, petering out to no more than a ridge in the red sandstone face. Carefully he squatted down beside her. He spoke gently and patted the velvety head. She whined softly and tried to stretch, almost as though wanting to show him where it hurt. He felt her legs gently. There didn't seem to be any broken bones but she had a nasty gash on one front leg and another on her flank. The blood had dried and the wounds looked stiff and sore. A silver disk told him her name was Nell.

'How long have you been here, Nell? Without

food or water...' She pricked her ears at the sound of her name but she was obviously weak. The problem was how to get her back up. Could he even get out of the quarry himself?

Down at Darlonachie Castle Polly Pringle paced the floor of Garden Cottage trying to push away her anxiety.

'George, are you sure you didn't see Andrew after school? Did he say he would be late, Willie?' she demanded for the umpteenth time.

'No, Ma,' the boys chorused wearily, then turned to grin at each other. There was eleven months between them and what one did the other did too. They were often in trouble, late for school, late home, boots not cleaned, trousers torn. It made a change for Andrew, their elder brother, to be earning their mother's wrath for once. Secretly they were very proud of him. He was the brightest pupil in the school and he was kind and reliable. It never occurred to them that Andrew could be in serious trouble, even danger. 'Here's Father home,' Willie called. 'Maybe Andrew's been helping him at the gardens.'

'Is it that time already?' Polly ran outside to meet her husband but Joe had not seen their eldest son either. Polly was distraught. 'George, Willie, keep an eye on wee Josh,' she commanded sternly. 'I'm going up to the castle to see if Victoria is in the kitchens. She usually helps her granny after school. Andrew always sees the wee lassie home safely. Maybe she knows where he's gone.'

'Aw Ma, Victoria Lachlan's not a wee lassie now. She'll be ten in November.'

'Well, she's always adored Andrew and he's taken care of her since the day she started school. They're always chatting. If anyone knows, it'll be Victoria. It'll be dark soon...'

'Not for another couple of hours yet, lass,' Joe comforted but Polly could see the anxiety in his eyes, and the frown lines on his brow. He was worried too.

'Your meal's on the table, Joe. Eat it up. You must be tired,' Polly said softly. 'I'll not be long.' She reached up and touched his cheek. Joe and her four boys were Polly's whole world. It was true she had craved for a wee girl when Josh was born so much later than the other three, but they were all healthy and strong and she was thankful for that.

Jane McCrady had been the cook at Darlonachie Castle for as long as Polly could remember. She had just finished serving dinner to Sir William Crainby and his son, Luke, when Polly entered the kitchens. Victoria was standing on a stool scouring the copper pans in the big sink. They looked at Polly in surprise.

'What's wrong, Polly? Sit ye down here and get your breath back,' Jane McCrady said with such motherly warmth Polly wanted to cry. Victoria got down from her stool and came to stand close beside her, brown eyes wide, sensing the older woman was in trouble. She loved Mrs Pringle and her husband, Joe. Jane McCrady, her great-grandmother, was the only living relative she had, but the Pringles had always welcomed her into their home. She didn't like to see Andrew's mama so pale and upset.

'It's Andrew,' Polly whispered. 'He's never been home. Did he walk home frae the school with ye, Victoria? Did he say where he was going? That he would be late? Can—'

'Calm down, Polly. I'll make you a cup o' tea,' Jane McCrady interrupted. 'Now, lassie, did you come home from school with Andrew as usual? Tell Polly if he said anything while I make some tea.'

'We always walk home together,' Victoria said, 'but this afternoon Andrew said he was going somewhere. He said it was a secret.' She pouted and Jane McCrady knew she had not been pleased with Andrew. 'He always takes me with him when he's looking for birds' nests, or for fish in the burn, but he said I was too little to go this afternoon. He said it was a long way and it might be rough. He wouldn't tell me where, not even when I said please. Six times. He shook his head and he left me when we got to the wood.'

'Which direction did he take?' Jane McCrady asked.

'Through the wood, but I don't know after that. But when we were eating our pieces at midday I heard Angus Bell whispering about some fox cubs he'd seen.'

'Foxes! Oh Jane.' Polly put both hands over her face. 'D'ye think he's got caught in a trap in

11

the wood?' She stood up. 'I must go and tell Joe. We must search before it gets dark.'

'Drink your tea first,' Jane McCrady urged, but Polly was already at the door.

Too late Andrew realized he should have gone for help before trying to rescue the collie on his own, but he was here now, stuck on the ledge. It was too late to be afraid. There was nothing but fields on either side of the quarry. No one would hear even if he shouted. He assessed his position. Further to his left was a slightly bigger protrusion of rock than the way he had come down, but it was further away. He needed to be able to reach high enough to lift the collie on to it and then follow himself. He had to try. He bent and talked softly. Her brown eyes were trusting, reminding him of Victoria's. As he slid his arms under her he prayed she would not struggle or they would both end their days in the bottom of the quarry.

Andrew was tall for his age, but not quite tall enough. He was desperately afraid he would overbalance and fall from the ledge with Nell in his arms, but she lay still as a statue. He strained up towards the ledge, on his toes now, pressing into the rock face. He had almost given up hope of reaching when the collie seemed to understand what he needed. She eased herself from his outstretched arms on to the ledge. She was safe, but it had cost her. He could hear her panting and the soft moan of pain. He scrambled on to the rock he had used to descend, but he needed to reach the one where Nell lay so still and so near the edge. There was nowhere to put his feet. He reached out one gangly young limb. Again Nell seemed to know instinctively. She eased herself backwards until he could stand beside her. Four more times they repeated this manoeuvre but a jagged rock carved his leg and for a moment Andrew felt sick and dizzy with the severe pain, but with one last effort he lifted Nell on to the soft grass at the edge of the quarry and scrambled after her. He lay face down, trembling with relief, knowing his knees were shaking too much to bear his weight until he recovered. Thank goodness he hadn't brought Victoria. He had been sorely tempted to relent when she pleaded so eloquently.

Eventually he got to his feet and stood looking around him wondering which way to go and where Nell lived. As though in answer she struggled to her feet and moved slowly in the direction she wanted to go, before she collapsed on to the grass. Andrew lifted her in his arms and set off up the slight incline. Once across the field he could see the peaks of roofs in the field below. He rested a while, feeling the ache in his muscles and the pain in his leg. It was bleeding quite fast but his mother always said bleeding would clean the wound. He pulled up his stockings. He would be fourteen in July and he would wear breeches then and go to work, like his father, or at least he hoped he would. There were thousands of men who couldn't get work and last year hundreds of people had marched from Tyneside all the way to London to protest.

He was very tired by the time he reached the farm. He realized at once this was Langmune and the tenant was a Mr Rennie. He was barely known in the village and rumour had it that he was a short-tempered, miserable sort. Andrew chewed his lip anxiously as he made his way through the yard. A man came out of the dairy. He stared at Andrew. He set down his empty pails and, as far as he was able, he hurried towards them. Andrew set down his burden with relief. As he straightened he met the man's eyes, saw the incredulity and relief there. He also heard the rasping breath.

'Nell...' he breathed hoarsely. 'You found her.' He bent and patted the dog's head. She had pricked her ears at the sound of his voice, now she tried to wag her tail. 'A-ah, laddie. How can I thank you. Where did you find her?'

'In the quarry, sir. Maybe she was chasing off the foxes. She was trapped on a ledge. She's hurt, but I don't know where.'

'Aye.' The man crouched beside his beloved bitch. He ran his hand gently over her belly. 'She's having pups. The fall will have brought them early...' He looked from Andrew's legs up to his face. 'She's not the only one who is hurt either. That's a nasty gash you've got. It's bleeding fast. We must bathe it and bandage your leg. Can you manage to carry Nell just a bit further? To the house?' He held his chest and gave a rueful smile. 'Asthma,' he wheezed. 'I'm not as fit as I used to be.'

14

Andrew looked at the grey eyes and the man's pale smooth skin. This must be Mr Rennie then, but he didn't seem like a crabby old man. Andrew lifted Nell in his arms for the last time and carried her into the house, setting her down, as Mr Rennie instructed, in front of the fire but not too close.

An elderly woman came bustling from the pantry. She stared from one to the other, then down at Nell.

'You've found her? She's alive? Thanks be to God.'

'The laddie found her. Rescued her too, I'm thinking, judging by his wounds.'

'Aye, that leg's bleeding fast. I'll attend to it. What's your name, laddie?'

'Andrew Pringle from Darlonachie Castle. My father is head gardener there.'

'Bring me the iodine, please, and some water and bandages, Miss Traill. I'll attend to Andrew if you will make some warm milk for Nell. It's been three days now. She's bound to be weak and she's going to have her pups early, I reckon. I expect this laddie could do with some food too, once I've dealt with his wounds. All your knuckles are bleeding, I see.'

'They'll be all right.' Andrew brushed his wounds aside. 'It's just my leg.'

'Yes. I'm sorry, but this is going to sting. It's very deep. You need stitches. If I bind it up to stop the bleeding will you promise me you'll go straight to Doctor Grantly and let him deal with it? I'll write a letter telling him to send the bill to me, but tell him I need a reply.' He gave a whimsical smile and looked Andrew in the eye. 'You promise to see him as soon as you get back?'

'Is it really bad enough to need the doctor, sir?'

'Yes, it is. You're a brave laddie and we don't want anything to go wrong. It's a nasty cut. I'll attend to Nell's wounds when she's drunk some milk.'

'Will she have her pups soon?' Andrew asked.

Mr Rennie hesitated. She would have them very soon, he thought, and they'd probably be dead. He didn't want the boy to witness that.

'I expect she'll have them in a day or two.'

'Can I come and see them?' Andrew asked eagerly. 'I always wanted a dog but Ma says she has enough to feed with me and my three brothers.'

'I expect she has at that.' Mr Rennie nodded. 'I doubt if Nell's pups will survive this time after all she's been through, but if any of them do, you can choose the name. And come up to see Nell whenever you like. Can you read?'

'Of course I can read.' Andrew stared at Mr Rennie indignantly. 'Mr Nelson, the schoolmaster, says I'm one of his best readers, but I enjoy it.'

'Very well. I'll write a note and send it down with one of my men. Will you be at church on Sunday?'

'We usually go.'

'I'll tell you how Nell is getting on then. But

16

remember, I don't expect any of them to survive from this litter.'

'Thank you, Mr Rennie.' Andrew's blue eyes glowed. 'I'd love to come to Langmune again.'

Miss Traill smiled at his eager face as she brought him a plateful of freshly baked soda scones and cheese as well as pancakes spread with her homemade raspberry jam. It was only then he realized how hungry he was, and how late it was getting.

'Are you going to be a gardener like your father?' she asked.

'I don't think so. I like helping him and growing things but there's only two apprentices at the castle now. There used to be six when Father was young. Anyway I'd rather work with animals if I can get work. I shall be fourteen in July.'

'And you're leaving school then?' Mr Rennie asked.

'I must. I have three younger brothers. It's time I earned my keep.'

'I see.' Mr Rennie eyed him shrewdly.

'Thank you very much, Miss Traill. I was hungry. Now I must get home or Ma will wonder where I am.'

'Don't forget to see Doctor Grantly,' Mr Rennie insisted. 'And, Andrew, there's plenty of jobs about a farm for a laddie who is keen to work. You can come here any Saturday you like. If you like the work, and if you're any good, I'll find you a job in July.'

Andrew stared at Mr Rennie, his mouth

17

slightly open with surprise. 'You really mean that, sir?' he breathed incredulously.

'I never say anything I don't mean, laddie. You'll find that out if you come to work for me at Langmune. You'd need to board at home though. It's too much work for Miss Traill having young men in the bothy, but you could save up for a bicycle.'

'I could, yes I could, if I have a job and earn some money.' If Andrew's leg had not been so sore he would have skipped out of the door and all the way home. He couldn't wait to tell Victoria he had rescued a collie dog and then been offered a job.

When he reached the corner of the wood Andrew knew he ought to get home but he had promised Mr Rennie he would see Doctor Grantly and home was nearly two miles in the other direction, besides the blood had seeped through the pad and dressing. So on he trudged. Mrs Grantly opened the door and showed him into the surgery but Doctor Grantly soon appeared and Andrew was thankful to lie back on the leather couch while the doctor took off the bandages. He felt dreadfully weary.

'It's very deep and it will need stitches but I'll be as gentle as I can.' Andrew's face was white by the time the stitches were finished and there was a sheen of perspiration on his brow and upper lip. Doctor Grantly washed his hands and opened the envelope. He smiled.

'Mr Rennie doesn't really need an answer, Andrew. He is worried about you and he was

18

making sure you came to me. Anna...?' he called for his wife. 'Would you ask Bennet to yoke the pony and trap please? I will take Andrew home now.'

'Oh no! Please. I can walk. Ma would be furious.'

'She will certainly be worried. It's getting late. Anyway I would like to see her. Don't worry, it will not cost your parents anything. Mr Rennie tells me you're a hero. He thinks the world of his collie dog and he's grateful to you. It was rather a stupid thing to do, Andrew, to go into the quarry on your own,' Doctor Grantly added gravely. 'If you had fallen in no one would have known where you were.'

'I know. I'm trying not to think of it,' Andrew admitted. 'I don't tell lies, doctor, b-but I don't want Ma to know, if I can help it.'

'Very well, but promise you will never do anything like that again.'

When Doctor Grantly drew up at the gardener's cottage a group of men had gathered and they were about to set off in search of Andrew. Polly was beside herself with anger and relief and finally burst into tears. Joe had to soothe her and Andrew felt guilty and weary and wondered whether he might burst into tears himself and show himself up in front of the estate workers. He was thankful when Doctor Grantly intervened.

'Andrew will tell you all about it tomorrow, Mrs Pringle, but for now he needs to get to bed and have peace and quiet. He also needs plenty of fluids. He has lost a lot of blood. Make sure he rests his leg tomorrow. We don't want the bleeding to start again.'

'Yes, doctor,' Polly said meekly and ushered her eldest son to his bedroom without more ado. Before he went to sleep George and Willie crept in to say good night.

'We never get off so easily with Ma,' George said, grinning. 'You're lucky, Andy.'

'They were really worried,' Willie said, 'we all were.'

'I'll tell you about it tomorrow,' Andrew said sleepily, then he remembered, 'but I think I've got a job for when I leave school.'

'A job...?' they echoed in unison, but Polly came and swept them away.

The following morning Victoria was at the Pringles' cottage before Joe had left for work. She was sure she had been awake all night worrying about Andrew and picturing him lost in the woods with his leg mangled in a trap and unable to move. Both Joe and Polly assured her Andrew was fine and sleeping like a baby.

'He'll tell you all about his adventures tomorrow, Victoria. He usually does,' Polly said, smiling. 'In fact, you're probably the only one who will get the whole story out of him,' she added dryly. 'But if ever he worries me like that again...'

'You'll hug him and put him to bed just the same, Ma,' George said with a yawn, pulling on his braces as he clattered down the wooden ladder from the loft, where he slept with Willie

20

and Josh.

Andrew had all the resilience of a healthy youth and by the middle of the following week he was well on the way to recovery. True to his promise Mr Rennie had sent word that two of Nell's five puppies had survived and one of them was to be Andrew's. He chose the smallest and named him Mick.

Not all the residents of Darlonachie village were so happy though. Doctor Grantly wished with all his heart he could cure the world's ills but that very morning he had received a telegram informing him of the death of his only sister, a widow living in Lancashire. News of Agnes's unexpected death was hard enough to bear but the future of her young adopted son caused Peter Grantly even greater concern.

'Are you thinking of bringing the child back to Scotland, Peter? I mean to live? To attend our wee school, the same school as...' Anna Grantly's low voice faltered into silence. She watched her husband's restless fingers smooth out the telegram for the fourth time.

'There's nothing else I can do. I stole him from his own family,' he added almost under his breath.

'You didn't *steal* him, Peter...' Anna rose and moved round the breakfast table to lay a gentle hand on her husband's shoulder. He was a tall, distinguished looking man with his thick hair streaked with silver and blue eyes that could twinkle at a child or darken with compassion for a bereaved family. Now he held his head in his

21

hands, his shoulders bowed.

'Who am I to play God? I took the laddie away from his own flesh and blood. Now I see the damage I have caused.'

'That's nonsense, Peter. You did it for Agnes and she loved Mark dearly.'

'I know.' Peter Grantly nodded. 'That night... when he was born...so unexpected and so frail ...I felt it was God's will. Agnes longed for children. Adopting was her only option, but it was wrong of me.' He rubbed his brow.

'Dear Peter, you acted with the best of intentions, as you always do where your patients are concerned. Mark brought Agnes great joy. He couldn't have had a more loving mother, or a better home.'

'But now he is an orphan. I was wrong to take him from his own kith and kin.'

'Mark was an orphan anyway, and he has enjoyed many privileges with Agnes which he would never have had. None of us could have guessed she would die so young.'

'We don't know for certain he is an orphan. His father...'

'Ten years have passed and the father has never come forward. We shall never know who he is after all this time,' Anna said briskly.

'I suppose you're right.' Doctor Grantly sighed, drawing a hand across his eyes.

'Well then, Peter, stop blaming yourself. You acted with the best of motives.'

'Maybe, but it doesn't help young Mark now. I must leave at once to deal with the funeral

arrangements. I shall bring him back with me.'
He looked up into his wife's face. 'Will you
mind very much having a child in the house
again, Anna?'

'Not at all.' Anna Grantly smiled. 'On the few
occasions Mark has spent holidays with us it has
been a pleasure. I never heard a child ask so
many questions.'

'Aye, he's a lively laddie. He told me he
wanted to be a doctor.'

'Well I wouldn't count on that!' Anna chuckled wryly. 'By now he's probably decided he
wants to be everything from a boxer to a train
driver.'

'I expect you're right, Anna. I do thank you,
my dear.'

'Whatever for?'

'For agreeing to give the laddie a home with
us. It helps ease my conscience. It doesn't do to
try arranging other people's lives.'

'We must forget about the past. There are only
three people who know what really happened
during that dreadful night nearly ten years ago.'

'Three of us.' He sighed, then straightened his
shoulders, knowing what he had to do, but was
it possible to keep a secret in a small community?

Try as he might Peter Grantly could not put the
night of Mark's birth out of his mind. The train
chattering over the rails seemed to mock him.
'You took him away...you took him away...You
were wrong to do it, you were wrong...'

He gazed unseeingly at the signs of spring: the fat green buds of the trees and hedges, primroses holding their pale perfect faces to the sun, a little bird darting by with grass for a nest. Even the happy gambolling of several lambs in a field close beside the line did not gain his attention. His mind was on that fateful November night in 1917.

It was nothing short of a miracle that one baby had survived considering the complications. Half an hour later, with all the skill and knowledge he could call upon, he had brought another frail and wrinkled mite into the world. Amazingly he had given a pitiful whimper, but it had been enough. He breathed. He lived. But not all his years of learning, or his patient skill, had been enough to save the life of the innocent young girl who had borne the infants. Peter rubbed a hand over his eyes, trying to banish the memories which flooded his mind.

Two

Before he boarded the train Dr Grantly had called on Jane McCrady. He had told her of his sister's death and of his plans to bring Mark back to Darlonachie to live with himself and Anna, as their nephew. He had watched anxiously when the colour drained from her lined face. She had proved herself to be a woman of great courage and strong character, but as he held her arm in a gesture of support, he had felt her tremble.

'If you agree,' he said gently. 'I see no reason why anyone should know his true identity. Mark is small for his age, but he is a wiry, happy wee fellow – or at least he has always been so until now. He is bound to grieve for the woman he believes to be his mother. My sister loved him dearly.'

The old woman nodded silently, feeling the awful tightness in her chest.

She watched the doctor take his leave. Was it possible to keep such a secret in a small community such as this? If the boy discovered his real family, would he blame her for allowing him to be taken away? Would he blame Doctor Grantly? Should she have suggested he make his home with her now? But what future could she give him. She was an old woman, a cook whose home was a cottage which was tied to her being able to carry on her work.

'Mistress McCrady, the soup's burning,' the young kitchen maid said urgently. 'Shall I give it a stir?'

'Aye, aye, you do that, Milly.' Jane McCrady slumped on to a chair beside the long scrubbed table in the centre of the kitchen.

'Ye're awfy pale,' the girl said with concern. She had never seen Mrs McCrady sitting down in the middle of the morning. 'Will I make ye a

25

cup of tea?'

'Yes please, Milly. You're a good lassie.' Milly's eyes widened, then she grinned. That was praise indeed. She was more often being told off for daydreaming. Her mother insisted Mistress McCrady was the best cook in the county and she was lucky to get work in the castle kitchens. Her mother helped with extra cleaning at the castle on the rare occasions when the laird gave a dinner party, or, even more rarely, if there were guests to stay. Mrs McCrady was both cook and housekeeper now, and as much a part of Darlonachie as the laird himself.

Her mother liked to reminisce and Milly liked to hear of the old days when Lady Crainby was alive and there had been the butler and footmen and maids for nearly every room. Half the castle was closed now and Sir William cared little for traditions.

'There's only Mistress McCrady left who knows about the old days, and the old ways, and how to train a girl to the standards of a gentleman's household,' Milly's mother insisted. 'So you pay attention, my girl.'

'But if the laird doesna worry, why should we?'

'Because the young laird will marry and there'll be a new Lady Crainby one day. She will want things done the way they're done in London, or at least in the best country houses. We don't want her bringing new folks here because Darlonachie folk aren't good enough.'

'Will there be parties and dances again if

26

Master Luke gets married?' Milly asked.

'That will depend on his wife, and whether she's wealthy. Things are changing, lassie, and not all for the better. Everybody thought it would be a better world after the war but it isn't. So, you make sure you keep your job at the castle and you'll have a full belly and a bed at night.'

Jane McCrady sipped the tea gratefully, aware that Milly was watching with both concern and curiosity. The doctor's news had disturbed her. Surely God must consider her a wicked woman, she thought. Why else would He have given her so much grief to bear in a single lifetime? It was all very well the Reverend Dewar assuring her the good Lord always gave His children strength to carry their load, but recently she had felt her strength ebbing and her conscience was troubled anew.

Later, she stood at the sink preparing vegetables, but for once her mind was not on her work. Her thoughts were with Victoria, her great-granddaughter. Would her beloved bairn ever forgive her if she discovered how she had been cheated? Ever since she could toddle the child had been like a ray of sunshine, lighting the darkness which had clouded both their lives. She never complained. At seven she had stood on a stool in the castle kitchen eager to help wash dishes. Now at ten years old she was a bright, intelligent child with a passion for books, but she never neglected her tasks; but it was her ready smile and the happiness she radiated which brought joy to Jane's heart. She was full of enthusiasm, whether she was learning to cook, or following Joe Pringle around the gardens, asking questions about his plants. Jane knew she couldn't bear it if Victoria blamed her when she discovered the secret surrounding her birth.

Rain and wind battered the windows of the little cottage later that evening reminding Jane McCrady of the flood which had almost wiped out her family. It was twenty-four years ago, but the memory of that night would remain with her until her dying day. She shuddered.

'What's wrong, Granny?'

'Nothing, 'tis nothing, ma bairnie, just the wind. Hear how it howls. There'll be storms before morning I shouldn't wonder. It always reminds me of –' her voice sank – 'of that night. The night the bridge was swept away.'

'Tell me about it, Granny?' Victoria pulled a low stool up to the old lady's knee and bent her head on to her lap, as she had done as a small child. Slowly Jane McCrady began to stroke the soft, dark tresses, and as her hand moved her thoughts turned to the past, as they did often of late.

'Lady Crainby had been on a visit to her own family in Fife. She had received a letter to say her mother was seriously ill. Master Felix had recovered from the measles so she took him with her, and the baby, Mary. Nanny went with them too. Master Billy and Master Luke still had measles so they had to stay behind.

'I was head cook at the castle by then. Polly Pringle's mother, Mistress Cole, was my best friend and she was the housekeeper. It was a happy place...' She sighed. 'Albert, your great-grandfather, was head coachman. We had Jenny, our bonnie lassie... She loved bairns, and they loved her. When she was fourteen Lady Crainby gave her a job as an upstairs maid, but after Master Billy was born she helped Nanny in the nursery. Time went by and more babies came along...

'Willie Lachlan was under-coachman. He lived next door to us. He was a kind, gentle man, six years older than Jenny. We were happy when they married. He would have been your grand-father, lassie, and he would have been so proud o' ye...' Her voice shook a little but she went on. 'Even after Elizabeth was born Lady Crainby asked Jenny to bring her own baby and continue helping Nanny.'

'The baby, Elizabeth, she was my mother?'

'Aye.' She sighed. 'She was three years old. The laird sent word down to say Albert was to take the coach and meet her Ladyship at the station. It was a night such as this, only worse. It had rained the day before, and all through that night. It was still raining as darkness fell again, and the wind was howling like a banshee by the time the coach was ready to leave for the station. Willie Lachlan was like our own son. He was afraid the coach would get stuck in the muddy lanes on the way to the station so he went too. It was a dreadful night...' She stopped and stared into the fire.

Eventually she went on in a low voice. 'Nanny had been taken ill with the measles. She was too ill to travel with them. Jenny knew the children would be frightened and tired and her Ladyship was not used to caring for them herself. The coach was ready to leave when she grabbed her coat and bonnet and ran out to join her father and her husband...' She stopped talking again. The hand on Victoria's head trembled, but she kept very still, waiting.

'They were nearly home – so very nearly home...' Jane McCrady's voice quavered. 'Some of the men thought the coach must have been almost over when the bridge was swept away. The coach, the horses...everything...went down into the water. The river was in spate. They were swept away.'

Victoria trembled as she pictured it in her head. 'D-did they all drown, Granny?'

'All of them.' She shuddered. 'They were trapped... Couldna get them out...' Jane's voice shook. Even after all these years the memories of that dreadful night were as vivid as ever.

'And the little girl? Elizabeth...?'

'Puir wee bairn, she cried sorely for her mama. There were only the two of us left.' She stared unseeingly into the embers, her lined face sad, her thoughts faraway. 'The laird was a true gentleman, kind and considerate, even in his own grief. Two new coachmen had to be hired so I moved here, to Burnside with wee Elizabeth. Nanny came back. The laird said Elizabeth should spend time in the nursery with Master Luke while I carried on as cook. Luke would be about fourteen months old and Master Billy was seven or eight. He was the eldest and went away to school. Master Roddy, the laird's nephew, used to join them for lessons and games. They all treated Elizabeth more like a sister than the bairn of a servant.'

'Was she a happy little girl, my mama?'

'Aye, I think she was. She had a sunny nature and everyone was kind to her. But as time went on, without her Ladyship to take charge, things began to change. The boys often came down to the kitchen with Elizabeth. They liked to eat with us when Sir William was away in London. Master Billy loved bread and butter pudding...'

'But he went to war? Mrs Pringle told Andrew he was very brave, but he never came back, did he?'

' 'Tis true, my bairnie. War is a cruel state. His cousin Roddy had been fighting in France already...' she said slowly, reliving events in her mind, searching her memory as she had done so many times before. She shook her head as though clearing it of unwelcome visions.

'They were very brave to go to war...' Victoria prompted softly.

'Brave – or maybe foolish. Or maybe the world forced them to go. Able-bodied young men who didna volunteer were sent a white feather...'

'A white feather? But why?'

'It meant they were cowards. Sir Rodderick Manton had been injured and he was at home for Master Billy's coming of age party. We scarcely recognized the young man who had gone so readily to war.' She frowned. 'I think he was sick, but the doctors didn't agree. He was no longer the carefree boy we had seen galloping his pony across the glen, laughing and singing, joining his cousins here at the castle. He looked haunted, desperately troubled. Some of the men who fought beside him said he suffered terrible nightmares. But I shouldna be burdening you with such things, my bairn.'

'Mrs Pringle tells Andrew stories about the war,' Victoria said. 'She says it's better to know how bad it was, then men will not be so keen to fight again.'

'Perhaps she's right. The men around Darlonachie, and as far as Lockerbie and Annan and Dumfries, all have stories to tell, those who were lucky enough to return. Many of them fought beside Master Billy or Master Roddy. They still tell of their bravery but it was little comfort to Lady Manton, the laird's sister. She never recovered from Master Rodderick's death. He was their only child. People say she died of a broken heart. But lassie...' Her fingers stopped their gentle stroking and she raised Victoria's face to hers. 'Life is not always as kind to us, as we would wish, but it is God's will. We have to accept it. We have to be strong even...even when we are full of grief. Remember that, Victoria. "The Lord giveth and the Lord taketh away."

Never give up. We must soldier on. Remember that, lassie,' she said urgently. 'There'll always be another dawn, and blue skies to follow the grey.'

Victoria nodded without understanding. She would have liked to ask more about Elizabeth, her own mother. Recently she had begun to wonder about her father too, but she sensed that Granny was lost in memories that brought sadness to her heart. She drew away from her lap and moved to the chair on the opposite side of the fire, finding it hard to understand why terrible things should happen in the world.

She had always felt happy and secure with Granny at the castle, or here in their cosy cottage, but now she understood why Sir William sometimes looked sad too. He had lost two children in the floods, and Master Billy, fighting in France. He had not taken a new wife as Sir Joshua Manton had done, but he still had Luke. One day he would be the Laird of Darlonachie and there would be a new Lady Crainby if he married. Milly said there would be would be footmen and more maids at the castle then, and parties and dances.

Unknown to Victoria, her grandmother's thoughts were on the last grand occasion the castle had witnessed. Although she was small for her age, by the time she was fifteen, Elizabeth was a capable young cook and a tireless worker. She had proved this on the cold February day when Darlonachie had celebrated the coming of age of the young William

Crainby, heir to Darlonachie Estate.

Jane McCrady's nimble fingers stilled. Her eyes took on a faraway stare. Try as she would she had never been able to put her finger on the significance of that night when Master Billy had celebrated the approach of manhood. Yet she was convinced that something had gone dreadfully wrong. Something which had changed all their lives.

Three

The young Master William was convinced it was his duty to fight for the freedom of his country. In spite of the pleading of his father, and of his aunt, Lady Christina Manton, he was determined to follow his cousin's example.

'Cousin Roderick has been in the army for almost a year now, and he's younger than I am,' he argued.

'But you must see the change in him, Billy dear?' Lady Christina said, wringing her hands in sorrow. 'Did he not tell you of the horrors which...which waken him in the night...?' She broke off, her pale face crumpling as she struggled to hold back the tears. Even for the sake of her beloved nephew and her brother, she could not bring herself to describe the nightmares, the sweat drenched body of her own brave son –

then worst of all the harsh sobs which followed. 'Did you not talk with Rodderick, Billy?' she asked in a hoarse whisper.

'We had so little time, dear Aunt. His leave was so short. I was honoured that he came north for my sake. Now I must follow his example and do my duty for my king and country.'

Jane McCrady knew nothing of the horrors of war, but she would never forget the black despair she had felt nine months later. She would have given her own life willingly if only her beloved Elizabeth could live. Had she not borne enough sorrow with the loss of her husband and her daughter? But it had not been God's will to spare her beloved granddaughter.

That autumn night when Elizabeth died, it had been almost as bleak and stormy as the night her parents were swept away in the flood. But it was not the weather which had caused her death. She had died in childbirth. For the second time in her declining years Jane McCrady found herself nurturing a defenceless child – her great-granddaughter. Her faith was sorely tested by the death of Elizabeth, barely more than an innocent child herself. She had prayed for strength, and time to succour the small scrap of humanity Doctor Grantly had placed in her arms. She had named her Victoria after the late queen.

There had been no father to offer love, or support; no grandfather, or great-grandfather either. If she had to live her life over again, Jane Mc-Crady knew in her heart she would make the

35

same decisions she had made that night, just as she would always wonder, had she been wrong? Had she committed a sin?

Sir William had asked no questions when she had kept Victoria in her pram in the castle garden, or in the kitchen beside her. She had been a contented baby and she had grown into a happy child.

'That bairn's too old for her years,' Polly Pringle often remarked if she came upon Victoria standing on her stool to help in the kitchens, or kneeling to weed in the gardens beside Joe Pringle, Polly's husband. Polly had been an upstairs maid at the castle before she married Joe and produced four sons of her own, but she still had a very tender heart for the smiling little girl with her childish prattle.

'Send young Victoria down to play with our brood,' she would say if Jane McCrady was busy with the season's produce, bottling fruit, making jams and chutneys or pickling beetroots or onions. 'One extra bairn makes little difference to me and the lassie should have young company.'

'She enjoys Andrew's company. She says he shows her how to climb trees or where to look for birds' nests... And she loves looking after young Josh and pushing him in his pram.'

'Aye, aye, and he smiles like an angel when she's around.'

Doctor Grantly called at the schoolhouse the evening he arrived back from Lancashire.

'Come in, come in, doctor,' Harry Nelson greeted him. 'I'm pleased to see you're back again. Did you bring your nephew home with you?'

'You heard of my sister's death then? It doesn't take long for news to get around in this community, does it?' the doctor said wryly.

'No, it does not, and what people don't know they soon invent,' Harry Nelson added. 'But I was sorry indeed to hear of your loss.'

'Thank you. It was rather a shock.' A look of pain passed fleetingly over his face. 'She didn't mention her illness. I think she was anxious to protect young Mark, but he's an intelligent boy. It has been a shock to him too...'

'Yes, it must have been. But you are prepared to give him a home, I understand? He will be attending the school here?'

'Yes, for a time at least. Losing his mother, and his home, changing schools and losing his friends, they are big changes for a ten year old.'

'They are, but we are a caring community and children soon adapt. If he is as intelligent as you say, doctor, perhaps he will present a welcome challenge for one of my pupils. Another enquiring young mind will be beneficial to them both.'

'Andrew Pringle, you mean. But he will be fourteen soon and he has been offered work up at Langmune Farm. It seems a waste of a good brain.'

'I believe Andrew will use his brain whatever he undertakes. His parents will welcome the money with three more sons to feed and clothe.

But it is not Andrew I'm thinking of. It is young Victoria Lachlan.'

'What makes you say that?' Doctor Grantly demanded sharply.

Harry Nelson looked at him in surprise, seeing his face was paler than usual. He must be under a lot of strain. 'Apart from Andrew Pringle, Victoria is by far the brightest pupil I have in the school and she thrives on challenge. Competition will be good for her. Besides they have much in common. They are about the same age and they are both orphans. I hope they will get along together and help each other.'

'Oh, I see...' Doctor Grantly passed a hand over his brow.

'You are tired. You have had a lot of anxiety this past week, doctor,' Harry Nelson said with sympathy. 'Take a dram before you go?' He went to the big sideboard and drew out a crystal whisky decanter and poured two measures. 'Things will fall into place, don't you worry. Your nephew will soon settle in. Shall I expect him on Monday morning? There's no use putting it off – the ordeal of a new school will loom large on his small horizon.'

'Yes, you're right. And, yes, I am tired. I shall be guided by you regarding Mark's education, but I expect him to attend Dumfries Academy in due course.'

'I see...' Mr Nelson said as he nodded. 'So you hope he will be fit for university? Maybe even follow in your own footsteps perhaps?'

'Perhaps.' Peter Grantly drained his glass and

stood up, drawing a weary hand across his brow. 'I shall make sure he is at school on Monday morning.'

The two men parted amicably and with mutual respect.

Victoria was eager to learn to be a proper cook. Already she could make the crispest of pastries, and a smooth egg custard, which was more than Milly could do despite Jane's efforts to teach her. When she was not helping her grandmother she became Joe Pringle's shadow around the garden.

'The bairn knows more about plants already than the two lads will ever know,' Joe would say when he lost patience with one of the young apprentices. The truth was Victoria was keen to learn from anyone who had time to answer her questions, including the laird himself. He had found her wandering around the empty schoolroom and taken her to the library to show her pictures of wild animals and exotic flowers. When the village school was on holiday he had given her a book of fairy tales with beautiful illustrations. It was one of her most treasured possessions. When she was not at school, or helping in the kitchens or garden, her favourite refuge was the library. The laird encouraged her to read any of the books which took her fancy. In fact he guided her choice of reading with infinite patience.

Lady Christina Manton, the laird's sister, had gone into a decline after the death of Rodderick, her only son. After her death Sir Joshua Manton had married the widow of a squire with a daughter of her own. The new Lady Manton had called unexpectedly one afternoon and discovered Victoria reading in the library.

'She was really sharp and nasty with Victoria,' Milly reported indignantly to Jane McCrady. 'I heard her telling Sir William he shouldn't allow her in the library.'

'What did the laird say?' Jane McCrady asked. She had no wish to take advantage of Sir William Crainby's tolerance.

'Och, he shrugged his shoulders. He said Victoria always took care of his books and she should be encouraged to read whenever she had the opportunity. Lady Manton said servants should be kept in their place, and that the standards at the castle were appalling, and she didn't see how poor Luke would ever be fit to be the next laird.' Milly mimicked Lady Manton's waspish tones.

'Oh dear. Perhaps I'd better tell Victoria to stay out of the library.'

'But she loves the books!' Milly protested. 'Anyway, folks say Sir William doesna care for the new Lady Manton.'

'That's gossip. We don't know what he thinks, Milly,' Jane McCrady cautioned, knowing the young maid listened at half-open doors, then frequently let her tongue run away with her.

'Well, he's always stiff when she and her pasty-faced daughter call. Ma says Sir Joshua and the first Lady Manton often came to dinner

40

in the old days, but the laird hardly ever invites them to dinner now.'

'The first Lady Manton was Sir William's sister and they were very close.'

'Ma says a lot of things have changed since the war. I wish the laird would invite people to dinner again.'

'It would mean a lot more work for all of us if he did. Remember that, Milly.'

Four

There was great excitement in school as the children awaited the arrival of Doctor Grantly's nephew. The doctor was well known and respected in the community so the boys were squabbling over who should sit beside him.

Mark Jacobs was not nervous about having a new schoolmaster or about his lessons, but his young heart was sad at leaving everything that was familiar and he had loved his mama dearly. The thought that he might never again see his best friend, Jimmy Witherspoon, had also troubled him until Aunt Anna promised he could invite his friend to visit in the holidays.

He soon found that his main problem was being able to understand everyone. He couldn't tell what the children were saying when they all gabbled together.

41

The boys were surprised and disappointed when Mr Nelson seated the new boy beside Victoria Lachlan and instructed her to help him get to know the ways of the school.

'And Andrew, will you introduce Mark to the other boys and show him the toilet at the end of the yard?'

'Yes, sir.'

Many times in the ensuing years Andrew looked back on those days when Mark Jacobs came to Darlonachie School and wished he had had the foresight to push him into the toilet and flush him away. Such violent thoughts were alien to Andrew's nature and he was ashamed whenever they came into his mind, especially since he was honest enough to admit Mark was a likeable kid. He was bright and eager to learn, and his upbringing had made him more polite and mannerly than the rest of the pupils. In fact, Andrew had quite liked the doctor's nephew during the short time they were both pupils together. It was only later he began to envy Mark Jacobs.

Victoria felt honoured to be seated beside the new boy, but she was less pleased to discover he was better than her at mathematics.

'How did you get on at school today, and was the doctor's nephew there?' Milly asked with eager curiosity when Victoria returned from school that first day. Jane McCrady listened intently.

'He's sitting next to me,' she said proudly. 'His name's Mark Jacobs.'

42

'Is he a nice laddie?'

'Mmm...He's all right...' Victoria screwed up her small face thoughtfully. 'But he talks funny. He says "bewks" instead of books and "skewl" for school, and things like that. I think he must be a bit deaf. Sometimes he doesn't understand what I'm saying.' Then she added honestly, 'But he's better than me at mathematics'

'Is he?' Milly was surprised. 'I thought you were Mr Nelson's brightest star – teacher's pet according to Georgie Pringle.'

'Och, Georgie is jealous because he doesn't like school. There was only Andrew who was better than me before. I didn't mind that because he's older and he's nice. I'm better than he is at spelling and I got a better mark for my essay, but I'm a day older than Mark Jacobs so –' her dark eyes gleamed – 'I'll ask Andrew to help me so I can beat him at mathematics.'

'Andrew will not be there much longer. His pa was telling us he's saving up to buy a bicycle so he can get to Langmune in time for the morning milking when he starts work.'

'I know.' Victoria sighed. 'Why do people have to go to work...?'

'Ach, lassie, you know well enough there'd be nothing to eat and no clothes to keep us warm if we didn't work to earn them,' her grandmother said reprovingly.

Victoria nodded. She was more aware of this than most children. She might have been sent to an orphanage if she hadn't had a great-grand-mother who worked so hard and loved and cared for her.

'But why are there so many books if we haven't time to read them? Andrew says Mr Rennie has books about farming and he's going to lend them to him. And he gets magazines about farming every week. One is called *The Scottish Farmer* and the other is *The Farmer and Stockbreeder*. Andrew is going to read them too.'

'Och, you and your books!' Milly scoffed. She had never read anything since she left school. She flounced away to the dining room to make sure she hadn't forgotten anything before Mistress McCrady went in to check.

'You'll miss Andrew when he starts work, my lassie,' Jane McCrady said reflectively. 'He's a good laddie. Mr Rennie must think so too or he wouldn't have offered him a job when there are so many men without work. Will you walk to school with Georgie and Willie next term?'

'Oh no. They're always late, then they get into trouble.'

'But it's a long lonely walk in the winter.'

'I shall run fast and I shall call for Mary Hardie. She lives at the last cottage, at the side of the long wood.'

'Yes, I know. Her father is a ploughman at Home Farm. But it's a long way to her house on your own.'

'But I'm not little any more, not like when I started school. Andrew gave me piggyback rides on the way home because my legs were short and I couldn't keep up.'

'Aye, he's always been a kind laddie, has Andrew. I hope he gets on well with Mr Rennie and his housekeeper.'

'Miss Traill is old but she is going to give him a hot dinner at twelve noon on the dot, every day except Sundays.' Victoria repeated Andrew's words exactly. Her grandmother smiled. Andrew and Victoria had always confided in each other. She would miss his company more than she realized.

'Wee Josh will be starting school soon.'

'Yes, Mr Pringle says I can take him to school after the summer holidays. Then Josh will be on time and only Georgie and Willie will get into trouble.'

'I see...' Jane hid a smile. Victoria and the head gardener were great friends. Joe admitted he had missed her lively chatter when she started school. He looked forward to the holidays as much as she did herself.

As spring turned to summer Victoria and Mark became good friends, sharing a love of learning which few of the other pupils understood. Mark missed his mother badly and it comforted him to know that Victoria had no parents either. He found the village and the school quiet after the bustle and friendships of a larger school, but he became accustomed to the Scottish accent and picked up some of the local slang, much to his aunt's dismay and the doctor's amusement. He was learning to share Victoria's enthusiasm for catching tadpoles, her patience when searching for a bird's nest, and naming the wild flowers. Later he joined in her search for hazel nuts, or gathering brambles to make jelly. Mark sensed a reserve in Andrew Pringle but the older boy was generous in his sharing of country lore, showing Mark how to identify animal footprints in the mud beside the burn, or explaining the difference between a hare and a rabbit.

Andrew had become a working man shortly before his fourteenth birthday and Victoria missed his company around the castle grounds and in the gardens where he had often helped his father. Mark went to stay with his old school friend for two weeks but he was happy to return to the village. Jimmy Witherspoon returned with him. Both boys enjoyed accompanying Doctor Grantly on his rounds. While he visited his patients they investigated a burn or climbed a tree to search for birds' nests. Jimmy would have liked to make a collection of eggs to show his school chums back home, but Victoria had said it was cruel to rob little birds of their eggs.

Then came a day when Doctor Grantly had to make a call at one of the cottages near the castle. No sooner had he closed the car door behind him than the two boys were speeding along the back drive in search of Victoria. Mark had often listened with envy as she and Andrew discussed the castle grounds and the gardens. He was eager to see for himself. They came to the high wall which surrounded the kitchen gardens and fruit orchard but they could see no gate and no way to get in.

'Listen...' Mark said, 'that's Victoria's voice. I can hear her talking.' He put both pinkies to his mouth and gave a piercing whistle.

In the garden Victoria was picking the fat green pods from the peas ready for her grandmother to cook that evening, and as she worked she chattered to Joe Pringle who was on his knees weeding. At the sound of the whistle Victoria almost dropped her basket. Excitedly she sat it on the ground and returned the whistle.

'What's that ye're doing? Trying to deafen me, are ye?' Joe Pringle asked with a twinkle in his eye.

'Oh no. Andrew showed me how to whistle like that,' she lowered her voice conspiratorially. 'Now it's a secret code for when Mark needs me.'

'The doctor's laddie? But why would he be near here?'

'I don't know. Mark?' she called in her light young voice.

'I'm here. How do we get over this big wall?'

'You'll have to come round to the gates...' Swiftly Victoria issued directions. 'It's quicker if you come to the kitchens. I'll meet you.'

Jane McCrady's first impression of Mark was his wide smile, and hair the colour of polished chestnuts, like Victoria's. His was short and neatly brushed with a parting which could have been drawn with a ruler, but there were bits which wanted to curl, as Victoria's did, in spite of the neat plaits she wore to school. Jane's hand shook. Carefully she set down the pan of soup.

Was she the only one who saw the resemblance?

Victoria was ushering the boys out into the garden to introduce them to Joe and to show them all the plants he grew.

'Och, lassie,' Joe chuckled, 'Doctor Grantly will have plants in his own garden.'

'He does have a garden, but not like yours, sir,' Mark said earnestly.

Joe blinked at the boy. No one called him sir. He was an ordinary gardener. 'Mr Hardy comes to take care of it but he only grows potatoes and cuts the grass. He doesn't grow vegetables like this –' Mark gestured with a wave of his arm – 'and we don't have fruit.'

'In that case, young Victoria, ye'd better pick a few strawberries for your friends to sample.' Victoria needed no second bidding.

The boys had tasted a variety of samples by the time Doctor Grantly eventually found them. He looked harassed and anxious.

'I'm so sorry, Mistress McCrady. I never thought of them wandering so far.' He looked at her keenly, noting her pale, lined face.

'He's a fine boy,' she said, but her voice shook. She cleared her throat. She was glad Milly was busy in the morning room setting the table for luncheon when the three youngsters came into the kitchen.

'Oh.' Victoria said, her voice flat with disappointment when she saw Doctor Grantly. 'Mark and his friend were going to help me shell the peas for Granny. They've never done it before.'

'Well, young lady,' Dr Grantly smiled at

Victoria, 'I'm sorry if I've come too soon, but I do have other calls to make.'

'Couldn't you leave us here, Uncle? We could easily walk back home, couldn't we Jimmy?' His friend nodded.

'I don't think so, boys. Forgan House is nearly a mile further than the village.'

'Please, Uncle. We wouldn't be a nuisance. Victoria has so much to show us...'

Doctor Grantly chewed his lower lip. His eyes met Jane McCrady's.

'They seem to get on well...' she said slowly, the words forming of their own volition. 'Leave them be. They can sit outside to shell peas. I–I don't think the laird would mind for once.' Dr Grantly raised his eyebrows and rubbed his jaw.

'You want them to stay?'

'If it will please them.' She couldn't tell the doctor how guilty she felt at keeping them apart. She sat down heavily on a kitchen chair and pressed a hand to her chest. Hard work never killed anyone, but tension...Yes, tension was another matter. It brought a weight to her chest. Guilt, relief, anxiety for the future. Every night she prayed she would live to see Victoria grow to womanhood.

Twice Mr Nelson had told her Victoria would make an excellent teacher but education needed money as well as intelligence. It would mean sending Victoria to the academy in Dumfries and she would have to stay in the hostel there during the week. Jane just managed to scrape by already. 'The Lord will provide' it said in the

49

Bible. It was another of the Reverend Dewar's favourite texts, but how could He provide? She was an old woman. How much longer could she continue to give satisfaction with her work. Sir William never complained or interfered but Master Luke was taking over the running of the estate and when he married there would be changes.

Five

The bond between Mark and Victoria strengthened as time went on. They spent most of their free time together and Doctor Grantly felt a growing concern.

'There's no harm in friendship,' his wife reassured him. 'They're still children and it's good that Mark has found someone to share his interests.'

'Yes...He has settled better than I dared to hope after such an upheaval in his young life and I realize Victoria's companionship has helped him a great deal, but...'

'Victoria will not hold him back from his studies. She seems as keen to learn as he is. I'm astonished that she is able to provide the competition he needs.'

'Why should that surprise you? Because she is

a girl?'

'Of course not! Girls are as intelligent as boys, though not always as knowledgeable about the same things. But Victoria Lachlan has such a different background...'

'Don't forget she has the same blood in her veins,' Peter Grantly warned morosely. 'Why shouldn't she have the same potential? Mr Nelson gives her all the help he can and Sir William encourages her to use his library. According to Mark, he even selects books for her himself. She reads more widely than Mark.'

'Yes, but he is more knowledgeable about mathematics and science,' Anna said in quick defence.

'I know.' Dr Grantly smiled broadly. 'You leap swiftly to his defence, my dear, like a mother hen with her chick. Does that mean you have grown attached to Mark?'

'Yes, I'm afraid it does,' his wife admitted slowly. 'How the time has flown. It doesn't seem possible he's been here a year already. I couldn't bear to lose him now.'

'There's no reason why we should lose him.' He patted her shoulder reassuringly.

'I don't know.' She gave a slight shiver though the June day was warm. 'He spends all his spare time up at the castle since we bought him a bicycle.'

'Precisely. I feel he is up there too often,' Peter Grantly said. 'He tells me Victoria helps her grandmother and sometimes he helps too, or spends time with the Pringle boys in the woods.'

He frowned thoughtfully. 'I fear Mistress Mc-Crady is growing more frail as the months pass. Victoria is a good, considerate child. It's such a pity...'

'What is?'

'It's a pity Victoria has only her great-grand-mother to support her.'

'Do you think Sir William would put them out of their cottage if she was unable to carry out her duties as cook?' Anna asked with concern.

'No, Sir William would never put Jane Mc-Crady out of her home. He will never forget the sacrifices her family made for his wife and children. That is not his way, but he will not be here forever. In any case, there are several empty cottages on the estate these days. Things are not so prosperous since the war. There are fewer workers on the farms too. I heard a rumour that the laird is hiring a live-in maid to help Mistress McCrady in the kitchens though.'

'Why are you concerned for Victoria then?'

'They would have no money to live on if Mistress McCrady was unable to earn a living. Mr Nelson is convinced Victoria would make an excellent teacher, but he knows she will not have the opportunity.'

'Are you thinking we should help Victoria, as well as Mark?' Anna asked.

'No. Mark will need many more years of education, and all the support we can give him, if he is to become a doctor. We have our own son and daughter to consider too, and soon we shall have our first grandchild.'

'That's true,' Anna said, nodding eagerly. 'If only Annabelle lived nearer...'

But her husband's mind was not on his own daughter. 'There are many people in need...' he said, his voice troubled.

'You mean those patients you help even though they cannot pay?'

'And those who are too proud to admit they need my help because they have no money. And those who are beyond help. The world was supposed to be a better place when the war finished but there's little sign of improvement, even here in the countryside. I'm told it is ten times worse in the towns where men cannot get work and women and children die for lack of nourishment. It is two years now since the general strike but still many men are unemployed.'

The gardener's cottage and the two coachmen's cottages were near the back of Darlonachie Castle, forming one side of a square courtyard. Adjacent to the head coachman's cottage were the stables and beyond them one of the workshops had been converted to a garage for Mr Luke's new automobile. The remaining estate cottages were further away, scattered in various parts of the grounds, the woodmen's being near the sawmill and the old mill cottage near the ruin which had been a grain mill until the war. The joiner and two other handymen lived in a little row of three. The workers from Home Farm nearly all lived close to the farm steading, and then there were the two elderly gate keepers in the lodges at the end of the east and west drives.

Victoria knew several generations of her family had lived in the main coachman's cottage until the flood, which had taken her grandfather and great-grandfather. It was in tiny Burnside Cottage where Victoria had been born. She loved it dearly, with the box bed where Granny slept, and the cosy hearth in the winter time. The burn ran by the end of the long sloping garden. Wild primroses grew on its banks in the spring-time and bluebells gleamed beneath the surrounding trees.

Burnside Cottage was about half a mile from the castle via the gravel track but there was a short path through the small copse on the other side of the castle gardens. Victoria knew the surrounding grounds like the back of her hand but Mark was always eager to explore and to know more about the castle and its families.

'There was nothing like this where we lived in Lancashire, even though we lived in a village,' he said to Victoria. He described the mill towns where workers lived in long rows of back-to-back houses and smoke darkened the sky from the tall mill chimneys. Victoria couldn't imagine such places.

One of their favourite haunts was a rocky outcrop in the middle of the copse. It was not far from the castle but to them it was a small world of their own. Wild flowers grew in the cracks and crevices and the tops of the two highest rocks were purple with heather in the autumn.

From the top of the highest rock they could look out over the little copse to the glen spread out below them and the lands of Darlonachie all around, with the river flowing fast and free to the Solway Firth. On clear days they could see beyond the Firth to the Cumberland Hills to the east and the Galloway Hills to the west. Mark shared Victoria's love of the view stretching out to the horizon.

Sometimes he would stand on the topmost peak with the wind blowing through his hair and his arms spread wide and shout out the words.

> Behold! A giant am I!
> Aloft here in my tower,
> With my granite jaws I devour.

Then he would run down the hill chasing Victoria until they fell together on the short grass and their laughter filled the air.

When the wind was keen and rain threatened, they took shelter in the hollow between the two large rocks. A smaller outcrop joined the two and made a welcome overhang, giving protection from wind and rain, except when the wind blew from the south. It had become their favourite meeting place. Mark was happy to lie there with a favourite book while he waited for Victoria to finish her tasks.

Their imagination knew no bounds and the small cave became everything from a palace to a dragon's den, a dungeon to a fortress. Neither could have guessed they had been conceived in that very place, when the girl who gave them life had been only a few years older than themselves, and every bit as innocent. They knew nothing of the effects alcohol could have on a sensitive young man trying to drown the memories of suffering, of deaths too horrible to contemplate, a man desperate to overcome an abject fear of returning to the hell known as war.

The days were growing shorter when Sir William waylaid Jane McCrady in the upper hall.

'I believe I mentioned the new maid I have engaged to help you, Jane? She will be arriving this week.' He gave her a kindly smile. 'Her name is Eve Ware. She was recommended to me by Lady Manton. I understand she has done some cooking, but I rely on you to train her in the ways of Darlonachie. I hear you are passing on your skills to young Victoria already?'

'Och, the bairn has been around the kitchens since she was born. She never stops asking questions so she canna help but learn.'

'Then I'm pleased we shall be assured of another excellent cook in our kitchens.' He smiled and went on his way, but Jane sighed heavily. Victoria should have had a better life than a servant. She loved her books; Mr Nelson praised her ability and he was not a man who gave credit easily. She shook her head wearily.

'The laird has engaged a woman called Eve to help me in the kitchens,' she told Victoria later. 'So, ma bonnie bairn, you'll not need to spend so much of your time helping your old grandmother in future. You can roam around the countryside in the fresh air with Mark, or read your books in peace. Life will be easier for both of us.'

Three weeks after Eve Ware started work Jane McCrady knew how wrong she had been. The woman was both sly and lazy and it felt as though her own work had doubled instead of halved. She was frustrated beyond endurance. She rarely gossiped, so Victoria was surprised to overhear her talking to Polly Pringle in the garden.

'I can't rely on Ware to cook anything,' she said in exasperation. 'She told Milly she had been hired as assistant cook and she has no intention of doing a maid's work, yet she doesna ken the difference between oatmeal and pearl barley, she canna boil an egg, she can't even make a custard without it curdling. I don't know where she learned to cook – if she ever did. My bairn can peel the vegetables in half the time it takes her to do them. I canna trust her, and that's worse than having nobody.'

'Maybe she lied about having cooking experience,' Polly said. 'She certainly lied about her age. If she's only twenty-nine then I'm still a bairn!'

Victoria didn't wait to hear any more. She was meeting Mark and she was not interested in ages. Anyone over fourteen was old in her eyes. Andrew had always been her best friend and confidant, but he seemed different since he started work up at Langmune Farm. He wore a flat cap now and his legs were bound around with sacking above his clogs. Georgie said he had started shaving and he was thinking of growing a moustache, and he put oil on his hair to make it lie straight because the other men teased him about his wavy locks. Victoria had always loved his curly hair and the twinkle in his blue eyes. She didn't want him to change and she missed him terribly.

As the weeks passed Victoria found herself sharing her grandmother's dislike of Eve Ware. She had a vicious tongue. She took credit for things she hadn't done and she tried to get Milly into trouble, blaming her for mistakes she had made herself. Jane McCrady knew Milly's faults well, but dishonesty was not one of them. She was not taken in by Eve Ware's lies, but disagreements made for tension. The atmosphere in the kitchens was no longer pleasant and welcoming. Victoria was uncertain whether she should help her grandmother or whether her presence in the kitchens made things worse. She sensed the Ware woman's resentment and it puzzled her. She had always been welcome around the castle and all she wanted was to help Granny.

Victoria and her grandmother had always eaten their meals with Milly and the other servants. There had been no mistress at the castle for so long that things had grown increasingly informal. Sir William liked it that way and Mr Luke couldn't remember when things were different. He had an easy, friendly manner and the servants and tenants liked and respected him. Jane McCrady had been in charge for more years than he could remember and she had always provided good food, well presented and correctly served. The standards below stairs had never fallen, not even when Mrs Cole, the housekeeper, retired. Jane McCrady had simply continued to supervise the indoor staff, ably assisted by Miss Frame who was in charge of household linens and furnishings and kept the upstairs maids on their toes.

Sir William had never enjoyed the formality of the vast, cold dining room. Both he and Luke preferred to dine in the morning room. This arrangement did not please Eve Ware. She had believed she was stepping up in the world when Lady Manton procured a place for her with Sir William Crainby of Darlonachie Castle. She was aware the woman had only used her influence with a view to furthering her own plans for a match between her daughter, Henrietta, and Mr Luke. It pleased her even less when she discovered two large golden Labradors stretched out in front of the fire while the two gentlemen ate their meal.

She was determined to make changes, so she insisted Milly must set out the meal in the main dining room.

'And there's no need for you to go telling the old woman in there,' she hissed, jerking her head towards the kitchen where Jane was making pigeon pie.

'But we never...'

'You do now. I'm here to take charge!' Eve snapped, 'It's time things improved around here, so don't argue. Lady Manton was right, the old woman should have been sent packing long ago. She says the castle needs another Lady Crainby to take charge and raise the standards.'

'Is that right,' Milly sneered. 'She'll be trying to wed that whey-faced daughter o' hers to Mr Luke next if she—'

'That's exactly what she intends to do,' Eve said haughtily, 'and you'll know a difference then. Miss Henrietta will probably send you off with a flea in your ear when she becomes Lady Crainby.'

'Who says! Her father was only a squire, and not a very wealthy one either, if the rumours be true.'

'Well, she's Sir Joshua Manton's heiress now. He has no children.'

'He did have. Master Roddy was killed in the war. And most of the money belonged to the first Lady Manton, Sir William's sister. My ma told me...'

'That's all in the past. Miss Henrietta will inherit and she'll marry Mr Luke.'

'Heaven preserve our poor young laird if he takes her for his bride,' Milly muttered and went off to shiver in the huge dining room while she set out the silver and polished glasses which had not been used for years. The long table seated two dozen persons comfortably and she wondered whether she should put one man at each end, or seat them nearer together.

Sir William Crainby rarely complained, but that evening he and his silver-topped cane came down the stone stairs right into the kitchen, bristling with irritation.

'Mistress McCrady, whatever possessed you to open up the main dining room? You know how much I dislike eating in there.'

'The main dining room, Sir William?' Jane looked up startled. 'I gave no such order.' She looked at Milly and saw a triumphant gleam in her eye. She glanced at Eve, with her mouth pursed so tightly her lips were scarcely visible. 'We shall rectify the error immediately, sir,' Jane said hurriedly.

'Good. Don't let it happen again.'

He stomped out and back up the stairs as Eve said loudly, 'That was a daft idea of yours, Milly. Go and set dinner in the morning room.' Milly drew herself up ready to explode but Jane spoke quietly, her voice weary.

'Just do it, Milly, as quickly as you can.' Milly opened her mouth to protest, met her eyes, and closed it again. They both knew the truth. They turned their backs and went about their tasks, leaving Eve fuming, knowing her plans to change things stood little chance of succeeding unless Miss Henrietta became Lady Crainby. More humiliating was the fact that Milly had not even bothered to argue. The old witch knew who to blame.

There were many more incidents as the weeks passed and the tension tired Jane McCrady far more than work had ever done. Instead of join-

61

ing the rest of the staff for their evening meal, she took to leaving the castle as soon as coffee had been served upstairs. Victoria quickly adapted to this. Each evening she prepared a meal for herself and Granny to eat in the peaceful atmosphere of the cottage. She enjoyed this new routine. She was eager to learn and now she had the opportunity to make real meals for the two of them. Under her great-grandmother's guidance her confidence grew. She learned to cook dishes she had never been allowed to try before. They began to look forward to this time together, neither of them realizing how precious it would prove to be.

In November 1930, soon after Victoria's thirteenth birthday, she realized how different Mark's future would be from her own, and that of most children around Darlonachie. She began to dread losing her dearest friend. They had developed an uncanny knack of reading each other's thoughts, almost without the need for words.

She had always accepted that her own future would be working beside Granny in the castle kitchens, absorbing her knowledge of foods and cooking, learning to balance menus, budgeting and presenting dishes. One day she would follow in the footsteps of her ancestors for Granny McCrady's mother and grandmother had cooked at the castle. It was a family tradition and Victoria accepted it as the natural course of things. She looked forward to repaying her great-grandmother for her love and care. Now that nebulous thing called the future seemed to be approaching fast.

She was getting good at creating appetizing dishes from basic ingredients, but she still loved books. She longed to learn more of people in other lands, of faraway places, of past customs and times, and kings and queens. She would miss going to school and listening to Mr Nelson. She comforted herself with the knowledge that Sir William had always given her the freedom to read the books in the castle library and there were enough there to keep her reading for a lifetime.

Inevitably the time was approaching for Mark to move to the academy in Dumfries where he would board in a hostel during the week, returning to Darlonachie only at weekends.

'Uncle Peter has arranged it,' he told Victoria glumly. 'He says it's the only way if I want to pass the examinations so that I can go to university. I do want to be a doctor, but I wish you could come too, Victoria.'

'I expect it costs a lot of money,' Victoria said, practical as always.

'I hope Papa would not be disappointed because I want to be a doctor instead of a colonel in the army, as he was.'

'You could become a doctor and then join the army and look after the wounded soldiers,' she said soothingly.

'Victoria, you're a genius!' He hugged her. 'That is what I shall do.'

'I wasn't being serious!' Victoria wailed in alarm. 'It'll be awful when you go to Dumfries. But it'll be terrible if you go travelling in foreign lands with the soldiers. I shall never see you again.'

'Of course you will. I shall always, always, come back to see you. And I'll write lots of letters. You will write to me, won't you? I don't think I shall like going away. What will you do, Victoria?'

'We shall be fourteen next November. We shall both leave Darlonachie School after the summer term, but you will go to the academy. Granny needs my help. Milly says there will be lots of parties when Mr Luke gets married next year. Ware is horrid. She says Granny is too old, it's time she hung up her pinafore and stayed at home.' She looked worriedly at Mark. 'She is my great-granny so I know she's old, but I do try to help her as much as I can, but Eve Ware doesn't like me being in the kitchens. I cook at home instead but sometimes Granny is too tired to eat the meals I make.'

'Shall I ask Uncle Peter to call on her? He could make her a bottle of medicine. Auntie Anna calls them his magic potions. I'll ask him to make a special one. I know he likes Mrs Mc-Crady. I heard him saying so to Auntie Anna.'

'I don't know,' Victoria said anxiously. 'It depends if they cost a lot of money.'

That evening at supper Mark mentioned Victoria's concern about Mrs McCrady.

'I shall visit her tomorrow,' Peter Grantly said

64

immediately. 'And you can tell Victoria not to worry about the cost. We owe Jane McCrady a great debt.'

Doctor Grantly was aghast at the deterioration in Jane McCrady. He had eaten his own lunch earlier than usual so that he could call at Burnside Cottage in the early afternoon. According to Mark she had taken to resting for an hour in her own home when luncheon was over at the castle.

There was no reply to his knock. He peered in the window and saw her lying in the alcove which contained the box bed where she slept. She was fully clothed except for her stout laced shoes which stood neatly side by side. Dr Grantly frowned. Until the arrival of Eve Ware he knew Jane McCrady had worked in the castle kitchens all day, returning to her cottage only after the evening meal.

It seemed a pity to disturb her brief rest. In his heart he knew there was no magic to keep the years at bay, no potion for eternal youth. Mistress McCrady must be seventy-five or -six, he guessed. She was fortunate to have kept her health and strength so long. It was a good thing Victoria would be leaving school next summer. She would help her grandmother and eventually take over as the castle cook.

Doctor Grantly knocked at the door again then lifted the latch and walked quietly into the room, closing the door behind him. Jane McCrady stirred wearily. She opened her eyes. She stared at the doctor in dismay. He reached out a hand

and patted her arm.

'Don't jump up, Mistress McCrady. It's not good for you. I didn't mean to startle you. I was passing and thought I might find you at home...' His words faltered before her shrewd stare.

'Sit ye down, doctor. Tell me what brings you here while I put my shoes on again.' She sighed heavily, unaware that she did so.

Peter Grantly bit his lip. This was one patient he would give everything he had to be able to promise another ten years of life, but every instinct told him it was not to be. His heart felt heavy as he took the chair on the opposite side of the empty grate.

Jane McCrady glanced at the clock on the wall.

'I come back to my ain hoose at midday since Eve Ware started at the castle.'

'Mmm...so I see.' A ghost of a smile lifted Peter Grantly's lips. 'I've not heard much good spoken of Miss Ware so far.'

'Oh? I suppose my wee rascal has been telling tales to the boy?'

'To Mark? They share many confidences, I believe, but it was not from Victoria I had a poor opinion of Miss Eve Ware. Joe Pringle has little time, or respect, for her. Neither has Billy Wright from the Home Farm. He tells me he would like to throw the cream and eggs in her sour face.' He smiled slightly as he quoted the sentiments of the outspoken young herdsman.

'I see...Well, doctor, I must confess I find the woman more hindrance than help around my

kitchen. I'm wearied by her carping at young
Milly. The castle was a happy place, considering
all the troubles we've had since her ladyship
died. Since Eve Ware arrived there's an atmosphere that sickens and tires me. Now there you
have it...'

'Couldn't you ask the laird to move her
upstairs?'

'No.' She shook her grey head. 'Lady Manton
persuaded him I needed help. She recommended
Eve Ware. The laird thinks he's doing me a
kindness, but she's less of a cook than my
bairn.'

'I understand from the local gossip that Lady
Manton favours a marriage between her daughter and Mr Luke.'

'Aye we-ell, I suppose ye'll hear all the talk as
ye do your rounds, doctor, but I dinna think it
was gossip ye came for?'

'No. Victoria is concerned for you. Mark
doesn't like to see her upset so I promised to call
on you. He insisted I should bring you one of
my magic potions...' He gave her a wry smile as
he drew a medicine bottle from his overcoat
pocket.

Jane McCrady frowned, then she returned the
smile. 'Would that it could work magic, doctor,
would that it could.' She reached out and took it
from him. 'But I'll give it a try, if only to stop
that bairn o' mine worrying. She tries hard to
make life easier for me. She kindles the fire as
soon as she gets in from school and she can cook
a wholesome meal better than many a woman

three times her age.'

'You don't take your meals at the castle any more then?'

'Not since Ware arrived. She...she resents Victoria being anywhere near the castle. I fear she's jealous because Sir William and Mr Luke speak so freely with her, but they've known her since the day she was born. Their familiarity with Victoria makes Ware worse than ever. The bairn is enjoying cooking "real meals" as she calls them, and she's careful with the fire.' She chuckled. 'She'll make a fine wee cook before long.'

Her lined face sobered and she looked directly into Doctor Grantly's eyes, her expression troubled. 'As a matter of fact, doctor, I'm glad of a chance to talk to ye in private. It is in my mind that I might not have too long on this earth and...' She held up a hand. 'No, no let me finish. This has been on my mind ever since the boy came back to the village.'

'A-ah...' Peter Grantly expelled a long breath.

Six

Doctor Grantly had no difficulty guessing what was on the old lady's mind. It was a subject he had pushed to the back of his own, but now he had to face it.

'I think it is time I told them they are brother and sister. I can only pray they will forgive my sin in parting them.'

'No. Please, Mistress McCrady, not yet,' Peter Grantly pleaded. 'They're children still. They wouldn't understand...'

'Understand why I was so wicked? Why I gave away my own flesh and blood? No, I know they will not understand, but...'

'You were never wicked. You are one of the best loved and most respected women in Darlonachie.'

'That's as maybe, but no one knows what I did that night.' She shuddered and stared into space.

'Please, I beg of you...?' Peter Grantly took her work-worn hands in his and clasped them tightly. 'Please don't tell them yet. Remember, Mark believes he has lost his parents. He is just beginning to feel secure again. My wife loves him dearly. Soon he must face another change when he moves to Dumfries Academy. He wants to be a doctor, you know.'

'So Victoria tells me.'

'Yes, he will miss Victoria's company. If we burden him with the past he will be filled with confusion. He will not know who he is, or where he belongs. Please,' he said urgently, 'for Mark's sake, keep our secret a little longer.'

'And Victoria? Suppose I don't live long enough to explain?'

'I promise you, I give you my word on all I hold sacred, and I will tell them the truth together, when the time is right for them to know. When they are older and understand more of life. Will you trust me? Please?'

Jane McCrady would have withdrawn her hands but he held them firmly in his. She gnawed at her lower lip, as he had seen Victoria do when she was troubled, and as Mark did.

'I don't know...' she sighed. 'It is my duty to tell them the truth. Victoria knows nothing of how babies are gotten. She has asked a little about her father, but nothing serious yet.'

'Please leave it with me. I promise I will choose a time which is right for both of them, and I will tell them exactly how it was.'

'I confess it is a secret I have dreaded having to tell, but only a coward would avoid the truth.'

'You have never been a coward.'

'Not intentionally perhaps.' She looked into his eyes and seemed reassured by his conviction. 'Very well, I shall leave it to your judgement to choose the time, and to tell the truth.'

He breathed a sigh of relief and released her

hands. His own gaze moved to some unknown horizon.

'The truth...' he murmured. 'I fear we shall never know the whole truth after all this time.' He spoke softly, almost to himself, then he brought his clear gaze back to her face. 'Did you ever discover anything more...? Anything afterwards...?'

'Nothing.' She shook her head in distress. 'There had been a letter of course but...'

'A letter? I never knew of a letter? Did it...? Was it from the father...?'

'I never saw the letter, doctor. I only know there was one because I found the envelope beneath the bed. You will remember Elizabeth developed a fever? How we feared for her life as she tossed about in her delirium?'

'I remember clearly.' Peter Grantly's thoughts went back to that February morning in 1917.

Elizabeth McCrady had been sixteen, small for her age but a vivacious child with the happiest of smiles and dark laughing eyes. That morning she had been burning with a fever, tossing restlessly on her narrow bed in the room upstairs, her eyes wild, recognizing no one, not even her beloved grandmother. There was no sense in the words which came in gasps from her lips. It was due to her restless state he had noticed the blood and bruises. Mistress McCrady had noticed at the same time when she kicked aside the sheet and blankets. She had stared in dismay. She assured him it was not Elizabeth's usual monthly period. He knew most

71

of the women used pieces of material from worn towels or sheets, folded to make a pad. In a thrifty household like the McCrady's these were washed and dried to use again and again. There could be few secrets between women living in the same house regarding their time of the month.

Jane McCrady had stared at him, her eyes wide with disbelief. She consented to him examining her granddaughter more closely. He had not needed to explain. The child was torn and sore. She had been raped, possibly more than once. He had made up a soothing balm and by the time the fever had passed much of the soreness had abated.

'Elizabeth never told you what happened the night of Master Billy's coming of age?'

'Never. She was a changed girl from that night on. She rarely spoke. She refused to venture outside during the day. She was like a ghost. I've been over it all in my mind many times.'

'Tell me again what happened the night of the party?'

Jane McCrady was very still, except for the constant wringing of her hands. Her eyes had a faraway look.

'The castle hadna seen so many people since the funeral of Lady Crainby and the two wee bairnies. But that night there was a different atmosphere. I remember it well – as though they were all determined to enjoy it, as if it was their last day on God's earth. You'll remember times were troubled, the war was dragging on. More and more men were being called to service. The young laird...he was determined to do his duty and fight for his country. His cousin, Rodderick Manton, arrived but he had only a few days before he had to return to his regiment. There had been little cause for celebrations but there was a false gaiety about them all, a wildness, a – a sort of desperation...' She shook her head as though trying to clear it.

'And drink? Was there...?'

'Oh aye, there was drink. Champagne and wine from the cellar with the dinner. Great bowls of punch. They sent down for more. Some of the guests were staying overnight. As the evening wore on the older couples went home, the young ladies who were staying went to bed, but the young men...' She frowned. 'Sir William left them to it eventually. They drank more than they would have done if Her Ladyship had been alive. Master Luke was about thirteen or fourteen. He had been sent to bed when the ladies retired but he kept creeping out on to the landing to watch the revelry through the banister. We had been preparing food and getting the rooms ready for days before – everyone had worked hard. We all loved Master Billy. We'd been up since five o'clock. Elizabeth had worked as hard as any, helping to serve the meal, later clearing the dining room, continually collecting glasses and bringing them to wash. The bairn was dead on her feet. At midnight I told her to go home to bed for there would be more work to do with breakfast trays and clearing up.

'"I'll collect the dirty glasses from the library, then I'll go home," she said. "Will you be long, Granny?".' The old woman sighed. 'I can hear her voice yet, concerned and loving. Victoria is so like her...'

'And did she go home?' Doctor Grantly prompted gently.

'I thought she'd gone. I didna see her again. As soon as I got back to the cottage I went straight to sleep, down here.' She indicated the alcove. 'I thought Elizabeth was asleep upstairs. Next morning I called her. There was no reply. I was a wee bit later than I'd intended. I thought she must have crept out and gone to work already. It was several hours before the break- fasts were finished. Elizabeth was not at the castle. I hurried back here...' Jane McCrady drew a hand over her face as though she could wipe away the memory.

'She was here, at the cottage all along?'

'She was huddled in her bed, shivering as though with an ague, her teeth chattering. Her clothes were soaked. She must have been out all night. There had been rain, a cold February drizzle. I remember that. Her hair was still wet, though she had rubbed it with a towel. I could see the bairn had been crying but I couldna get her to talk. She wanted to hide herself beneath the blankets like a rabbit in its burrow. I tried to get her warmed up and dry. I made her hot milk but she turned her face to the wall. I knew some- thing was very wrong, but I couldn't get a word out of her, then or ever...I was needed back at the castle. She was still shivering when I returned home at night. Next morning she was worse. I sent for you...'

'Yes, I remember. So, the letter? You're sure it was for Elizabeth?'

'Yes, it had her name written on the envelope. There was no stamp. It had the castle crest. It must have been delivered by hand.'

'But you have no idea who could have sent it? It was not from Sir William?'

'The laird? Oh no.'

'The young laird, Master Billy, I meant. Thanking her for...for birthday greetings maybe?'

'No...' She frowned. 'Master Billy was always in trouble from Nanny for his handwriting. He was left handed, you see, and his writing sloped the wrong way. No, it wasna his. There was always writing paper and ink in the library. It could have been any of the guests...' Her voice trembled. 'I didna think any of the young gentlemen would have done such a thing, but who can tell when the drink goes to a man's head?'

'Indeed, you're right. It drives out sense, and even normal decency. I've seen too many loving husbands beat their wives when they're worse for drink.' He sighed. 'Thank you for going over everything with me, Mistress McCrady. I didn't want to distress you. I hoped...'

'That's all right, doctor. It's a relief to have someone...someone who understands. I've been over it all in my mind so often.'

'Well, you can talk to me any time, you know

that. And thank you for trusting me to break the news to Mark and Victoria. I shall do my best to choose the right time, and to help them understand. They're sensible children.'

Primroses faded from the grassy verges and the hillsides were clothed with sheets of gold as the whins burst into bloom; in the woods the scent of bluebells mingled with the pine, and hedges were adorned with veils of white lace where the hawthorn blossomed. Birds flew hither and thither, some still building or rebuilding nests, others already feeding an early brood. In the ponds the frog spawn developed tails and arms and legs. At thirteen years old Mark and Victoria were still young enough to delight in all the changes that nature wrought to their small world.

There were changes at the castle too. Master Luke was twenty-eight years old and Lady Manton and her daughter, Miss Henrietta Crossjay, had worn down his resistance to marriage. Or rather, he knew the succession of his family's estate depended on him providing an heir. Henrietta was not without charm when she chose to exert it. She criticised the lax way the castle was run, but not in front of Luke.

Sir William declared himself too old for changes. He liked his comfortable lifestyle. He continued to take his favourite old Labrador and his playful young spaniel into the morning room at breakfast time and into the library in the evenings. If he happened to see Victoria in the

76

vegetable garden with Pringle, or making her way to her grandmother in the kitchen, he often waylaid her, drawing her into the library to show her a book he had discovered, and which he believed would interest her. Sometimes her bright brown eyes and eager young face reminded him vaguely of his late sister when she was a child. These habits of her future father-in-law irritated Henrietta intensely. She vowed to make changes, including disciplining the servants.

The wedding was fixed for July but in the meantime Henrietta discovered Luke was usually too busy overseeing his estate to keep her company as she desired, or conducting some business of his own further up the glen. He explained that the farms and woods needed his constant attention if they were to be preserved for another generation.

'Surely you understand, Henrietta? Farming has not been profitable since the war ended. Our government is importing shiploads of cheap grain from America, as well as frozen lamb and wool from Australia, and butter and cheese from New Zealand. Many of our tenants are struggling to pay their rents.'

'Then give them notice to move out. Choose tenants who are more efficient and who can pay higher rents,' she snapped.

Luke turned to stare at her in astonishment. 'But your own father was a tenant farmer...?'

Henrietta flushed and scowled at him. She drew herself up and pushed out her narrow chest.'My father was a squire!'

'I know he rented a large sheep farm in the Borders but I think even he would have struggled had he been living now. You must understand, my dear, Darlonachie tenants have been loyal to my family for many generations. It is true attitudes have changed since the Great War, but we value the loyalty of those who remain.'

'Rubbish. You're so old fashioned and bound with tradition!' Henrietta scoffed. 'You may not allow me to make changes outside the castle but I shall certainly make some inside.'

'Not too many, I hope.'

'The servants need discipline. There hasn't been a Lady Crainby to keep them in order for years. That old woman who does the cooking for instance, she'll have to go. Then there's—'

'Mistress McCrady? Why, she's as much a part of Castle Darlonachie as I am. Her family have worked for mine for generations. More than that, she is a wonderful cook. Most of the big houses in the county would have taken her from us if they could.'

'Pity they didn't then, her and her brat!' she muttered under her breath, but she was too wise to argue out loud until she had Mr Luke Crainby's wedding ring securely on her finger.

Nevertheless, she made her personality felt in the castle kitchens through judicious comments and hints in the ear of Eve Ware. The tension increased. Jane McCrady never knew when Miss Henrietta Crossjay would be present for lunch or dinner, or what sort of substitute dish she would request on a sudden whim. The atmosphere grew more and more fraught. Jane looked forward to the end of each day when she could return to her own cottage and the meal Victoria always had waiting for her.

'I must say, my bairn, you'll soon be a better cook than I am,' she smiled at Victoria as she finished the last spoonful of a lemon pudding, which was as light as any she had made herself.

'It was out of your recipe book,' Victoria said, beaming with pride. 'I followed the instructions.'

'It's a wonder you can still read that old book, lassie. The writing has faded so. All the recipes are in my head these days.'

'I know. I have started copying all my favourites into a book of my own. Look, Mr Nelson, the schoolmaster, gave me this as a prize.' She brought a leather bound exercise book from the dresser drawer. 'I shall keep it for recipes.'

'How did you earn a prize, lassie? You never told me.'

'It was at Easter. I got it for the best essay in the school. It had to be a theme taken from the Bible so I invented a story about a good Samaritan.'

'And you beat Mark?'

'Yes, he was second. But he beat me at mathematics,' she added fairly.

It was an exceptionally warm day for June and Jane McCrady was feeling tired after baking bread. The fire had to be kept well tended to get the oven hot enough. Large though it was, the kitchen was sweltering. Eve Ware was supposed to have peeled the vegetables and plucked a chicken ready to make the midday meal but when Jane went into the scullery there was no sign of her. The chicken still hung from the hook where Billy Wright had hung it earlier that morning when he brought it up from the farm. The basket of vegetables was just as Joe Pringle had brought them from the garden.

Jane wiped a weary hand across her brow. She opened the door which led to the walled kitchen garden.

'Have you seen Ware?' she called to Joe Pringle, who was on his knees weeding the rows of beetroot.

'I havena seen her but I heard her. Screeching at young Milly, she was. I reckon the lassie must have committed murder, no less.'

Jane nodded and went back inside. She climbed the stairs to the long passage leading from the servants' quarters to the main hall feeling weary and exasperated. The lunch was going to be late and Sir William always liked his midday meal on time. He had taken to having a short rest afterwards, as she did herself these days. It seemed to have become a part of growing old, this constant weariness, this dragging of the footsteps. Oh, to be young again, she thought with a wistful sigh.

She heard Ware scolding Milly, her voice raised unnecessarily. She relishes the task, Jane McCrady thought with irritation. She opened the door of the morning room.

'Eve, you were supposed to have plucked that chicken two hours ago and you have not even started on the vegetables. Will you—'

'I'm not your kitchen skivvy!' Eve Ware flashed back sulkily.

'Then who do you think will do such things? I gave you the choice of baking the bread instead, but you refused to do that. Now come immediately, both of you. Sir William willna mind a trace of dust, if there is one, but he will mind if his lunch is delayed.' Jane knew her tone was sharper than usual.

Milly followed at once, clearly relieved to be rescued. Eve dawdled. Jane took the chicken and a chair outside the kitchen door and proceeded to divest the bird of its feathers with swift efficiency. She was glad to take the weight off her feet if only for five minutes. When she returned to the scullery to remove the innards, Eve was lounging on a stool watching Milly peel the vegetables.

'Well, you could get on with the stuffing, Eve, if you don't want to help Milly with the vegetables.' Jane's voice was sharp. The woman had no sense of urgency.

'I need a recipe for that. Stuff it yourself.'

'A recipe! Even Milly can make stuffing. Milly, leave the vegetables to Eve and begin making the breadcrumbs, please.'

Afterwards Milly told Polly Pringle that Eve Ware had done everything she could to provoke Mistress McCrady into losing her temper but the old woman had gritted her teeth and got on with the cooking. Lunch had been late and Sir William had been annoyed. Eve blamed Mistress McCrady in the loud voice she always used when she wanted other people to hear.

'I had never seen Mistress McCrady upset before. Her face went white. She told Eve Ware she could take over the cooking from now on. She was going home. She turned and went out of the door.'

The tension had been building in Jane for weeks but that morning was the last straw. She walked home, feeling the increasing tightness in her chest. She knew it would have done her good to lose her temper with Ware, or to drag her before Sir William and tell him she was both useless and idle. Instead she bottled up her emotions as had become her habit since the death of her husband all those years ago.

Once inside her own cottage she bent, intending to unlace her shoes.

Seven

Victoria didn't hurry home from school that warm summer afternoon. Mark walked part of the way with her, chatting together as was their habit, until the path brought them to the edge of the small wood. They were both conscious they were nearing the end of their last term together at Darlonachie.

Afterwards, all Victoria could think of was that she should have hurried home. It was to Polly Pringle she had run, sobbing out the news of her grandmother's collapse on her ample chest. No amount of reassurance from Polly could convince her she could not have saved her beloved granny from death's clutches. George and Willie, newly home from school, had run all the way back to the village to bring Doctor Grantly, but there was nothing anyone could do to console Victoria.

Andrew came home from Langmune and ate his meal quickly and in silence. Then he persuaded Victoria to walk with him to the top of the hill behind the castle, way beyond the little wood and the places Victoria had been in the habit of exploring with Mark. Andrew was deadly tired himself after a long day mowing hay, the cycle ride to the farm and home again, helping with the milking before the field work began, and again when it ended, but he knew exhaustion was the only way Victoria would sleep that night.

They said little as they walked but when the ground was rough or steep Andrew would hold out his warm, work-roughened hand and she slipped hers into it, glad of his help and his re-assuring strength. At the top of the hill the wind was fresher but Andrew found a small hollow and they sat together on the short grassy turf with only an odd ewe and lamb for company.

'See that clump of trees on the far side of the

glen, across the river?' Andrew said. 'Langmune House is behind them and the farm steading is on the other side of the slope.'

'It looks a long way away, Andrew.'

'It is from up here. It's about three miles up from the village.'

'That's a long way every morning and back again at night.'

'Och, it's not far on the bike. It seems longer in the winter when it's dark both ways. I'll take you one day, Victoria. You'd love the farm and all the animals. You'll love Mick, my wee dog. We have two pet lambs now and chicks and ducklings. We always have calves around the place. Last year we had a Clydesdale foal and we have four lovely mares for working the land.'

'You love the farm, don't you, Andrew?' Victoria's voice was wistful. When she was very small, even before she went to school, it was Andrew who had taught her about the woodlands and the meadows and the animals and birds. Now she was teaching Mark. All that was finished now. Would the laird allow her to stay in the cottage? She would have to earn her living. Her eyes grew wide and dark and then silent tears welled and streamed down her pale cheeks. Quietly Andrew drew her against his chest. It was hard and muscular although he was not yet eighteen years old. He stroked her long dark hair with a gentle hand until the tears stopped, then he tilted her face to his and looked earnestly into her eyes.

'You know I shall always be your friend, Victoria. You can come to me if you're worried or in trouble. Or if anyone ever lets you down...' His thoughts went instinctively to Mark Jacobs. The lad was destined for a wider world and greater things than Victoria's. Would he desert her? Look down on her in the future? 'If ever anyone hurts you, Victoria, come to me. He'll have me to reckon with...' He was unaware that his voice was unusually harsh until Victoria looked up at him in surprise. She shivered and his arm tightened around her shoulders.

'Come on, lass. It's time we went home to bed. The air's growing cool now.' He got lightly to his feet and pulled her up. For a moment he held her close then he kissed her brow. 'Remember you've still got us, Victoria. My brothers may be a rowdy lot but we're your family now. Mother and Father have always thought the world of you and wished they had a daughter like you.' He didn't allow her time to think or to answer. 'Come on, I'll race you as far as the burn.'

Victoria knew it was the custom for a simple service to be held at the deceased's home. Afterwards the men accompanied the coffin to the kirkyard while the women waited behind and made refreshments for the mourners, but there were no men in the family and Victoria couldn't allow her beloved granny to take that last journey alone. It was the Reverend Dewar and Mr Luke Crainby together who persuaded her to allow the service to be held in the little village kirk which Jane McCrady had attended almost every week of her life.

'Afterwards it is but a step or two to the churchyard, my dear,' Reverend Dewar said. 'I know there will be many people who wish to pay their last respects. Jane McCrady was highly respected in our community for her courage and her generosity of spirit.'

Even so, Victoria was astonished at the number of people who crowded into the little church with its pretty stained glass windows above the altar, and the shining brass plaques, including one for the young laird William Crainby who, it said, had given his life in the service of his country. The laird was there and Mr Luke, seated in their own box pew. Victoria walked between Polly and Joe Pringle, her head held high in spite of her wobbly chin and the effort to hold back her tears. Andrew joined them in the front pew. He had cycled home at midday but he was going back to Langmune later and staying up at the farm all night to make up time while the good weather lasted for making hay.

She was surprised to see Doctor and Mrs Grantly and Mark in the other front pew. She looked again at Mark and saw his eyes were as red as hers must be and knew he was sharing her sadness, even though he could not possibly miss Granny McCrady as she did.

After the funeral was over Sir William Crainby came over in time to hear Polly telling her that her home was with them from now on.

'You know how dear you are to Joe and me, lassie. I want you to stop calling me Mrs

Pringle. I'll understand if you can't call me Ma, as my laddies do, but what about Aunt Polly?'

Victoria tried to protest, but it was no more than a bewildered, half-hearted whimper.

'You canna stay in the cottage on your own, Victoria. Andrew doesna mind. He's already moved back into the loft with his brothers. You'll have the wee back room to yourself.'

'That is a splendid solution,' Sir William agreed, patting Victoria's shoulder. 'You can leave Burnside as it is, and go back there now and then. We shall not need it. There are four empty cottages on the estate already.'

'B-but I have no money. I must find work to pay for my keep...' Victoria protested. 'I shall leave school. I must look—'

'All right, child. Don't distress yourself.' It didn't occur to Sir William to consult his son, even less his future daughter-in-law, as he proceeded to arrange Victoria's future. 'You are used to helping your grandmother with the cooking, and you know Milly. You can start work at the castle as soon as you are ready. I will pay Mistress Pringle for your board and lodging. Every six months you will receive your wages. Does that suit you, Mistress Pringle?'

'Thank you, sir.' Polly was overwhelmed. She had not even considered money. All she wanted was to comfort the bairn.

Within weeks Victoria changed from a happy schoolgirl to a work-worn servant.

Eve Ware bitterly resented having the old

woman's brat foisted upon her and she informed Miss Henrietta Crossjay at the first opportunity.

She never missed a chance to humiliate Victoria or to find her the dirtiest of jobs. Victoria already knew how to clean and blacken the cottage range and buff it until it gleamed. She had taken pride in doing it every Saturday morning for her grandmother for the past year. True, the range in the castle kitchens was huge and it meant a very early start, but it was not the hard work which made her unhappy, it was Eve Ware's constant malice, her niggling criticism. She was unfair and unreasonable. When Victoria did get a chance to cook any dishes it was always Eve who took the credit.

'She's jealous o' ye,' Milly repeated at least once a day. 'She knows ye're a better cook than she is, even though ye're new out o' school.'

'But she's a woman.'

'Makes no difference. She makes horrible beef stew. The meat is so tough even the dogs choke on it. The last time she made it the laird and Mr Luke sent it back, but she made us eat it.'

Milly remembered the happy, laughing girl Victoria had been and she did her best to cheer her, but if Eve heard the slightest sound of a giggle she raged at both of them and added more chores, often repeating things they had already done, scrubbing the floor again, wiping down shelves, or scouring the copper pans. There were guests for dinner more often now that Mr Luke's wedding was drawing nearer. Two extra live-in maids had been hired for upstairs, making four in all, as well as Mrs Baxter who came in to do the laundry on Mondays and Thursdays, and Ware, Milly and Victoria. Life became one of constant grind and carping for Victoria. However hard she tried she never seemed able to satisfy Eve Ware. She began to lose confidence in her own abilities. She was often too tired to eat by the end of a long day. At night she fell into bed exhausted. Polly worried about the thin, sad-faced waif she was becoming.

Eve Ware's angry resentment was nothing compared with Miss Henrietta Crossjay's fury when she heard Sir William had hired Victoria Lachlan to help in the castle kitchen.

'Your father hired a girl for the kitchens. He never even consulted me!' she said, storming into the estate office to find Luke. She was oblivious to the presence of John Swift, the farm manager. Luke looked up in surprise at her entrance, and nodded assent when Swift asked to be excused.

'What is it, Henri? I'm rather busy.'

'Don't call me Henri! I've told you before.'

Luke replaced his pen in the inkstand with a sigh. 'Five minutes. That's all I can spare. What's troubling you?'

'Troubling me? Did you know your father has taken on another servant for the kitchen – that brat belonging to the old woman!'

'Victoria? Of course I know, but Victoria is no brat. She's a fine worker and one day she'll be as good a cook as her great-grandmother. She's probably a darned sight better than the Ware

89

woman already.' This statement infuriated Henrietta even more.

'Eve Ware was well recommended. She worked for a friend of my mother.'

'That's probably why they recommended her then – to get rid of her.' He chuckled.

'Don't be ridiculous! There's nothing wrong with her cooking as far as I can see.'

'That's because you never eat anything she actually cooks. You only nibble lettuce leaves and bits of carrot and celery. You're too busy watching your figure.'

'You wouldn't want a bride who looked like a ship in full sail coming down the aisle, would you?' Henrietta pouted, swaying her hips provocatively, inviting compliments which were not forthcoming.

'Oh, I don't know...' Luke grinned and she was aware how attractive he could be. 'I think I'd enjoy someone warm and cuddly in my bed on a cold winter's night.' He was surprised to see Henrietta flush because he knew she was no innocent maiden.

The truth was he knew very well who he would like for his bedmate. Maggie Lennox was always warm and welcoming. She was the wife of one of his tenants and he had seen a lot of them in recent months because Tobias Lennox had been badly injured by a runaway horse and he had been unable to carry out his work. Luke had taken more interest than he might have done and he had provided help from his own estate workers. Maggie had been employed by Tobias

Lennox as his housekeeper. He was a kindly man. He knew she was alone in the world and as his wife she would have a small measure of security. Besides, he was afraid she might be tempted away to a less isolated farm, and he didn't want to lose her. Now Maggie was repaying his kindness by caring patiently for his badly injured body, and doing her best to carry on the small farm.

Luke had often heard of Cupid's arrow, but he had believed it to be a fairy tale, until the day he met Maggie. He had felt an instant attraction for her. As weeks passed into months he was certain she felt the same, but he was too honourable to put it to the test. He knew her first loyalty would be to Tobias. He sighed deeply now as he looked at Henrietta's angry face.

Sometimes he wondered if he could go through with his marriage to his uncle's stepdaughter. He was surprised that his father seemed to favour the match considering he had little patience with Uncle Joshua's second wife, or Henrietta's whims. Of course his father's dearest wish was to see his grandchildren and to be assured there would be another generation of Crainbys at Darlonachie.

Luke felt no compunction about marrying Henrietta even though he did not love her. She was conveniently available, very available, and moderately suitable. The estate badly needed an injection of capital in the present economic climate but he doubted whether there would be much of his aunt's fortune left by the time

Henrietta and her mother had had their way. He knew she did not love him either. Recently he had wondered whether she was capable of loving anyone, but she had set her heart on being Lady Crainby. He had a feeling she was going to be sadly disillusioned with the reality. Perhaps he ought to warn her.

'If you are intending to entertain the local gentry once we are married you will need someone to assist Ware. Victoria Lachlan is intelligent and capable, especially for her age,' he said soothingly, adding cheerfully, 'and she will not take up so much of your household budget while she is so young.'

'Money! That's all you think about these days.'

'It's an essential commodity, my dear, and rather scarce.'

'So you keep saying but I'm telling you now we shall need a lot more servants once we're married and start entertaining as befits our position in the county.'

'So why are you objecting to my father hiring young Victoria, pray?'

'Because I expect to hire my own staff. I already have my eye on a housekeeper. She will expect to offer her opinion on the servants who are under her control.'

Luke frowned. 'I don't see why we need a housekeeper after all the years we have managed without one. I meant what I said about keeping costs to a minimum until conditions improve,' he added sternly. 'Half the tenants are behind with their rents already. Even the saw-mill is not bringing in as much as it should. The best wood has already been taken to build the ships for the war and now wood is being brought in from Scandinavia for house building.' His attention moved back to the account book he had been discussing when she rudely inter-rupted.

'Oh, spare me the lecture!' Henrietta snapped. 'Are you going to tell your father he must get rid of the Lachlan girl or shall I?'

'You can tell him if you feel so strongly, my dear, but I wouldn't advise it,' he added. 'Re-member he is still the laird, and what's more he's always had affection for Victoria.'

Henrietta chose to ignore both the warning and the steely note in his voice.

Sir William stared at Henrietta as though she had taken leave of her senses.

'You intend to get rid of Lachlan! My dear girl, Victoria is as much a part of Darlonachie as I am. Her family have always worked at the castle.'

'In a few weeks' time I shall be mistress here and I do not consider her suitable,' Henrietta said with a haughty toss of her head. The laird looked at her over his steel framed spectacles.

'Your opinion matters little, Miss Crossjay,' he said calmly. 'Victoria Lachlan will have work at Darlonachie for as long as she wishes to stay, and I hope that will be a very long time, like her family before her.' Even Henrietta could not fail to see the steel in the laird's eyes, or miss the implication that she had overstepped her position.

Her stepfather and Sir William had once been good friends, as well as brothers-in-law, but she knew his regard did not extend to her or her mother.

She pursed her mouth, turned on her heel and left him to his books, but she seethed with anger and vowed she would get rid of the Lachlan brat one way or another. She would make the girl's position untenable. She had been favoured far beyond the status of a servant by Sir William, all because she pretended to share his enjoyment of fusty old books. Henrietta had never been fond of learning herself and she couldn't believe that any woman could find pleasure in reading books. Her chief interests were her looks and cultivating a position in society.

Victoria had grown up around the kitchens and gardens at the castle and she knew well enough the tasks which needed to be done, which of them must be a priority according to the season and those which could be set aside until time allowed. Granny had said it needed organization to use the time available each day. Even Milly was familiar with the general routine and she welcomed Victoria as an ally against Ware.

'I miss your grandmother as much as you do, Victoria,' she sighed one day, after Eve Ware had been screeching at both of them. 'She was always fair and she showed me how to do things. She never raged like Ware. She said no task was too menial for working hands and we all had to learn. I dinna ken what she meant exactly,' Milly confessed, 'but at least she was kind.'

Victoria nodded silently, swallowing the lump in her throat. She missed Granny dreadfully. Polly Pringle had said her sorrow would ease as the time passed, but months had passed in a daze of grief and weariness and she missed her beloved granny more than ever.

She missed Mark's company too. Several times he had cycled to the Pringles' cottage to see her during the school holidays. He couldn't understand why she was never there to talk to him.

'I only see her in church on Sundays,' he told Polly earnestly, 'and that cross-looking woman hurries her away after the service. We never get time to talk. Please tell her I miss her.'

Polly repeated Mark's comments to Victoria. Andrew was seated at the table finishing his meal. He was surprised Mark Jacobs still wanted to spend his free time with Victoria now that their paths had changed so radically.

'We should all make time for our friends, lassie,' Polly said.

'How can I?'

'Mother's right, Victoria. Surely you get free afternoons if you work on Saturdays and Sundays? Even at the farm we only do essential milking and feeding at weekends, unless it's hay time or harvest or lambing. I promised to take you to the farm one day. Do you remember?

When is your next day off?'

'I don't get a day off yet,' Victoria said. 'Eve Ware is off on Thursdays and Milly gets Monday and Saturday afternoons, but Ware says I haven't earned free time yet.'

'What?' Joe Pringle demanded, lowering his newspaper. 'Ye've earned it more than any o' the rest.'

'Milly thought we might spend an afternoon together, but Ware said I would have to work for a year first.'

'That's ridiculous,' Andrew exclaimed. 'You start at six every morning. It's half past seven now and you've just finished. That's more hours in a week than we do!'

'Aye, 'tis so,' Joe frowned thoughtfully. 'While ye're under this roof, lassie, I think it's my duty to speak up for ye.'

'Dinna speak out o' turn, Joe,' Polly urged. 'Ye'll only make it worse for Victoria. She might lose her job...'

'All right, I'll be careful.' He sighed. 'But I shall tell her the lassie must have some free time every week. This is the nineteen thirties. Men went to war so we could enjoy a bit o' freedom.'

Joe tackled Eve Ware the next day. Only when he threatened to go to Sir William Crainby did she grudgingly agree to arrange it. Even then she said Victoria could have three hours off once a week, and that included the hour and a half to attend church on Sundays. Joe had no idea about workers' rights. He had had mixed feelings about the general strike five years ago; he had always felt he was treated fairly by the Crainby family.

'That's not enough. All the castle servants go to the kirk.'

As soon as Henrietta returned from her honeymoon Ware complained to her. She was sure of her support, but she knew if her Mrs Crainby ever discovered the truth about her references as a cook she might not be so pleasant. Henrietta didn't relish another confrontation with Sir William, but neither would she allow a gardener or a maid to dictate to her.

'Tell the chit she can have Friday afternoons off so long as she completes her weekly tasks, then see that she is kept busy. An hour off will be sufficient.'

Eve Ware informed Victoria of the arrangement, but there was a malicious gleam in her eye. She was preparing a rice pudding at the time. Victoria couldn't believe her eyes as she added the rice to the milk in a large enamel dish. She spooned in the grains, frowned, stirred and added more. She did the same again, and added more.

'It doesn't need—' Victoria began.

'What are you gaping at? Get on with your work and don't stand there idling!' She added more rice and stirred again. Victoria's eyes grew rounder, but she turned and went into the scullery. An hour later she saw Ware draw the pudding from the oven and stir it. Victoria knew the grains had not had time to swell but Ware scowled and brought another bag of rice from the cupboard and poured it in. Victoria hurried out of sight. Milly was peeling vegetables in the scullery and Victoria tried to stifle her laughter. She found it hard to stop and the tears ran down her cheeks.

'C-come into the laundry,' she gasped at last. Once there she said, 'Ware is supposed to be making rice pudding. She keeps adding more and more rice... I think she's making a brick.'

Sure enough when it was time to serve the midday meal Ware went to lift out the pudding. It had thickened and swelled until it was all over the oven. Victoria groaned inwardly. She knew she would get the job of cleaning it but as she caught Milly's eye it was all they could do not to explode with laughter. Ware glared at the dish. It was so thick and so hard it was impossible to get it out of the dish.

'Don't stand there staring!' she yelled at Victoria. 'Boil some milk and make custard. I'll tell her Mrs Crainby the pudding has been delayed.'

'I'll tell her,' Milly said and darted out of the door before Ware could prevent her. Milly knew she would have blamed Victoria, as she always did. Later they laughed until their sides ached.

'It was almost worth having to clean the oven just to see Ware's face!' Victoria told Polly later.

As the months passed it did not occur to Victoria to complain to Sir William, or anyone else, about Ware's vindictiveness. She and Milly made the best of things and helped each other

98

when they could. Victoria felt she was fortunate to have a home with the Pringles and a measure of independence, however small.

Whenever Mark had holidays from school he cycled over to the Pringles' on Fridays, eager to share his news and the changes which were happening in the world at large. Victoria had little opportunity for reading but she appreciated Mark keeping her informed. Andrew borrowed newspapers from Mr Rennie, as well as farming papers, but it didn't occur to him that she might be interested too.

During the winter months Andrew was rarely at home himself so he didn't notice Victoria had scarcely any more free time than before. He enjoyed his work at Langmune. Even though it meant more work, he liked the steamy warmth of the byres in winter when the cows were housed and the wind whistled outside. Hay and turnips were carted into them twice a day and the byres were swept and cleaned and the manure removed with wheelbarrows. During the short dark days the horses and carts were loaded with manure from the midden and taken out to the fields to be spread. Hard work kept the men warm and steam from the manure rose in the crisp frosty air.

There was ploughing to be done whenever the frost lifted. Ted Holmes, the elderly cowman, fell ill with bronchitis and was confined to his cottage for several weeks so the work increased.

Mr Rennie himself had always suffered from a weak chest and as he grew older he had become increasingly prone to attacks of breathlessness, especially when the winter winds blew. He had begun to rely on Andrew to keep him informed and to see that his orders were carried out. The housekeeper, Miss Traill, relied on him too. He was polite and thoughtful; he never tried to take advantage. She had started making him a big breakfast and a midday meal now. The other workers knew Mr Rennie discussed the farm and the animals with Andrew during meal times. Young though he was the two older farm labourers seemed to accept this. He had proved he was not afraid of hard work, but neither did he let them take advantage of his youth and enthusiasm. They began to respect his ideas and his suggestions for making their work easier, or their day more ordered. It was this intelligence and commonsense which Mr Rennie had recognized the day Andrew rescued his collie bitch and he appreciated their discussions.

At the castle things were changing too. Henrietta Crainby was expecting a child and her condition did not improve her temper or her pettish ways. Mr Crainby seemed to spend more and more time on the estate. Six weeks earlier Tobias Lennox had died, leaving Maggie a young widow at High Bowie. Women without sons usually gave up the tenancy on the death of a husband but Mr Crainby had suggested Maggie should keep on the small farm at the head of the glen. He had promised to give her whatever help she needed. He had not asked for anything in return, or acted dishonourably, but there was a new lightness in his step and a new tolerance towards the unreasoning tantrums of his pregnant wife.

Victoria began to look forward to the Thursdays when Ware went away to visit her sister. She and Milly were supposed to serve a selection of cold meats, pickles and cheeses for both lunch and dinner. The other maids complained because there was never enough.

Victoria began making soups in addition to the cold collation. This proved a welcome addition as winter approached, so she experimented further. Only Milly knew it was Victoria who had made the extra dishes. As she regained her confidence Victoria made some of the puddings her grandmother used to make. She tried bread and butter pudding with a golden Demerara topping, queen of puddings topped with crisp meringue, and Eve's pudding served with creamy custard.

'Even her Ladyship cleared her plate today,' Milly would report with glee, or, 'His Lordship says it seems years since he enjoyed such bread and butter pudding.'

Victoria began to enjoy herself. She started to plan the dishes she would try out on Ware's day off. Sometimes she brought her grandmother's old recipe book with her if the dish was more complicated than usual, or when there were several accompaniments required, as there were with the roast duck with orange sauce. Milly was useless at cooking but she was a willing helper and always peeled and chopped the vegetables and any other tasks which saved Victoria's own time. She had learned how to make the batter for the Yorkshire puddings as soon as she was old enough to hold a wooden spoon, but now she had to cook them. Sometimes it was a struggle to get the fire drawing to make the oven hot enough. Twice she burned her arm and almost dropped the tin.

Then came a day when Eve Ware developed a cold and changed her mind about visiting her sister. She came into the kitchen as Victoria was getting in the leeks from Joe Pringle, ready to make leek and potato soup. She had planned to follow it with roast pork and apple sauce.

'And what d'you think you're doing?' Ware demanded sharply, making Victoria jump so much that she dropped the leeks on to the newly washed floor, scattering bits of soil everywhere. Milly looked at Ware in dismay.

'I was just—'

'I can see what you were doing. Stealing leeks from the garden – you and that wretched gardener. I saw him handing them in to you.'

'I was not stealing them. I intended to make soup. It is such a cold day—'

'I shall tell you when soup is required. Now get this floor swept and scrub it clean. I need some hot milk. I am going back to bed but I shall be up again by lunchtime and I expect to find everything spotless.'

Victoria didn't dare cook that day.

'They didn't look very happy upstairs when I said there was only cold meat and pickles for lunch,' Milly reported. 'Mrs Crainby said it was time she hired an assistant cook for when Eve Ware has her day off. Mr Crainby said he usually enjoyed his meals better when it was her day off and what was different today? She told him Ware was unwell. She never guesses it is you who cooks on Thursdays, Victoria. Of course, she always picks and pokes so I reckon she doesna ken good food when she tastes it – except for your caramel custard. She would eat the whole dish o' that. Ma says it's a craving because o' the baby...'

Ware's suspicions had been aroused and she began to check the foods in the larder, but Joe Pringle always brought a supply of vegetables from the garden and Billy Wright brought extra milk and cream and eggs on Thursdays. Now that he understood, he delighted in thwarting Ware and brought a couple of chickens, rabbits, partridges, pigeons, pheasants, salmon or whatever was available. When there had been a pig killing Eve Ware never dealt with it herself as Granny McCrady had done so she didn't know how much had been brought fresh to the kitchens and how much had been cured.

Victoria enjoyed the challenge of pitting her wits against Eve Ware. On Wednesday evenings she spent ages poring over her grandmother's recipes and when she was not too tired she copied some of her favourites into her own book.

'Billy Wright said I was to tell ye he has a nice plump goose ready for ye to cook on Thursday,

Victoria,' Joe Pringle said with a grin one evening.

'Oh? I don't know much about cooking a goose,' Victoria gasped.

Andrew looked up from the *Scottish Farmer* magazine and winked at her.

'You'll manage fine.'

'It's nearly the same as a duck, lassie, only it will need longer,' Polly said reassuringly. 'Ye're a natural wee cook anyway, like your grandmother said.'

'But it will take me a while to pluck it and get it ready and Eve Ware doesn't always leave at the same time in the mornings since she was ill. I'll search Granny's recipe book to see what she has written about accompaniments.' A little later she looked up at Polly. 'I can make the sage and onion stuffing, and the apple sauce and the gravy, but I think I must take her book with me for the instructions on how to truss it and fold the skin so that the stuffing doesn't come out.'

'Don't look so worried, lassie,' Polly soothed. 'Though I must say I could never have tackled a goose at your age.'

Jane McCrady's recipe book was well thumbed and many of the pages were loose but to Victoria it was the most precious thing she possessed and she tucked it under her arm as she hurried over to the castle that Thursday morning. It contained a lifetime of hints and ideas, as well as her grandmother's own recipes for cooking and baking. Victoria only had to look at it to realize what a lot she had to learn before she could call herself a cook. Sometimes she wondered how Eve Ware had dared to give herself such a title when there were so many things she didn't know.

Bill Wright arrived early at the scullery door with the day's supplies. 'I've rough plucked the goose, Miss Victoria. Thought ye might be in trouble if the feathers flew everywhere!' He grinned at her. 'Give it a good singeing when ye've cleaned it out, and make sure ye dinna burst the gizzard.'

'Thank you, Billy.' Victoria smiled up at him. 'I want this to be a special dinner for Sir William. Ooh! How heavy it is! I'd better get started on it right away.'

'Good luck, lassie. I'll bet them upstairs have no idea what ye can do, and ye no more than a bairn yet.'

Victoria drew herself up as tall as she could but Billy Wright was a man in his forties with a family of his own. He grinned at her and went on his way, wishing his own children were half as capable and willing to work.

Both Milly and Victoria worked hard and by the time the meal was over and the dining room cleared they were exhausted. As they sat down with the rest of the servants to eat their own meal Milly beamed.

'Sir William said that was the best meal he could remember eating.'

'Aye, but his memory isna very good these days, according to Mrs Crainby,' Mrs Baxter muttered.

'There's nothing wrong with his memory,' Milly defended the laird indignantly. 'Anyway Mr Luke said the goose was delicious – they've eaten all the plum sauce.'

'Mmm,' Mrs Baxter said as she nodded vigorously, looking across at Victoria. 'It's tasty, and it's tender. Ye're not a bad wee cook when ye try. Your grandmother would have been proud o' ye.'

'Thank you,' Victoria said, catching Milly's eye and her raised eyebrows. Mrs Baxter rarely praised anyone. In fact she grumbled constantly, especially since Mr Luke's marriage. Although she worked an extra day, and earned more wages each week, she complained bitterly about the amount of ironing she had to do for Mrs Crainby.

It took Victoria and Milly some time to scour all the saucepans and put away all the serving dishes and restore the kitchens and the dining room to order after the meal.

'What shall I do with the carcass and the skin frae the goose?' Milly asked.

'Well, Granny would have made stock for soup,' Victoria said slowly, 'but if we did that Ware would find out we'd—'

'What would I find out?'

Both girls spun around to see Ware herself standing in the doorway. She was sniffing the air like a bloodhound.

'You...you're back early!' Victoria stammered, her cheeks burning guiltily.

'I knew you were up to something. All that

whispering together yesterday. What's that smell? What have you been doing while—'

'Ahem...' Henrietta Crainby coughed. 'I did ring but apparently no one heard.'

'Oh ma'am, I'm so sorry. It's these stupid girls! They—'

'Yes, Ware, I leave them to you. I came down to tell you Mr Luke found the goose delicious. Indeed the whole luncheon was excellent today. I thought this was your day off. I wondered how you had contrived such a special treat for Sir William's birthday. I should have guessed you had sacrificed your free time.'

Ware gaped a moment, her mouth slightly open then she simpered, 'It was a pleasure, ma'am. I'm so glad Sir William was pleased.'

Milly gasped aloud. Ware quelled her with a scowl.

'Thank you, Ware. We are all impressed. I knew my mother's friend would not have recommended you if you had not been an experienced cook.'

Ware flushed but she remained silent. Henrietta Crainby nodded, picked up her skirts and retreated.

Victoria was unaware of the mixture of contempt, disbelief and pity reflected on her face as she stared at the older woman.

'It's plain to see how you carry on when I'm not here to supervise,' Ware said coldly. 'This kitchen is filthy. You can start by wiping down every shelf, scrub the tables and then you will scrub every inch of the floor.'

'But...' Milly began

'And if it is not to my satisfaction you will do it again. Get on with it, girl, and don't dare argue with me.'

Victoria and Milly turned away, gazing at each other in dismay. They were exhausted by their morning's labours. As she turned to leave Ware spied the tattered recipe book lying open on the long wooden dresser. She knew at once what it was. She had seen the old woman referring to it and adding notes now and then. She gathered it up into the folds of her dress and took it to her room.

The door to the laundry was always left open when Mrs Baxter was ironing. She had overheard everything. Her sympathy was with the girls.

'Hey, you two, come in here,' she hissed softly.

Victoria and Milly went dejectedly into the laundry. 'She's gone,' Victoria told her. 'There's no need to whisper.'

'Ware is a jealous, spiteful bitch. I wouldn't have believed it if I hadn't heard her with my own ears, taking credit.' She nodded at Victoria. 'If you take my advice ye'll give the floor no more than a wipe over with wet cloths. She'll be none the wiser. I saw the pair of you scrubbing it early this morning and there's nothing wrong with it except for a bit of grease where ye moved the goose from the oven to the serving platter. Scatter a wee bit of soda over it and it'll be all gone by the time ye wipe it with the cloth.'

It was much later when Victoria remembered the recipe book. She went to get it but it was nowhere to be seen. Neither Milly nor Mrs Baxter had seen it. They searched everywhere. The evening meal had been served and cleared away before Ware appeared to inspect the kitchen.

'Have you seen Granny's recipe book?' Victoria asked at once. 'I left it on the dresser.'

For a moment Ware hesitated, then her eyes narrowed, her lip curled. 'Do you mean that tattered old bundle which someone left lying around?'

'It was not a tattered old bundle. It was the most precious—'

'Well, miss! There's no place in my kitchen for such filthy rubbish. I threw it in the fire. That's the end of it.'

'You threw it in the fire?' Victoria gasped incredulously. Her face had gone alarmingly white.

'I did. Now get out of here before I throw you out.'

'No. No. You can't have burned Granny's book. You can't...' Barely aware what she did Victoria darted at Ware, pummelling her corseted figure. Taken unawares by the small hurtling figure the woman stumbled backwards, crashed into a kitchen chair, and then on to the floor in an undignified bundle of skirts. Victoria stood over her, her brown eyes blazing. 'How could you? You're a wicked, horrible, lying woman...' She began to sob, great wrenching sobs.

Milly watched helplessly. She had never seen Victoria lose control before. She wished Mrs Baxter was still here, but she had left ages ago.

Ware scrambled to her feet, her pale eyes glaring, her face screwed up with fury. 'You... you attacked me! You have injured me. You'll pay for this. Oh yes, I'll see you pay. I shall speak to Mrs Crainby. Don't you ever come back in here. There's no place for you now. Nor anywhere else. You'll never get a reference.'

Victoria was too distraught to take in what she was saying, but Milly understood only too well. Jobs were hard enough to get, but without a reference it would be impossible.

'Come on, Victoria. Come home now,' she urged, wrapping her arms around Victoria's shaking shoulders.

Eight

Stripped to the waist Andrew Pringle was washing himself at the outside pump when Victoria returned to the cottage. He knew at once she was upset. A great tenderness welled up inside him as she tried to stifle her sobs. He had always had a deep affection for her, an urge to protect. But he was a man now and his feelings were changing.

'Whatever has upset you so, my wee Vicky?'

He set the rough towel aside and opened his arms. Like a child she ran into them, feeling his strength as he held her close. 'Did you burn the goose? Is that it?' Over her head he saw his mother come to the cottage door. His desire to hold her increased but he slackened his grip as he met his mother's questioning gaze.

Polly had seen Victoria brushing away tears as she came up the path.

'The g-goose was fine. Even Mrs Crainby enjoyed it. Sh-she c-came down to the kitchen to tell us. She n-never does that...'

'Then what's wrong?' Andrew asked.

Haltingly Victoria recounted the day's events, but it was only when she repeated Ware's words about losing her job and having no reference to get another one that the full implication hit her. She drew back and looked up into Andrew's face, her eyes wide with shock and horror.

'Did you really hit her, lassie?' Joe Pringle asked. He had joined his wife in the doorway. 'It's what I'd like to have done many a time.'

'I don't know...I d-don't know. What shall I do without a job?'

Andrew's arms tightened again; anger at the Ware woman surged in him.

'I canna think it will be that bad,' Polly soothed. 'Anyway she had no business burning a book that didna belong to her. I know how much you treasured your granny's recipe book, lassie. It was like her Bible – a part of her life. The laird will understand how important it was to you.'

'B-but it isn't the laird. Ware was going to tell

111

Mrs Crainby. I don't think she likes me either, but I've never done anything wicked before.'

'Come away inside, bairn. You're tired out. It's been a long day with all the excitement.'

Reluctantly Andrew allowed his arms to fall to his sides, ignoring his mother's shrewd glance.

'Mrs Crainby thinks Ware cooked everything,' Victoria said dully.

'How could she think that?' Joe demanded.

Victoria explained.

'And Ware didn't tell her you had done the cooking?'

'No,' Victoria said as she shook her head. 'Wh-what shall I do without a job? The laird will stop paying my lodgings.'

Polly thought she was like a small wounded animal and she drew her into her arms and cradled her against her ample bosom.

'You'll always have a home here with us, lassie, whether or no the laird pays your lodgings. To tell the truth I never thought of him offering such a thing when I asked you to come and live with us. Joe and me, well we've always wished you were our wee lassie. We want you here, all of us.'

'Don't you worry, Victoria, we'll not starve,' Joe reassured her.

But Victoria did worry. The Pringles had three boys still at school. They needed food and clothes. Andrew contributed to the family's expenses but she knew he was saving up every penny he could earn. She didn't know what he wanted the money for but she knew it was important to him.

Then there were her clothes. She had grown out of the clothes she had worn to school. She was taller now and she blushed at the sight of her swelling chest. Polly had taken in the seams of one of her own dresses. It was lilac and suitable for her to wear to the kirk on Sundays. At the castle all the servants were provided with dresses and aprons and caps for work, but if she had no work she would have no clothes either. She had to earn her living. The Pringles were generous but she couldn't accept charity from them, or anyone else.

'Listen to me, Victoria,' Andrew said, seeing the anxiety clouding her brown eyes. 'Go to bed and have a good sleep. Everything seems worse when you're tired. You're supposed to be free tomorrow afternoon anyway, and she did tell you not to come back, so if you wake up in time you can come with me to the farm.'

'Can I?' Victoria brightened, but only briefly. Her shoulders slumped. 'Ware always leaves me jobs to do on my day off. She didn't give me any for tomorrow. She doesn't intend me to go back.'

'There'll be other jobs, don't you fret,' Polly tried to comfort her. 'I'm sure Sir William will give you a reference. He's always had a liking for ye. Or we could ask the doctor or the schoolmaster. They both speak highly of you, Victoria. They enquire about you whenever I see them.'

Victoria went to bed but she didn't sleep well. At five o'clock she heard Andrew creeping down the steps. She rose and washed her face in the cold water from the ewer and quickly pulled on her clothes.

'Wait for me, Andrew, please?' she whispered. Together they ate a hurried snack of bread and dripping and a mug of buttermilk then crept outside.

Andrew fashioned a pad from his folded raincoat and tied it to his crossbar. He grinned at her as he used to do when he gave her piggybacks home from school. They wobbled precariously and, in spite of her heavy heart, Victoria couldn't help laughing as they pedalled away down the track towards the village. When they had left the village well behind and the track to Langmune began to rise more steeply, they walked side by side while Andrew pushed the bike.

'I don't want to make you late for work,' Victoria said.

'We're in good time.' He turned to smile at her. 'Anyway I shall set you to work and we'll soon catch up. The main thing is to get the cows milked and have the churns at the road end in time for the milk lorry. The driver is usually there by a quarter past seven so we can't afford to waste time. Old Ted, the cowman, isna very fit since he had the bronchitis, so it's up to me to get moving. Maybe you'll help carry the milk from the byre to the dairy?'

'I'll do anything if it will help,' Victoria promised.

'That's fine then. The milk has to be cooled

before it goes away to the creamery. We pour it over a water cooler and catch it in the churn below. It's important not to let the churns run over and waste milk down the drain.'

'Ooh, I hope I can manage all right.'

'You will!' Andrew assured her with a grin. 'If you come often to Langmune on your day off I'll teach you to milk a cow too.' His face sobered when he saw the shadows return to Victoria's eyes.

'I may not have a job at all,' she said recalling the previous day's events. 'I hate the Ware woman,' she added vehemently. 'Granny's book was the most precious thing I had in the entire world.'

Andrew tucked her hand in his. 'You'll make a recipe book like Mistress McCrady's, Victoria. I heard her tell mother more than once that you were a born cook. But I know it meant a lot to you and I don't blame you for disliking Eve Ware. Nobody at the castle has much good to say about her. Father thinks Mrs Crainby only keeps her because she wants to assert her authority.'

'I suppose so,' Victoria said unconvinced. Instinct told her Mrs Crainby disliked her because she had always been at Darlonachie and the laird had always been kind to her. Mr Luke had always been friendly too. Some of her earliest memories were of him getting down on his hands and knees on the castle lawns, persuading her to climb on his back while he pretended he was her horse. He often accompanied her into

115

the kitchens too. Granny said he missed his elder brother and his school friends so he was lonely when he came home. She cooked all his favourite foods. He had read her stories and helped her learn her letters and numbers. Once he had tried to teach her to ride his pony but she had fallen off and they had both been in trouble.

'What are you thinking about that makes you so sad, Victoria?' Andrew asked, breaking into her reverie.

'I–I was thinking how friendly Mr Luke used to be when I was young. Granny always said we must not forget we were servants at the castle, even though the laird and Mr Luke treated us so kindly. I've never been anywhere except the castle. I don't want to leave, Andrew...' Her chin trembled and she shivered. 'I hate Eve Ware, b-but I d-don't want to go away to live.'

'We don't want you to go away either, Victoria,' Andrew put his free arm around her shoulders and hugged her. 'It wouldn't be the same without you around. Let's wait and see what happens. After all it's only Ware's word against yours and Sir William is still the master and he's known to be a fair man. Look, here we are and here comes Mick!' He grinned and squatted down as a collie dog bounded up to them, his tail wagging, and ears pricked in welcome.

Andrew hugged him, then held out a hand. 'Paw?' The little dog obediently lifted one silky white paw and put it trustingly into Andrew's hand. 'Now you try, Victoria?' He grinned up at her. There was no doubting how much he loved the dog, or that the feeling was mutual.

Vicky felt almost envious. She bent down in front of the collie, stroking the silky fur of his head. It was black and tan with a little patch of white, but all four paws were white. Mick hesitated then in response to her soft voice he lifted a paw. Victoria took it gently and patted his head, delighted that he had offered her his greeting too.

'Go back to your kennel now, old boy,' Andrew said and pointed towards the farm house. 'I'll introduce you to Miss Traill, the housekeeper, at breakfast time, Victoria. We need to get busy with the milking now.' He led her towards the long whitewashed building which he called the byre.

'How warm it is!' Victoria said in surprise.

'Aye, the cows give off a lot of heat.' As he talked he cleaned the channels where the muck and urine had collected and which ran all the way from one end of the building to the other behind the two rows of cows. 'Mr Rennie used to be at the milking when I first started working here,' he explained. 'He insisted we clean up the night's dung before we bring in the buckets and stools for milking. Ted and his wife and daughter will be here soon. You can fetch the luggies and stools from the dairy if you like, Victoria. It's the square building across the yard.'

'What are the luggies?'

'The milking pails. You'll find them sitting upside down in a row. They have one handle and

117

fit between our knees. When we've milked the first few cows we take the milk to the dairy in the ordinary buckets. I'll set up the water cooler and show you what to do to fill the churns.' He grinned. 'There's always a job for everybody who comes to Langmune.'

'I'd like to help. There's something warm and comforting in here with all the cows munching and looking contented. Don't they mind being tied by their necks?'

'I don't know, lass,' Andrew said as he grinned. 'I canna speak cow talk.' His expression grew serious. 'Tying them into their stalls is the only way to keep order but I suppose they must be glad to be free when they get out to the fields. You should see them gallop across the field and kick their heels in the air the first day they get out after the winter. They lick themselves to groom away the dust and dirt. They can't do that when they're tied up so we have to groom their flanks with a metal curry comb. Whenever we have time to spare on a wet day there are always the cows to groom.'

'You love the farm and the animals, don't you, Andrew?' Victoria said softly.

'Aye. Aye, I do.' Andrew stopped brushing the channels for a moment and looked her in the eye. 'I dream about it sometimes – having a wee farm of my own, and – and a wife and bairnies to run around and enjoy it with me. Of course I know it'll never happen but I'm saving up. Even if I can't have a farm I shall try to rent a cottage with a big garden so I could keep a few pigs and

118

hens of my own.'

'Granny's cottage has a big garden,' she said wistfully. 'It goes right down to the burn, but it's grown wild with no one to keep it.'

'Aye,' Andrew said thoughtfully. 'I'd forgotten that. Maybe...' He broke off as a cool breeze came down the byre when the door opened to admit an elderly looking man and two women. 'This is Ted Holmes and his wife, Edna, and their daughter, Rosie. They help with the milking and Rosie looks after the dairy and keeps everything clean, don't you Rosie?'

'I try to, but you're never satisfied, Andy Pringle. What's your name?' she asked, staring hard at Victoria.

'This is Victoria Lachlan, a friend of mine,' Andrew replied before Victoria could open her mouth.

'OK, Victoria.' Rosy grinned. She was about twenty, Victoria thought, plump and rosy faced with freckles on her nose. Although Andrew was not quite nineteen Victoria got an impression that Rosie admired him and was trying hard to gain his approval. Her heart sank.

As the milking progressed Victoria found she had no time for thinking. The milkers emptied their luggies into two larger pails in the middle of the byre and as these were filled Victoria carried them to the dairy to pour into the D-pan above the cooler. Seeing how small she was Andrew found her a wooden block so that she could reach higher without so much effort and to avoid spilling. She kept a watchful eye on the milk churns which caught the milk after it had trickled over the ridges of the cooler. Each one held ten gallons and she found them heavy to move when they were full. Rosie came into the dairy with some of the milk.

'Am I getting behind?' she asked.

'Och no, bless ye,' she giggled. 'It's nice tae have help. We take it in turns to bring the milk across to the dairy when we're on our own.' Seeing Victoria struggle to move a full churn she showed her how to tilt it on its rim and roll it. 'I handle plenty o' these fellows,' she muttered, giving one of the churns a kick. 'It's my job to clean and sterilize them when they come back frae the creamery. Sometimes they're stinking.' She pulled a face and Victoria laughed.

'Do you like working on the farm, Rosie?'

'Never done anything else. Youngest o' six, ye see. The rest are married, working on farms on the estate, 'cept oor Dickie. He's the black sheep, works in a mine in Yorkshire. He went on the march in the big strike. Ma thinks he's gone to hell.'

'I see...'

'Hey, come on you two! Stop gossiping and bring the buckets back,' Andrew called, but there was laughter in his voice. 'We're waiting to empty our luggies.'

'Proper slave driver he is!' Rosie said, but she grinned up at Andrew and gave him a flirtatious wink which made Victoria blush. She felt young and gauche beside Rosie.

Ted had finished milking his last cow and set

120

his luggie to one side. 'Dinna empty that, lassie, or ye'll be in trouble. 'Tis beestings for her calf.' He jerked his head towards a young heifer with a bloody string hanging from her.

'Oh!' Victoria gasped. She wondered what the trailing stuff was. She'd never seen an animal being born. She looked in the luggie. It looked like thick yellow custard. A middle aged man came striding down the centre of the byre.

'Ye're early this morning,' he boomed grumpily. 'I'd better take this and get on wi' feeding the calves.'

'Here, you can take this one as well,' Andy said rising and lifting his stool from beside a young animal with a painfully swollen udder. 'She wouldn't give much this morning but it will be enough to feed her calf.' He turned to Victoria. 'The young calves get their own mother's milk. It's rich, see. It would set like scrambled eggs if you heated it. Some people make beestings custard but I can't fancy it. Mr Rennie calls it colostrum. He says it helps the young calves fight diseases if they get the first milk from their mothers. We leave them to suckle for a day then we take them away and feed them from a bucket.'

'And who would you be then?' The newcomer asked abruptly.

'Victoria Lachlan.'

'Victoria, this is George Green. GeeGee we call him. He's always grumpy this early in the morning. Must be the name for he's like that young brother o' mine.'

Ted Holmes took out a pocket watch and flicked it open.

'We're a good half hour earlier this morning. You must have worked hard, lassie.' He gave Victoria a toothless smile.

'Aye, made a difference, she has,' his wife said as she nodded. 'I'll get away home and get the porridge boiling.'

'Fair enough,' Ted said. 'I'll saddle up the horse and cart while ye get the churns measured up and sealed, Andy.'

'I shall not be long this morning. Victoria seems to have got them all well filled for us.' Andrew showed Victoria how to measure the gallons according to the dents on the side of the churns, then he put the heavy lids on tightly and sealed them with a lead seal. 'We write down the date and the gallons we have sent away in that book. Mr Rennie keeps a record as well, up at the house. He'll ask when we go in for breakfast. We check it with the creamery figures to make sure they pay for the right amount. Some of them can't be trusted.' As he talked he deftly rolled the churns out of the door.

Ted came round with the horse and cart and they lifted the churns in together. 'I'll take them to the road end and drop them off,' Ted volunteered.

'You're sure you can manage?' Andrew asked.

'Aye. I expect this wee lady is ready for her breakfast after the work she's done. Will Miss Traill feed her? She could come to us if ye like?'

'Thanks, Ted, but Miss Traill always makes

122

more porridge than we can eat. She feeds some to the cats. Come on, Victoria.' He lifted a big shiny can from the stone table in the dairy. It was like a miniature milk churn with a handle. 'This is the house milk. Miss Traill always sets it out in a big shallow bowl then she skims off the cream ready for the porridge next morning. There's always too much so she churns it into butter on a Friday. You'll see her making it today.'

'Granny used to make butter, until Billy Wright's wife started doing it for her down at Home Farm, don't you remember?'

'So she did. I'd forgotten.'

Victoria was surprised to find Miss Traill looked as old as her grandmother. Andrew introduced them but the elderly woman was quiet and wary and Victoria felt uncertain of her welcome.

The main kitchen at Langmune was large and warm with a big black range with a water boiler on one side. On the adjacent side of the room there were several doors which Andrew told her led to the scullery, the pantry and the wash house, but a fourth door, almost in the corner, was open. It was the dining room and an elderly looking man was seated before the fire, apparently waiting for Andrew to remove his boots and bring him a report of the day's milk consignment.

Miss Traill took the milk can from him and carried it into the pantry. Through the open door Victoria could see a row of stone tables down one side. On one of these stood two large creaming pans. There were shelves with bowls of eggs. On the opposite side a ham and a side of bacon hung from large hooks in the ceiling. The ham was shrouded in muslin. Later Andrew explained it was to keep the flies off during the summer. Along the back of the pantry there were shelves right up to the ceiling. They held jars of preserved fruits and jams, pickled onions and beetroots. There was also a crock of salt and a large chest which Victoria guessed held the bags of flour and oatmeal. In many ways the kitchen premises were a smaller version of the castle kitchens, but they were huge when compared with the tiny sculleries of the cottages and the kitchen-cum-living rooms where all the cooking, eating and living was done.

There was a well scrubbed table in the centre and a wide dresser along one wall. This was filled to capacity with blue and white dishes of every shape and size, but all with the same matching pattern. In one corner a rocking chair had been pushed back and beside it was a rolled up rag rug. Victoria guessed that Miss Traill sat in front of the kitchen fire at the end of the day. Under the chair a big tabby cat lay fast asleep.

In the pantry Miss Traill stood on a small stool to cut extra slices of bacon from the flitch.

'I'm s-sorry if it is an inconvenience to you, having me for breakfast, I mean,' Victoria said diffidently. 'Mr Holmes said I could have some breakfast with his family but Andrew—'

'Ted Holmes offered you breakfast?' The

housekeeper's eyes widened and she turned to look at Victoria more closely. 'And how, I wonder, did you manage to earn such approval? Did you help with the milking?'

'No. I don't know how to milk a cow so I carried the milk to the dairy.'

'That's the hardest job. 'Tis no so hard to sit beside a cow and milk her. Now I see why Ted felt you'd earned your breakfast. In here Mr Rennie is the boss. I've no doubt he'll invite you to break your fast with him presently, when Andrew gets round to telling him you're here.'

'I see. Is there anything I can do to help you?'

'Aye.' Miss Traill looked keenly at Victoria as though making sure she had heard aright, and that the offer was genuine. She nodded her grey head with its neat bun. 'You can take the milk can into the scullery and rinse it with cold water. I wash it in hot water later so don't be wasting any now. Then you can lay an extra place for yourself in the dining room.'

'In the dining room?'

'Aye, 'tis Mr Rennie's custom. He sticks to some of the genteel ways he knew as a young man so he always eats in the dining room. I eat with him these days, so does Andrew.'

'I see...' Victoria said uncertainly.

'Mr Rennie was not brought up to farm life. His family were not gentry exactly, but they were...different, wealthy and educated. He keeps up some of the refinements he was accustomed to. When we first came to Langmune the men in the bothy and the two live-in maids

125

always ate in here at the kitchen table. He invited me to eat with him,' Miss Traill said. 'Now Andrew joins us. He enjoys the laddie's company since he got used to him being around.'

Victoria nodded and went to the scullery with the milk can. When she returned she began to smooth down her apron before entering the dining room.

'Oh dear, how grubby I am!' she exclaimed in dismay. 'I should have brought a clean apron with me.'

Miss Traill turned to look at her. 'Aye, you should. That will not do. I must lend you one of mine, though it will likely go round you twice.' In fact Miss Traill was as thin as a sparrow but she was taller than Victoria.

'It fits beautifully now that I have tucked it up,' Victoria said with satisfaction. 'At least I am clean again. I will launder it and send it back with Andrew. Granny always got cross with maids who wore dirty aprons.'

'She brought you up well then. Now go and lay a place in the dining room.'

Mr Rennie looked up enquiringly when Victoria entered. Andrew quickly introduced her and the man greeted her gruffly, but his blue eyes were shrewd and she knew he missed nothing of her appearance although he returned to his discussion of the work for the day ahead. He was a tall gaunt man and Victoria could hear the breath rattling in his chest whenever he spoke more than a couple of sentences.

A few minutes later she thought she had never enjoyed a plate of porridge and cream so much in her life. She helped Miss Traill clear away the empty bowls and carry in the plates of bacon and eggs, with potato scones and a large plate of freshly made soda scones. Even Mr Rennie ate a hearty meal and Victoria wondered how he stayed so thin when he didn't seem to go out much.

After breakfast Andrew returned to the kitchen to reclaim his boots.

'We have to go fencing in the far field today, Victoria. I hadna expected that when I asked you to come today. Some of the neighbour's cattle have been straying on to Langmune land and he never mends his own fences. I hope you will not be too bored.'

'You know I'm never bored,' Victoria said. 'If there's anything I can do to help I'll come with you, but Miss Traill has promised to show me a brood of chicks, and you said there was a new litter of piglets and three pet lambs. Perhaps I could help with them if I stay here?'

'She's a handy wee maid, Miss Traill,' Andrew said earnestly to the housekeeper. 'Shall I take her with us in the horse and cart or can she help you until midday?'

'We-ell...' Miss Trail frowned. 'I'm not used to company these days...' She looked searchingly at Victoria. 'If you want to help, and so long as you don't mind the company of an old woman instead o' Andrew, there's plenty you can do. There's the butter to churn today.'

'Then I shall stay here until you return,' Victoria said and smiled at Andrew.

He grinned back at her. 'You're not sorry you came?'

'Of course not.' Her face clouded. 'What would I have done at home? Only think about Eve Ware.'

'Och, I didna mean to remind you of that woman. I'll be back at noon, then I'll take you to see the piglets.'

Victoria watched him stride across the farmyard with a jaunty step. 'He's so happy here...' she said wistfully, almost to herself.

'Aye, he seems to be. Now, lassie, we'll feed the hens first and I'll show you the chicks. Maybe later you'll collect the eggs for me when you know where all the hen houses are.'

'Yes, I'd like that. And I'll help you churn the butter. I used to turn the churn for Granny if I was home from school.'

'Andrew told us you were a bright pupil at the school,' Miss Traill recalled. 'He said you had to leave when your grandmother died.'

'He was a bright pupil himself,' Victoria said. 'Mr Nelson, the schoolmaster, said he was one of the best. He thought it was a waste of a good brain for him to be a farm worker, but Andrew has three younger brothers so he wanted to earn some money. Besides, he loves the animals. He wants some of his own one day.'

'Aye? So Mr Rennie has the right measure o' the laddie then.'

Miss Traill was not used to chatter but Victoria

didn't mind. There was so much to see and do at Langmune. She was used to working and she sang to herself as she turned the butter churn.

'She seems a cheerful child,' Mr Rennie remarked, hearing her as he passed the open door of the scullery.

'Aye. She's not shy o' work either. She has worked at the castle since her grandmother died, but if I'm reading the signs right there's trouble there when she has time to think about it. Maybe that's why she's singing, to escape her thoughts.'

'Well, we both know life is never smooth for any of us, Miss Traill.'

'Aye, 'tis so.' Miss Traill sighed.

Except for her employer there were few people who knew of her own past. Her father had been a minister in the market town of Hawick where Mr Rennie's family had owned several woollen mills. She had been engaged to be married to a young man who worked as a clerk in one of the mills. Shortly before their wedding Bruce had been killed in a freak accident while walking between some of the machines at the mill. It had taken her a long time to get over the tragedy and the doctor had recommended a complete change of scene with plenty of fresh air.

It was about that time that Mr Rennie had had a serious quarrel with his father. He had refused to take his place in the mills. He had moved to Dumfriesshire and taken over the tenancy of Langmune, using the legacy from his mother to buy cattle and sheep to stock the farm, as well as horses, for working carts and a plough and other equipment from the outgoing tenant.

There had been two married men and their families and several single men in the bothy at that time, before the war claimed some of them. Mr Rennie had needed a respectable house-keeper to take charge of the maids and to feed the men. Miss Traill had applied for the post. She had welcomed hard work as an antidote to grief. She had been at Langmune ever since. She had learned a lot, but she had never forgotten her lost love.

After some years Mr Rennie had reached an agreement with Sir William Crainby and between them they had repaired one of the derelict cottages. Now there were three married men with families working on the farm. The bothy was empty and Andrew was the only single man. A woman came up from the village three days each week to help with washing and ironing, but she refused to do anything outdoors.

Miss Traill didn't mind. She liked the poultry. She had even learned to milk in her younger days. Now it was as much as she could manage to look after her hens and rear enough new chicks each year to keep the numbers up. She had not welcomed Andrew in the beginning. Young men had healthy appetites and that meant extra work. She was beginning to feel her age now the years were creeping on. But Andrew had proved a pleasant lad and gradually she had begun to make most of his meals.

His presence had breathed new life into the household, for both herself and Mr Rennie. Andrew repaid her by making sure she was well supplied with logs and sticks to light the fires. Mr Rennie felt the cold badly and suffered from the damp chill of winter so she always lit a fire in his bedroom, except in high summer. When he had time Andrew topped up and trimmed the paraffin lamps for her, a task she had never enjoyed. Mr Rennie was planning to bring electricity to the farm and it couldn't come soon enough for her.

Andrew had mentioned the girl who had moved in with his family after the death of her grandmother, but Miss Traill was surprised that he had brought her to Langmune. She was even more surprised by Victoria's readiness to help with whatever tasks the day demanded.

There were so many things to see and so much to do that Victoria could scarcely believe it was milking time again. This time she was prepared for the routine.

'You'll both have a long walk home,' Miss Traill said. 'I've set out some scones and cheese and a jar of freshly made lemon curd. Be sure to eat up before you start the milking, Andrew.'

Andrew looked at Victoria and smiled. 'I think you've won Miss Traill's approval, Victoria.'

'I do hope so,' she said with feeling. Her brow creased and he knew her thoughts had moved back to Eve Ware and her job. At least he had managed to take her mind off her troubles for most of the day.

131

'Come on, jump on the cross bar and we'll ride down hill together for part of the way.'

'It's been a lovely day, Andrew!' She settled herself between his thighs while he held his coat in place along the bar. Soon the breeze was catching her cap and blowing strands of hair across Andrew's face. It smelled of lavender and his arms tightened involuntarily. She half turned towards him, laughing into his face.

'This is wonderful, feeling the wind in my hair. I wish we could go on for ever.'

'So do I, so do I,' Andrew answered softly. 'Unfortunately we're nearly at the bottom of the hill. We'll have to walk for a bit before we can both ride again.'

The last stretch from the village to the castle was mainly a gentle incline and Andrew pulled Victoria back on to the cross bar. It was worth the effort of pedalling a bit harder to hold her close. They were only fifty yards from home when they met another cyclist riding towards them.

'Hey, you're back.' Mark Jacobs slithered to a halt beside them.

Andrew had no option but to put his feet on the ground and stop. Victoria jumped off and ran straight to Mark, hugging him fiercely.

'Oh, Mark! It's so good to see you.' Her greeting was warm and spontaneous.

Andrew watched. Moments before his spirits had been soaring with the lark. Now they sank like lead. 'We're nearly home,' he said stiffly. 'I'll leave you now.' Without waiting for a reply

132

he pedalled furiously away. Mark Jacobs would always come first with Victoria, he reminded himself sternly. How could he have forgotten how close they were. Contrary to all his expectations Mark had not neglected Victoria for other friends since he moved to the academy. Nor did he consider himself too clever to discuss things with her. They were as close as ever and they had a rapport which Andrew envied.

Looking out of the scullery window Polly Pringle had seen the meeting, and witnessed Victoria's eager embrace. Of course they were little more than children yet, but she was surprised Mark Jacobs had remained such a constant friend to Victoria now his own life had moved on, and his future seemed likely to be far removed from hers. As he came closer Polly noticed Andrew's slumped shoulders, the bleakness on his lean face. Ah, the awful pangs of first love, she thought and her heart ached for her firstborn child. He was almost a man now, but the capacity for hurt did not grow less with age. Men learned to hide it better.

Nine

'Victoria! How are you?' Mark said. 'Mistress Pringle told me you were upset over trouble at the castle. She said Andrew had taken you to his farm to get your mind off things.'

'Yes.' Victoria frowned. 'Yes, I suppose that is why he took me with him.'

'What upset you? Was it that woman?'

'Eve Ware.' Victoria nodded. All the joy had gone out of the day. The sun had gone down and a chilly wind was springing up. She shivered, missing the warmth and shelter of Andrew's body.

'Are you cold? I'll leave my bike here. We'll go up to our cave then you can tell me. I've things to tell you too.'

'All right.'

Mark propped his bike against a tree and took her hand. Together they went along the narrow path through the wood and up to the shelter they still regarded as their cave.

'Tell me your news first, Mark,' Victoria said. 'It can't be as bad as mine.'

'It's good news. Do you want to hear?' He looked anxious, almost guilty.

'Of course I want to hear, Mark, especially if

it's good news.'

'I've had good results in all my exams. Well, all except Latin,' he admitted honestly. 'Even Uncle Peter is proud of me.'

'He has always been proud of you, Mark. We all are.'

'We-ell, I'm not sure about that. He gives me some very strange looks sometimes. Anyway I'm to be moved up a year but I'm to have extra lessons in Latin.'

'That's splendid news, Mark.' Victoria was genuinely pleased for him despite her own bleak future. 'Do you think you'll be able to keep up?'

'I think so. It will mean extra work most weekends, though. It takes such a long time to become a doctor. Anything which will shorten the time would be worth working for, don't you agree, Victoria?' He looked at her, his brown eyes, eager for her approval. 'I hope I can manage it.'

'Of course you'll do it,' Victoria said robustly and squeezed his arm.

'Here we are,' Mark said happily, and bent to brush away the debris from a small tree trunk they had often used as a seat. They sat down side by side. 'Now tell me what upset you yesterday?'

Victoria recounted the events of the previous day. She left nothing out.

'I've never lost my temper like that before but I felt so – so...Granny's recipe book was like having her beside me. But I've never hit anyone – ever. I don't know if I did hit her, but she said

135

I did and she says I shall lose my job. I don't know what I'm going to do. She said I wouldn't get another job without a reference.'

Mark's fists had clenched and his jaw set. 'I wish I was a man and I could...I could confront her, or...'

'There's nothing anyone can do,' Victoria said forlornly. 'Polly said your uncle might give me a reference, but I would probably have to go away from here and live in some other house.'

'Oh, Victoria! I don't want you to go away from here! I know Uncle Peter would give you a reference. He thinks it's a pity you couldn't go to the academy like I do. Mr Nelson told him you were as clever as I am, but I knew that anyway.'

'Well, I can't go so it's no use talking about it,' Victoria said tensely.

'No, I'm sorry. I wish I knew how to help you. I could ask Aunt Anna if any of her friends could find you work.'

'Would you ask her?' Victoria asked.

'Of course I will, as soon as I get home. Come on, you're getting cold.'

As they drew near the edge of the wood Joe Pringle was leaning against a tree. He had been waiting for them and he saw Victoria's face was streaked with tears.

'Mark is going to ask his uncle if he will give me a reference,' she said as they drew level with Joe.

'I would like to help if I can, Mr Pringle,' Mark said earnestly.

'Aye, we all would, laddie. But we had better wait until after tomorrow. Victoria, Mr Luke wants to see you tomorrow morning at nine o'clock at the castle, in the library.'

'Oh!' Victoria clapped a hand to her mouth and looked up at him with wide frightened eyes.

'Och, lassie! There's no need to look like that. Mr Luke has known you all your life. He's a fair man. He wants to hear your side of what happened.' His eyes twinkled. 'Young Milly came by the gardens on her way home. She said the laird and Mr Luke had both complained about the cooking today. She said the custard was lumpy and the beef was like string. Maybe the Ware woman will realize she can't manage without ye.' He didn't tell her he had taken the opportunity to let Mr Luke know it was Victoria who had cooked the goose and the rest of the dinner, with only Milly to help her, and a bit of support from Mrs Baxter with the dishing out.

'Maybe everything will be all right, Victoria,' Mark said encouragingly and squeezed her hand.

'I'll never, never lose my temper again if Mr Luke says I can stay,' Victoria vowed fervently.

'I'd been waiting a while at Mrs Pringle's before you returned,' Mark said grinning, 'so I'd better get home before Aunt Anna sends a search party. Let me know if you want me to ask either of them for help.'

'All right.' Victoria gave him a wobbly smile.

'I'll walk with you to your bicycle, laddie,' Joe Pringle said. They watched Victoria until she

137

was out of sight. 'I don't think the laird, or Mr Luke, will let her go on the word o' Eve Ware,' Joe said, 'so maybe it would be best not to trouble your aunt and uncle, eh?'

'You mean you don't want me to tell them? But Victoria was so upset about her granny's recipe book. She treasured it.'

'Aye, I know. I think the Ware woman is jealous. It was a nasty thing to do, to destroy her book, but Victoria will manage.'

Joe watched the boy pedal away down the track towards the village. He was a nice laddie, he decided, in spite of his family and his education. He frowned. Mark Jacobs reminded him of someone but he couldn't think who.

Although Victoria was tired after the fresh air and the work at Langmune, she found it difficult to sleep. She couldn't help but worry and wonder what Mr Luke would say to her.

The following morning she presented herself at the library a few minutes before nine o'clock. Her hair was drawn back into a neat bun but nothing could stop the tiny curls which curved about her brow. Her apron was snowy white but her stomach was churning and her hands felt clammy with nerves as she knocked on the familiar door.

Mr Luke was there already and he bade her enter. He was seated at the library table. His expression was quizzical as he looked up at Victoria, but she was too nervous to notice the glint in his eyes. For the first time he realized that Victoria was no longer a child. She was on

138

the verge of womanhood and she was going to be a very attractive woman indeed.

'Don't look so worried, Victoria. Sit down on that chair and tell me what happened between you and Miss Ware.'

Victoria bit her lower lip. 'I – I was angry with her...I know I shouldn't have lost my temper and I'm sorry.'

'Are you?'

Victoria looked up swiftly. 'Well – well yes.'

'When you were small, Victoria, I often teased you and made you cross. I don't ever remember you losing your temper, though. Miss Ware must have done something very bad to provoke you. Come on, what was it?' Victoria stayed silent. 'I need to know so that I can resolve this – this quarrel to my own satisfaction.' It may not satisfy Miss Ware, he thought, and it certainly wouldn't please his wife after the heated discussion they'd exchanged on the subject of staff in general and Victoria Lachlan in particular.

'Well?' he demanded, with an impatient edge to his voice. 'Did she give you extra work to do?'

'Oh no! She often does that anyway. She was annoyed so she took my recipe book. It was Granny's. She had kept it all her life since she was a girl. It had all her recipes, and other things in.' Her voice shook with emotion even now.

'I see. Yes, I can understand that is something you would treasure, Victoria,' Mr Luke said and his voice was gentler. 'What has Miss Ware

139

done with it?'

'She burned it!' Her dark eyes glittered with remembered grief and anger.

'Burned it?' Mr Luke echoed incredulously. The woman's mad, he thought, mad and jealous. 'No wonder you were upset.' He steepled his fingers together and frowned. He would like to dispense with Ware's services but it was his wife's domain. 'You're so young still,' he muttered, more to himself than to Victoria. He looked up at her. 'I have it on good authority that it was you who cooked the goose and the rest of the meal on Thursday. Is that correct?'

'Yes, Mr Crainby,' Victoria said in a low voice and lowered her head. 'I'm sorry.'

'There's nothing to be sorry about. It was an excellent meal. I expect it made Miss Ware angry, you being so young and making such a good job. I'm astonished, but you always were a bright little thing and you've spent most of your life around the kitchens, helping your grand-mother. You couldn't have had a better teacher. Perhaps it would be better if you worked in an-other part of the castle, away from Miss Ware?' he mused 'But it would be a pity to remove you from the kitchens...'

'You mean I can stay here at the castle?' Victoria looked up, her brown eyes full of hope.

'Yes, you can stay, Victoria, but I do hope there will be no more problems.' He sighed heavily. Domestic staff were not his affair but he had felt it imperative to see that Victoria Lach-lan was treated fairly, and it was not as though

140

Ware was much of a cook, despite his wife's claims. In fact she was barely passable even as a plain cook. 'I think we were spoiled by the standard of your grandmother's cooking,' he said, speaking his thoughts aloud. 'Do you think you could be civil to Miss Ware for four days each week?'

'Only four days?' Victoria's face expressed alarm.

'Yes, four days. Ware will have two days off each week and I shall make it plain that you must do the cooking during her absence, and that you must be allowed to choose whatever is within your capabilities.'

'Oh, that would be wonderful!' Victoria clasped her hands together, her eyes shining. 'I wouldn't need to hide my cooking from Ware then. I love to cook and I know I shall get better...' Her eyes pleaded for understanding.

'If the goose is anything to judge by I think you are well on the way, Victoria. You have one day off, too, I believe?

'Half a day, on Fridays.'

'Ah, is that so?' He frowned. 'From now on you will have all of Friday off. So –' he assumed his sternest expression – 'can I trust you to get along with Ware for the other four days?'

'Oh yes, Mr Crainby! I promise I will never lose my temper with her again. I promise.' Victoria's eyes were shining and her knees felt weak with relief.

That might not be so easy as you imagine, Luke thought cynically.

His supposition proved only too correct. Eve Ware never lost an opportunity to find fault or provoke her. She insisted on tasks being repeated for no real reason, and generally treated her as a slave, but Victoria stuck to her resolve and gritted her teeth. She could not risk losing her job again. Milly had reported some of the gossip from the upstairs maids. One of them had overheard Mr and Mrs Crainby quarrelling because he insisted Victoria should be given another chance. Next time she would not be so lucky. Milly and Mrs Baxter sympathized with her and they all looked forward to the days when Ware visited her sister. They hoped she would go to another job but they knew it was a vain hope. She had a comfortable position and good wages at the castle and Mrs Crainby appeared to support her no matter what she did.

In spite of her vow to obey Ware and never to grumble again, there were many nights when Victoria felt almost too tired to undress, and many more when the tears would not be held back. Once or twice when he came home late Andrew heard her crying and he longed to comfort her. He felt helpless. She was too young to marry, even if he had had anything to offer a wife. Worse than that, Mark Jacobs always came to see her at least once a week and there was no doubt Victoria welcomed his company. She looked for him eagerly on Friday evenings when he came back from the academy for the weekend.

Victoria looked forward to her day off each week more than she had ever believed possible. She longed to go with Andrew to Langmune again, but time passed and he never suggested taking her again.

It was a Friday when Victoria was away from the castle that Henrietta Crainby gave birth to a baby daughter, Charlotte Anne Mary Crainby. Joe Pringle brought the news when he came home from work that evening, but it was Milly who filled in the details as soon as she saw Victoria the following morning.

'The midwife had been here half the night and she said the bairn wouldna be born for hours but Lady Crainby insisted on sending for Doctor Grantly. He told her the same thing and went away to take his surgery and do his house calls. Lucy, her maid, said she was furious,' Milly announced with relish. 'But they were right. The wee thing wasna born until half past four in the afternoon. You should have heard the screams and tantrums coming from Mrs Crainby's rooms yesterday.'

'Why did she scream?' Victoria asked innocently.

Milly gave her a strange look. 'Some women do, or so Ma says –' she shrugged – 'and you know what a fuss she makes at sight o' a spider. So you can imagine...'

'But surely she was not frightened by her own baby?'

'Victoria Lachlan, there's a lot ye dinna ken for all ye read so many books,' Milly muttered

143

in exasperation. 'Oh God, there she goes again! What can she want this time?' She went off to answer the persistent ringing of Henrietta Crainby's bell.

On her birthday Mark proudly presented Victoria with a thick volume of Mrs Beeton's *Book of Household Management*.

'It's not the same as your granny's book, Victoria, but Aunt Anna says it is the best she can recommend, wherever you go.'

'I do thank you for such a splendid book, Mark. I shall have to earn my living somewhere if not at the castle, so please thank your aunt too.' She smiled and gave him a hug, but in her heart the years seemed to stretch ahead with grey monotony. Recently George had teased Andrew about walking out with a girl from the next village. Andrew had aimed a cuff at his younger brother's ear but he had not denied it. Victoria couldn't understand why the news should depress her so badly.

As time passed George and Willie taunted their eldest brother about various girls. He had grown into an attractive man with his crooked grin and white even teeth, and the wave of brown hair which flopped over his brow when he was not wearing a cap. His blue eyes sparkled in his tanned face, but behind his cheerful facade Andrew had dreams of his own – quite impossible dreams, he often chided himself. He worked hard at Langmune but on the rare occasions when he attended the village dances he

144

was as light on his feet as any and he was popular with both the men and the girls.

Sometimes he went to see a film at the cinema in Dumfries and Victoria was always certain he had taken a girl. She hated it when she heard him creeping in late and climbing up the loft ladder.

Ten

In the autumn of 1935 Mark was preparing for life at the university in Edinburgh. During the last three summers he had spent a lot of his spare time accompanying Uncle Peter on his rounds.

'I'm sure he will make a first class doctor,' Peter Grantly said to his wife.

'And of course you're not prejudiced!' Anna teased.

'Of course not. I may have pushed him a bit with his studies but he has a natural compassion and he's keenly observant.'

'He's going to miss Victoria,' Anna reflected.

'Yes.' Doctor Grantly frowned. 'Yes, he is but I think it will be good for him. It is time he made other friends. He depends on Victoria too much for moral support. He will have to be more self reliant – the way Victoria has had to be.'

'I didn't think she would stick it out at the castle with that Ware person. Mrs Baxter says

145

she's the most spiteful woman she's ever met and she takes all the credit for Victoria's cooking.'

'Mmm, I agree her abilities are wasted, but we have problems enough of our own, at least until we see Mark through university, and there'll be his training after that. It would please me greatly if he decided to join me in the practice here.'

'Oh Peter, don't set your heart on it. You know he has always said he would join the army once he qualified as a doctor.'

'I suspect it was Victoria who put that idea into his head, but I can't imagine she will want him to go to the army now that they are both older and have a bit more understanding of life. I'd like to believe the Great War was the war to end them all, but I'm not convinced.'

'Well dear, as you said, we have enough problems without worrying about things which may never happen. Are you going to tell Victoria and Mark they are twins now they're nearly eighteen? I think it is time and you did promise Mrs McCrady...'

'Humph!' He scowled. 'The time is not right.'

'Will you ever think it's right?' Anna asked. 'They're young adults now. Anything could happen...'

'Another reason why it's good Mark is going away. It will keep them apart.'

'He has asked Victoria to write to him every week.'

'They can't get up to much mischief in letters. I believe Mark would feel guilty that he is going to university while Victoria is working as a servant for the Crainbys. He might refuse to go. No dear, I shall know when the time is right. We must encourage him to bring home new friends. Wean him away from Victoria.'

'I don't think we shall ever do that. There's an uncanny bond between them.'

'Well, I refuse to tell them yet.'

Andrew Pringle was as pleased as Doctor Grantly that Mark Jacobs was going away. He would meet lots of educated girls. Surely he would make new friends. Once he was at university he would soon forget Victoria. He might look down on her when he had his fine education though, and the last thing Andrew wanted was to see Victoria hurt.

'Victoria, can I ask you to do me a favour?' he asked one night when he came home from work.

'Of course. What is it?'

'You shouldn't agree so easily!' George teased. 'He might want to borrow a pound note.'

'Get on with you!' Andrew aimed a fist at the air above his younger brother's head, though both George and Willie were almost as tall Andrew now and both of them were working at farms on the estate.

'What did you want, Andrew?' Victoria asked curiously.

'Will you bake me one of those special chocolate cakes like you baked for Mother's birthday?'

'A chocolate cake?' Victoria's heart plummeted. Did he want it for one of his girlfriends?

'When I told Miss Traill about you making a cake for Mother she said she'd never had a birthday cake in her life and it was too late now. But it's not too late. She is seventy next week and it would be a surprise. Mr Rennie says I can get the extra eggs and milk from the farm. I'll give Mother the money to buy the flour and cocoa and whatever else you need from the grocer's van on Thursday. Will you make a list? Will you do it?'

'Of course I will. But how will you carry it on your bicycle?'

'Mr Rennie has offered to lend me his car. Can you believe that? He suggested I drive down here at lunchtime next Friday. It's your day off, isn't it? Will you come back with me?'

'Oh Andrew! I'd love to come.'

'You would? Even though you'll miss Mark? He always comes on Fridays because you're off.'

'I want to come to Langmune.'

'Wonderful!' Andrew grinned and lifted her off her feet to swing her round as he used to do when she was a child. But she wasn't a child any more and her heartbeat quickened at the feel of his strong arms and his hard chest. She hoped he hadn't noticed. When he set her back on her feet he laughed down into her face and his joy made her laugh back at him. 'I never dreamed Mr Rennie would be so keen to give Miss Traill a surprise. Certainly I never thought of him suggesting I use the car. He's going to buy her the biggest box of chocolates he can find, all tied up

148

with a ribbon. I've to drive him down to Annan. Goodness knows why he ever bought the car. It's nearly always me who drives him and he only goes to see Doctor Grantly, or to the bank.'

'Well, he must trust you with it, son,' Polly said proudly. 'They have three cars up at the castle now, I hear. Though how they can drive more than one at a time, I can't imagine.' Polly remarked.

'The new one is Mrs Crainby's,' Victoria said. 'She calls it The Wild Rose. It has beautiful cream leather seats. She won't let her own wee girl in it in case she makes a mess.'

'A mess?' Polly scoffed. 'With one prim and proper wee girl? I'd have thought they would have had another bairn by now.'

'Milly says Mrs Crainby doesn't want any more children.'

'As if Milly could know that!' Polly muttered. 'They still use the Hillman to go to the kirk. I've seen them. So why did they need the Bentley?'

'Mr Luke drives it when he goes to town on his own,' Victoria said.

'To town? All on his own-io?' George gave a mocking laugh. Victoria glanced at him curiously. 'He might set off in the direction of Annan but rumour has it your wonderful Mr Luke and his car are seen on the road up to the head of the glen nearly every day. He used to ride his big black stallion up there at one time, before Maggie Lennox was a widow. Now he takes the car and he can't hide that in the stable at High Bowie.' He winked at Victoria. She gave him a puzzled frown.

'You talk in riddles.'

'And you, sweetheart, are far too innocent for your own good.' He began to hum one of the songs Gracie Fields had made famous about the Isle of Capri. Then, barely above his breath, he sang some of the words, all the time holding Victoria's puzzled brown eyes with his twinkling blue ones:

Can you spare a sweet word of love?
She whispered softly, its best not to linger
Da-da, daa, Da-da daa Da-da dee...

'Get on with you!' Polly scolded, batting her arm in his direction and giving him a disapproving frown. He chuckled wickedly, escaped halfway up the loft ladder, then he leaned down to sing clearly:

She was as sweet as a rose at the dawning
But somehow fate hadn't meant her for me.

He wagged a finger at Andrew.

'Hey big brother, it's time you educated our wee fledgling. She's far too innocent for this wicked world.' He cocked his head at Victoria and grinned wolfishly before he disappeared.

'He's a terrible laddie!' Polly said shaking her head and pursing her lips. 'Now, lassie, be sure and make a list of the things you'll need for the cake.'

Victoria knew Polly was deliberately changing

the subject but she let it pass, determined to ask Andrew what George had meant at the first opportunity.

'I used the baking tins from the castle on Eve Ware's day off when I baked your cake, Aunt Polly, but I'd better not try that again. Granny had her own baking tins. We left all those things at the cottage, didn't we?'

'Aye, that we did. I thought you might be glad o' some of them for your own house one day, and it's not as though the laird needs the cottage.'

'I must go and have a look for them.'

'I'll come with you,' Andrew said promptly. 'We'll go now.'

'You'll need matches to light a lamp,' Polly reminded them. 'It gets dark early now the days are getting shorter and it will be dark inside.'

'All right if I borrow yours, Ma?' He reached up to the mantle shelf and pocketed the box of matches, then he shepherded Victoria outside.

'Do you go to the cottage with Mark?' Andrew asked. The words were drawn from him, though he knew he had no right to ask.

'Oh no. Mark and I usually go up to the cave – well, it's not a real cave, but it's where I used to play houses. It's dry and sheltered from the wind. I've hardly been in the cottage since... since...'

'I'm sorry, Victoria.' Andrew took her hand in his and squeezed it gently.

'I'm glad you offered to come with me.' She looked up at him with her wide brown eyes and

151

his heart jolted. George was right. Victoria was far too innocent for her age, but then she never went anywhere except with Mark Jacobs and he always seemed just as naıve. That wouldn't last long when he got away to university though.

'I hear young Milly has a boyfriend,' he said, wondering whether girls talked much about relations between men and women.

'Oh she has! It makes her more dreamy than ever,' Victoria said, and laughed. 'She says she's in love...' She frowned. 'Have you ever been in love, Andrew?' She was unaware of the yearning in her voice.

'I've never loved any of the girls I've taken to the pictures or to the dancing, if that's what you mean, Victoria.'

'You haven't?' Victoria beamed at him. The world seemed brighter, even though it was getting quite dark as they walked through the little wood.

Andrew opened the sturdy oak door of the cottage. People rarely locked up their houses. There was a film of dust everywhere but otherwise it was as they had left it after Joe and Andrew had moved Victoria's bed and bedding and her own clothes to the Pringles' cottage all those years ago. Polly had helped her store the spare blankets with camphor and lavender in the wooden blanket box. There was Granny's treasured tea set in the top of the cupboard, and various cooking utensils lower down. Below them the pans and baking tins had been neatly stacked. Polly had taken down the curtains which used to hide the box bed where her grandmother had slept. She had said they would only get dusty and harbour the moths.

Andrew trimmed the wick and lit the lamp which still stood in the middle of the table. Victoria looked around and memories came flooding back. The grate was empty now and the flagged floor bare of the bright rag rugs which had made the little cottage seem so cosy, but Granny's rocking chair still sat on one side of the fireplace. There was a musty, damp smell and it seemed cold and forlorn. She swallowed a huge lump in her throat and turned quickly, bumping into Andrew, unaware he had come up behind her until she collided with his chest. A stifled sob shuddered through her and Andrew's arms encircled her, holding her close against his chest.

'I shouldn't have brought you back here,' he said gruffly. 'Perhaps I shouldn't have asked you to bake a cake...'

'Oh, I'm glad you did, Andrew! I want to do it.' She sniffed hard and brushed away her tears but she didn't draw away from the comforting circle of his arms and Andrew was glad. He stroked her shining brown hair gently. She leaned against him feeling safe and warm. 'It's ridiculous...' She tried to laugh at herself, but it was a wobbly croak. 'It's five years now. I'm nearly eighteen,' she said firmly. 'Granny would tell me it's time I behaved like a grown woman.'

'You've been very brave, Victoria. We're all proud of you.'

'I – I don't know what I would have done without your mother and father, Andrew, and you and the boys. I'm sorry I could never call Aunt Polly "Mother" as she hoped I would do. I couldn't have had a better one if she'd been my very own.'

'She knows how you feel, Victoria, and she's pleased enough with Aunt Polly. And you know we all love you.'

'Do you, Andrew? Truly?'

'Truly.'

'I've been so fortunate to have you all. I could never have stayed at the castle if it hadn't been for your support.'

Andrew's arm tightened involuntarily and his fingers stilled. 'Are you very miserable there, Victoria? Is the Ware woman still as nasty?'

'Sometimes I think she's getting worse, but I've learned to cope with her. I'm not a child any more, and Mrs Baxter and Milly, and your father, and Billy Wright – they all know what she's like so I know it's not my fault when she starts shouting. I don't know whether I feel contempt or pity for her when she takes credit for the meals I've cooked. I think she knows I've no respect for her. I do most of the cooking now.'

'But that's unfair! You should be paid for what you do, Victoria, and have more free time, as she does.'

'I don't mind about that side of things. I'm learning all the time. Where else would I have an opportunity to cook so many dishes and experiment? Things will change one day.' He could feel her smile against his fingers as he stroked her cheek. She made no effort to draw away from him and Andrew savoured the precious minutes of holding her close.

'What sort of change? You think Ware will leave?'

'I doubt if she'll ever leave of her own free will, but Granny used to say everyone gets better with practice and one day I shall be ready to find another job. But for now I hate the thought of leaving Aunt Polly and – and all of you, everyone I love. I shall need a lot more courage to take such a step.'

'I hope you never leave us!' Andrew said sharply, unaware that his arm had tightened.

'There aren't many places near here that employ a cook. I've thought about it often, especially when Ware has been especially horrid. Mark says nothing lasts forever however bad it seems.'

At the mention of Mark Jacobs Andrew held her away to stare down into her face. 'Do you love Mark, Victoria?' The question was torn from Andrew.

'I shall miss him terribly. He always understands what I'm thinking,' she said slowly. 'Sometimes I don't even have to say any words but he seems to know how I feel.' She half turned her head to look towards the box bed beside the fireplace. 'I was born in there, Andrew. Granny, and Aunt Polly, they say nice things about my mama. B-but I never knew her...'

Andrew forced himself to hold her gently, and his hand moved soothingly up and down her spine.

She leaned into him again. It was quite dark outside now and it seemed right to confide the things which troubled her. 'I don't even know who I am – who my father is...I feel as though half of me is missing. Since Eve Ware found out she's always making nasty remarks. Twice she has called me a bastard.'

'The bitch!' Andrew's jaw tightened. 'How did she hear, do you know?'

'She said she had it on good authority from Mrs Crainby that I was spawned in the gutter.'

'She thinks of herself as a lady? Yet she talks like that – to a servant?'

'Granny never wanted to talk about...things, but I'm sure she would have told me if she had known who my father is. Don't you think so?' She raised her face to his.

It was so close. Andrew was sorely tempted to kiss her lips. He lowered his head, then drew back sharply. It would be a betrayal of his parents' trust as well as Victoria's while she lived under their roof, as one of the family.

'If your grandmother had known, other people would have known too, Victoria. But it doesn't matter who your father is. You are the one who matters. We all know you're a brave, sweet person.'

'Mark said something like that. It doesn't matter who I am, it's what I do with my life that counts.'

'I see...' So she had discussed all this with Mark Jacobs already. Andrew's arms fell to his sides. 'It's getting late. We'd better look for those cake tins and get back home.'

'I suppose so. Andrew, what did George mean about Mr Luke and...and everything.'

'Och, he was blethering. You know George.' Andrew knew he had spoken too quickly, too heartily. Victoria was not a child any more, and she was no fool either.

'He was hinting about Mr Luke doing something wrong, but what? You may as well tell me or I shall have to ask George himself, or pester you as I used to do on the way home from school when you found a bird's nest and wouldn't tell me. Come on...? Tell me!'

'Well...' Andrew sighed. 'Blast that young brother of mine and his big mouth.'

'He said there were rumours. What sort of rumours?'

'Doesn't Milly ever tell you the gossip?'

'Milly? We don't get much chance for long talks when Ware's around, and when she's not, well, all Milly talks about is her Jem. So...?'

'Och, it's gossip. Some folks reckon Mr Luke has a lady friend up the glen. A young widow she is now. Her husband was a tenant. Mr Luke has let her stay on as the tenant herself.'

'But surely that's a kind thing to do.'

'It would be, but I believe he does go up there more often than seems necessary, even if he has to advise her about running the farm. He was acquainted with her before he married Mrs

157

Crainby but she had a husband then. Gossip has it that she was his first love and he only married to please his father and get an heir. Don't ask me how anyone can possibly know that.'

'So that's what George meant when he sang that song – and of course the song goes on: "she wears a plain golden ring on her finger". I knew George was talking in riddles!'

'Of course he was.' Andrew thought it was better not to mention the latest rumours which were going around the glen about Maggie Lennox's child...

'George thinks Mr Luke is still visiting this young widow?'

'Yes,' Andrew sighed. 'I suppose you're shocked now, Victoria. I know you've been brought up to believe the Crainbys are on a higher plane than the likes of us, but they're only human. It's best not to listen to gossip.'

'Not even if it's true?'

'We don't know whether it is or not.'

'Perhaps not,' Victoria conceded, 'but Mr Luke does go away a lot and sometimes he doesn't return for his meals then Mrs Crainby gets bad tempered with everyone. Some of the upstairs maids say they're always quarrelling. So...perhaps it's true.'

'Does it shock you that Mr Luke might love someone else when he has a wife?'

'We-ell...I wouldn't like it if I had a husband and he spent his time with someone else – another woman I mean. But...' She frowned. 'I've always liked Mr Luke. I can't believe he would

158

be deliberately cruel.'

'I don't think he is cruel exactly, but he's not faithful to his wife.'

'No, and that's a sin, isn't it, according to the Bible? But ...sometimes Mrs Crainby has such a sharp temper and a spiteful tongue, perhaps I can feel a wee bit sorry for him. Perhaps I can excuse him a little bit?'

'Oh, Victoria!' Andrew threw back his head and laughed. 'You have all the wisdom of Solomon. You may be as innocent as George says but you certainly consider all angles. Come on, let's get these baking tins and get away home.'

The cake turned out splendidly and Polly insisted Victoria must use one of her best plates to present it to Miss Traill. She had sandwiched the two sponges together with a chocolate butter cream and the covering was beautifully smooth and shiny made from boiled cream and chocolate. She had added three tiny sugar violets; Polly thought it was beautiful. Victoria was her own sternest critic but she was secretly delighted with the result.

Joe Pringle came home early for lunch on Friday and he brought with him a bunch of chrysanthemums from the castle greenhouse. They were huge balls of bronze, yellow and white.

'I asked Mr Luke if I might bring you a few for the old lady's birthday,' he beamed. 'He said Mr Rennie was one of the best tenants on the estate. I think he meant one of the few who is still managing to pay all his rent. Anyway, he said it was a pleasure to send a few flowers to his housekeeper. He was in good spirits himself. He asked me to cut a bunch for him and place them on the back seat of the Bentley.' He winked at Polly.

'Mmm, and I can guess where he was taking them,' she said darkly.

'I do hope Mrs Crainby doesn't find out,' Victoria said. 'Your flowers are one of the few things she praises, Uncle Joe. She has brightened up the castle with them since she started giving dinner parties. She always has fresh flowers in the hall in case any of the ladies call unexpectedly.'

'She hasn't opened up any of the rooms that Sir William closed down during the war, has she?' Polly asked with interest.

'Only the nursery wing and two rooms for the new nanny. But she sorted out some of the furniture. She was talking of holding a ball and bringing in caterers to make the food but Mr Luke has promised to take her to the Hunt Ball instead.'

They had finished eating their midday meal when Andrew arrived, driving Mr Rennie's car. He manoeuvred it carefully on the narrow track until he could turn it round.

'You looked like a king, sitting up there behind the wheel,' his father teased.

'I feel like one,' Andrew said grinning. 'Are you ready, Queen Victoria? Did you get the cake finished?'

'I did, but you can't see it until we get there. Aunt Polly helped me pack it in a box and I shall hold it on my knee.'

'So don't go too fast or drive over any bumps,' his mother cautioned.

'What's in the parcel?' Andrew asked, 'and where did you get the flowers?' He looked at his father with raised eyebrows.

'It's all right, son. Mr Luke gave permission. He says Rennie is one of his best tenants.'

'Aye, so he is. Langmune is the only farm on the estate to have electricity, except for the castle and Darlonachie Home Farm.'

'Electricity? You never told us that!' Polly said. 'I wonder if we shall get it soon.'

'I doubt it. Mr Rennie paid for it himself. It's wired to the main farm buildings, the house and the cottages. We have an electric light in the byre now. It's wonderful on dark mornings. Mr Rennie had to guarantee to use a certain amount before the electricity company would agree to bring it over the hill to Langmune. It's come to us from the Lockerbie side.'

'Imagine that! He must have plenty of money.'

'It isn't from farming then,' Andrew said glumly. 'He gets an income from his share in the mills which his father used to own.' He looked at Victoria sitting beside him, clutching the box. 'What did you say was in the wee parcel?' he asked curiously.

'It's a new apron for Miss Traill, for Sunday afternoons. Aunt Polly and I made it between us.'

'Victoria made it herself,' Polly said. 'I only added the bits of embroidery to make it a wee bit special. How do you like Victoria's new dress? She made that too. She can use the treadle sewing machine better than I can myself now. I wish I'd kept my mother's old hand one.'

'I was going to tell her how smart she looks.' Andrew grinned at Victoria sitting very erect beside him. He guessed she was nervous of riding in the car while he was driving. 'It's quite safe, you know,' he teased as they chugged slowly down the track.

Eleanora Traill was astonished when Andrew and Victoria entered the kitchen at Langmune. Shyly Victoria wished her a happy birthday, while Andrew grinned from ear to ear and echoed the good wishes. They presented her with the cake and flowers and the small parcel.

'Well, I never! Well, I never...' She was speechless. She looked from one eager face to the other, shaking her grey head incredulously. 'Never in all my life have I had a birthday cake,' she said gruffly and bent over the box to hide her emotion. Carefully she lifted out the large chocolate cake. 'My, it looks too good to eat. Wherever did you get it?'

'Victoria made it,' Andrew said with pride.

'At Andrew's request,' Victoria added quickly. 'He bought all the ingredients.'

'I don't know how to thank you both. Such kindness.' She turned as Mr Rennie came from the dining room where he had been taking his after dinner rest. Although his breath rasped in his chest he was smiling warmly as he presented Miss Traill with a big box of chocolates beautifully tied with a blue satin bow.

'This is for me?' His housekeeper stared at him in amazement.

'Not everyone manages three score years and ten,' Mr Rennie reminded her. 'We're very proud of you, Miss Traill.'

'Well, I never!' she gasped again and Andrew and Victoria laughed merrily.

'And you, young lady.' Mr Rennie turned to Victoria, eyeing her shrewdly. 'It is too long since you last came to visit us. You're a proper young woman now. And a pretty one at that.' His eyes twinkled unexpectedly at the blush which stained Victoria's cheeks. 'We're very pleased to see you, aren't we, Miss Traill?'

'That we are.'

'In that case, you willna mind if I leave Victoria with you, Miss Traill,' Andrew said, 'while I get on with the work? It will be milking time before we know where we are and I must be back here for my afternoons and a piece of your birthday cake. Unless you're going to eat it all yourself?'

'Ach, laddie I can't think of anybody more deserving of a piece.'

'Right then, I'll be back later.'

'If I may, Miss Traill,' Victoria said when Andrew had gone, 'I've come to help you feed the poultry and collect the eggs. And make the tea.'

'Now there's a kind offer, Miss Traill. Seize it

while you can. It's not every day you get the chance, and this is a very special day,' Mr Rennie put in.

'You knew, Mr Rennie! You knew what Andrew was planning, didn't you?'

'Ooh...I may have heard a wee whisper.' Mr Rennie smiled. 'Now, if you'll excuse me, I'll go back to the fire.'

They watched him move slowly and close the dining room door behind him. Miss Traill looked at Victoria with anxious grey eyes. 'I don't know how he's going to get through another winter,' she said in a low voice, shaking her head. 'Such a bad chest he has. It never seemed to have cleared this summer.'

'He is in good hands,' Victoria heard herself saying soothingly. 'Andrew says you give him every care.'

'I try, lassie, I try, but neither of us gets any younger.' She sighed heavily and Victoria realized how worrying it must be. If anything happened to Mr Rennie, Andrew would lose his job, but Miss Traill would lose both her job and the only home she had known for most of her life.

'If you'll tell me what you would like me to do I'll get on with it while you have a seat beside the fire,' Victoria suggested. She went across to the rocking chair and drew it up beside the kitchen range and spread the thick rag rug in front of the fire.

'Thank you, lassie.' Miss Traill sat down with a grateful sigh.

'Now, what shall I do first?' Victoria asked with a smile.

'You have grown into a young woman, and a kindly one at that.' Miss Traill nodded approvingly. 'I did the churning this morning, but I havena made the butter into pats yet. Could you do that for me?'

'I haven't had much practice at making the patterns,' Victoria admitted, 'but I can work the water out without spoiling the texture. Where do you keep the scotch hands?'

'It doesna matter about the patterns. The scotch hands are in the bucket of cold water in the scullery.'

Victoria went to get them. 'Oh! You've got an electric cooker.'

'Mr Rennie insisted on buying it when he put the electric in. Too complicated for me, I like my range. I understand it.'

Victoria smiled. She could imagine Granny probably would have said the same. 'Do you have an instruction book?'

'I do. Do you know anything about them? Do you have one at the castle?'

'We have had one for two years now but I'm not allowed to use it and Eve Ware hides the instructions.' A mischievous smile brought a fleeting dimple to Victoria's cheek. 'We tried it one day when it was Ware's day off. It boiled the potatoes dry and they burned. Another time I put a pudding in the oven but it didn't cook enough.'

'It will take a bit of getting used to. You can

165

read my instruction book if you like.'

'I'd love to see it, but I'll get the work done first.'

Victoria dealt with the butter then she went out to feed the hens and ducks. She thoroughly enjoyed wandering from hut to hut gathering the eggs in the big wicker basket. When she returned she saw that Miss Traill was dozing in front of the fire so she crept outside again to look around the farmyard and find the young calves, hoping she might see Andrew, but he was working in the fields. She did see a tiny hunchback piglet in a little wooden house in the barn. When she returned Miss Traill was just wakening up.

'Ach, I'd meant to make fresh scones for tea and look at the time. I'm getting too old for the churning. I think I shall have to stop it. Does your mother buy her butter from the grocer's van?'

'Aunt Polly does, yes.'

'Of course I'd forgotten you stay with Andrew's family.'

'I'll make a scone while the fire is nice and red, if you like.'

Victoria soon found the various ingredients. Miss Traill kept everything tidy and in its proper place, something Eve Ware seemed incapable of doing. It was a fault which irritated Victoria even more than the woman's sharp tongue and petty criticism.

The scones were cooling between the folds of a clean tea towel when Andrew came in for tea before starting the milking. Mr Rennie joined them.

Miss Traill cut her birthday cake. 'The first I ever had,' she repeated several times that afternoon. She seemed pleased, and not the least bit critical as Eve Ware would have been. Victoria breathed a sigh of relief. It was lovely to be in such an easy atmosphere. Even Mr Rennie praised her and indulged in a second piece of cake.

'It's a big cake, and it's delicious. I think we must send out a piece for each of the men,' Miss Traill announced, 'and Ted's wife and Rosie. Will you take them, Andrew? I'd like them to share in my little celebration. I'm fortunate to have reached my allotted span, as it says in the Bible.'

'It was such a simple little celebration for someone who has lived seventy years, and yet Miss Traill seemed so very pleased,' Victoria said as she and Andrew prepared to leave Langmune when the day's work was done.

'I've never seen her so overcome. Even Mr Rennie had a twinkle in his eye. I heard them both telling you to return before too long. Will you come again, Victoria?'

'Oh yes. I'd love to come, that is if you don't mind?'

'Of course I want you to come! I...' Andrew broke off, knowing he could never tell Victoria how often he longed for her company.

'Maybe I could borrow Mark's old bicycle. He'll not need it when he is in Edinburgh.

Anyway, he's learning to drive the doctor's car.'

'Mmm,' Andrew muttered. Mark had everything to offer her, he thought bitterly. 'Do you think he will keep up his weekly letters?'

'Oh, yes, I'm sure he will,' Victoria replied with conviction, unaware that she was twisting a knife in Andrew's heart. Darkness was falling and with it an evening chill. Victoria pulled her thick shawl more closely round her, wishing she had worn her winter coat over her thin dress. She had wanted to show it off to Andrew.

'You're cold,' he said. 'Come on, we'll see if we can still ride the bike together, at least downhill to the village. You're not that much bigger than you were the last time you came.'

'That's ages ago. I must be bigger.'

'I doubt if you weigh any more. You're just a different shape. Come on, let's try.' Bugger Mark Jacobs, he thought. For this evening Victoria is here and she's mine.

Victoria blushed at Andrew's comment on her changing shape. She was glad it was getting dark so that he wouldn't see and think her gauche and silly. Milly often told her about kissing and cuddling with Jem. Victoria's face flamed at her own thoughts. She wanted to be close to Andrew.

Andrew stood with legs astride his bike, one hand on the handlebars.

'Come round this side. You can't have forgotten how we used to manage to ride two to a bike?'

'Of – of course not.' Victoria struggled on to

168

the crossbar while he held the bike steady. His arm at her back was firm and strong. She felt so safe with Andrew. She looked into his face and smiled shyly. It was light enough for him to see her and he grinned back, sorely tempted to kiss her.

'OK? Let's give it a try.' They wobbled dangerously and Andrew put one leg to the ground to stop them falling over. 'Put one arm round my back, Victoria. It will steady us. At least if we fall off we'll fall together.' He chuckled softly and his breath stirred her hair and tickled her ear. She did as he asked, feeling his muscular body beneath her arm. Once she had overcome her initial shyness she found she liked holding him close, snuggled against his chest.

'That's better! Feel safer now?' They were gathering speed without Andrew needing to peddle as the track wound downhill. Victoria could feel the wind rushing by. 'OK?'

'Wonderful,' she breathed and her arm at his back tightened slightly. Andrew wished he could hold her this close forever.

He knew lots of girls. Sometimes he walked them home from the dances or took one to the pictures. He had had offers of more than friendship from one or two but so far he had never been tempted, as some of his pals had been. Two of the boys he had known at school were already married with children but he had no desire to be rushed into marriage. For some time now he had known there was only one girl he wanted. If Victoria married Mark Jacobs and he made her happy he would accept it, but until then he would bide his time.

As they cycled down to the village he was blissfully aware of her body closely moulded to his. He prayed he could keep his emotions under control whilst she was so close. He suspected Victoria was still as innocent as she had been when she left school, unless Milly had educated her on the facts of life. He didn't think Mark Jacobs was the type to hurt her or cause her harm; in fact, Andrew was honest enough to admit he would have liked the lad if he had not been so jealous of the bond he and Victoria shared. Apart from himself and his brothers she didn't meet any other boys.

'Would you like to go to the dance in the village hall next week, Victoria?' he asked before he could stop himself. 'George and Willie will be going too,' he added when she hesitated.

'Oh.' Victoria was disappointed he was not asking her as his partner. 'I – I've only danced around the table when Aunt Polly showed us what to do. Would I be able to dance at a proper event?'

'Of course you would. Ma said you were light as a feather on your feet. I – I'd like you to come, Victoria. Are you afraid Mark would disapprove, is that it?'

'Mark? I doubt if he would think anything about it. It's...well, it's...I don't have any dresses for dancing. I've never needed anything like that.'

'Ma will help you make one – that is, if you'd

like to go. I'll tell you what,' he said with a flash of inspiration, 'I'll buy the material for your birthday present. Miss Phipps always keeps rolls of silk and satin as well as the muslin, doesn't she?'

'Oh, Andrew, would you?' Victoria turned to him, her eyes shining in the faint light, but the movement almost overbalanced them and they wobbled precariously. Victoria squealed and clung even more tightly to Andrew. When he regained his balance he laid his cheek briefly against her hair and his heart sang.

'I hope you will come up to Langmune again soon.'

'Oh, I shall. I saw the tiniest wee piglet all on his own. Miss Traill let me feed him with a bottle, like a baby.'

'Och, that's Squeaker. He was the runt of the litter. We didn't think he'd make it but he's a survivor.'

'Oh, I do hope he is. Miss Traill said I could feed him whenever I'm there. She allowed me to read the instructions for her electric cooker. She says I can try using it if I go to Langmune with you next week.'

'Next week? You'll come so soon?'

'You think I should wait a while?' Victoria asked doubtfully.

'Oh no. If you don't mind spending your day off at Langmune I'd love you to come. And I'm sure Miss Traill appreciated your help today.' He didn't ask whether she thought Mark would object. He wondered whether she would tell him, but Victoria was so open and frank he was sure she would never deceive Mark deliberately. 'She ought to have a regular maid instead of a washerwoman, but it would mean another wage to pay and I don't think Mr Rennie likes the idea of anyone else living in his house.' This was true, but both Miss Traill and Mr Rennie were getting older. Changes were coming quicker than any of them could have guessed.

'Aunt Polly, Andrew has promised to take me to the dance in the village. Would you help me to make a dress? Please?'

'Why, lassie, I'd be delighted.'

'Andrew says he will buy the material for my birthday.'

'Good for him. We'll go to Miss Phipps and see what she has and choose a pattern. Oh my lamb, I'm pleased to see you going out and enjoying yourself at last. I'll tell Joe. We'll buy you some new shoes to go with the dress. I wish I was eighteen again,' she chuckled merrily.

It was the first time Victoria had indulged in dreams of dresses, other than for work or to go to the kirk. Polly was sure she didn't earn anything like the money she and Joe felt she deserved. She regularly saved a small sum in the Savings Bank, as Polly had encouraged her and the boys to do. She always had a decent winter coat and hat and sturdy shoes but Polly doubted whether she had much money left to spare for finery.

There was no doubting her excitement and

Polly guessed it was because the boys were taking her to her first dance. Each evening they wound up the gramophone and put on one of Joe's records of Harry Lauder to practise the steps around the kitchen table.

Miss Phipps was a kindly little woman of indeterminate age. She never seemed to look any different, with her grey hair twisted into a neat bun and her grey eyes peering through spectacles which always rested near the end of her small straight nose. She eyed Victoria carefully.

'I have a nice bolt of crepe de chine in a lemon colour, and another in turquoise. The silk and the satin are a little more expensive...'

'Oh no, nothing too expensive, Miss Phipps. Andrew is buying it for my birthday. I shall be eighteen next week, the first of November.'

'Och, dinna worry, Victoria. I'm sure Andrew has given us enough to pay for whatever you fancy. He said I was not to skimp,' Polly insisted.

'Mmm, what about the blue muslin, Miss Phipps. Perhaps I could trim it?'

'Better have the blue silk, lassie, if it's blue you fancy,' Polly said.

'You have such rich brown hair and lovely dark eyes, Miss Victoria. I do think the lemon would suit you best of all.'

Victoria chewed her lip and looked at Miss Phipps. That lady smiled kindly.

'It is in the middle of the price range and I have satin ribbon which matches exactly. I shall

173

make you a little gift of a length if you decide on the lemon. After all, it's not every day a girl is eighteen and your grandmama was always very kind to my mother when she was alive, bringing her tempting morsels to coax her to eat.'

'I didn't know,' Victoria said.

'Maybe we should choose a pattern first,' Polly prompted, anxious to get home before it was pitch dark. 'Miss Phipps is usually closed by now.'

'Oh! I'm so sorry!' Victoria said in dismay.

'That's all right m'dear. I have new patterns from both Butterick and Weldons. The low waists and long straight bodices have all gone.'

'We don't want anything too difficult,' Polly said quickly. 'I'm more used to sewing shirts and trousers with a family of men.'

'I'll be pleased to lend a hand with the cutting and pinning if you have any problems.' Miss Phipps beamed at them both. 'Some of the patterns seem quite simple. It's a case of getting the tucks in the right place on the bodice and sewing the long seams without puckering. Some of them go from the shoulder to the hem in the latest patterns. Some have a flare to the skirt and that would be better for dancing.' She held up a pattern for their inspection but the bodice was only held in place by two thin straps.

'Oh! I could never wear anything so – so naked,' Victoria gasped.

'It has a wee bolero to go with it,' Miss Phipps pointed out, but Victoria blushed and shook her head.

'This is a similar style but it with a square neck which you could cut lower for dancing, if you wished. It has pretty sleeves. The pattern is good value as it gives a variation in necklines.'

'I think that would suit Victoria very well,' Polly said. 'So long as you're sure it's not too difficult?'

'I think you'll find it quite simple and it's a pattern which can be adapted for other dresses, a round neck with a collar for Sundays, a sweetheart neck in muslin for summer, various trimmings, or add a sash...'

'Shall we take that one then, Victoria, and the yellow crepe de chine?'

'If you're sure we're not spending too much money. I know Andrew is saving up to buy his own pig.'

'Och, he dreams of being a farmer like Mr Rennie but it'll never be more than a dream, I reckon. Anyway, it was his own idea to buy the material for your birthday and we want him to be proud of you, don't we?'

'Y-yes, oh yes.'

In the end Miss Phipps was infected by their enthusiasm and she offered to cut out the pattern herself and pin up the material.

'You come back tomorrow evening, Miss Victoria, and I'll fit in on for you and show you what to do. I used to enjoy teaching sewing when I was younger. It will be a pleasure to pass on a few hints to you, child.'

Victoria could scarcely contain her excitement by the night of the dance. The yellow dress had turned out better than she had dared to hope and Miss Phipps was right about the colour. It suited her fresh, clear skin and it seemed to bring out the red-gold lights in her hair. Milly had told her long hair was out of fashion and she should have it cut in a short bob. When she mentioned this to Polly it was Andrew who protested vehemently.

'You have lovely hair, Victoria. Please don't cut it to look like all the other women. Tell her Mother, please?'

'I think Andrew's right. It would be a real shame to cut off her bonny curls,' Joe declared before Polly could decide.

'I believe my men are right, lassie. You do have lovely hair and it's a shame it's hidden away under your cap most of the time. If you want it short for the dance we could put it up on top of your head and thread some of Miss Phipp's satin ribbon through it. What do you think?'

'All right,' Victoria agreed. She didn't care so long as Andrew approved.

Her only disappointment was that she didn't have a bicycle yet. In his last letter Mark had promised to ask his uncle to deliver his bicycle to the cottage for her. Mrs Grantly had seen Aunt Polly in the village and told her Dr Grantly had taken it into Mr Crabb's cycle shop and asked him to check it over.

'Dr Grantly willna ken you need it to go to the dance,' Polly said, 'and I didn't like to tell Mrs Grantly.'

'Och, don't worry, Victoria,' Andrew grinned.

176

'You're light as a feather. If we can manage to get to Langmune we'll surely manage down to the village with you on the crossbar, but be sure to wear your coat over your new dress.' Secretly Andrew was glad the cycle was not ready. It was only three miles to the village and downhill most of the way. He didn't mind walking back if he had Victoria for company. No doubt George and Willie would pick up partners at the dance and probably walk them home afterwards. He would have Victoria to himself.

Andrew planned his work carefully so that he would be finished as soon as the milking was over. He had reckoned without Ted developing pains in his chest and having to leave halfway through the milking; then one of the older cows had decided to calve three weeks early. It turned out to be twins and Andrew's conscience would not allow him to leave until they were safely delivered.

He pedalled furiously to get home in time. George and Willie were trying to persuade Victoria to go with them, leaving him to follow later.

'I'm as strong as Andrew,' George boasted. 'If he can balance you on the crossbar then so can I. You'll be safe with me.'

'Don't trust either of them, Victoria.' Andrew skidded to a breathless halt.

'Oh Andrew! I – I thought you weren't coming,' Victoria said tremulously. She didn't trust George and Willie not to go off with their pals and leave her standing alone like a wallflower.

177

'I'll bring her. Get on your way, you two.' He turned to Victoria. 'I'm sorry. Please wait. I'll not be long...'

'You canna go to a dance without eating first, Andrew!' Polly announced, hands on hips, ready for a confrontation.

'Your mother is right, Andrew. The main thing is, you're here now. Surely it doesn't matter if we're not there for the beginning?'

'Maybe you're right at that.' Andrew grinned his spirits rising again. 'If we're a bit late the other lads will have got fixed up with partners. I shall be able to keep you all to myself.' His eyes widened as they returned to the lamplit room. 'Or at least I shall have a damned good try. You look lovely, doesn't she, Ma?'

'She does that!' Polly smiled fondly at them both, but Joe took his pipe from his mouth and eyed his eldest son shrewdly.

'I hope you'll look after her then,' he grunted. 'Remember she's part of the family. She lives under our roof.'

'Of course I shall look after her, Father. You should know by now I'm more reliable than those two flirts. They have a different partner for every dance.'

'That's not what I meant, son, and I think you know it,' Joe said quietly. Andrew flushed and his gaze fell beneath his father's penetrating blue stare. Had he guessed how he felt about Victoria? Did he realize he was seizing every opportunity to be with her now that Mark Jacobs was away? Did he disapprove? Surely his father didn't believe he would do anything underhand to get Victoria for himself. He scowled as he went to wash in the candlelit scullery, yanking off his shirt as he went.

'I'll make him a good big sandwich to eat while he changes or he'll be dashing off without anything to eat,' Polly said.

'I'll do that.'

'No, no, lassie. You sit still. The lads will dance the feet off you tonight. You're looking pretty as a picture. We don't want you spilling anything on your new dress.' Victoria grinned at her. Aunt Polly made her feel like a twelve year old, while Eve Ware treated her like a forty-year-old slave.

Andrew settled Victoria securely on his bike, enjoying the feel of her supple young body so close to him. He didn't care if they never arrived at the dance. George was the one who was the expert dancer. He fancied himself as Fred Astaire. Willie and himself were passably good.

Long before they reached the village hall they could hear the lilting strains of the music.

'It's a good band tonight,' Andrew said, 'two accordions, a pianist, a fiddle and a drummer. Sometimes the drummer brings his sister along to give us an occasional song.'

'I – I'm beginning to feel nervous,' Victoria said and snuggled closer to Andrew's chest as though for protection. She trusted Andrew. She was sure he would not go off with his friends and leave her alone. A sudden thought occurred to her. 'Have you arranged to meet one of your girlfriends?' she asked turning sharply so that she could see his face.

'Hey, steady on, Victoria!' Andrew chuckled, putting both feet on the ground to prevent them over balancing, but he still kept an arm around her. 'You make me sound like some kind of Lothario! You don't think I shall have eyes for any other girl when I've got the prettiest in the hall already, do you?'

'Andrew Pringle! You sound like a well practised flirt. When did you acquire such a silver tongue?' Victoria's voice was tart but inwardly she was delighted with Andrew's praise and she was glad of the darkness to hide her blushes.

Andrew laughed, his long day forgotten, his tiredness evaporated. 'You haven't seen much of the local lads since you left school but you will know a lot of them. They'll get a surprise when they see you. So, Miss Victoria Lachlan, may I remind you, you're my partner tonight!' he said sternly.

'As though I would forget!' Victoria chuckled merrily. 'But I'm still worried I shall not know how to do the steps.'

'You'll be all right with me, or with Willie. Usually we have a mixture of modern and Scottish dances. You'll enjoy it, Victoria. I'm glad you agreed to come. Did Mark never offer to take you dancing?'

'Mark? I don't think he ever thought about dancing when he lived in Darlonachie, but he is learning to dance now that he is at university.'

'Is he indeed? Did you tell him you were

180

coming to the dance tonight?'

'Yes, of course. I asked if I could borrow his bicycle, remember?'

'And he didn't mind you going without him?'

'Goodness no. Why should he mind? He's not here.'

'No, he isn't, is he.' Andrew felt his spirits rise.

A dance was finishing as they entered the village hall together and Victoria blushed, feeling all eyes were fixed on them. Many of them were. It didn't take long before Willie and George were plagued with questions about their eldest brother's new girlfriend. Some of them remembered Victoria from school and they were quick to ask her to dance.

'Remember, Victoria,' Andrew said seriously, as yet another partner led her away, 'keep the last waltz for me.'

The only dance Victoria didn't enjoy was a quickstep with George as her partner. He was so quick and light on his feet but he did so many fancy steps and moves she couldn't follow him. She stopped in the middle of the dance floor.

'George Pringle! You're trying to make a fool of me!' she accused hotly.

'Lord, Victoria, keep your hair on! Course I'm not.'

'Well then, you're showing off.' The couple next to them stopped too and began to laugh. Victoria's face flushed.

'That's right, lassie, you tell him off. None of the other lassies can keep up with him and his fancy steps either, but none of them dare tell him so.' There was general laughter all around the little group which had gathered but Victoria felt mortified. She was thankful when the music stopped. She looked around wildly for Andrew and almost ran into his arms for the next dance, a reassuringly familiar Gay Gordons.

'Don't let George get to you, Victoria,' Andrew said softly. 'He is one of the best dancers around these parts but he likes to show off a bit.'

'I don't suppose he'll ask me again, but I shall refuse if he does,' Victoria retorted, still feeling ruffled.

'Well, I wouldn't mind if you refused them all, so long as you dance with me,' Andrew said, his blue eyes sparkling, making Victoria's heart give a strange sort of flip. 'Tell George to ask you for a waltz or a Scottish dance next time.'

At the end of the evening Victoria's feet were aching but she had thoroughly enjoyed her first real dance. She had met again several people she had not seen since she left school and it had been good to exchange news and hear about their lives. Most of them were pleased to have a job of work. The girls all seemed to have the same desire: to settle down with a husband and have children of their own. Even the boys she had known did not seem to have any ambitions like Mark and his burning desire to be an army doctor, or Andrew wanting to rent a farm of his own. So she had made no mention of her own aspirations to be one of the best cooks in the county.

There had only been one unhappy moment and that had been when she saw Andrew returning to the hall from the direction of the cloakrooms. A pretty dark-haired girl was hanging on to his arm, laughing up into his face. He laughed at her quip, but he released her grip and went to ask another girl to dance. Victoria did not recognize her feelings as jealousy, but Willie had seen her watching and drew her on to the floor for the next dance.

'I see you're keeping an eye on our big brother, Victoria. He usually has his pick of the girls, even if George is the best dancer in the hall.'

'And you, Willie? I hear you have a different girl at every dance?'

'Och no, that's George. There's only one I fancy and she's not here tonight.'

'Oh? Do I know her?'

'Shouldn't think so. She's younger than we are and she didn't go to Darlonachie School. Her parents rent the little farm next to where I work. Sometimes I see her bringing in the cows for milking in the summer. I keep teasing her and asking when I shall see her at the dance but she's only been once and she never came back.'

'Do you think she likes you?'

'She seemed to but she's a bit shy, so I'm not sure.'

'Well then, you should ask her to come to the dance as your special partner. I would never have come if Andrew hadn't asked me.'

'What, not even with George and me?'

'No. You would have gone off and left me. Andrew has always looked out for me, even when I started school. I know I can trust him.'

'And you never did trust George and me,' Willie chuckled, 'I remember now. You always had a soft spot for Andrew. And for wee Josh, of course.'

'I've always loved Josh,' Victoria said warmly. 'He was like a little brother to me.'

'Aye, and he's the brightest o' the family, like you and Mark Jacobs, always got his nose in a book. Of course, you always helped him with his lessons so he had an advantage.'

'But he always wanted to learn. You and George never even wanted to go to school,' she reminded him. 'You were always late.'

'Aye, so we were.' He grinned unrepentantly. 'Mr Nelson wants Ma and Pa to let Josh go to the academy in Dumfries. He thinks he should be a teacher.'

'Do you think they will?'

'Depends if they can afford it. They're thinking about it now that we're all working.'

'I wish I could earn better money and pay them more,' Victoria said as she sighed.

Willie's steps faltered and his arm tightened.

'Don't talk like that, Victoria! Old Crainby pays them generously for your board and lodgings. They wouldn't accept any more. Don't you know you're the sister we never had? Look how Ma enjoys helping you sew dresses and things. It would be mighty stupid her trying to teach George and me to make dresses, wouldn't it?'

'Oh I don't know...' Victoria teased, grinning up at him, 'you could always become a tailor.'

'Ah-ah! Tailor my foot!'

'Hmm, maybe your foot would be better with a bit trimmed off to stop it treading on my toes?' Victoria asked innocently.

'Victoria...' he growled. 'You're getting too cheeky for your boots. I'll...Gee, did you see the scowl Andrew gave me as he passed us. He must think I'm ill treating you.'

Minutes later Andrew came purposefully towards her. Then the band struck up for the last waltz of the evening. Andrew had known it would be and he was determined not to take any chance of someone else claiming her. They waltzed easily together. Victoria felt it seemed so right being in his arms, and when the lights dimmed and Andrew held her closer she closed her eyes and felt she must be in heaven. She could feel his cheek resting lightly on the top of her head and his breath was soft and sweet against her forehead. She wished it could go on for ever.

Then it was all over. The lights went up. Girls made a dash for the cloakroom to collect coats, afraid their boyfriends might leave without them if they were too long. Victoria was not used to such a mêlée, and she was too well mannered to push forward, so she was one of the last to leave, buttoning her coat as she went. Andrew was waiting patiently in the shadows at the side of the hall, holding the handlebars of his bike in one hand. She ran straight into the curve of his free arm. Immediately, involuntarily, it encircled her, holding her against his chest.

'Did you enjoy it, Victoria?'

'It was wonderful!' She reached up to kiss his cheek in gratitude, but he moved his head and their lips met. His arm tightened, holding her. His lips lingered longingly on hers, so soft and warm, so innocent. His father's warning came back to him. She trusted him as a brother, but that was not the way he felt. Slowly, reluctantly, he lifted his head.

'Yes, it was...wonderful,' he breathed against her cheek. He sighed and with a tremendous effort he reverted to brotherly mode. 'Button up your coat.'

Eleven

Every night of the following week Andrew was late home. Several times they were all in bed when he came in. Polly always left him a meal but sometimes he was too exhausted to eat and twice Miss Traill had made him a meal before he left. His lean jaw was tense with strain and fatigue. Both Victoria and Polly worried about him, albeit for different reasons.

'You should move to a farm without a dairy herd,' George told him. 'You'll not catch me working all the hours God sends for someone else.'

'Aye,' Willie agreed. 'Give me sheep any day, but don't ask me to milk cows seven days a week. You must be mad, big brother.'

Usually Andrew took both teasing and criticism in his stride, giving as good as he got from his two younger brothers. Tonight he snapped at them angrily and a pulse beat rapidly in his jaw, a sure sign of tension.

'We know you've never wanted to work anywhere else but Langmune, son,' Polly said quietly, 'but you're exhausted and I'm concerned about you. We all are.'

'It'll pass.' Andrew's tone was unexpectedly curt. He had always treated both his parents with consideration and respect.

Polly frowned. 'What will pass? Maybe we can help?'

'Nobody can help. Ted Holmes has had a heart attack. He's bad. His wife is looking after him so we're two milkers short.'

'Well, that's not your problem,' George said irritably.

'Be quiet,' Joe admonished. 'So what's happening up there, Andrew?'

'The cows still have to be milked. There's only Rosie to help most of the time and they're worried sick. Ted's cottage depends on him keeping his job and providing his own helpers for the dairy.'

'So that's why you've been so late home?' Polly frowned. 'What does Mr Rennie say about it?'

'What can he say? He's not fit himself. He hasn't been at the milking for more than eighteen months now. You can't pick an experienced herdsman up off the village street. He understands Ted's anxiety and he doesn't want to put him out of his home. There'll be men looking for jobs at the November term but they would need Ted's cottage as well as the job.'

'But Mr Rennie must realize you can't go on working like this much longer?'

'He does.' Andrew frowned and bit his lip. He looked up but his eyes sought Victoria. Then he put his head in his hands. 'I can't decide what to do. Miss Traill has suggested I should move into Langmune to live. Mr Rennie agreed so long as she is sure she can manage having an extra man living in.'

'Well, it makes sense, laddie.' Joe nodded. 'It would save you time and energy biking there and back every day.'

'Yes, but I think Miss Traill has other reasons for suggesting I move up there. Mr Rennie has had some frightening breathless attacks recently. She gets anxious. I believe she would like somebody else there at night. It would be a permanent arrangement.'

'So what's stopping you?' Polly asked. 'Miss Traill is making most of your meals anyway these days. You can bring your washing home to me once a week.'

'You don't understand, Mother. If I'm living there Mr Rennie will have to deduct my board and lodging. I wouldn't be contributing here and Josh...'

'Mercy me, son, you don't need to consider Josh. We've already decided he will go to the academy if that's what he wants. We don't need your money when we're not feeding you. You're all independent now. How do you think we managed when we had four of you to feed and clothe? We only have Josh to think about now so you do what is best for your own health and happiness. Do you want to leave Langmune?'

'No. Oh no...' There was no doubting Andrew's conviction.

'I could come up this Friday and help Miss Traill,' Victoria said.

Andrew looked up, his eyes brightening. 'You'd still come, Victoria? Even if I was staying up there.'

'Of course I'd come if I can be useful.'

'I would leave you my bike,' Andrew said eagerly.

He looks brighter than he's looked all week, Polly mused, looking from her son to Victoria.

'I'm sure Dr Grantly will be bringing Mark's bike for me any day now,' Victoria said. 'I love the farm and the animals. And Miss Traill doesn't seem to mind me being there now she's got used to me.'

'She likes you to be there. We all do, even Mr Rennie. I'll tell them tomorrow that I'll move up there at the weekend then.'

'Why not straight away? When Ted's ill and you're so busy?' Polly asked.

'It's the first of November on Friday. Victoria's birthday.'

'That doesn't make any difference, you've given me my birthday present already,' she grinned mischievously. Then she went on more seriously, 'Granny never made a fuss of birthdays. In fact she always seemed sad. Anyway, I would enjoy spending the day at Langmune.'

'There you are then, son,' Polly said on a note of relief, flashing Victoria a grateful smile. 'I'll pack you up some clean washing and you can take it with you in the morning.'

'All right.' Andrew nodded wearily, trying and failing to stifle a huge yawn.

They all knew it was the most sensible arrangement but both Polly and Victoria felt the house seemed empty without Andrew. Victoria looked forward eagerly to Friday.

The evening before her birthday they were surprised when lights illuminated the cottage windows.

'Whatever can that be?' Polly asked in alarm.

'Sounds like a car,' Willie muttered. 'There's someone knocking at the door. Must be a stranger looking for the castle.'

Joe went to open the door himself. 'Why Doctor Grantly! Is anything wrong. It's not Andrew?'

'There's nothing wrong. I'm sorry, I didn't mean to alarm you. I've come to deliver the bicycle. Mark insisted I must deliver it in time for Victoria's birthday and I know that's tomorrow.'

'It's very kind of you,' Victoria said as she

smiled up at him. 'I hope Mark has not been pestering you with reminders. He never forgets because his birthday is the day after mine.'

'Mark didn't need to remind me, lassie. Yours is one of the few birthdays I shall never forget,' he said gravely. Victoria looked puzzled but Polly nodded understanding.

'Of course,' she said softly. 'Victoria's birth, Elizabeth's death... It was so very sad.'

'Yes.' Dr Grantly's face wore a pained expression. 'It is always a miracle when a child enters the world, but when the young mother dies giving birth –' he suppressed a shudder – 'it was a night I shall always remember with regret.'

'I see...' Victoria said uneasily. 'That's probably why Granny didn't like being reminded either.'

'Oh, lassie, she felt she had been well blessed to have you, as we all do,' Polly assured her, making an effort to dispel the sudden sadness. 'And you'll have a bicycle to go up to Langmune tomorrow now that Doctor Grantly has been kind enough to bring you Mark's.'

'Ah...' Peter Grantly began to smile. 'I will bring it to the door and you will see it in the light of the lamp. Mark's bicycle was getting a bit rusty so I traded it in for a lady's model. It's not a new one, but Mr Crabb assures me it will be reliable. He has added lights front and back as a gift from my wife.' His eyes twinkled. 'She didn't want Constable Munro pulling you up for riding in the dark, even if he is an attractive young bobby.'

'Oh, thank you. It's very kind of you and Mrs Grantly, doctor.' Victoria felt slightly overwhelmed by their generosity, but there was more.

'Mark asked me to purchase a bicycle bag to fit on the back. It is his birthday gift to you. He said it had to be leather so that it will be waterproof in case you wanted to go shopping. Mr Crabb fixed it on. I believe my wife has put Mark's waterproof cycling cape inside. Come and have a look.' They all trooped to the door. Polly carried the oil lamp and held it high.

'Why, it looks brand new!' Willie exclaimed.

'It has chrome wheels and handlebars,' George said admiringly, walking round it. 'We'll have to put it in father's shed to keep it dry.'

'Aye, you do that, laddie,' Joe said. He scratched his head and frowned. The doctor and his wife had certainly been generous. Did they have some reason of their own for treating Victoria so well? Polly was wondering the same thing.

Victoria was speechless. She suspected most of the bicycle was brand new. 'I can't believe it!' she gasped. 'How can I ever thank you all...'

'It's a pleasure, my dear. We are very grateful to you. We realize how homesick Mark has been during his first term. I believe your letters, so regular and dependable, have been the only things that have kept him going.' He sensed the Pringles relaxing, but if only they knew.

'Oh, but Mark is happier now. He has made new friends and he's more settled,' Victoria said.

'Maybe he is, but it's thanks to your good common sense and advice. We went up to see him. He misses you and he waits for your news every week. I wish there was more we could do to repay you.'

Victoria could scarcely wait for morning to ride her new machine up to Langmune. She could spend most of her free days up at the farm now. Already she was missing Andrew more than she had expected. She had relived the night of the dance every night before she fell asleep, and most of all she clung to the memory of her first real kiss. She felt she would never forget that as long as she lived. It was like waking up from a long dream. She felt alive, aware.

She was up as soon as she heard George and Willie getting ready to go to work.

'Happy birthday, sleepyhead!' they chorused. Grinning widely they tossed her a brown paper parcel.

'They're from us, but it was Andrew gave us the idea,' George grinned.

'The wee parcel is from Josh.' Willie added. 'He worked in the gardens to earn some pocket money, then he bought it from Mr Nelson.'

'Mr Nelson the schoolmaster?'

'The very same. He belted us often enough but he was aye soft with you. "Victoria Lachlan is the best in the class," he used to say. Josh says he remembers you well. He offered to look for a book while he was in Dumfries, one you would enjoy.'

'It's a book of poetry,' Victoria exclaimed

happily as she unwrapped the small parcel. 'Oh, indeed I shall treasure it. I've missed not being able to use Sir William's library.'

'Open ours before we go,' Willie urged boyishly as he spooned up the last of his porridge.

It was a heavy, unwieldy parcel, well wrapped in brown paper and string. George chortled as he watched her puzzled expression.

'Clogs!' she gasped. 'Brand new clogs.' She fingered the gold studs which ran all the way round.

'Andrew said you got wet feet when you were helping in the dairy,' George told her. 'We thought if you were to keep going to Langmune you should have some working footwear.'

'They're too nice to wear in the dairy and the byre,' Victoria insisted.

'Course they're not!' Willie scoffed but she could tell he was pleased.

'The clogger in Dumfries made them. Take them with you today. They'll keep your feet warm and preserve your shoes.'

'You're all so good to me.' Victoria ran across and gave both boys a big hug.

'Eh, any more of that, pretty lady, and we'll never go to work today,' George teased, his cheeks a little redder than usual, his eyes bright.

'Well, you'll need to hurry,' Polly added, bringing their sandwiches from the scullery. 'Here, don't forget these or you'll be mighty hungry by night. Victoria, lassie, if you're going to Langmune will you ask Andrew to send his dirty washing then I'll have it ready for when he comes down on Sunday afternoon. And here's a pair of good thick socks I knitted to wear with your clogs,' she added, beaming happily. 'The lads are right. You'll need something warm and dry to wear at the farm.'

'Do you mind me going, Aunt Polly? Perhaps I should stay here and help you?'

'Och, awa' wi' ye, lassie,' Polly said gruffly. 'You spend plenty of time on this family, helping Josh with his lessons, and cooking a meal now and then. That's a real treat for me. If you enjoy going to the farm that's good enough for me. You get little enough pleasure slaving away at the castle all week.'

'It's better than it used to be. I write down all the recipes I use now and how they could be improved, as Granny did. I shall soon have my own recipe book. And I use the electric cooker when Ware's not there.' She gave a triumphant grin. 'Miss Traill showed me her instruction book and it's nearly the same. You have these hot rings on top but you can turn them up or down with quarter turns of a dial, from low heat to high, so the vegetables don't boil dry and burn as they did the first time I tried.' She shuddered, remembering her panic, thinking she had set the kitchens on fire. 'The oven is a bit funny to use, but I'm getting used to it as well now.'

'Good for you, lassie. I wonder if we shall ever get the electric. It would be grand for the lights but I don't know how I would manage the cooking. I'll bet you make a better job of it than the Ware woman, for all she keeps the instructions to herself.'

'That's what Milly says. Mrs Crainby is having guests to stay soon. They're coming from Berwickshire. We think they must be quite wealthy, the way ma'am is preparing for them. She told Ware she was making up some special menus for the five days they'll be here, but Ware is still taking her two days off during their stay. I'm looking forward to cooking different dishes on my own.'

'Better you than me, Victoria,' Polly shuddered. 'I'd probably be so nervous I'd burn everything. You do enjoy the cooking, don't you, lassie?'

'Yes, I do.' Victoria laughed and hugged her. 'This is the best birthday I've ever had. Now I'd better go or Andrew will think I've changed my mind.'

'And a very disappointed man he'll be when you do, my lamb,' Polly whispered to herself as the door closed behind her, 'but my poor laddie will never be able to offer you the life Mark Jacobs will give you when he becomes a doctor.' She sighed heavily and went to the bottom of the ladder to call Josh up in time for school.

The milking was almost finished when Victoria pedalled into the farmyard at Langmune. Rosie was carrying her last two pails of milk across to the dairy.

'Hello, Victoria,' she called cheerfully. 'Happy birthday.'

Victoria blushed and grinned back at her.

'Thank you, Rosie. I must be later than I thought if you're almost finished milking?'

'We're a bit earlier than we've been lately. Ma has come to help this morning. She's tired of staying in the house and she says Pa sleeps such a lot.'

'How is he?'

'Not very well.' Rosie's cheerful mask fell away and Victoria saw there were dark shadows beneath her eyes as though she had not been sleeping. 'He's worried to death about the cottage. We haven't dared tell him yet, but Dr Grantly told Ma he'll never be fit for a herdsman's job again. He says there's a danger he might take another heart attack, but even if he gets better from this one he'll only be fit for light work a few hours a day.'

'Oh, Rosie. That's awful.' Victoria stared in dismay at the older girl's troubled face.

'I shouldna be troubling you with my family's worries,' she said as she grimaced, 'but to tell the truth, it's nice to see you again and have somebody to talk to.' She gave Victoria a lopsided smile. 'And life's not all bad. Allan asked me to marry him when he realized how bad things are with Pa.'

'Is he your – your...?

'My man. Aye. We've gone around together these past six years, but he never mentioned marriage before. He says he thought Ma and Pa depended on me to make up their dairy team. He works down at Beechwood Farm and he helps with the milking there some of the time. Now he wants the two of us to take a dairy of our own, with a wee cottage. There are not many jobs where a wife can keep on working when she marries so it would suit us fine, like Ma and Pa. He even said he'd have Ma to help if they want to live with us.' Rosie lowered her voice. 'Mind you, I havena told her any o' this yet. She's enough to think about.'

'I'm sure she has.' Victoria nodded. 'I'll not breathe a word.'

'Trouble is, Allan needs to decide by the November term and that's only four weeks away. The farmers take on their new workers then. Shush, here comes Ma. Andrew will be popping his head out o' the byre any minute now. He's been looking out for you for the last half hour, and he's whistling like a blackbird courting his mate because you were coming.'

'I don't believe you,' Victoria said, blushing furiously.

'Are you two going to stand there gossiping all morning?' Andrew called on cue, a pleased smile splitting his tanned face.

'See, what did I tell ye?' Rosie laughed aloud and went on her way to the dairy.

'Well, hello, and whose is this posh bicycle?' Andrew whistled coming up closer. He grinned at Victoria and there was no doubting he was pleased to see her. Victoria's spirits soared.

'Dr Grantly brought it over last night. He traded Mark's old one in with Mr Crabb.'

'He's done you proud, Victoria. Does that mean you'll keep coming, or will Mark object?'

'Object? Why ever would Mark do that?'

'You tell me.' Andrew raised his eyebrows.

'I can come whenever I'm free, now I have my own bicycle.'

'I hope you'll come often then, now I'm living up here.

Victoria felt her eighteenth birthday had been the happiest day of her life and yet she had spent it working, helping Miss Traill, feeding the poultry, churning the butter, and then helping Andrew at the byre. It was almost dark before the afternoon milking even began and Victoria saw how good it was to have the electric lights for working with the cows, as well as saving time trimming lamps.

Miss Traill insisted she must stay to share the evening meal with them. She had made a roast chicken and two kinds of stuffing, Brussels sprouts and carrots, creamy mashed potatoes, bread sauce and gravy, as well as potatoes roasted in goose fat and beautifully crisp. They were one of Victoria's favourites. To finish they had a trifle made with Miss Traill's famously light sponge cake and bottled raspberries laced with her home-made wine, and a layer of chilled egg custard topped with cream.

'That was delicious.' Victoria sighed happily as she cleared the last spoonful from her dish. 'I never knew I was so hungry.' Miss Traill beamed with pleasure.

'It's the fresh air, lassie,' Mr Rennie said, 'and the work you've done today.'

'And Miss Traill's excellent meal,' Andrew

199

added gallantly.

'Yes, yes, that too of course,' Mr Rennie agreed with a smile. 'I see why she favours you, young man!' he twinkled. 'You know how to keep the right side of her.'

'I'm so full I think I shall never be able to pedal home,' Victoria groaned softly. 'But I must be on my way as soon as we have washed the dishes.'

'There's no need for you to help, lassie...' Miss Traill began.

'If you wash, I'll dry them. We'll give Miss Traill a rest,' Andrew volunteered.

'You will?' Victoria raised her dark brows. 'You never volunteered to help with dishes at home.'

'Maybe that was a wee bit different,' Mr Rennie suggested, exchanging a knowing smile with Miss Traill. 'Leave them to it. Rest while you can,' he advised.

Andrew and Victoria were perfectly at ease chatting and chaffing each other as they cleared away the dishes. Afterwards he insisted on seeing her part of the way home.

'Andrew, there's no need. You've had a long day already.'

'And so have you, and you will be up as early as I shall tomorrow morning. Besides...I want to come. I don't like you going off alone in the dark. That's the only bad thing about you coming up here in the winter.'

In the event Andrew cycled beside her and they were almost at the village before Victoria realized how far they had come.

'I'm nearly home! You have to go all the way back alone,' she said with remorse.

Andrew dismounted and propped his bike against a tree.

'It's worth it, Victoria.' He was standing very close now, one hand on her bicycle. 'I like living up at Langmune but I do miss you. All of you,' he added quickly. Quite apart from his father's warnings he felt he had to go cautiously with Victoria. She was so capable and adult when it came to work, but he was certain she was as innocent as a child in the ways of men and women. He was convinced she still regarded him as an elder brother, but he hoped she might begin to see him as a man in his own right now that he no longer lived under the same roof. He hoped she would always regard him as a trusted friend, but he wanted more than that. Were those feelings reserved for Mark Jacobs? He tortured himself with that thought, knowing how much more Mark could give her. Right now, though, he was away. All's fair in love and war, he told himself. Letters might keep him in touch, but they were not the same as touching in the flesh.

'We miss you being around too,' Victoria told him, breaking into his chaotic thoughts.

'You do?' He hugged her. For a second he hesitated then his arms tightened and he bent his head and kissed her mouth. It was soft and yielding and his lips lingered on hers, reluctant to draw away. Victoria showed no more inclination to end the kiss than he did.

''Night, Victoria,' he said huskily at last.

As Victoria cycled the last three quarters of a mile she kept lifting her gloved hand to her lips as though imprisoning Andrew's kiss there for all time. Her heart sang. She was beginning to understand why Milly talked incessantly about Jem and why she longed to be with him all the time.

Four days later they received word that Ted Holmes had died peacefully in his sleep.

'That will mean changes up at Langmune,' Joe said. 'I expect Mr Rennie will want to hire another family for the dairy. I wonder if the man's wife and daughter have anywhere to go?'

'There are a few empty cottages on the estate,' Polly said doubtfully, 'but they will need work to pay the rent.' It was one of the worries for everyone living in a tied cottage, loss of the job meant loss of the home.

It was the first thing Polly told Victoria when she arrived home that evening.

'Poor Rosie. Though I think the real sadness will be for his wife, Edna.' Victoria went on to tell Polly about Rosie's boyfriend and his plans for the future.

On Victoria's next visit to Langmune she learned that Rosie and her mother were moving to Beechwood Farm.

'The farmer has hired Allan as head herdsman now that he can supply his own helpers,' Rosie told her. 'The present dairyman is moving on. Mother is moving in with Allan and me. He's getting a cottage with the job, and free milk and firewood and fours sacks of potatoes a year. It's not as nice as here and we shall miss the electric light, but –' she shrugged her shoulders – 'beggars can't be choosers. Anyway, we're getting married in six months when Ma has had time to accept things.'

'I shall miss you when I come to Langmune,' Victoria said.

'Maybe I'll see you at the dancing if Andrew brings you with him. I shall be nearer to the village at Beechwood and I shall get Allan to take me.'

'That will be lovely. I'll look for you if I go again.'

'Och, I'm sure Andrew will want to take you once things settle down here. I heard a rumour Mr Rennie has hired another herdsman already, with his wife and son. They're moving from a farm in Wigtownshire.'

'Oh, Andrew never said.'

'It's only just happened. Anyway I expect he has more important things to talk about when he sees you.' Rosie grinned impudently, bringing a blush to Victoria's cheeks. 'You should hear him singing "Dancing cheek to cheek" when he knows you're coming up here. We can't shut him up.'

As Christmas drew nearer Milly seemed to grow even more absent-minded and lethargic than usual. Surprisingly she was less talkative too and Victoria wondered if she was sickening for something. Ware was constantly nagging her about one thing or another but Victoria had to admit the older woman did have cause. Milly didn't seem able to concentrate on anything.

'I hope you're feeling better today,' Victoria greeted her on the morning of Ware's day off. 'We have to make a Christmas tea party for the children this afternoon. Mrs Crainby has invited some young friends for Miss Charlotte. I would like to bake some biscuits and a chocolate log with a robin on top.'

'Some bairns are lucky.' Milly gave a big sniff as though holding back tears and Victoria looked at her more closely. She looked terribly white and her cheeks were hollow. She frowned.

'Do you feel worse this morning, Milly? Are you...?

'I feel awful. I'm never going to feel better, ever again.'

'Of course you will, but if—'

'Oh, Victoria! I'm going to have a bairn!' she wailed.

Victoria stopped, holding a saucepan in mid-air, her mouth open in surprise. 'But–but you haven't got a husband...H-how can you have a baby?'

'You should know. Mark Jacobs is a doctor, isn't he, and he's your friend. I expect he knows things Jem and me dinna ken about babies, doesn't he?'

'I – I don't know what you're talking about, Milly...?' Victoria frowned, genuinely puzzled.

Milly stared at her. 'No, I don't believe you do,' she said incredulously. 'Whatever do you talk about, or write about in the letters you get every week?'

'Oh, Mark tells me about his studies and his new friends and his fears about the situation in Europe. He says if things don't improve there could be another war.'

'War? That's all I need, for Jem to run away and get himself killed and leave me wi' his bastard.'

'His...?' Victoria's face went pale. That's what Ware had called her. 'D-did you...d-did Jem...?'

'Of course me and Jem. I've never even kissed anybody else.'

'B-but h-how?'

'Don't you know anything, Victoria Lachlan? You've been friendly with Mark Jacobs a lot longer than Jem and me. And you go off to see Andrew Pringle every week. You should—'

'I don't! I – I mean I go up to Langmune to help Miss Traill.'

'Och aye?' Milly put her hands on her hips and stared at Victoria defiantly. 'Well, you can go and tell that tae the seagulls. You'll be getting a bairn next.'

'Why? What did you do? You and Jem?'

'You don't...?' Milly stared at her in disbelief. 'I thought you were educated and that you knew everything about everything, but ye dinna, d'ye?'

'I don't know much about babies, except I loved wee Josh when he was a baby.'

'Wee Josh!' Milly began to laugh hysterically. 'It's years since he was a baby. You must ken

205

how a woman gets a bairn...' But Milly could see by the expression on Victoria's face that she didn't know. Of course she had no mother to tell her things and Milly couldn't imagine Polly Pringle giving the dire warnings her own mother had given her. Not that they'd done any good. She hadn't heeded her mother, she thought dejectedly.

'Milly? What did you do?'

'Well, when a man and woman get together – you know and – and they kiss, and you have certain feelings...then you kiss some more and he puts his tongue round yours...' Milly giggled, 'and then...and then it leads to-to more, and you get a baby in your belly...' Milly's giggles suddenly turned to sobs, great hiccupping sounds. Tears streamed down her face.

Victoria put an arm around her shaking shoulders and tried to comfort her, but there was so much she didn't understand and Milly's explanation alarmed her.

It took precious time and two cups of tea before Milly had calmed down enough to do any work and Victoria judged it best to leave the subject of babies and Jem alone if they were ever to get through the day's work together.

She couldn't put Milly's words out of her mind. Later she would think about things, in the privacy of her own room. For all the many books she had read there were a lot of things about life that she didn't understand. She considered some of the things Mark had told her about his studies in biology, about plants and the monk called Mendel who had discovered genes and why some people had brown eyes and some had blue. But nature study with Mr Nelson at Darlonachie School had never included such things and Mark had not gone into detail, and he had never even mentioned how babies were made. Of course, she knew the chickens and the birds hatched out of eggs, but she had never actually seen a calf or a pig being born.

Ware had called her a bastard with such venom that she had known it was not pleasant so she had looked it up in her dictionary. The meaning given was a child born of parents who were not married, but she had never had a father so how could her parents have been married? When asked, Polly simply told her to ignore Eve Ware and brushed the whole thing aside as unimportant.

Her grandmother had avoided her questions too. She had learned not to delve too deeply. Now she realized there were things she ought to know, questions she needed to ask, but who would answer them? Who could dispel this new anxiety which she felt. She had kissed Andrew and she had enjoyed it. In fact, she longed for him to do it again, and again. She had felt her stomach clench. Surely it could not be so wrong to enjoy the touch of his lips on hers, yet Milly had said...Victoria frowned. What exactly had Milly said? And did she know? Everyone understood her brain was a little slower than most. Could she be trusted to understand and tell the truth?

The preparations for the children's party claimed Victoria's attention as she turned the chocolate sponge on to sugared greaseproof paper and concentrated her attention on rolling it into the shape of a log. She enjoyed such tasks. Lady Landour had arrived from Berwickshire again, with her three children. They were to stay over Christmas. Lord Landour was in London but he would join them on Christmas Eve. At Darlonachie the main festivities were usually held at New Year, while Christmas Day was no more than another Sunday. This year things were to be different at the castle, at least while there were guests. Mrs Crainby had already told Victoria she would have no days off during the fortnight around Christmas but she had promised she could have the extra free time when their guests had departed. Surprisingly there was no such ban on Eve Ware's usual days off.

Victoria felt saddened that she would see little or nothing of Andrew, or of Miss Traill and Mr Rennie, during the festive period. She knew the demands of the castle kitchens would allow her little time even with Aunt Polly and Uncle Joe and the boys. However, she insisted she must have a few hours free to spend with Mark before the New Year. Mrs Crainby had agreed reluctantly to this so long as she returned to the castle to help cook the evening meal for Hogmanay.

Although she would never admit it Mrs Crainby now accepted that Lachlan was a far better cook than Ware would ever be, and the girl was cheaper to pay. She knew her father-in-law paid board and lodging directly to the Pringles on her behalf so she felt no compunction in paying Victoria little more than she had earned when she started work at thirteen. Thankfully Sir William rarely interfered with such matters these days. He seemed content to spend his time in the library with his books, or ambling around the gardens and nearby woods with his faithful old Labrador, Goldie.

Andrew was bitterly disappointed when he heard Victoria would have no time to spend with him for two whole weeks. His own work was equally demanding; the animals needed the same attention whatever day it was. It was not only lack of time with Victoria which bothered Andrew though. He had noticed a reserve in her recently which had not been there before. Every time he accompanied her down to the village after a visit to Langmune he looked forward to experiencing the sweetness of that first lingering kiss, but after the briefest peck Victoria jumped on her bicycle and pedalled away. He knew there was something troubling her. Sometimes he felt she wanted to talk, but always she hesitated.

It did nothing to help his spirits when his mother mentioned that Victoria had spent the whole of one precious afternoon with Mark Jacobs. He had arrived in his uncle's car and they had walked up to the old cave, their favourite childhood haunt. They had spent considerable time talking together. Had they only talked,

Andrew wondered miserably. Afterwards Mark had driven her to the doctor's house for afternoon tea with his uncle and aunt. He had brought her back to the castle in time to change her clothes and cook the Hogmanay dinner. Fortunately for Victoria it was to be served later than usual because Mr and Mrs Crainby and their guests planned to stay up to welcome in the New Year of 1936.

Twelve

One of the loveliest surprises at the beginning of the new year had come from Mr Rennie. Andrew arrived with a box carefully strapped to his bicycle. Polly and Victoria were changing their clothes ready for Sunday morning service at the kirk.

'Mr Rennie has decided to buy a new wireless now that we have electricity up at Langmune,' Andrew announced. 'He knows how much Victoria enjoys listening to the news when she's at Langmune so he thought you might all like to have his battery wireless.'

'Oh, my word!' Polly exclaimed, staring almost fearfully at the object Andrew was unwrapping.

'That's wonderful. How thoughtful of Mr Rennie to think of us,' Victoria said, her eyes shining with excitement.

'I hope this accumulator battery has travelled all right,' Andrew frowned, unpacking the oblong glass container. There is a spare one but I'll bring it next time I come. You need to take these to Mr Crabb for topping up with acid, Mother. Mr Rennie had two so that he was never without the wireless. Once you get used to listening in you'll not want to be without it either.'

'I don't know about that,' Polly said doubtfully.

'The man isn't in the box, Ma. It's only his voice. He's not going to jump out and bite you,' Andrew teased. Victoria could have hugged him. He looked young and happy and when he laughed she was sure her heart skipped a beat. He caught her gaze and raised his brows. She blushed shyly, and bit her lower lip.

'So when are you coming up to Langmune again, Victoria?'

'I shall have my usual day off again from Friday.'

'Good. We'll see you then shall we, so long as it's not snowing?'

'All right.' She smiled. 'It seems ages since I saw everyone up there. How is the new man? Has his son improved? Has his wife settled in?'

'Humph.' Andrew frowned. 'They're not turning out too well. I reckon Mr Rennie will be looking for a replacement come the May term.'

'So soon? Oh dear. What—'

'You'll see for yourself.' He inclined his head

211

towards his mother and she guessed he didn't want to discuss problems at Langmune.

It was from the wireless that Victoria learned of the death of Rudyard Kipling whose books Sir William had loaned to her. She had derived real pleasure from some of his poems and stories. Only two days later this was followed by news of the death of King George on the twentieth of January.

Closer to home was Milly's plight. Jem had agreed they must marry but he could not afford to rent a cottage of his own and the jobs for married farm workers wanting tied cottages had all been taken at the November term.

'We'll have to stay with his mother,' Milly wept as she poured out her troubles to Victoria. 'My pa is furious. He says we've made our ain bed and now we must lay in it. Ma keeps crying, saying I've brought shame to her family. My brothers wanted to fight Jem.'

'Poor Milly,' Victoria sighed, 'perhaps they will not think it's so bad once they see your baby. Now, please can you peel the potatoes and carrots so that I can get on with lunch?'

'You don't care! You're as bad as the Ware woman!' Milly sobbed hysterically.

'I do care and I'm truly sorry, but you know we both need to earn our wages,' Victoria said desperately, 'and Eve Ware never organizes the work for the days she is off. She leaves everything to be done.'

'Wh-what do I care if the pampered folk upstairs dinna get their meal on time.' Milly sniffed and blew her nose loudly.

'Well, at least I try to give you lighter work to do when Ware is off,' Victoria said, 'so please get on with the vegetables, or shall I ask Stella to do them?'

'I'll do 'em,' Milly muttered sulkily. For a while they worked in silence, each deep in their own thoughts. Since Ware had discovered Milly was expecting a child Victoria felt she had been as spiteful as it was possible for one human being to be to another. Although the young maid, Stella, had been employed as a general to do the scrubbing and attend to the fires Ware seemed to take delight in giving these tasks to Milly, including carrying in the heavy buckets of coal and baskets of logs and carting them up the stairs.

'I'm sorry I was nasty, Victoria,' she said, breaking the silence. 'I know you do your best for me. I don't know how much longer I can stand Ware and her vicious tongue. She's trans-ferred her spite from you to me – well, some of it,' she added dolefully. 'Do you ever think about leaving?'

'Oh yes, often,' Victoria said promptly. 'One day I shall.'

'Trouble is I need the money,' Milly mourned, 'more than ever now. Ma says she'll knit some wee jackets and leggings and a blanket if I buy the wool.'

'Aunt Polly is going to crotchet a shawl for you. I've ordered white wool from Miss Phipps. She says it will be in next Thursday and she will send it up with Mr Blake, the fish man.'

Milly mumbled her thanks. She looked so wretched that Victoria's heart ached for her. Again and again her thoughts turned to the mother she had never known. Had she suffered as Milly was doing? There must have been someone like Jem, or like Andrew perhaps? But who was he and what had happened to him? Why had he not married her mother? Milly's plight made her realize the shame and anguish her mother must have suffered. Yet Granny Lachlan had never made her aware of it. She had always felt loved and cherished. Even Sir William had always welcomed her at the castle, and even in the nursery.

The weeks passed and Mrs Crainby informed Ware that Lady Landour and her children would be returning for a week at Easter. They were planning to take a picnic down to the Solway, near Annan, if the weather was favourable.

'I expect you to prepare some dainty cakes and savoury pasties,' she said to Ware, but her eyes were fixed on Victoria. 'Make sure you have all the ingredients in readiness. Lachlan, you must miss your day off. You may take it when Lady Landour has departed.'

'Yes, ma'am,' Victoria nodded, 'but if you please, ma'am, I have not had the days I missed at Christmas yet.'

Ware shot her a venomous look. Mrs Crainby tutted impatiently. 'You must arrange such things with Ware,' she said coldly.

'Well, I would like time to spend with my

friend, Mark Jacobs, during his Easter vacation from university,' Victoria persisted.

'Again?' Henrietta Crainby's eyebrows rose. 'Surely he has found more suitable friends than you by now, Lachlan.'

'He does have other friends but we have been companions since we were at Darlonachie School together. We write to each other every week. We have things to – to discuss when Mark comes home.' There was a stubborn note in Victoria's voice, but Henrietta thought she detected urgency too. Her eyes narrowed and she looked Victoria up and down with a curl of her lips. Victoria flushed with indignation. She thinks I'm the same as poor Milly. If only she knew. That was the very thing she wanted to avoid and Mark had promised to explain to her about what he called procreation. She couldn't possibly wait until the summer.

'Oh, very well.' Henrietta Crainby pursed her lips impatiently. 'You had better take two or three hours off, to meet your "friend", if he has not changed his mind in the meantime,' she added. In her mind there could be only one reason for a student doctor to continue meeting a kitchen maid.

While Victoria was up at Langmune the following Friday she told Andrew about the impending visit of Lady Landour.

'Mrs Crainby says I must miss my usual days off and take them later, but I need to see Mark while he is on vacation. I insisted I must have a few hours free.'

'I see,' he said coolly, 'you can get time off to see Jacobs but not to come up here.'

'Oh, Andrew! You know how much I love to come up here, but it would take most of my few precious hours cycling up and back again.'

'Of course it would, m'dear,' Mr Rennie said, as he came slowly to the dining table. 'But you should insist you get your days off when they are owed to you. You must be firm about it. Perhaps you will pay us an extra visit when you have arranged it?'

'Oh yes, I'd love to do that.'

'There you are then, Andrew. Is that not a good compromise?'

'I suppose so, if it ever happens,' Andrew said morosely.

'Of course it will happen. Victoria will insist, won't you, my dear?'

'I will.' Victoria nodded with new determination. 'I will arrange it.'

'Aye, I'd be glad of your help for an extra day now and then, lassie,' Miss Traill said. 'I've a fair number of broody hens waiting to sit, and some already on eggs. Chicks will be hatching over the next six weeks. Then there's the lambing. There's always a pet lamb or two to feed. Andrew will be glad of your help with them, will ye not, laddie?'

'If Victoria can tear herself away and come up here, I shall be glad,' Andrew replied stiffly.

Victoria frowned. What had she done to displease him so? She had never known him to be petty or childish. She was sure of her welcome at Langmune now though and she vowed she would insist on getting the free time she was due.

As soon as they had eaten afternoon tea she accompanied Andrew to the byre to prepare for the milking as had become her usual routine. He had taught her to milk one or two of the quietest cows and she had begun to enjoy it. Andrew usually milked a cow in a nearby stall and sometimes they chatted quietly as the milk thrummed steadily into the pail.

Today Andrew seemed preoccupied and cool towards her and she felt awkward. She was uncomfortably aware of the new herdsman's son, Horace Doig. She had noticed him watching her on her previous visits but today he seemed to be leering at her whenever she looked up and there was an unpleasant sneer on his thick lips. He looked dirty and unkempt and she couldn't suppress a shudder. His mother had the same appearance. Her lank dark hair trailed untidily around her shoulders instead of being caught up in a neat bun; her skin looked sallow and greasy and her harden apron was filthy. No wonder Andrew found them so unsatisfactory.

The father, Tom Doig, seemed quite different. His skin had a freshly scrubbed look and his flat tweed cap was turned back to front for milking so that the peak didn't rub against the cow. He had a quiet voice and a calm manner which soothed the nervous young heifers. He smiled at Victoria and asked which of the cows she preferred to milk.

'Just the quiet ones,' she said, smiling back at him.

Every time she went to the dairy to empty the pails of milk over the cooler Horace Doig seemed to follow with his own, even if his was only half full. Twice he brushed up against her and she felt trapped between him and the wall. Andrew came into the dairy to empty his own pail the second time and Horace Doig gave her a calculating stare and a nod before he moved away.

'Is he bothering you?' Andrew's voice was still cool.

'N-no, but I don't like him.'

Eventually the day's work was over and Victoria went inside for her evening meal. Andrew was a little late.

'There's a cow calving,' he said. 'I'll not come with you tonight. You'll be all right?'

'Of course.' Victoria knew her own tone was as cool as Andrew's. She didn't know what she had done to offend him but she had her pride too. Mr Rennie looked from one to the other and frowned.

'Surely Victoria can wait for you, Andrew? Will the cow calve soon?'

'It's hard to tell. It's Butterfly. It's her second calf so she shouldn't have any difficulty but she had twins last time and one of them was dead.'

'Ah yes, I remember. But I think it is more important to see Victoria safely on her way.'

'Oh no. Andrew mustn't neglect the animals for me,' Victoria protested.

'Are your lights working all right?' Andrew asked.

'Yes, George brought me a new battery for the front lamp so it's bright.'

'Do Andrew's brothers look after you well, when he is not there?' enquired Mr Rennie.

'Oh yes. They're like my own brothers. I could never have wished for a kinder family.'

'That's good to hear.' Mr Rennie smiled and nodded his satisfaction.

Victoria didn't see Andrew purse his lips in frustration. That's the trouble, he thought morosely, she never thinks of me as anything but a brother, even now I've moved out of the house. He was almost sure the cow would not calve for a couple of hours and he could easily see her well on her way down the track and be back in time, but frustration, combined with the demon jealousy, prevented him offering.

They left the house together. Victoria collected her bicycle from the shed beside the house but she walked with Andrew to the stone shed where the cow was pacing restlessly.

'How do you know she's going to have a calf soon?' Victoria asked.

'Instinct...' Andrew shrugged. 'Experience, I suppose. Mr Rennie taught me a lot before his chest kept him confined to the house so much, and Ted Holmes was good with cattle. I learned a lot from him.'

'I – I see...' She paused but Andrew said no more. 'Well...goodnight then.'

'Night.' Andrew resisted the temptation to pull

her into his arms and kiss the breath out of her. He turned his attention to the cow instead and Victoria mounted her cycle and pedalled slowly away from him, her heart heavy.

Esther Doig was a slovenly woman and her cottage reflected her character. She had never bothered to hang curtains at the windows, and the few rag rugs which lay on the floor rarely had the dust and dirt shaken out of them. It was through one of these naked windows that Horace spied the flicker of Victoria's bike lamp as she set off for home. Only one light tonight, he noted with satisfaction.

Although there was a narrow footpath between the buildings through the farmyard, the proper track for vehicles and bicycles was like a figure seven, with the long leg running along the length of the stack yard before turning at a sharp angle down the side to join the main farm road down to Darlonachie. The farm cottages were almost at the junction.

Horace slammed out of the door, across the vegetable patch and vaulted over the picket fence, his piggy eyes gleaming malevolently. He reached the main track before Victoria had cycled round to it. He crouched in the shadow of the hedge, ready to pounce when she came into view. He had made enquiries about Victoria Lachlan. A few drinks in the village pub had loosened more than one tongue. She had no family of her own, didn't even know who her father was if the gossip was true. She was a bastard and she had no right to look down her pert little nose at him.

Victoria's mind was on Andrew; her spirits were low as she pedalled through the darkness. In all the years she had known him he had never been withdrawn and cold towards her. What had she done to displease him? She was too pre-occupied to notice the shadows. They held no fears for her. She had wandered the woods and fields since she was a child so it was a shock when one of those shadows launched itself from the hedge, knocking the breath out of her as she landed on the track with her bicycle on top of her.

Before she could gather her wits the cycle was flung aside and a heavy weight pressed her into the ground. She was vaguely aware of the front wheel of her bicycle still spinning in the air beside her head, while the lamp shone uselessly at the sky.

'Let me go!' she gasped, struggling violently when hands began fumbling all over her. Her eyes were becoming accustomed to the dark-ness. She knew by the shape and weight the figure must be a man but she couldn't see his face. She squirmed and struggled, but her strength was puny against the solid weight.

'You think you're too good to look in my direction, do you?' Horace Doig sneered, bring-ing his face so close to hers she could feel hot breath and smell the onions he had eaten.

'Let me go! Why did you run into me? Stop it! What d'you think you're doing?'

'Ye ken fine what I'm about,' he mocked.

221

'Ye're not so innocent as ye pretend. Made enquiries, didn't I? Ye're just another bastard. Like mother like daughter, eh?' He gave an evil laugh. Victoria's struggles were futile beneath his legs and heavy body and his hands seemed to be moving everywhere at once. She managed to aim her fist at his face but he only jeered at her and ripped her coat open with such force the buttons shot into the air. Immediately his hands groped inside, feeling the softness of her breasts beneath her jumper. He squeezed cruelly. Victoria screamed.

'Hod yer whisht, woman!' he growled. 'Keep still, will ye!'

'No. No!' Victoria struggled in terror, helpless against his brutish strength.

He laughed, a sickening, throaty sound. 'I like a woman with fire in her. More pain for you, more pleasure for me, eh?' He tugged at the hem of her skirt and yanked it up. Victoria screamed, and screamed. He struck her face with the back of his hand but she was too petrified to feel the pain, or the warmth of blood where her teeth had cut her lip. She couldn't stop screaming.

'You silly bitch!' He clapped a rough hand over her mouth to stifle the noise. 'There's nobody to hear, or come to your rescue! Be quiet, I tell ye, or I'll knock your teeth out the next time.' But the instant he allowed her to breathe she screamed again, and again, struggling frantically. He uttered a string of foul oaths, jerked her scarf off and gagged her. He pulled it so tight she thought she must suffocate.

After Victoria had gone Andrew cursed himself for letting her go alone. He leaned on the door of the shed and put his head on his arms. He had never felt so miserable in his life. In the silence he thought he heard a scream. Probably an owl catching its unsuspecting prey, he thought. It was a melancholy sound and matched his mood. He opened the shed door and went inside to take a closer look at the cow, but Mick was barking now, a frenzied, agitated bark and he paused, frowning. Mick was a good watchdog, not easily upset by vermin or a passing cat. Before he had time to close the door behind him the sound came again, then again.

'Victoria?' He slammed the door shut. She must have had a nasty tumble from her bike to scream like that. He started to run across the yard, his feet instinctively finding the footpath in the darkness. Once past the shadow of the stone buildings he saw the light shining upwards from her cycle lamp. He ran even faster. Moments later he saw the dark heaving huddle on the ground, heard panting and scrabbling.

'Doig!' He bellowed the name in fury. He seized the collar of the man's jacket, jerking him to his feet. He smashed his clenched fist into his face. Horace Doig was taken by surprise. He hit the ground with a thud. Andrew was beside himself with fury. He pulled the man to his feet and punched him again, and then again, feeling the pain in his own knuckles as they connected with Doig's teeth. He gave one final punch. Horace Doig sprawled on the ground and lay still.

He turned to Victoria. She had crawled to one side and scrambled to her feet, her arms crossed tightly over her chest. She had lost her hat and her hair hung down.

'Oh, Victoria!' he said, his voice thick with emotion and remorse. 'Are you all right, lass?' He put his arms round her, drawing her against his chest. 'Dear Lord, you're shivering like an aspen leaf.'

She yelled his name in warning. He spun round and managed to deflect the worst of Horace Doig's fists in yet another onslaught. He was blind with rage for what he had done to Victoria. He hit the man squarely on the jaw, then twisted his arms behind his back before he could recover.

'Pass me your scarf, Victoria.' He spoke tersely. She obeyed without question. He bound the man's wrists.

'Now walk,' he commanded Doig.

'Where?' Doig spat blood and at least one tooth on to the ground. He swore profusely.

'To the cottage. Be thankful I'm not taking you to Mr Rennie. He'd call Constable Munro for certain.' He hauled Victoria's bike on to its wheels, then drew her to his side with his free arm. He spoke quietly. 'We'll go back to the house. You've had a nasty shock. We'll tidy you up then I'll take you home.'

It was not far to the herdsman's cottage and Andrew banged on the door. Tom Doig opened it. As soon as he saw Horace his eyes lifted to

Andrew, and beyond him to Victoria standing shivering in the shadows.

'Oh Lord, not again. Not again...'

He sounded almost ready to weep, Andrew thought. He felt sympathy for the man who surely deserved better than such a wife and son.

'Stop moaning, y'auld bugger, and untie ma bloody hands,' Horace Doig lisped through the gap where three teeth were missing now. There had been only one gap before.

Andrew put a comforting arm around Victoria's shoulders and led her towards the yard and the farmhouse beyond, wheeling her bicycle with his free hand. In spite of his strength and warmth she couldn't stop shivering. As they drew nearer the lighted shed they heard a slithering sound and then a thump.

'The cow!' Andrew exclaimed. 'I'd forgotten about her...'

'What was that noise?' Together they peered over the door in time to see the calf lying behind its mother where it had fallen to the ground. The caul was still over its head.

'I must clear its nose or it'll suffocate,' Andrew said urgently, struggling with the bolt of the door, but the cow had heard them. She spun round and nosed the calf protectively, mooing and licking off the skin with her rasping tongue. Victoria felt Andrew relax against her but she was staring in horror at the bloody skin trailing from the cow. She had never seen an animal being born, not even a kitten or a puppy. If that's how babies came out, then surely they must get in the same way? That's what Doig had meant to do to her? She gave a shudder of revulsion. She shook her head violently, trying to wipe it from her mind.

'She's cleared it herself.' Andrew's attention was on the cow and calf. 'It'll be all right now,' he said with satisfaction. She glanced up at him. He was so matter of fact, so pleased. He glanced down and saw her shiver. 'Come on, Victoria, let's get you inside and warmed up.'

Miss Traill was sitting in her rocking chair beside the fire when they entered. Her eyes widened. She got stiffly to her feet.

'Oh, lassie. You've fallen off your bike. Are you badly hurt? Here, come to the fire.' She frowned when she saw the buttons had been torn from Victoria's coat. Her eyes took in her dishevelled state and the mud on her back. Her eyes narrowed.

'However did this happen? Ye're shivering, lassie. Come closer. Are ye hurt?'

'It's the shock, Miss Traill,' Andrew said quietly. 'I—I thought I should bring her in. Clean her up...Then I will take her home myself.'

'What happened? Tell me the truth, Andrew...'

'Th-that m-man knocked me off my bicycle,' Victoria stammered through chattering teeth. 'He-he t-tried...' To her dismay Victoria began to cry. She couldn't stop. Her shoulders shook with sobs.

'Hush, Victoria, hush,' Andrew urged in alarm. 'You're safe now. Horace Doig willna touch you again if he knows what's good for

226

him.' But Victoria shuddered and cried all the more. Her thoughts were all mixed up with what Doig had tried to do and then the slippery calf and bleeding cow.

'Let her cry, laddie. It'll get it out of her system. I'll make her some hot milk and lace it with brandy. That will warm her up and help to calm her in a few minutes. Give me your coat, lassie. It will brush up fine when it's dry.' She guided Victoria to the rocking chair and gently pushed her into it. 'Will you go and ask Mr Rennie if we can have a glass o' brandy, Andrew?' He nodded and tapped on the dining-room door.

'Come in,' Mr Rennie called gruffly and Andrew knew he was reluctant to be disturbed. He was reading and he peered over his spectacles.

'Andrew? Something wrong? Is it the cow? You need a veterinary?'

'No. I'm sorry to disturb you, sir. Miss Traill asked if we could have a nip of brandy for Victoria. She – she's had a bit of a shock.'

'A shock? Is she in the kitchen?'

'Yes, but we don't want to disturb you.'

Mr Rennie was already struggling to his feet, setting aside his paper and spectacles. He followed Andrew to the kitchen, lifting a crystal brandy decanter from its stand as he passed the long mahogany sideboard. 'Victoria!' He looked sharply at her pale face and shivering figure, hunched in Miss Traill's rocking chair.

'It's the shock,' Miss Traill pronounced. 'I

thought hot milk laced with brandy would warm her up, and maybe calm her.' She frowned and shook her grey head, clearly angry about something.

'This was more than a fall from her bicycle, I take it,' he said grimly, reading the signs of Miss Traill's displeasure.

'It was that – that vile fellow! He jumped out of the bushes and knocked her off. He – he attacked her. Andrew heard her scream.'

Mr Rennie turned to look at Andrew, his breathing more laboured now. 'You reached her...? In time?'

'Yes. We don't want to disturb you, Mr Rennie. Won't you return to your papers?'

'The man must go! He must leave Langmune at once! Now! Tonight. It was bad enough him stealing eggs and potatoes to sell in the village, but this! This is—'

'Please, Mr Rennie, don't upset yourself,' Andrew pleaded in alarm as he listened to the rasping breaths. 'I will take Victoria home, all the way. It is what I should have done anyway,' he added in a low voice, lowering his head, disgusted by his own petty jealousy of Mark Jacobs.

'Wait until she is calmer, then you may take her in my car, Andrew. Tie her bicycle on the back.'

'Please, I don't want to be a nuisance. It's getting late...' Victoria shuddered convulsively.

'It's all right, Victoria, you're not going anywhere alone,' Andrew hurried over and crouched beside her, putting a comforting arm around her shoulders, holding her against his chest.

'Bring her through to the dining room, you too, Andrew. It's warmer in there. We need to talk and I...I need to sit down.'

'Do as he says,' Miss Traill said. 'I'll bring through the hot drink in a moment. Andrew, your knuckles are bleeding.'

He looked down at his bruised fist and grim-aced. He pulled a handkerchief from his pocket and wrapped it round his bloodied fingers.

In the dining room Mr Rennie sank into his chair and bid Victoria be seated on the opposite side of the fire.

'Bring up a chair, Andrew. We must decide what has to be done. You tell me the father is a decent, hard-working man, as his last employer said?'

'He is. I can feel sorry for him with such a wife and son, but—'

'Their last employer made no mention of their faults. I must conclude he wanted rid of them. And so do I. I am not so tolerant. He must leave Langmune first thing tomorrow.'

'Can I tell you what I think, Mr Rennie?'

'Of course, Andrew.'

'We canna put the whole family out on to the road.'

'No, it was the son, Horace, isn't it?'

'Aye, that's his name. But if we put him out of the house he will hang around the village and in the area for as long as his mother is here. I'd never know where he was lurking.' His glance rested on Victoria. 'I suspect something like this has happened before. I would feel happier if I knew where he was. If he's working here we can keep an eye on him.'

'But I will not tolerate such a – a thug around my farm, Andrew.'

'No, sir, but if you were to give his father a month's notice perhaps they would all leave together, maybe go back to where they came from. In the meantime, we would know where Horace Doig is living.'

'We-ell...' Mr Rennie frowned, considering. 'Maybe there's something in what you say. But it is going to leave us very short of labour until the May term, if they all leave.'

'There's only Tom Doig who is worth employing,' Andrew said truthfully. 'I feel sorry for the man, saddled with such a burden.'

'Very well. We'll do as you say, Andrew. Please tell Mr Doig I wish to see him immediately after milking in the morning. I shall give him a month to find a place elsewhere. I shall also have a quiet word with Constable Munro.' He looked towards Victoria, huddled over the fire. 'A word of warning to Horace Doig would not go amiss. He's getting off too lightly as it is, but perhaps it is for the best. It would be a stressful business if he was charged with assault.'

'That would never do,' Andrew agreed hurriedly, knowing they were both considering Victoria. He looked up as Miss Traill came in with a large enamel mug of hot milk from which brandy fumes arose.

'Here now, lassie. Drink this and here's a shawl to put around you.' Although her voice was as brusque as usual there was kindly concern on her lined face. Mr Rennie watched her attend to Victoria and realized his elderly housekeeper had developed a real affection for this girl who had come into their lives as unexpectedly as Andrew himself had done the day he rescued Nell. It must be seven or eight years ago now. How time has flown, and how much fitter I was then, Mr Rennie remarked to himself. He sighed heavily. Victoria heard the sigh and looked anxiously at Andrew.

'I think I ought to go now. I have disturbed you enough, Mr Rennie.'

'No, no, you're not disturbing me, child. You must finish your drink or Miss Traill will be offended.' Victoria sipped at the milk obediently but it was very hot. She was not used to anything alcoholic and the brandy tasted strong. Miss Traill was not used to alcohol either so she had carefully measured two full sherry glasses of brandy into the milk, hoping it would be sufficient to achieve the desired results.

When Victoria had drunk all the milk Andrew led her through to the kitchen. Miss Traill had her button box beside her and was busily plying a needle and thread to Victoria's coat.

'I've found four buttons all the same, although they are not exactly like the ones you had, Victoria. He had even torn the material. I do hope my repairs will be satisfactory. My old eyes are not so good as they used to be.'

'Oh, Miss Traill! How kind you are.' Victoria's chin wobbled and her eyes filled with tears. 'I have been such a trouble to you. I promise I will not return until Horace Doig has gone away from Langmune.'

'Oh lassie, dinna say that. I want you to come. We all want you to come. Andrew will make sure that animal doesna touch you again, will ye not, laddie?'

'I certainly will. Victoria, I think you will have a nasty bruise on your cheek by morning. Here –' he lifted her coat from Miss Traill's lap as she snapped the last thread – 'put on your coat and I'll get you back home.'

'My legs feel very wobbly,' Victoria said as she accompanied him out to the car.

For the first time that day Andrew gave his old familiar chuckle and hugged her against him. 'I don't know how much brandy Miss Traill put in the milk but it certainly smelled strong. You're probably feeling the effects of it.'

'I certainly feel warm and safe now,' Victoria giggled, then blinked. 'I sound as bad as poor Milly.'

Andrew settled her in the car, wound up the engine and climbed in beside her. All the way home she chattered. Andrew smiled to himself. He had never known Victoria to be so talkative. They were almost back at the cottages when she turned to him.

'Milly told me she got her baby because Jem

kissed her, and then he kissed her a lot and they made her baby.' The car swerved. 'That's not right, is it? That cow tonight...?'

Andrew drew to a halt but he kept the engine running. He didn't want to break Victoria's mood for confidences. He knew it was the effects of the brandy which had loosened her tongue but he had to know. 'You mean you don't know how a woman gets a bairn, Victoria? You didn't really think they were found under gooseberry bushes, or brought by a stork, did you?'

'You're laughing at me. Milly said—'

'And you believed she got hers through kissing? Is that why you didn't want me to kiss you good night?'

'I didn't believe...Well, I mean I don't know. I didn't see how kissing made seeds or eggs or...How was I to know?' Her voice rose indignantly and Andrew knew he dare not laugh or she might slap him in her new intoxicated state. 'Aunt Polly never said how babies are made when I asked her, and Granny never wanted to talk about when I was born. There's always been some kind of secret about it. Anyway, I have asked Mark and he is going to bring me some books to read when he comes at Easter. He says I need more education...'

'Does he now?' Andrew looked at her keenly. 'Why couldn't you ask me rather than Mark, Victoria?' He had turned to face her now and he held her shoulders so that she couldn't turn away from him. He saw her flushed cheeks deepen in colour. Even with the brandy inside her she couldn't blurt out that she wanted him to kiss her and she never felt that way about Mark. She stared back at him. 'Are you afraid of me, Victoria?'

'Oh no. I would never be afraid of you, Andrew.'

'Do you trust me to tell you the truth?'

'Yes, of course.'

'Well, it needs a lot more than kissing to make a baby, honestly. All the kisses in the world couldn't make a child. Surely with your intelligence you must know that.'

'Well, I never thought about it until Milly said—'

'Milly only told you half the story. Kissing can lead to – to other things. Especially if a man and woman love each other.' Andrew swallowed hard. Would she be frightened if he took her hand and let her feel the desire which was rising in him? Maybe tonight was not the right time after her ordeal with Doig. 'Some day, Victoria, when you love someone, it will all become clear to you...' His voice was husky. He put a finger below her chin and raised her mouth to his. 'So now you know that kissing on its own is harmless, can I claim a kiss Miss Victoria Lachlan?'

'Oh yes. Yes.' She threw her arms around his neck. Andrew knew it was the brandy which had overcome her inhibitions but he had no intention of turning aside such an invitation.

A little while later the blood was singing in his veins. There was a fire in Victoria's kisses which did not owe everything to the brandy. He knew

234

he could take advantage of her in her present mood. He could teach her everything she wanted to know. He didn't need books. Reluctantly he drew away from Victoria's soft sweet lips.

'It's very late. I must get you home,' he said gruffly, breaking the spell.

Driving back to Langmune later Andrew wondered what sort of fool he was to let Victoria go so easily. Would Mark Jacobs only give her books to read? Would he give her a lesson in biology? Or would he...? Andrew couldn't bear the thought. He slapped his forehead and said aloud to himself, 'You're a fool, Andrew Pringle. A slow, damned silly fool.'

Thirteen

Polly tried to persuade Victoria to stay at home the following morning but she was too conscientious to miss her work. Her face was bruised and she had a thumping head, whether from the blow or from too much brandy neither of them knew. Ware remarked on her appearance as soon as she entered the kitchen, her curiosity aroused. Andrew had told his parents the truth and asked them to warn George and Willie in case Horace Doig appeared in the village. Polly advised Victoria to say she had fallen off her bicycle in the dark. Although this was true in part Eve Ware sensed there was more and she persisted with her questions.

'At least it gives me a rest frae her wasp's tongue when she's getting at you,' Milly said dolefully. She and Jem were to be married quietly the week before Easter but she was not looking forward to moving in with Jem's parents and his two sisters and younger brother.

'My father doesna want Jem near our house. His folk dinna want me. They havena room for us, and I dinna want to go there,' she repeated for the umpteenth time.

'It's a pity you and Jem can't milk cows, then he could have applied for a job as dairyman with a tied cottage of his own,' Victoria said.

'Jem does milk cows. He learned frae his father when he was ten. His boss has twelve cows and Jem helps him to milk them nearly every morning.'

'I didn't know that. They have thirty-five cows at Langmune,' Victoria said slowly. 'Andrew would like to have more but there's no room in the byre.'

Her thoughts turned to Andrew. He and the other men at Langmune were going to have a lot of extra work to get through when Tom Doig and his family left at the end of the month. She felt it was all her fault. Andrew had tried to reassure her.

'I told you they wouldn't be at Langmune long anyway. Mrs Doig and Horace are useless and he's a thief and a liar.'

It had turned out that Horace was not Tom

Doig's own son. Somehow that didn't surprise Victoria. He had confided to Andrew that his wife tricked him into marriage after he got drunk one night. Evidently she had recognized a decent if simple soul in Tom Doig. She had told him she was having a child but she didn't tell him it was not his, not until their first quarrel by which time they were married. Even so Victoria knew if it had not been for her the Doigs would have stayed at Langmune until the end of May and by then other dairymen would be looking for jobs and Mr Rennie would have hired another family. Andrew had tried to make light of the situation for her sake.

'We'll manage,' he said cheerfully. 'Jocky Conley will help before and after school. He's thirteen, nearly fourteen, so he'll be leaving in the summer. He wants to work with cattle instead of horses. He's a good lad and observant.' Victoria hoped fervently that the boy would prove suitable

'Victoria!' Milly snapped. 'Ye were miles away. Ye havena been listening to me, have you?'

'Sorry. What did you say?' Victoria blinked and brought her thoughts back to her own work with an effort.

'I asked if there was any chance Jem could get a job there. At Langmune?'

'I shouldn't think so.' Victoria frowned. 'Mr Rennie usually employs a man with a family to help with the milking. Most of the wives either milk the cows or carry the milk and do the dairy work, some do both.'

'I could wash milk cans,' Milly muttered. Anything to get away from her parents and Jem's mother, she thought dolefully.

Victoria thought no more about the conversation. They had a lot to do with the additional work for Lady Landour and her family. Miss Charlotte was not a happy child and Victoria hoped she would get on better with her young visitors this time.

Milly gave Jem no peace until he agreed to go to Langmune to enquire about work but she warned him not to mention Victoria in case they got her into trouble.

'How did you know we needed someone?' Mr Rennie asked in surprise.

Jem mumbled a garbled story which made Mr Rennie frown impatiently. He had been taken in with the Doigs. He was not about to make another hasty decision, although it was worrying him that the spring cultivations and the lambing were already demanding every spare minute of Andrew's time, and that of the other men, and Tom Doig himself was still working in the byres.

'If you already have a job why are you leaving before the May term?' Mr Rennie asked suspiciously.

Jem bit his lip. 'I'm getting married. We need a house.'

'I see. Your present employer hasn't offered you a cottage then?'

'No, sir. He said he would have given me one

if he'd had one empty. He's a good boss. I've worked for him since I left school.'

'Indeed? I don't suppose he knows you have come here looking for work?' he asked dryly, 'or that you will be leaving him in the lurch if I offered you a job?'

'Aye, he kens all that, sir. Milly said I should-n't have told him, but he's been good to me. Anyway, I would need a reference.'

'You certainly would. I have always employed a herdsman with a wife or a family to help with the milking and attend to the dairy work.'

'Aye, it's what I thought.' Jem nodded de-jectedly and made to leave.

'There is a possibility we could find you work, but only until the May term. You would need to look for another job and another house then. It is only a couple of months.'

'Anything would be better than living with my folks,' Jem said eagerly. 'And Milly says she would wash the milk cans and milking pails. She canna make butter, though. But she might learn?'

'Maybe...' Mr Rennie said absently. 'I appre-ciate the fact that you have been honest with your present employer. It is almost midday. If you care to wait I will discuss this with my foreman, Andrew Pringle.'

'Andrew? I ken Andrew.' Jem flushed. 'He'll ken all ma history,' he mumbled.

'Is there something you wish to hide?'

'It's just that...that I've got to get married. Sharpish. My lass is expecting a bairn. That's why we need a job with a house.'

'I see. I hear Andrew coming in now. If you wait in the kitchen I will discuss this with him.'

'Yes, I know Jem Wright,' Andrew nodded. 'He was a couple of years older than me at school. He's a bit slow, but he hasn't moved around much so he must be a reasonable worker.'

'That's what I thought. He's desperate for a cottage. He's getting married. In a hurry.' Mr Rennie grimaced. He looked up. 'I hope you will never make that mistake, Andrew. Never allow yourself to be pushed or rushed into things you may regret.'

'I – I hope I shall not.' Andrew flushed, but he didn't take offence. He was honest enough to admit to himself that he had been sorely tempted to make wild and passionate love with Victoria. It was only his love and respect for her which had held him back. Even now he half regretted his self-control. Whenever he thought of her in his arms, kissing him back without her usual shyness, his body ached for her.

'You're certainly going to be busy when Tom Doig leaves,' Mr Rennie went on. 'Though I don't think you'll miss his assistants.'

'Too right I won't. It will be a relief to see Horace Doig off the premises. I don't trust him.' He didn't tell Mr Rennie that Doig had tried to lay a trap for him in the hayloft. The trap door had given way as he entered the shed below. He had jumped clear but the hay had tumbled down and half smothered the two calves below. 'We could have done with a woman for the dairy, though,' he said, bringing his thoughts back to the conversation.

'Would it be worth giving the fellow a trial then? He says his wife would help with the dairy, but whether she will once they get the cottage remains to be seen. She is expecting a child in July.'

'The Doigs have made us all cynical,' Andrew grimaced. 'His wife is called Milly. She works beside Victoria at Darlonachie Castle. I believe she is a bit slow but I think she would do her best, if only for the sake of having a place of her own.'

'I see. That probably explains how they knew we should be short of a dairy family. Right then,' Mr Rennie said decisively, 'if his references are all right, we'll give the two of them a trial.'

'I'm surprised he's willing to move into the cottage for such a short time, but I'd be glad of their help. Young Jock Conley is a good lad. He's small for his age but he's keen. He has a pair of sharp eyes and he's not slow to learn.'

'Yes.' Mr Rennie nodded. 'I will pay the lad if he proves useful once the Doigs have gone. His father has always been a good horseman. They're a decent family. Perhaps we should stick to people we know in future.' He gave a wry smile. 'I recall you were not too keen to have the Doigs from Wigtownshire. You've been proved right. Now would you ask Miss Traill if she has a bowl of soup for the fellow

while I write a letter for his employer, request-
ing a reference?'

Milly couldn't believe her good fortune when
she heard Jem had got the job and a cottage at
Langmune. Jem's reminders that they would
only be there for a couple of months, and that
she would have to help in the dairy, could not
curb her enthusiasm. She went around Darlonachie in a complete daydream. The Landours
made extra work and Ware's temper flared, but
Milly was content.

Victoria was delighted for her and relieved
that Andrew would have Jem's help.

'Surely washing milk cans and pails canna be
any worse than scrubbing pans here,' Milly muttered, with her head half inside a large copper
soup cauldron. 'Ware burns everything to the
bottom. Will she ever get used to that electric
cooker? Oh, and we'll have an electric light in
our wee cottage. My ma is fair jealous.' Milly
talked incessantly and jumped from one topic to
another like a grasshopper, while Victoria wondered how she would cope with Ware without
Milly's support.

'It will not be the same here without you,
Milly.'

Victoria enjoyed Mark's visit during his Easter
vacation. As usual he borrowed his uncle's car
and parked it outside the Pringles' cottage, then
they walked through the wood together to the
little cave. Mark was a head taller than she was
now, though he was not quite as tall as Andrew.

The old affection and easy camaraderie always returned.

'It's like putting on an old pair of slippers, being with you, Mark.' She grinned up at him.

'I'm very flattered to be like a pair of old slippers, Victoria Lachlan! New slippers would be bad enough.' His eyes danced. He seemed more relaxed than usual. He had an air of contentment and more assurance than he had ever had. 'But I do know what you mean. You and I, we pick up the pieces as we left them, as though we'd seen each other an hour ago.'

'That's exactly how I feel too,' Victoria said as she nodded.

'I brought you the books to read. I had no idea you had such a gap in your education. After all, it was you who taught me so much about nature. You always read such a lot, and you always seemed to know more about history and geography and literature than I ever did.'

'But we never did serious things in biology at Darlonachie School. Nobody seems to want to talk about getting babies.'

'No, we didn't, but we were children then.' He grinned down at her. 'We learned about seeds and bees pollinating, and tadpoles growing into frogs.' He sighed reminiscently. 'But I would have thought your girlfriends must have talked about getting babies and such like?'

'Which girlfriends? I only see Milly and I'm beginning to think that getting a baby was as big a surprise to her as anyone. She says she had no idea it was so easy. But she still wouldn't talk about it and it was always a taboo subject with Granny. Aunt Polly goes all pink and shy.'

'I suppose it's not a topic for the tea table,' he said as he smiled.

'Not with Aunt Polly anyway. But Mark, I saw a calf being born at Langmune the other week! I thought it was horrible seeing all that blood and slime but it made me realize how ignorant I am about such a lot of things. Then Andrew confirmed what I'd begun to suspect. He laughed, but he told me it took a lot more than kisses to get a baby...' Her cheeks flamed as she recalled that night when Miss Traill had given her too much brandy. She still wondered exactly what she had said and done with Andrew, but the memory of his mouth on hers, his arms around her, she would never forget that, or the wonderful feeling which flooded her insides with liquid fire.

'Ah, Andrew eh?' Mark raised a quizzical eyebrow, and Victoria blushed again.

'Don't look at me like that, Mark Jacobs! We didn't do anything wrong.'

'I'm glad, Victoria.' Mark's face was gentle now, as was his voice. 'I've learned an awful lot myself since I began studying to be a doctor. And there are some things you can't learn from books. No one can tell a person how to feel, or how they will react. Not just babies, but living and dying and...' He sounded impatient with himself, and life in general. He turned to look at her, staring into her eyes. 'You know how I had set my heart on joining the army as a doctor,

244

believing it would have pleased my father because he was a colonel in the army? Well, now I'm not sure it's what I want, or where I'm needed. You should see some of the poverty and suffering in parts of the city, Victoria. Even the poorest people in the countryside don't starve to death, but many of them in the city do. Around here they might poach a rabbit, eat pigeon's eggs, or even steal a chicken. In the cities it seems so much worse.'

'Well, I shall be glad if you don't go to the army,' Victoria said firmly.

'You're not the only one.' The anger in him faded and his eyes took on a dreamy look. He took hold of her hand and played with her fingers. When he looked up again Victoria knew instinctively that what he was going to say would be of major importance to both of them.

'What is it, Mark? You're not going to give up your studies, are you?'

'No. Oh no, it's what I want to do more than ever now. But I've met someone...someone who understands how I feel and what I want to do with my life. This is the 1930s, for goodness sake, and men and women are still dying of tuberculosis, little children too! People without work can't afford to eat, even less pay for medicines or a doctor.' His hand tightened on hers, curling their fingers together. 'Victoria, I've met a girl. Her name is Catriona. Her father is a doctor. She works in one of the hospitals. She's training to be a nurse. I haven't told Uncle Peter and Aunt Anna, or anyone else, but I know you will understand.'

'But I'm sure your aunt and uncle will understand too, and be pleased for you, so long as you continue with your studies.'

'It's not that. It's Catriona...'

'But she must come from a respectable family. Her father is a doctor you said.'

'He is a different sort of doctor to Uncle Peter. He has a few wealthy patients, enough to keep his household going. He treats the rest of his patients, but he knows they can never pay him. They can't afford a doctor. The thing is, Victoria, I've accompanied him several times on his rounds already. During my summer holidays I have promised to stay with his family and help him. His surgeries are crowded. I fear my aunt and uncle will not be very happy about it. I shall not tell them until the summer vacation starts.'

'They may understand better than you think,' Victoria said uncertainly.

'I doubt it.' He grimaced and released her fingers. 'You are the only one who understands me, Victoria. Perhaps it's because we've been friends since our school days, or more likely because neither of us has parents of our own. Anyway, I wanted you to know everything, and about Catriona.'

'Thank you for telling me.'

'I'm afraid Aunt Anna may blame Catriona. She introduced me to her father, and she shares his work whenever she can. I love her dearly and one day I hope we shall marry, but–' his mouth tightened – 'I am my own man when it comes to making decisions about my life. I shall not be doing this to please Catriona, but to please myself, and those patients I may be able to help. Will you promise not to mention her to anyone? I wouldn't like Uncle Peter to hear from someone else.'

'I promise,' Victoria said promptly, never considering the complications which might arise. 'I know nothing of treating the poor people in the cities, but I do know that money alone can't bring happiness. Mrs Crainby lives in a castle and has servants to care for her, but she never seems truly happy. We never hear her laughter, even when she is with her own child. I hope you will be truly happy, Mark, whatever the future holds for you.'

'Thank you, Victoria,' he said as he smiled warmly. 'I knew I could count on your support. He leaned forward and kissed her cheek. 'I hope you and Catriona will meet one day. She says she needs some cookery lessons, and you–' he tapped the parcel of books – 'you may learn a little about caring for the sick and elderly, as well as making babies, or bandaging up their knees.' He grinned knowingly but Victoria blushed at the thought of having children of her own, not least how she would get the children and the man she loved to be their father.

Easter was over and Lady Landour and her children were to depart soon after breakfast. It was Ware's day off but she had given instructions for Victoria to make up a picnic hamper for them to eat on their journey.

When Lady Landour came to the kitchens in person Victoria was surprised and flustered. 'The hamper is almost, packed, m'lady. The lemonade is freshly made. I will add it now for the children.'

'The chauffeur will collect it in half an hour. It was you I came to see, Lachlan. I have a proposal to make to you.'

'A – a proposal, Lady Landour?' Victoria frowned.

'I know your family have been at Darlonachie for several generations and you believe your loyalties are with Mr and Mrs Crainby. However, Ware is head cook here now and she is unlikely to move on at her age.'

Ware was loitering in the old butler's pantry. Her ears pricked at the sound of her name. She opened the door a crack to listen.

'You are young and must look to your own future,' Lady Landour went on brightly. 'Lord Landour praised your cooking when we stayed here at Christmas. I have taken particular note of it myself during our present visit.' She did not add she had made a return visit so soon specifically for that purpose, or that Henrietta Crainby irritated her as much now as she had as a social climbing schoolgirl when they had found themselves attending the same finishing school for young ladies.

'Lachlan, I am offering you the post of head cook at our country house in Berwickshire. You would have your own room and use of a staff sitting room. This is used only by the butler, housekeeper and cook. It has a radio and comfortable chairs. You would have full board, of course, plus one guinea per week.' Victoria gasped. That was a lot more than she earned now. 'You will be provided with three of everything – white aprons, dresses in dark green and white caps. You will have four hours free one afternoon per week plus three days off each month. So? What do you say to that?' She smiled confidently.

'I – I don't know...' Victoria was flabbergasted. 'I – I thank you, but...'

Lady Landour's smile slipped a little. She had expected Victoria to seize such an opportunity. Lady Landour had made discreet enquiries and discovered Henrietta was paying a mere pittance of what the girl could earn in the right circles. She had traded on the girl's loyalty long enough.

'Your offer is – is a generous one, m'lady. But I have never been away from Darlonachie...' Victoria said slowly, her dark eyes still registering shock.

'I see. It would be a big change perhaps, but I think you would be comfortable and happy with us. My husband is often away from home, but when he is there we like to entertain. I believe you enjoy experimenting, at least according to Mr Luke...?'

'I do, oh indeed I do, your Ladyship. I would love to work for you if – if only it was not so far away.' She thought of Aunt Polly and Uncle Joe, of Josh who was like her younger brother, but most of all she thought of Andrew.

Lady Landour frowned. 'You would need to give notice here, of course, but I understand you have no family of your own to consider. This is my card. Please write to me and tell me how soon you will be available. I will make travel arrangements for you.'

'I thank you, but—'

'I'll send the chauffeur to collect the hamper shortly,' she said in a louder voice. 'Thank you, Lachlan.' Moments later Henrietta Crainby's heels could be heard clicking down the steps.

'Ah-ha, there you are, Deborah,' she simpered sweetly. Then with a scowl: 'Why is the hamper not ready, Lachlan? How dare you keep my guests waiting! Get a move on, girl.' She hooked her arm through Lady Landour's, ushering her out, while hiding her chagrin that her guest had had to come down to the kitchens in person.

She was convinced Deborah Landour had only gone to pry and to discover whether Darlonachie had one of those Swedish cookers which never went out. An Aga she called it and she had gone on and on about it at Christmas. Henrietta couldn't care less what sort of cooker they had, or how old fashioned and worn things were below stairs, so long as her friends didn't know. It was all very well for Lady Landour, she thought pettishly. Her husband made his money from his properties in the city, as well as owning a large country estate. Her own husband never tired of telling her how bad things were in the country, how few of the tenants managed to pay their rent in full, and how many repairs needed to be done.

'But...' Victoria stared at the backs of the two women as they retreated from the kitchen. She put the card in her apron pocket and shut the lid of the hamper with a thud. She would have been glad to escape from the castle kitchens since Ware and Mrs Crainby had come to Darlonachie, but she hated the thought of leaving everything that was familiar, and especially Andrew.

Lady Landour's offer had unsettled her. If only she could have been sure of earning her living nearer home, of having employment that was secure. Ever since Granny McCrady died she had realized it was essential to work to be independent. Even around Darlonachie there were men desperate for employment, and women anxious to earn a pittance to help to feed and clothe their children. According to Mark, unemployment was worse in the city and it was a big problem in some other countries too. He feared young people might become involved in serious rebellion if things didn't improve.

Polly was astonished when she heard about Lady Landour's proposal. 'It's a grand chance, lassie. I'm glad somebody realizes what a good cook you are, but oh, I do wish it wasna so far away.'

'So do I,' Victoria said dolefully. 'The staff in the big houses around here never seem to move, or at least I've never heard of any of them wanting a cook.'

251

'No, it's tradition, or at least it used to be before the war. Families usually stayed with the same laird, as my family did, and yours,' Polly mused. 'But things have changed. A lot o' the men never came back frae the trenches, and the women who went to work in the towns have stayed there. Even the big houses dinna employ as many maids these days.'

'No. Mrs Crainby says we're not getting a maid to replace Milly.'

'Maybe ye'd be wise to move to Berwickshire then, lassie. 'Twill be no pleasure working on your own with that awful Ware woman.'

'There is still wee Stella...What if I moved and hated it? Mrs Crainby would never take me back.'

'That's true.' Polly nodded. 'There's no milk o' human kindness in that woman.'

'It's my day off tomorrow. I'll tell Andrew and ask Miss Traill what she thinks.'

'Aye, lassie, you must tell Andrew, but do you think it's safe for you to cycle up to Langmune on your own while that–that fiend is still there?'

'Andrew said it would be safe, so long as he was there himself. Horace Doig and his family will be gone in another week.' She couldn't suppress a shiver. She had seen him once since that dreadful night.

'I'll make your lover-boy pay for what he did to me,' he had hissed.

It was lunchtime at Langmune before Victoria got a chance to mention Lady Landour's offer.

252

She was disappointed in Andrew's reaction but she didn't know whether she had expected him to congratulate her or to plead with her to stay in Darlonachie. He had done neither. He had gone quiet.

His brooding silence was not lost on Mr Rennie. How long would Andrew stay at Langmune if Victoria moved east, he wondered uneasily. Would he follow her to Berwickshire? He had come to depend on the young man who had such a natural instinct for the land and the animals, and who had been quick to learn about the business of farming since he came to Langmune. He sat up straighter. He didn't want to lose Andrew Pringle. He and Miss Traill would miss Victoria's visits too, but Andrew had become essential to Langmune and to him if he wanted to end his days here.

'It doesn't sound as though Lady Landour is a very sincere friend to Mrs Crainby if she approached you behind her back, Victoria?' Mr Rennie said mildly, raising one grey eyebrow.

'No, I suppose not,' Victoria conceded. 'It was certainly a surprise when she came down to the kitchens herself. I think she expected me to seize her offer.'

'What did my mother say?' Andrew asked abruptly.

'She said Lady Landour must consider me a good cook, but it's my life and only I can decide where I should be happy.'

'And what about Mark Jacobs? What does he say?' Andrew's mouth was tight.

'I only wrote to him last night, but it will not make any difference. He will write to me wherever I am and Berwickshire is no more difficult to reach from Edinburgh than Dumfries.'

'Who is Mark Jacobs?' Mr Rennie asked.

'He is Victoria's dearest friend,' Andrew said flatly, almost bitterly, before Victoria could reply. 'He's studying to be a doctor. Dr Grantly is his uncle.'

'Is he indeed?' Mr Rennie stroked his chin thoughtfully. He looked at Andrew's grim expression. A doctor would have a lot more to offer than a farm labourer. Andrew was too intelligent not to consider that. He was a kind and thoughtful young man. Was it possible he felt Victoria deserved a brighter future with the young doctor? Was he prepared to sacrifice his own happiness to that end? And what did Victoria want?

He sighed heavily. How blind young love could be. He had only loved once and he had been a very young man. His father had disapproved because his beloved Emmie came from a family of mill workers. He had been eighteen and ready to run away to Gretna Green with her, but Emmie had died from tuberculosis a month after her seventeenth birthday. His own health had always been precarious but there had been plenty of girls he could have married. None of them came near to filling the emptiness in his heart as Emmie had done. He didn't want to see Andrew tread the long path of life alone.

He had been glad to break away from his

father and his roots after the shock of Emmie's death. He had come as a stranger to Langmune and with one or two exceptions he had remained one. His father had never forgiven him for refusing to take over the family woollen mills. He had left the business to a distant cousin, but with a proviso that he should receive an income throughout his lifetime. It was this income which had helped him survive the rigours of farm life in moderate comfort. He had had much to learn and he had made many mistakes. Even when he was in moderately good health he had never managed to make much money, but he had improved Langmune – the land and buildings, the fences and drains.

Since the war the depression in farming had been severe and after his health began to fail he had made no profit at all once wages and feed bills had been paid. So what was he to do? Would the plan which was floating around in his mind be a kindness to Andrew Pringle, or merely a millstone round a young man's neck, binding him to Langmune for his own selfish reasons.

Victoria looked from one glum face to another and sighed. 'It isn't the money, useful though that would be, but Ware can be so spiteful, she makes all our lives miserable. I envy Milly coming to live up here at Langmune.'

'I hope she has no regrets herself,' Andrew grimaced, 'especially when she gets the milk cans to scrub. During the summer they smell vile unless the creamery workers rinse them before sending them back, and they hardly ever do.'

Victoria didn't say anything. Milly loved her Jem and now they would be working and living together. Surely that's what mattered.

'I came from the Borders,' Miss Traill said slowly. 'I don't have many contacts over there now but I have kept in touch with one very old friend. I will write to ask if she knows anything about Lord and Lady Landour and their staff. Don't make up your mind in a hurry, lassie. It sounds good, but it has to be what you want.'

'Thank you, Miss Trail, that's very kind of you.'

'Yes,' Mr Rennie agreed, 'it is a splendid idea.' It gives me some time to consider my plans for Andrew's future and Langmune's, he thought. Aloud he said, 'It is very thoughtful, Miss Traill, especially when Victoria has no family of her own to watch over her.'

'Oh, but I do have Aunt Polly and Uncle Joe and – and...' She blushed and looked at Andrew.

'And me,' he said and nodded, but he didn't smile. He was sick of being regarded as her brother. Surely even Victoria must realize it was not brotherly love he felt for her after the way he had kissed her when he had taken her home in Mr Rennie's car?

Fourteen

Later in the afternoon Victoria went with Andrew to the byre to help with the milking as she usually did when she was at Langmune.

'It's better to let people like Horace Doig know you're not afraid of them,' Andrew said. 'He's a bully, and sly with it. Anyway–' he gave one of his old boyish grins – 'I enjoy having your company. You do know that don't you, Victoria. I see too little of you now I don't live at home any longer.'

'In that case I shall certainly come to the byre.' Victoria smiled back at him, feeling warm inside because he missed her. 'Now that you have taught me to milk I enjoy it, you know, seeing the froth creeping up the pail, feeling the cow's teats going all soft and silky.'

'Do you, Victoria? I'm glad you understand and feel the way I do. I love the life here, you know. Even if mother and father had had plenty of money to educate all of us I would still have wanted to leave school and work with animals.'

'Your mother would be pleased to hear that, Andrew. It worries her because you were as clever as Josh but he's getting a better education than you had.'

'Gracious me! Ma has no cause to worry about me. You must tell her so.'

'It would be better if you tell her yourself sometime, then she would know it's true. You never said whether you thought I should accept Lady Landour's job?'

'I think only you know what your heart dictates, Victoria,' he answered gravely.

Victoria always felt secure and protected when she was with Andrew but she couldn't suppress a shudder when they entered the byre and she saw Horace Doig's malevolent stare and the sneer on his thick lips. Andrew sensed her unease and he led her to the far end of the byre. Tom Doig gave her a nod and a sad smile as she passed the stall where he was gently soothing a fractious heifer. She felt sorry for him being burdened with such a revolting person as Horace.

Andrew was the fastest milker so he always took the cows with the largest yields, leaving the ones which were nearing the end of their lactation for Victoria. As a result he filled the buckets faster. Mrs Doig was supposed to carry them to the dairy to empty over the cooler but she was slow and lazy so Andrew emptied some of them himself. He was making a second journey to the dairy when Victoria stood up with her stool in one hand and her milk luggie in the other, ready to move on to the next stall. She had believed Horace was milking at the far end so it was a shock when he rose up from the next stall and stood directly in her path.

'Excuse me,' Victoria said politely, 'I'm moving to my next cow.'

'When I say–' he grabbed her shoulders in a vicious grip – 'I told ye I'd make him pay, an' I shall. Didn't think I'd get a go at you as well though,' he leered and shoved his face close to hers.

'Let me go!' Victoria hissed. 'Ouch! You great oaf!' she shouted as he deliberately stamped on her foot with his dung covered clog.

'Horace!' his father called from the other end of the byre. Horace ignored him and tightened his grip.

'How d'ye like this, eh!' His hot mouth fastened on Victoria's, pressing her lips hard against her teeth. She clenched them furiously together so he twisted his head and bit hard on her lip with his remaining teeth. Fury raged through Victoria. She raised her stool and hit him on the side of the head. His grip slackened briefly. She pulled away from him, ready to strike again if he came at her. 'You bitch! I'll...'

'Ye'll dae nothing!' Tom Doig reached them. He grabbed his son's jacket. Horace jerked away from him in fury.

'Get awa' auld man! Mind yer ain business.'

'This is my business!' his father shouted back. He grabbed him again and shook hard. 'Ye've lost me another good place. This is the last time. I've had enough of ye! D'ye hear? Enough!'

Horace stared in surprise. This was the stupid, sad, old man who barely knew how to raise his voice.

'Enough eh!' he jeered. 'Jealous are ye 'cause I dared kiss the vixen wi' her big brown eyes!'

'Keep your filthy talk to yourself' now get out o' my sight! Out o' my hoose! Find yersel a—'

'What's this, Tom Doig? Ye canna put ma bairn oot.'

'I can. I have. I'll not have him under my roof, I tell ye. We'll never keep a decent job while he stays.'

'If he gangs, I gang tae!'

'Aye, dae that then. I've had enough o' the pair o' ye.'

'What? What...?' Mrs Doig's mouth opened and shut like a stranded fish. 'Why, Tom...ye canna mean it?' Her voice grew oily, wheedling.

Victoria wished she dared to push past them but the three blocked the gangway and she was afraid Horace Doig might make a grab at her. She could feel the hot blood on her mouth where he had bitten her. She wiped it on the back of her hand. It was a relief to see Andrew coming back into the byre with his two empty pails.

'What's going on?' He strode swiftly towards them. He saw the blood where it had run on to Victoria's chin. His eyes blazed as he turned to Horace Doig. Tom seized his arm.

'There's no need, lad. He's going! Now. To-night. I've had enough. I'm moving on Friday morning, back to Wigtownshire. He can do what he likes but not under my roof.' He looked at his wife. 'You can make yer own choice. I should hae done this when he left the school. He was nothing but trouble even then.'

'But what will he dae? Where'll he bide?'

'He can join the army. All he wants tae dae is fight and cause trouble. I dinna care what he does any longer.'

Andrew looked from one to the other then he stepped past them and took Victoria's arm.

'Away in and help Miss Traill with the supper,' he said quietly. 'We're nearly finished milking.' He frowned and licked his own lower lip. 'I could murder him for what he's done to you.'

'I'm all right now.' Victoria tried to smile but her lips felt swollen and all she wanted was to wash away the touch of that obnoxious creature.

The evening meal at Langmune was later than usual. As soon as milking was finished Tom Doig came to the house to speak to Mr Rennie. 'If ye could see your way to giving me a wee bit o' the money I'll be due on Friday, I'd be obliged tae ye,' he said, twisting his cap round and round between his hands. 'I've put the lad out this time. He'll need tae fend for himself, but I canna send him without a shilling in his pocket.'

'I believe you're a good man, Doig,' Mr Rennie said. 'It's a great pity you didn't do this some time ago. I know I can trust you to stay until after the morning milking on Friday so I shall pay you in full up to then. It is your affair how much you give your son.'

'I thank ye, Mr Rennie. That's mighty civil o' ye.'

'Have you any idea where he will go?'

'His mother has a cousin in Glasgow. He stayed there once before when the school put him out.' He frowned. 'He got in with a bad lot up there. Aye, I expect that's where he'll head for.'

'I wish you well then, Doig. You may give my name as a reference if ever you need one, but for yourself alone.'

'Thank ye, thank ye.' Tom Doig gave his weary smile and left.

As they gathered around the dining table for the evening meal there was an air of relief. No one was sorry to see the back of Horace Doig.

'For all the work he did we'll never miss him,' Andrew said.

They had almost finished eating when Mr Rennie cleared his throat. 'There's something I'd like to say to you, Andrew. I have been thinking it over all afternoon.'

'Then Victoria and I will clear the table and leave you in peace,' Miss Traill said quickly and stood up. Victoria did the same.

'No, no, sit down, both of you. Finish your meal. It is no secret what I have to say.' Indeed he wanted them both to hear his proposition, and Andrew's answer, though for very different reasons. He turned his attention to Andrew. 'Are you happy in your work, Andrew, here at Langmune?'

'Oh yes. You must know I am.' He flushed a little. 'Well, these past four months have not been very pleasant,' he added honestly, 'not with Doig's surly face and idleness to contend with.

But that's over.'

'Even without characters like Doig, what I have to suggest may not prove a kindness to you in the future, laddie.' Mr Rennie sighed, and made a steeple of his fingers. Andrew had often seen him do that when he was pondering a serious matter. He frowned, and his heart beat faster.

'Are you not happy with my work? Do you think I was responsible for the trouble with Doig?'

'No, no, not at all,' Mr Rennie said quickly. 'Indeed I'm not sure how we could have managed had you not been here. That is the point. I would like to be sure of keeping you here, Andrew.'

'But I'm not planning to go anywhere else...' Andrew frowned.

'Maybe not right now, but circumstances change. You have heard me say often enough that it is a struggle to make the farm pay since the war and the introduction of free trade. Food is being brought into the country by our great British navy, even from as far away as Australia and New Zealand, not to mention the grain from Canada and the United States of America.'

'Yes,' Andrew said, 'but you did think things might improve now we have a marketing board for our milk. I understand the way it is for other products, but people in Britain are still going hungry...It doesn't make sense.'

'Politics seldom do to ordinary mortals like ourselves,' Mr Rennie retorted dryly. 'The point is, I would like to make you a partner in the farm.' He gave a wry smile. 'I don't want to lose you, Andrew. I want to tie you to me and to Langmune.' Andrew stared at him wide-eyed, his mouth slightly open in astonishment. 'But would I be doing you a kindness if things get worse? When I die my income dies with me. It has gone a long way towards making the improvements I have made to Langmune, bringing in the electricity for one thing, keeping the fences in order when the landlord can't afford to do his share. One day I hope to have a telephone when the lines get a little nearer. But...' He frowned down at the tablecloth and fiddled with his cutlery.

'Surely there's hope things may get better,' Andrew said eagerly.

'Oh yes, there's always hope for better things to come, laddie, but none of us know for sure, or when that time will be. I want you to think carefully about what I've said though. If you decide to become a partner with me then half of the cattle, pigs, poultry and horses will be yours, as well as half the implements and the tenant's valuation, of course. It must be put in writing and signed. But half of the debts would be yours too if things get worse. Do you understand?'

'Oh I do, I do...' Andrew's eyes were shining. 'I don't need to consider. Farming is what I've always wanted to do.'

'Well, it is possible Mr Crainby may agree to take you on as a joint tenant and if he considers you make a good job of farming his land he may grant you the tenancy when I die, but of course all that is out of my hands. There would be one more condition...' He looked up and caught Miss Traill's eye. 'If anything should happen to me and you continue as tenant here, I shall stipulate that you provide a home for Miss Traill for as long as she lives, in return for the half of the stock I shall be transferring into your name.'

'Oh no, Mr Rennie. It is kind of you to think of me, but you canna put such a burden on a young man's shoulders,' Miss Traill exclaimed in consternation.

'This has been your home for as long as it has been mine, Miss Traill, and I have no wish to see your loyalty rewarded by turning you out.'

'Nor would I want to do such a thing.' Andrew smiled at her. 'I can't imagine you ever being a burden, Miss Traill. You have been good to me since I came to Langmune. We Pringles remember our friends, don't we, Victoria?'

'Yes, oh, yes.' Victoria put her hands together. 'I know how good and kind the Pringles are. And to have animals of his own is what Andrew has always wanted. He talked of renting my grandmother's house. It has a large garden. He planned to keep pigs there, and hens. Oh Andrew, it is a dream come true for you.' she said joyously. Andrew looked into her shining eyes and happy face and his heart beat faster. Maybe a struggling tenant farmer didn't compare very well with the prospects of a doctor, but dare he hope for an even greater miracle?

There was a lot more discussion and cautions

from Mr Rennie, but for tonight at least he knew he had made Andrew very happy indeed and Victoria seemed equally delighted for him. Would it make a difference to her own decision, he wondered.

'I must go,' Victoria gasped as the grandfather clock struck the hour. 'I should have been on my way an hour ago or more.'

'I'll see you down to the village,' Andrew said firmly, pushing his chair away from the table.

'Good night then, both of you,' Mr Rennie said as he smiled up at them. 'I shall retire to bed now, but first thing tomorrow, Andrew, you will drive me to Dumfries and we shall see my solicitor – unless you have changed your mind after you have slept.'

'There's no fear of that,' Andrew said, unable to control his smile.

Even when they reached the village Victoria and Andrew were still discussing Mr Rennie's proposal.

'Your father and mother will be so pleased for you when you come on Sunday and give them your news, Andrew,' Victoria said excitedly.

'I hope Mr Rennie has not changed his mind by morning,' Andrew said. 'However bad farming may be I'm sure I can make some sort of living if I'm given such a chance. Honestly, Victoria, I can't believe it.'

'It's because Mr Rennie knows what a good man you are, Andrew dearest.' Victoria turned to him and put her arms round his neck and kissed him firmly on the lips. Gently he stroked her

266

swollen lower lip with the pad of his thumb.

'I shall be truly glad when all the Doigs have gone on Friday,' he said vehemently. 'That way Horace will have no excuse to return.' He kissed her gently.

Andrew pedalled hard up the hill back to Langmune, exhilaration lending strength to his legs. He had almost reached the top of the slope when he became aware of the strange light in the sky ahead of him. His heart beat faster but he did not slacken speed. A deep foreboding was creeping over him. Twenty yards or so further on he rounded the bend. His worst fears were confirmed. 'Fire! Oh dear Lord, it's the house!'

Fifteen

The house at Langmune was one of the biggest farm houses on the Darlonachie Estate, second only to the Home Farm. It was one of the reasons Mr Rennie had offered for the tenancy and had been pleased and proud when he got it.

It was mainly constructed of red sandstone, which had been quarried on the estate. The main part was a substantial square but the back of the house, facing the farmyard, had a sloping roof which housed the addition of the wash house, coal store and pantry, as well as a back porch. It was this entrance which was in general use.

Along one side of the house was a small orchard with a flagged path leading to a semi-circular garden, and the front door which was flanked by sandstone pillars.

Miss Traill had never been in the habit of locking either door until the Doigs arrived. She had quickly discovered Horace was a thief and she had seen him prowling around the house in the evenings, causing Mick to stand outside his kennel and growl. So she bolted the front door now.

On either side of the front hall were the dining room and sitting room. Between them the staircase led to the two main bedrooms, each with a dressing room. All this Horace Doig had noted from furtive surveys, including the unlocked door. He did not realize the back of the house was quite different. A small passage off the kitchen led to a narrow back staircase used by both Andrew and Miss Traill. There had been four smaller bedrooms until Mr Rennie had one converted into a bathroom. Another twisting stair led to a large attic where the maids had once slept. Due to his deteriorating health Mr Rennie had recently moved downstairs to the front sitting room.

Horace Doig had vowed to wreak revenge but he had not reckoned on being put out by his own family. His bicycle, which he had stolen before leaving Wigtownshire, was propped against the garden fence, a parcel of clothes tied to the back and another large bag on the front. Everything was ready for him to make his escape to the station for the last train to Glasgow.

The lights had gone out in the farmhouse. They were all in bed. Armed with a bundle of dry hay and a box of matches, he crept stealthily through the orchard to the front, avoiding the dog kennel. He planned to start the fire beneath the stairs, trapping all of them in their bedrooms. He found the oak door securely bolted. He swore. Undeterred he moved to the dining room window. There were embers in the grate but the rest of the room was in shadow. He used his knife to release the catch then levered up the bottom sash until he could squeeze through. He worked with surprising speed, spurred by an insane desire for revenge. He crept across the room and opened a door. It led into the kitchen. He tried the other door and saw the hall and staircase. He had assumed there would be an alcove beneath the stairs but instead he saw there was a cupboard with a door which had been left slightly ajar. That was even better. He moved silently towards it and slipped inside, pulling it shut behind him. The darkness was intense. He bumped his head on the risers of the stairs and bent lower. He should have brought the lamp from his bicycle. It was too late now. He dropped the pile of hay, and struck a match. He looked around. The back wall was shelved and two glass oil lamps were ready to use when the electricity failed. On the top shelf were several candles and candle sticks. Horace grinned evilly and lit one of the candles. As he turned something feathery brushed his face. He jerked back, giving his head a hefty bump on the underside of a step.

'Bloody hell!' He rubbed his head with one hand and held up the candle with the other. 'A pair of bloody pheasants!' he muttered in disgust. Miss Traill always put the game to hang for a few days where it would be safe from the cats.

'Hello? Andrew? Is that you?' Mr Rennie called. He had been drifting into sleep when the noise disturbed him. He was sure he had heard someone speaking. 'Hello?' The only sounds were the usual creaks and groans of the house at night. He sighed and settled himself to sleep again.

In the cupboard beneath the stairs Horace Doig held his breath. Why was the old man downstairs? It was time to do the job and get out. He scattered the hay roughly with his toe and dropped another lighted match. It caught instantly. Triumphantly he turned to make his escape. He grabbed the knob. It came away in his hand. It had been waiting for Andrew to fix the screw. In semi-darkness and with panic rising in him he fumbled for the spindle which connected the two door knobs. In his haste he bumped it and heard it fall to the ground on the other side of the door. He was trapped. The flames were licking up the wall. He tried to stamp them out. Smoke billowed. It caught his breath. His eyes were stinging. He threw his weight against the door but it was solid, the catch firmly in place. He turned to feel along the shelves for a tool, a lever, anything. In his panic he knocked off one of the lamps. It smashed. Oil fuelled the flames. He banged on the door, uncaring who heard him now.

'Let me out o' here! Oh gawd, get me out!'

Bewildered by the noise Mr Rennie got slowly out of bed. He did everything slowly these days. Was that smoke he could smell? He tried to hurry. He could hear Mick barking. He groped for his torch and shone it round the room. Smoke was beginning to curl underneath the door. Smoke? Fire! He had to get out. He opened the bedroom door. The hall was full of smoke. He began to cough. His breath came in gasps. He couldn't get to the kitchen.

'Andrew! Miss Traill!' He tried to shout. I must waken them! Flames were licking at the carpet runner and the wooden wall beneath the stairs.

The front door was nearest. His heart was pumping erratically. He struggled with the bolts. Breathless from the exertion and the choking smoke, he pulled the door open at last. The draught caused a great whoosh. Flames shot up the staircase and across to the dining room. He slammed the door shut behind him. He breathed in the cool night air gratefully. The pain in his chest pinned him to the spot. He tried to breathe slowly, to gather his strength.

'Must tell Andrew, Miss Traill...' He staggered along the path, every step a milestone. He groped at the wall for support. In the flickering light of his torch he didn't see the uneven flagstone. He fell heavily. The world went black. He didn't feel Mick's cool wet nose trying to rouse him.

Andrew's breath was coming in great gulps by the time he reached the cottages. They were all in darkness but he hammered frantically on the Conleys' door. Ahead of him the farmhouse was well alight. He could hear Mick's frenzied barking. John Conley opened the door sleepily. Andrew pointed, bending double as he struggled to get his breath.

'Oh my God! I'll be with ye...'

'Send Jocky...Constable Munro, phone operator...fire brigade...' Andrew was already moving away. 'And the doctor...'

John Conley needed no more words. He was already shouting to his wife and son and pulling on his trousers over his night shirt.

The back of the house seemed to be untouched. Mick was barking, running frantically backwards and forwards between the orchard and the back door. Andrew knew he had to get into the house. The smoke made his eyes water and caught his breath. He ran to the back stairs.

'Fire! Miss Traill? Can you hear me?' he bellowed galloping up the stairs two at a time.

'I'm coming. Help Mr Rennie. The smoke seems to be coming from the front.' She began to cough. 'Front door's bolted...'

'Bring a blanket for him.'

'Yes. Help him. I'm all right.'

Andrew ran back down the stairs and pulled

open the hall door. The heat and flames leapt at him, singeing his hair and brows. He slammed it shut and raced out of the back door and round the side of the house. Mick jumped at him then ran before him barking frantically. He was almost in front of it when the sitting room window blew out like an explosion, sending glass everywhere. Andrew didn't notice his cheek had been gashed, he didn't see what it had done to his beloved dog, running in front; he tried to shield his eyes from the stinging smoke.

'Mr Rennie! Mr Rennie.' He knew it was hopeless but he had to try.

His foot caught something on the path, sending him headlong into the grass. He felt around, coughing and choking. He had tripped over a leg. Mr Rennie! He barely paused for thought. They were both going to die if they stayed here. He scooped his employer up in his arms and stumbled back towards the farmyard and the shelter of the calving shed. He looked around wildly for Miss Traill with the blanket.

'Have you seen Miss Traill?' he yelled at John Conley.

'Must still be in there. Ye canna go in now!'

'I must.'

Miss Traill lay at the bottom of the back staircase amidst a tangle of blanket and an eiderdown. The flames were still contained to the front of the house by the stout oak doors but the smoke was suffocating. Andrew lifted the elderly woman, seizing the covers at the same time. He stumbled out of the back door with his burden. John Conley and his wife and two other people were already passing a chain of buckets hand to hand from the horse trough in the yard. Andrew knew it was hopeless but they had to try.

'Mistress Conley, there's a new hosepipe fixed up in the byre,' he panted. 'Turn it on as fast as you can. Aim it over the end of the buildings, nearest the house. We must stop it spreading. We must save the animals.' He carried Miss Traill to one of the sheds and laid her on a pile of straw. As he covered her with a blanket she opened her eyes, but her face contorted with pain.

'Tripped. Leg...broken, I think. Mr Rennie...?'

'Lie still. Doctor's on the way.' He prayed silently that he was. 'Mr Rennie is over here. He's unconscious.' Andrew took the eiderdown and covered him carefully.

'Go on, laddie. Do what ye can.' She closed her eyes.

Jeannie Conley worked as hard as the men, plying the hose to wet the back of the house and the adjacent buildings. If the fire spread it would go from one building to the next, right round the square of the steading. Andrew had done what he could for Miss Traill and his employer, but he was desperately worried for them. He joined the chain of buckets, surprised to see that three men, including Mr McNaught, the neighbouring tenant, had come from the farm further up the hill. Tom Doig had come out to help. Constable Munro arrived with Jocky. They were all doing their best but they knew they had no hope of putting out the fire without the fire brigade.

'They're on their way,' Constable Munro said. 'It was Doris on the exchange. She put me straight through, and then to Doctor Grantly. He's arrived. He's in the shed, attending to two who are injured. He told Doris to put through a call for an ambulance before he left.'

It was a tremendous relief to see the Denis engine come trundling into the yard with two firemen in the front and another three seated on the side. They had jumped off almost before the engine stopped. A quick glance told them this was not a job for the ladders tied across the top. Between them they manoeuvred the pump to the ground.

'Where's the nearest burn?' one of them shouted. Andrew ran towards them, directing them to the pond below the hen houses.

'It's fed by the burn!' he shouted. 'It'll not run dry.'

Even with the help of the fire brigade it took hours before they were satisfied the house was safe and smouldering embers would not flare into life again and spread to the farm buildings. Then the questions began. How did it start?

'I don't know. I could see it on my way back from Darlonachie.' Andrew's voice tailed off remembering. 'Mick! Mick was barking! Where is he? Mick...' He looked around, calling. Two of the firemen exchanged sympathetic glances.

'If that's the collie dog ye're wanting, he's in the orchard. I lifted him from the path under the window and laid him under a tree.'

'Aw, Mick...' Andrew's voice shook. He gulped over the knot in his throat. 'He – he tried to tell me.'

'Aye. Collie dogs are intelligent beasts. It's a real shame, lad.'

Andrew nodded, holding his emotion in check with an effort. 'I have to go to him.' Mick had been his friend even before he started work at Langmune. Was his death a sign that his time had come to an end here too?

'There's nothing you can do for him. Just give us a minute, then you can see your dog. Have you any idea how the fire started?'

'It seemed to be worst in the hall.'

'If ye'll come down to the cottage,' Jeannie Conley said wearily, 'I'll make some tea and bread and jam. Andrew, laddie, ye look fit tae drop.'

'I hope Mr Rennie and Miss Traill will be all right,' he said.

'Ah –' Constable Munro touched his arm – 'Dr Grantly said Mr Rennie was in a bad way. He went with him in the ambulance. He asked if you would drive his car down to his house in the morning.'

'It's morning now,' Andrew said dully, looking at the first streaks of dawn lightening the horizon. 'It's time to start the milking.'

'Ye need something to eat first,' Mrs Conley insisted. They were making their way to her cottage when they saw Tom Doig running towards them, gabbling incoherently. Constable Munro lifted his torch to shine on his face. It was deathly white.

'Calm yourself, man. What's wrong now?'

'It's Horace. I thought he'd gone to the station but his bike's still here, propped against the fence, packed ready to leave.'

'He'll be in his bed!' John Conley's voice registered his contempt for Horace.

'No, no.' Tom Doig buried his face in his hands. 'His mother says he was muttering about "making the buggers pay" and he took the box o' matches from the mantlepiece. She – she thinks he st-started the fire...'

'Well, there was nobody alive in the front o' the house,' one of the firemen said, 'but maybe we'd better search what remains o' the back. He could have been overcome by smoke.'

'I didn't see any sign of him when I carried Miss Traill out.' Andrew frowned. 'The fire seemed to have started downstairs.'

'You go and have some tea, lad. You've a day's work ahead o' ye,' one of the firemen advised sympathetically. 'Bill and me, we'd best go back and check.'

'I'll go with you,' Constable Munro decided.

They found part of a clog first, then the metal cacker from its mate, but beneath the collapsed and blackened timbers of the staircase they could see the remains of a body.

Andrew felt sick at heart and totally exhausted. He slipped away to see Mick, but he knew there was nothing he could do for his faithful little friend. As soon as they had all drunk a cup of tea at the Conleys' cottage and eaten up

Jeannie's bread they gathered in the byre to get on with the milking. The cows were restless and dirty. The pall of smoke was everywhere and the night's noise and activity had made them jittery. The yields were well below the normal.

'But they could all have perished if the fire brigade hadna come in time,' John Conley comforted. 'And they'll be better tomorrow. That's more than can be said for Mr Rennie and Miss Traill by all accounts.'

Tom Doig was silent and white faced. His wife had not come out to help but they had all heard her screaming at him, blaming him for Horace's evil deeds.

Andrew knew Tom Doig was not to blame for anything but he was thankful the Doigs would soon be gone from Langmune.

Andrew tied his bicycle to the back of the doctor's car and drove to the village. Dr Grantly looked exhausted and dark stubble still covered his jaw.

'Come into the surgery. I see you need attention yourself.'

'I'm all right. But what about Mr Rennie? How is Miss Traill?'

'Sit down there. You'll need a few stitches in the gash on your face but I shall need to clean it up first. I fear it will mark you for life, lad. Your hair is badly singed too. I'll make a soothing salve for your forehead and cheeks. You're lucky it hasn't blistered. And what's this?' He turned Andrew's arm and held it up. It was only then he realized why it felt so painful.

'I must have done it when I was searching for Mr Rennie. Can I see them?'

'I'm afraid not,' Dr Grantly said gravely. 'Miss Traill should pull through. They had to operate on her leg. It's badly broken. But she's a brave lady, and tougher than she looks. So long as the shock doesn't cause pneumonia she should make a reasonable recovery in time – a few months at least...'

'A few months? Poor woman. And Mr Rennie...?'

'That's a different story.' He bent his head closer to clean Andrew's wounds.

'Tell me,' Andrew said in a hoarse whisper.

'They had a job bringing him round. He's having difficulty breathing, of course. He seems convinced you were trapped. He was agitated, calling your name. They were giving him oxygen and a sedative when I left.'

'Will he...will he survive?' Andrew asked hoarsely.

'I...' Dr Grantly looked into Andrew's weary face. 'I'm sorry, but there's not a lot of hope, I'm afraid. Mr Rennie was not a well man before all this.'

Sixteen

In the infirmary the screens were around Mr Rennie. Matron and the ward sister stood on one side of his bed, one of the most senior doctors stood on the other.

'Give him another sedative to calm him down,' the doctor said tersely. He had been called out during the early hours and he was irritable and short tempered.

Matron pursed her lips and frowned. 'There's something worrying him, wouldn't you say, doctor?'

'I can see that, matron, but he can't tell us anything while he is in this state.'

He moved on abruptly to do the rest of his rounds. Matron glanced back. Her eyes met Mr Rennie's eyes. Surely there was a plea, a look of desperation even? Instinct told her sedatives would not cure him unless they could deal with his mental anguish.

When the consultant had left she drew the sister aside and questioned her. 'I believe Mr Rennie called for someone called Andrew, matron, but Staff Nurse Kerr was on duty when he was admitted. She said he asked for his solicitor.'

'Do we know the name of his solicitor?'

'I don't know, matron.'

'Thank you, sister. I shall talk to Nurse Kerr later. Mr Rennie is a very sick man we must do our best to give him peace of mind.'

A couple of hours later Staff Nurse Kerr responded to matron's summons with trepidation. She was a strict disciplinarian.

'I believe Mr Rennie asked for his solicitor? Did he give a name?'

'Yes, matron. I didn't pay much attention. He needed help, urgently. Nurse Fellshaw was there when he was admitted. She's a junior but she cares about people. She said Mr Rennie was asking for her uncle.'

'Then she will know the name. Send her to me, please.'

Matron was strict but she was compassionate and understanding. She did not always agree with the doctors but she exercised diplomacy. She summoned all her tact as she faced Mr Rennie's consultant at the end of a long day.

'I understand you sent for Mr Rennie's solicitor, matron?'

'Yes. I hoped to give him peace of mind.'

'Instead of which Mr Rennie became even more distressed.'

'He tried to talk. There is something troubling him. I am convinced of it.'

'Your interference aggravated his condition, matron.' He swept away before she could reply. She pursed her lips. Mr Jenkinson, the solicitor had asked to see Miss Traill also. Before he left

281

he had come to see her.

'Thank you for your help, matron. I have had an enlightening conversation with Miss Traill. I think we have got to the root of the problem. I shall draw up a draft of our conversation and return tomorrow morning, with your permission. I shall read it to Mr Rennie. He is able to indicate his approval or otherwise with a shake of his head. He will be no more upset than he is in his present state.'

'I do so hope you are right,' Matron said fervently. 'A patient's peace of mind is very important, but I am not too sure what his doctors will say.'

'I shall come early then. Neither Miss Traill nor Mr Rennie has any close relatives, but there is a young man who lived with them at the farm. His name is Andrew Pringle. Miss Traill would like to speak to him. Would you be able to contact him? She says Mr Rennie has a high opinion of him. She shares it too. I gather he was something of a hero. He rescued them before the fire brigade could get there.'

'Doctor Grantly will probably know the young man.'

Andrew cycled to his mother's cottage after leaving Dr Grantly's surgery. He felt tired and depressed. Polly hugged him as she used to do when he was a small boy.

'We heard there'd been a fire but there are all sorts of rumours in the village. Victoria doesn't know yet. She'd already left for work before the

282

postie brought the news.' She stared at the wound on Andrew's cheek. It would leave a scar, but at least he was alive. He might have died if he hadn't been seeing Victoria home.

'I'll cook some bacon and eggs, son, while you tell me what happened. Will you be coming back here to sleep now the house is burned down?'

'It's not completely burned but there's not much left and we can't go near until the police and the firemen have examined it. They're fairly certain Horace Doig started the fire and then got trapped.'

'Such an evil thing to do.' Polly shook her head in disbelief.

'Tom Doig and his wife will have gone by tomorrow. I shall camp out in one of the sheds. I don't want to leave the farm unattended when Mr Rennie is away. Ma, Dr Grantly says he's very bad. I'll likely need to look for another job if he...if he doesn't recover.' There was no point in telling his mother what Mr Rennie had been planning. It was all too late now. 'Even if he survives he may not be well enough to return to Langmune.'

'He'll likely need a nurse.' Polly looked keenly at her son as she set his breakfast before him. Andrew was hungrier than he realized and he ate in silence and drank two mugs of strong tea, then yawned wearily.

'I think a good sleep would do you more good than anything, Andrew.'

'There's work to be done.'

'A couple of hours on George's bed would do you good. You'll not sleep so well in a shed tonight. Shall I pack you some blankets and some food?'

'I hadn't thought about that.' Andrew yawned again. 'Thanks, Ma. Maybe I will snatch an hour. Will you waken me?'

The hour was already past when Dr Grantly called in. 'I'm on my way to the castle and I saw Andrew's cycle. I have a message for him from the infirmary.'

'He's sleeping.' Polly flushed and chewed her lip.

'That's the best thing. Leave him for several hours if you can, Mrs Pringle. He will have a lot of responsibility whatever happens. Miss Traill would like him to visit her in hospital. I'm sure Mr Rennie will not mind him using his car.'

'D'ye think not?' Polly said doubtfully, staring at him with wide eyes.

'It makes sense. How else would he get in during visiting hours, especially when he has cows to milk?'

'I'll tell him what you said, doctor. How is Miss Traill?'

'I gather she is in considerable pain and she has a temperature. She is probably suffering from shock. Her leg is in plaster. At her age she may never recover completely.'

'She has been very kind to Andrew, and to Victoria. Joe was wondering whether Mr Luke will have the house insured?'

'Of course he will, but Miss Traill may not be

fit to...' The doctor stopped, frowning. 'You think the property may not be insured?'

'Maybe.' Polly shrugged. 'Rumour has it there are a lot of things being neglected on the estate.'

'I hope the house was insured. You will pass on the message to Andrew?'

When Dr Grantly arrived at Darlonachie one of the maids showed him straight in to the library. Four pairs of eyes turned towards him. The atmosphere was tense. Henrietta Crainby was glaring at her husband. Sir William was sitting in his armchair by the fire and Victoria was standing with her hands behind her back, her chin tilted proudly.

'Perhaps I should wait outside?' he said awkwardly.

'No, no. Come in, doctor. We were finished?' he raised an eyebrow at his wife.

'You were.' She glowered at Victoria. 'I demand an apology from this sly con—'

'Henrietta!' Luke interrupted sternly.

'That's what she is.' Henrietta Crainby stared at the doctor defiantly. 'She has ideas beyond her station!' Her lip curled and she went on furiously: 'She's been currying favour with my guests.' She ignored Victoria's protest. 'And,' she added triumphantly, 'she even pesters your own nephew, writing him letters and demanding time off to see him whenever he comes home for the holidays. As though he would want anything to do with a kitchen maid.'

'Henrietta, you forget yourself,' Luke Crainby said coldly. 'We have cleared up the matter of

Victoria's part in this. If she wishes to go to Berwickshire and earn twice as much money, who can blame her?' He shrugged apologetically at the doctor. 'But I still hope you will not accept Lady Landour's offer, Victoria.'

'You're moving, Victoria?' Doctor Grantly asked with surprise. 'Mark has not mentioned it. He will miss your company very much if you move so far away. My wife and I will miss you too.'

Victoria was grateful for his unwitting testimony to her friendship with Mark. There was nothing sordid about it as Henrietta Crainby continually implied.

'I have not made up my mind what to do, Doctor Grantly. Lady Landour offered me the post of Cook in her country house because she liked my cooking. I didn't ask her for anything. She came down to the kitchens herself to offer me a job. I was unsure so she gave me a card and asked me to let her know my decision. Someone removed the card from my apron pocket while I was off yesterday.'

'There, Henrietta, did I not tell you your friend envied us having a young cook with Victoria's talent,' Luke Crainby said. 'It was Deborah Landour who acted slyly. I suggest you give Victoria a couple of shillings extra to keep her here. If she leaves you will certainly need to look for someone instead of Ware.'

'I agree,' Sir William muttered gruffly from his armchair. 'This is where you belong, Victoria.'

'Shall you stay?' Dr Grantly asked, raising his eyebrows.

'I don't know.' She looked at Mrs Crainby. 'May I go now, ma'am?'

'Before you go –' Dr Grantly put out a detaining hand – 'I have some news. There was a fire at Langmune last night.'

'A fire? Last night? B-but...?'

'Andrew Pringle rescued Miss Traill and Mr Rennie. They are in hospital.'

'Andrew? Is he...?' Victoria's face was white. She felt sick.

'He has some injuries, but not serious.' Dr Grantly eyed her keenly. 'Are you all right, Victoria?'

'I – I was there yesterday—'

'You may go, Lachlan,' Henrietta Crainby interrupted harshly.

The door closed behind her and Doctor Grantly turned his attention to Luke Crainby, eyeing his pale face and the muscle twitching at his temple.

'How bad is the damage? Did you hear, doctor?' he asked.

'They managed to stop the fire spreading to the buildings, but the house was destroyed. Mr Rennie is seriously ill. He is asking to see you. His time may be short.'

'Come to the farm office. We shall talk there.' Luke Crainby looked haggard. Could the Pringles be right about the insurance?

Back at Langmune Andrew discovered Mr McNaught had sent one of his men to help tidy up, and he had offered the loan of tools and machinery if they were needed.

Then in the middle of the afternoon Jem Wright appeared. 'My boss heard about the fire. He knows your herdsman is leaving tomorrow. He says I can start with you right away if you want me.'

'But you haven't worked your notice.'

'He reckons you'll need me more than he does, with Mr Rennie in hospital, and no house and all that.'

'That's very decent of him...' Andrew said slowly. 'We could certainly use your help.' He lowered his voice. 'I don't think you'll find the cottage very clean though.'

'That's all right,' Jem grinned. 'Milly can't wait to get into a place of our own. She'll be scrubbing it from morning to night until she gets it the way she wants. We heard the house was burned to the ground.' He looked towards the blackened beams of the farmhouse roof.

'Not quite all of it, but we're not allowed near. The water and smoke made a lot of mess.'

'Aye.' Jem nodded. 'Milly says you can stay with us until they rebuild it.'

'That's kind of her.' Andrew said, genuinely surprised. 'I don't know what's going to happen about anything, but please thank Milly for me.'

Andrew felt guilty driving Mr Rennie's car without his permission but Miss Traill seemed so pleased to see him he decided it had been worthwhile.

288

'Mother has sent you one of her nightgowns,' he said, handing her the parcel.

'Oh Andrew, laddie. How kind.' Her voice shook.

'I'm not allowed near the remains of the house.' He explained about Horace Doig. 'I've had to borrow some of my brother's clothes.'

'How dreadful. What are we to do?' Miss Traill looked alarmed and anxious.

'Miss Phipps sent some material. It's a gift, for you. Ma is making a couple of nightgowns from it. She says I must take your washing to her. Mrs Grantly is sending you a crotchet bed jacket next time I come in.'

Miss Traill's eyes filled with tears. She looked old and vulnerable. Andrew patted her arm, resolving to bring Victoria next time, or even his ma.

'How kind people are in times of trouble,' she said. 'But I don't know how I shall pay my hospital bill. I kept my money in the house. It will be burned.'

'I could search your bedroom, when the firemen give permission.' He hadn't much hope.

'It was nearly all my savings for the past year,' Miss Traill said. 'I kept meaning to take it into the Savings Bank, but I thought it would be safe in the bottom of the chest.'

'Can you tell me which chest?' Andrew asked.

'The one where I stored the flour and oatmeal. It's in a tobacco tin underneath the bags.'

'In the pantry? It may be all right then. I'll make a search as soon as I can.'

'You're a good laddie, Andrew.' She smiled drowsily and Andrew left her to sleep.

He was not allowed to see Mr Rennie but the nurse promised to tell him he had been to visit.

'Did you say your name is Andrew? You're the one he believes is trapped.' She frowned. 'Would you write him a wee note? We'll read it to him. It may ease his mind.'

'All right.' Andrew nodded. 'Could I have paper and a pencil, please?'

Perhaps Mr Rennie had heard Horace Doig calling and thought it was him. He wrote a short note wishing Mr Rennie a good recovery, but his heart sank. His own throat was still sore from the smoke; what must it have done to someone like Mr Rennie? On a separate sheet he wrote an account of the investigation for the nurse to read out if they felt it would reassure him.

As soon as the Doigs departed Milly and Jem moved to Langmune. Jem's boss loaned them a horse and cart to move their few possessions. Milly set about scrubbing and by the first night the kitchen and bedroom were fresh and clean. Andrew elected to sleep in the shed until she got round to cleaning the second bedroom. He was not sure he wanted to sleep in the room which Horace Doig had occupied. Milly understood. She was convinced it was Andrew who had helped Jem get the cottage and the job and she was eager to repay him. She asked if she could use some of the distemper which Jem had seen in one of the sheds. It was a strange yellow green colour but Milly applied it to the walls

290

with enthusiasm and promised to add a border as soon as she could afford to buy one.

Although she had watched lots of cooking at the castle, Milly found it a struggle. There were disasters when things burned or milk boiled over, but nothing was as bad as the rice pudding Ware had attempted to make. The memory always brought a grin to her face. However, Andrew seized the excuse to eat at his mother's whenever he could.

Victoria was shocked by the devastation on her first visit to the farm.

'I appreciate now how beautiful it was,' she admitted to Milly, 'but the atmosphere has improved now you and Jem have replaced the Doigs.'

'We like it here,' Milly grinned. 'Jem is trying hard to please. He hopes Andrew will keep him on after the May term, but what will happen if Mr Rennie doesn't get better? The Conleys are worried. Gee-Gee is leaving. What does Andrew say?'

'He doesn't know any more than you do, Milly.'

'Mr Rennie must be serious,' Milly persisted but Victoria changed the subject and tried to be cheerful. She knew Andrew was worried. Mr Rennie had become agitated during a visit by Luke Crainby so the doctors had ordered no more visitors.

'Hi, Victoria.' Milly called her attention back to her surroundings. 'I thought you were going to sleep with your head on that cow. You've gone so quiet. How can you sit so close to them? I'd be frightened out o' ma wits.'

'You wait until you've had that baby then Jem will teach you to milk.'

'He tried to persuade me already, but he'll not get me that near to a cow's backside!' Milly declared.

'All the best herdsmen's wives help with the milking,' Victoria said, 'or so John Conley and Andrew keep telling me. Milking is easier than carrying the pails of milk to the dairy.'

'You enjoy it all, don't you, Victoria?'

'The company is more cheerful than Ware's.'

'It couldn't be worse,' Milly chuckled, 'but I think it's Andrew's company you really come for, Victoria Lachlan.'

'Don't talk rubbish.' Victoria pressed her cheek closer to the cow's flank so that Milly wouldn't see her heightened colour.

Earlier in the afternoon Victoria had taken Milly round all the hen houses and shown her how to feed them, care for the chickens, collect and clean the eggs and pack the ones to sell to the grocer. Already things were looking neglected without Miss Traill and she didn't have much faith in Milly keeping order. At the castle she had always needed supervision, but at least she kept her cottage a good deal better than Mrs Doig.

Polly had packed a picnic for their midday meal and after they had eaten it Victoria helped Andrew search for Miss Traill's money now the investigation was complete. Although the water had seeped through the pantry ceiling and was staining the walls, the chests and crocks looked much the same, apart from a white film and drips of water. The rows of bottled fruit and pickles still stood on the shelves, spattered with water and lime, but undamaged. They found the tobacco tin without difficulty. It felt like prying into Miss Traill's life.

'Will you come with me to visit her tonight, Victoria? We could tie your bicycle on the back of the car and leave it in the corner of the wood when we reach the road.'

'All right, if you think Miss Traill wouldn't mind.'

'She's never been ill in her life, not like this. I'd like you to come.'

Miss Traill smiled and her eyes lit up when she saw Victoria and Andrew coming down the ward.

'My word, Miss Traill, something is pleasing you tonight!' one of the nurses beamed. 'Ah, it's your handsome young man again,' she teased, ignoring Victoria. Andrew's fair skin coloured. This particular nurse was young and pretty. She had done her best to flirt with him after his last visit. He was glad he had brought Victoria. Miss Traill was pleased too. Victoria bent and kissed her lined cheek. Andrew gave her the tobacco tin.

'You found it? May the good Lord be praised.' Her relief was evident. She prised open the lid.

'You both deserve something for your honesty, and for taking trouble to visit me here. You could have kept the tin and said it was lost.'

'We'd never do that!' Victoria said aghast.

'I know that. If I'd had children of my own I should have wanted them like the two of you.' She took out a wash-leather bag and removed two crisp ten shilling notes and held them out.

'Please put them back,' Victoria said near to tears.

Andrew shook his head, deeply touched. 'It would be safer in the bank, Miss Traill. Would you trust my mother to take it to the Savings Bank? The Mackies have started running a bus from Darlonachie on Fridays so she enjoys going into Annan occasionally. Some of the farmers' wives go on it and take their eggs and butter to sell.'

'Of course I would trust your mother, Andrew. Will you tell her the nightgowns are a perfect fit and thank her? I hope I shall be able to repay her somehow.'

'She was happy to do it. Victoria helped her. Now please, put your money back in the tin.'

'It's such a relief. I wondered how I would manage to pay for my hospital bill,' she said with a grateful sigh. 'Did I tell you they are moving me to a convalescent home because I have no home since the fire?'

'I didn't know! Where? When?'

'Doctor Grantly arranged it. It's nearer Darlonachie.'

'Will they send Mr Rennie there too?' Victoria asked.

'I don't know.' Miss Traill looked at Andrew.

'They say he is very ill.'

'I think he must be.' Andrew nodded. 'Only his family are allowed to visit, but he has no family, has he?'

'No one close. No one he would want to see,' Miss Traill said. 'It's a pity you couldn't pretend to be his nephew. I'm sure it would have comforted him to see your familiar face, Andrew. It has comforted me to see you both.'

'It's too late. They know who I am.'

Miss Traill nodded and gave a frustrated sigh. Maybe if Matron came round again she could try explaining that Andrew had become almost like a son.

'There's the bell. We must leave now,' Victoria said. 'May I come to visit you another evening?'

'That would be kind, Victoria. The days are so long...'

Miss Traill was moved to the cottage hospital and settled down well, but Mr Rennie's condition showed no improvement. Then late one Monday Constable Munro cycled up to Langmune.

'I have brought a message for Andrew Pringle. That's you, isn't it?'

'Yes.' Andrew tensed. 'What's it about?'

'Mr Rennie. They want you to go in to see him.'

'Now? Tonight?' The visiting time was long past.

'That's what they said. Can you get in all right?'

'Yes, I'll take his car. I'll change into my boots

and grab a jacket. But I don't understand it. They refused to let me see him before.'

Andrew's heart was beating fast as he made his way to the ward, but Mr Rennie had been moved and it was a staff nurse who escorted him to the small room.

'He's very ill,' she warned. 'We were afraid you wouldn't get here in time.'

'But I've asked to see him so many times. Why now?'

'Matron insisted. She wants to see you afterwards. She will wait in her room.'

'At this time of night?'

'Sometimes she stays late if she feels it's necessary.'

Andrew's heart was heavy with sorrow even before he entered the tiny room.

He barely recognized Mr Rennie. He seemed to have shrunk into a shadow of the man who had been his employer. In spite of the oxygen mask the sound of his laboured breathing affected Andrew more than anything else. He felt as though his own chest was heaving too.

'I shall be at the desk if you need me, Mr Pringle,' the nurse said.

Andrew watched as Mr Rennie opened his eyes. He lifted one claw-like hand a few inches, but it was a greeting. He recognizes me, Andrew thought, and swallowed hard over the lump in his throat. He followed his instincts, as he had done when he rescued Nell. Mr Rennie was a man like any other and he was dying and Andrew was determined he should not die alone, or with strangers. He would stay as long as it took. He drew up the chair and took the bird-like hand between his warm, work roughened palms.

Mr Rennie turned his head, and with his free hand he pulled the oxygen mask down. Andrew thought he saw a glimpse of a smile. There was a light in his eyes anyway.

'And...rew.'

'Don't try to talk. I'm here and I'm not going away.' Andrew said. He squeezed the hand that lay in his. There was a faint nod in response. Mr Rennie's hair looked sparser and whiter than before, and as fine as a baby's.

'Must...talk...' Each word was slow and laboured. Andrew bit his lip. It hurt to hear him breathe, but he nodded, indicating he would listen.

'Take your time then, Mr Rennie.'

'Funeral...My solicitor.'

'I will see him and make sure your wishes are carried out,' Andrew promised. He felt a faint pressure in response.

'You're...good...laddie. Must see Mr...Crainby.' There was a long pause. 'Wish...more I could do...' The words came out together but their effect alarmed Andrew. Mr Rennie's chest was heaving in an effort to get his breath. 'For you...Not ins...ured.' He lay silent, struggling with his frailty.

'I think I understand. Langmune was not insured. I will see Mr Crainby, but please don't worry, Mr Rennie. The animals are all safe, and the buildings are undamaged.'

There was a faint nod. Andrew thought he had drifted into sleep. Then the piercing blue eyes opened again. 'He promised...' Each breath seemed to take a greater effort than the last. 'Miss Traill...'

'Miss Traill is convalescing. We found her money after the fire. She seems content. I give you my word I shall make sure she is cared for,' Andrew said. He couldn't promise to give her a home. Mr Rennie was dying. Without him there would be no farm, no home, and no work for any of them at Langmune. The future was unknown. Andrew felt sick at heart. This small ghost of a man had been such a vital pivot in all their lives, despite his failing health.

Seventeen

The funeral was a simple ceremony according to the instructions Mr Rennie had given three years earlier. Mr Jenkinson organized it but it was Andrew who hired a wheelchair and brought Miss Traill. Victoria accompanied them, making sure she was not left alone when Andrew was called to the head of the coffin, a mark of esteem. He was handed the first of the cords which would lower Mr Rennie to his final resting place.

'I'm grateful to both of you,' Miss Traill said afterwards.

Mr Luke Crainby and Doctor Grantly were amongst the mourners, but there were two men who seemed to be strangers. As Andrew turned away from the graveside Luke Crainby put out a restraining hand.

'It's a sad business, Pringle. I will come up to Langmune soon. Meanwhile I hope you will carry on as you appear to have been doing when Mr Rennie was alive.'

'I shall do my best, sir.' Luke Crainby nodded, replaced his hat and strode away. Andrew turned to look for Victoria and Miss Traill, but the two strangers accosted him. One was tall, the other small and slightly built. He had a slight North American accent, Andrew thought. His mouth was a tight line, his eyes resembled grey-brown pebbles, and looked just as hard.

'You think you were smart, worming your way round him –' he jerked his head towards the grave – 'but you'll not get away with it, you young fool.'

'Are you talking to me?' Andrew blinked.

'You're the scoundrel who worked for my cousin, aren't you?'

'I was one of Mr Rennie's employees.' Andrew frowned. Had the man mistaken him for Horace Doig? He straightened and lifted his chin. He was head and shoulders taller than the weasel of a man who was eyeing him so coldly. 'Who are you?'

'I am Rennie's cousin. This is my solicitor, Mr

Yanus. He will soon put a stop to your scheming.'

'I have no idea what you're talking about. Mr Rennie's solicitor is over there.' Mr Jenkinson was already striding towards them and Andrew turned away, intending to leave them. The little man's words rankled and he clenched his jaw in an effort to control his anger.

'Andrew Pringle...' Mr Jenkinson hailed him. 'Would you wait a minute? I need to arrange an appointment with you.'

'I'm the man you need to see. I am Rennie's cousin.' The man seized the solicitor's arm imperiously.

'Indeed?'

'Yes. This fellow is a scoundrel. He—'

'You're the grandson of Mr Rennie's father's cousin, I understand,' Mr Jenkinson corrected. Any qualms he had had about his client's plans for Andrew Pringle were forgotten. Miss Traill had endorsed her employer's opinion and the doctors had assured him there was nothing wrong with Mr Rennie's mental state. Now, after this briefest of encounters, he would have understood if Rennie had left all he possessed to the devil, rather than this obnoxious fellow.

'I am his only living relative and it is my right to—'

'Mr Rennie left a will,' Mr Jenkinson said, 'as I believe you know. It was witnessed and it is legal. This young man –' he looked at Andrew – 'knows nothing about Mr Rennie's affairs, neither did he try to influence him during the last weeks of his life.'

'You don't know that. You...you...'

'I do know. The doctors did not allow visitors, with the exception of myself and Dr. Grantly, and then only briefly. There is no point in you taking this any further.' Mr Jenkinson turned his attention to the tall man named Yanus. 'Mr Rennie had very little money. You must know he did not own any property, not even a house of his own. He rented Langmune and farming has been poor in recent years. The small income he received from his father's business died with him.' His eyes moved to the little man and there was a flash of contempt in his expression. 'I understand even that was frequently delayed. There has been none paid for at least three months. I shall be calling that in to pay the hospital bills.'

'You'll get nothing from me!' the man spluttered. 'All these years he's lived. He should have died long ago!'

'Only the good Lord decides that,' Mr Jenkinson reproved, raising one brow.

'I've kept the mills running. There would have been no income if I hadn't taken them over.'

'Perhaps not an income, but a large amount of capital, I suspect, all of which belonged to Mr Rennie's father and which would have generated interest. You would be well advised to pay up without delay. I shall demand interest, and maybe more. Now –' he took Andrew by the elbow – 'if you'll excuse us, gentlemen?' They walked away.

Andrew was bewildered but he had the impression the solicitor had rather enjoyed his confrontation. 'I don't know what he was talking about, but he is not a man I would want for a neighbour,' he said with feeling.

'I shall explain when we meet.'

'I have used Mr Rennie's car while he was in hospital, and again today to collect Miss Traill and bring her here, but I know—'

'No harm in that, my boy. I will call on you at two o'clock tomorrow afternoon.'

The following morning Andrew was finishing his breakfast at Milly's cottage when a car drew into the farmyard.

'It's Mr Crainby!' Milly whispered, peering through the curtains. Her face went pale. 'I suppose he's come to tell us we'll all have to move out.' Her chin wobbled. 'Just when I was getting everything nice.'

'Don't cry, Milly, love,' Jem said. 'I'll look for another job on term day. We'll get another cottage.'

'It'll not be as nice as this one and it willna have the electric. Even Ma is jealous o' us now,' Milly sniffed and blew her nose, then peered out of the window to watch Andrew accompanying Mr Crainby to view the remains of the farmhouse.

'It is even worse than I expected,' Luke Crainby said in dismay. He turned to look at Andrew and his face seemed to have gone white beneath his tan. He chewed his lip. 'I have to tell you, Pringle, Langmune is not insured. There will be

302

no money to rebuild the house.' Andrew remained silent. What was there to say? 'Mr Rennie was an excellent tenant. In fact, he was the best tenant we had.' Luke Crainby sighed. 'I thought this would be the last place to have a fire.'

'No one would expect such a thing, sir.'

'You know he sent for me?'

'No, sir. I didn't know.'

'The tenancy agreement states a year's notice should be given by either party, tenant or landlord, before it can be broken. Mr Rennie's death, with no widow, or son to carry on the lease, cancels that condition.'

'I understand, Mr Crainby.' Andrew's face went pale. 'It's not long to the May term. Do you plan to have new tenants in by then?'

'Mr Rennie asked me to consider you, as if you were his son. At least that is what I think he meant. His breathing was so bad. I believe he wanted you to have the tenancy for a full year from this May term to the twenty-eighth of May 1937. Do you want to take on the tenancy without a farmhouse, Pringle?'

'I – I – I don't know what to say, sir.'

'No, I suppose having no house would be a problem.'

'Oh no, it's not that, sir. It's...I mean I don't know how I would find the rent money, and buy stock to continue farming for a year. Mr Rennie talked of taking me into partnership, but...' Andrew spread his hands helplessly. 'We didn't get the agreement drawn up. I have been saving my money. I have always wanted to farm, but I havena enough yet to farm on my own.'

'I see...' Luke Crainby frowned. Had he misunderstood Rennie's wishes? 'Have you spoken with Mr Jenkinson yet?'

'Only about the funeral arrangements. He is coming this afternoon.'

'I see,' he said again, as though finding it difficult to make up his mind.

'I could manage the farm, sir, if you were to keep it on yourself,' Andrew said eagerly.

'That's not what I had in mind, nor Mr Rennie either,' Mr Crainby said. 'Whatever happens I must send up the estate joiners, and Mr Bristow, the builder. They will patch up the remains of the house. It wouldn't have much appearance but they could make it habitable for a man on his own, I suppose...' Luke Crainby was thinking aloud. 'I think Mr Rennie hoped I would grant you a tenancy in your own right after a year. He held you in high regard, Pringle.'

'Thank you, sir.' Andrew flushed with pleasure.

'Your father has always been an excellent gardener. Perhaps it is a gift you have inherited, but on a larger scale.'

'I don't know, sir.'

'Well, think it through when you hear what Mr Jenkinson has to say. I know Mr Rennie was concerned about his housekeeper. How is she?'

'She is convalescing, but she is worrying about where she will live when her leg has healed, especially now.'

'Yes. Life can be difficult,' Luke Crainby said

abstractedly. 'I will bring Mr Bristow and Mr Forsythe, the factor, to look at the house. They may have some ideas which would not be too costly, but it will never be the same. It was the house which attracted Mr Rennie to Langmune. We shall need to reduce the rent. We'll talk again next week.'

'Thank you.' Andrew watched his car disappear down the road then he turned back to the house, looking at it with fresh interest. The firemen had said the back stairs were safe enough and the floors of the back bedrooms were almost undamaged. If the wall to the front hall and the landing could be rebuilt as an outer wall it would leave the back rooms intact. It would be a strange narrow sort of house but it would be adequate. A dining room and front parlour had been important to Mr Rennie. They marked his status, but neither he nor Victoria had ever been used to such luxuries.

Victoria. What made him think of her now? He knew why. He couldn't think of a lifetime without her. His heart sank. What was the use of daydreams? Even if Luke Crainby allowed him the tenancy of Langmune for a year, there was no security, no guarantee he would get it for longer, no certainty that he could make enough to pay the rent and wages, let alone keep him and a wife. He needed capital to buy stock. If he had no stock there would be no income. His mind went round in circles.

Then there was Miss Traill to consider. She was as much a part of Langmune as Mr Rennie had been. Even if Luke Crainby allowed him to rent the farm for a year would she ever be able to climb the stairs again? If he was feeling in low spirits today, how must she be feeling? Her employer was dead, she had no wages, no home, not even a family to care. He shuddered. At least he had his parents, and they did care. Victoria cared too, even if it was not in the way he longed for.

At least he could cycle over to the convalescent home to see her. He could tell her Mr Crainby was going to patch up the back of the house and as long as he was allowed to stay at Langmune there would be a place for her too. It was not much of a promise, but perhaps it might reassure her for now. He felt too restless to settle to work. He took off his clogs and pulled on his best boots, then collected his bicycle from the shed. He set off for Darlonachie village and the large house two miles further on which had been converted into the convalescent home.

When he was admitted the matron greeted him warmly. 'This is a surprise in the middle of the morning. You have come to see Miss Traill?'

'Yes, if it is convenient?'

'Indeed it is. Seeing you will be a tonic, young man. She has been feeling very low in spirits since the funeral yesterday.'

'I guessed she would. I can understand that. We were all more dependant on Mr Rennie than we realized.'

'Miss Traill said work was the only cure for feeling sorry for oneself and she couldn't even do that. So I had an idea. I helped her through to the kitchens. At this very moment you will find her seated at the table peeling the vegetables.' The kindly face broke into a conspiratorial smile. 'And I have no doubt she will be keeping everyone in order in there. I understand she did a lot of cooking at the farm?'

'She is one of the best cooks I know,' Andrew said, 'including my own mother.' He grinned back at the kindly face, feeling his spirits rise for no apparent reason. 'Though I wouldn't tell Ma that, you'll understand.'

'Aye, laddie, I do. Come this way and we'll go through the garden and into the kitchen from the back.'

Miss Traill beamed with pleasure when she saw Andrew. 'I hadn't expected to see anyone for a long time after yesterday,' she admitted.

'I was feeling a bit down too,' Andrew said. 'Mr Crainby came up to see the house this morning. It's not insured. He says he can't afford to rebuild it but he's going to patch it up and make the remaining rooms fit to live in.'

'I see. Such a pity,' Miss Traill sighed. 'It was a lovely house.'

'It will be a bit ugly but there will still be the three bedrooms and the bathroom left upstairs,' Andrew said with more enthusiasm than he felt. 'If Mr Crainby does allow me to keep on the tenancy for a year there will be a home for you there as long as I'm there myself,' he said earnestly. 'I don't know how I shall manage and there will not be much money, but the kitchen garden wasn't damaged and the vegetables are growing well. We'd have eggs and milk, and the pig...' He looked down at his hands and the cap he was twisting. 'I'm sorry that's all I can offer you, Miss Traill, after all the years you've worked at Langmune,' he added gruffly.

'Ah, laddie...' Miss Traill swallowed the lump in her throat and brushed a tear away. 'You've offered me more, much more, than anybody ever offered me before. You're right, I have been wondering and worrying about where I'll go from here, an old woman like me. They're taking my plaster off next week. Even if the bones have healed, they say I might have a limp and I'll have to do exercises before I can leave here. Nobody would give me a job at my age.'

'But you can still peel the vegetables for the soup,' Andrew tried to smile as he glanced at the carrots in the bowl beside her. He was glad he'd come, even if he hadn't much to offer. It must be terrible not to have anyone in the whole world to care what happened to you.'

'I have a wee bit put by in the Savings Bank and thanks to you and Victoria I still have my year's wages. We'll get by, laddie, if the laird lets you take on the lease. Take each day as it comes, my father used to say. Have you seen Mr Jenkinson yet?

'He's coming to Langmune this afternoon. I expect he wants to settle any bills and things like that. Mr Rennie's desk and his papers were all destroyed in the fire. Most of the furniture was burned to ash.'

'Mr Jenkinson will have copies of anything important I expect. Did he manage to talk with Mr Rennie before he died, do you think?'

'I think he tried. Mr Crainby saw him, but he said it was difficult to understand him because he couldn't get his breath.'

'He had such good intentions.' Miss Traill sighed. 'At least he is at peace now.'

Mr Jenkinson had had another visit from Mr Rennie's relative that very morning. The man had been even more offensive and his attitude had made Mr Jenkinson determined to do all in his power to settle Mr Rennie's affairs quickly and get the best deal he could for his client's protégé, Andrew Pringle, and for Miss Traill.

Andrew could scarcely take in what he was saying as they stood together, staring at the ruined house.

'I know nothing about farming,' Mr Jenkinson said, 'but I knew Mr Rennie was finding it difficult to make a profit. His ill health didn't help, of course, and then he insisted on carrying out improvements and maintenance which the landlord should have undertaken. Anyway, Andrew Pringle, he has left you everything on the farm – that is animals, machinery and so on, but the money from his life insurance plus any remaining cash goes to Miss Traill.'

'I can't believe it.' Andrew stared at the solicitor. 'How did he manage to do it?'

'Miss Traill gave me the gist of his intentions so I was prepared. He had mentioned changing his will in your favour on two previous occasions so I was not entirely surprised. I hope you can manage to make a living, young man.'

'I shall have a good try,' Andrew said, stunned at his good fortune.

'If you need any help from me just come to my office. I've already seen Miss Traill. She said you had been in and you have offered her a home. I took the opportunity of telling her I have carried out Mr Rennie's wishes before he died. She is relieved and delighted.'

Mr Crainby granted Andrew the tenancy of Langmune for one year, with a promise to review it at that point. When Mr Forsythe, the estate factor, heard Miss Traill would be living at Langmune he suggested a small room should be built where the front hall had been, and also a downstairs toilet with a wash basin.

'It was such a fine house. I bitterly regret it cannot be rebuilt as it was,' he said, shaking his head. 'Money is short but it was a mistake not to keep up the insurance on Langmune.'

Andrew welcomed his foresight when it became clear Miss Traill would have had difficulty climbing the stairs. Between them Victoria and Milly had scrubbed out the house and lime-washed the pantry, the scullery and the wash house before Miss Traill returned. Everything looked fresh and clean and Miss Traill settled thankfully into the bedroom opening off the kitchen. Mr Forsythe had insisted it should have windows opening on to the front garden and the orchard.

Milly had given birth to a baby girl in July and she was making a surprisingly good mother. She had wanted to call her Ginger after Ginger Rogers but Jem and her mother had persuaded her to settle for Gracie after Gracie Fields. Every week Victoria fretted impatiently for her day off so that she could cycle to Langmune. She cleaned the upstairs and did the washing and helped Miss Traill with the cooking, but her favourite task was helping Andrew and Jem with the milking. Milly had tried to learn to milk but she was too nervous. Jem had been worried in case they lost their place at Langmune.

'I know the herdsman is supposed to supply a wife and a helper,' he said to Andrew, 'but Milly has tried. The cows sense she's nervous and it makes them nervous, so everything's worse.'

'Yes, I know.' Andrew nodded. 'I saw her fall off her stool. Do you like it here, Jem, apart from wanting the cottage, I mean?'

'Aye. I like it better than I expected, and the Conleys are good neighbours. Mrs Conley is mothering Milly and wee Gracie.'

'Well then, if Milly continues carrying the milk and washes the churns and equipment we should manage. Jocky Conley is a good worker and he wants to work for me.'

Mr Rennie had always kept an odd man as well as a horseman and a family to do the milking, but Andrew couldn't afford to do so, although he had one big advantage over Mr Rennie – he was young and strong and used to hard work. Making enough money to keep up the rent was his greatest worry.

Miss Traill would never be fit to do the work she had done before the fire and she refused to accept any money for wages.

'I'm thankful to have a home here, laddie. I don't do more than earn my keep now, and sometimes not even that. I don't know what we should do without Victoria's help and I don't like to see you working so hard yourself, and worrying about finding the rent.'

'I shall manage so long as we don't get any sick animals, or serious breakdowns with machines,' Andrew said.

'I could make you a loan to pay the rent for the first half year,' she said. 'Mr Rennie was well insured, and Mr Jenkinson claimed the money his cousin had owed. He has left me better off than I ever dreamed.'

'You deserve it, Miss Traill. You looked after him well all those years. I couldn't possibly take your money, but I thank you for offering. However hard things may get, I shall always be thankful to him for giving me a chance to be a farmer, even if I can't keep Langmune.'

The highlight of his week was having Victoria at Langmune for a whole day.

'I wish I could afford to pay you for all the work you do, Victoria,' he said one evening as they cycled back to Darlonachie together.

'Och Andrew, I don't need to be paid. I love coming to Langmune. I envy Milly being there all the time.'

'Truly, Victoria?'

'Honestly.' Then she chewed her lower lip. 'Only I – er...I shall not be able to come next Thursday. Mark is coming home and I promised to keep the day free for him. He said it was a special visit.'

'I see.' Andrew knew his voice had lost its warmth and he made an effort to sound more affable. 'Milly and Miss Traill will miss you,' he said, and wondered why Victoria's mouth tightened, why she was quiet for the rest of the ride to the end of the track. When they parted she gave him no more than a quick peck on the cheek and cycled off towards his mother's cottage. He blamed it all on Mark Jacobs. It didn't occur to him Victoria longed to hear him to say he missed her too.

His thoughts were glum as he cycled back to the farm alone. When Victoria had told him Mark was spending the summer vacation in Edinburgh, gaining experience with another doctor, he had given a silent cheer. Now Mark was returning and Andrew's spirits plummeted. He could never compete with someone like Mark Jacobs. Even if he managed to hold on to the tenancy at the end of the year he was barely making enough money to buy himself a pair of new clogs. He had been better off working for a wage.

He had had so many ideas for improving the farm when Mr Rennie was alive. Now he knew how difficult it was to keep it ticking over. Every month he set aside a sum towards the farm rent, which would be due at the end of November. He paid the wages and bought wheat for the hens and a few sacks of meal to feed the sow. As the days shortened there was less grass for the cows and he was forced to buy in cattle cake to supplement the hay and turnips to keep them milking. The milk he sold was his main, almost his only, income.

Every month he paid Mr Brood for the groceries he brought in his van, and Fraser Wood, the blacksmith, for shoeing the horses, and sometimes for mending the implements. The mower had needed a big repair before they could finish cutting the hay. Now John Conley and Jocky were getting the binder ready for harvest and found it needed at least one new canvas and probably a new knife. There were bills for electricity which he had never considered before. He couldn't consider asking Victoria to be his wife unless things improved. All in all, Andrew felt thoroughly despondent and Miss Traill was quick to notice.

'What ails you, laddie?' she asked the following morning at breakfast.

'I'm sorry,' he said, 'I was thinking...'

'About money and how you will pay your way?'

'Mmm...partly.'

'There's only one other thing makes you look so glum, and that's Victoria.' Andrew blushed to the roots of his hair. Were his feelings so obvious to everyone? Everyone except Victoria.

'Why don't you tell her how much you care

for her?' Miss Traill persisted. 'Is there any chance of her getting another day off, or even an afternoon, so that she could come and see you more often now you're too busy to go down to see her?'

'No.' Andrew shook his head. 'I'm not sure she would want to come more often anyway.'

'I'm sure she would. She—'

'She's not coming at all next week!' Andrew burst out with more anger than he realized.

'I see.' Miss Traill frowned. She knew she ought not to interfere but she hated seeing Andrew unhappy. 'Have you quarrelled?'

'No, not exactly. She has better things to do. Mark Jacobs is coming home. She has promised to save her day off for him. He writes to her every week you know. Long letters – at least according to Mother.'

'And you think Victoria loves him?'

'I suppose she must do.'

'You suppose? But you have never asked her?'

'No. How could I?'

'You've known each other all your lives and you would rather torture yourself than ask her a simple question? Shame on you, Andrew. I thought you had more courage.' Andrew flushed uncomfortably.

'Sometimes it's better not to know.'

'So that you can keep on hoping? No, no, laddie. It is better to face the truth than hide from it.'

No more was said but it seemed a very long week to Andrew. On Thursday Milly asked why

Victoria had not come.

'Mark Jacobs is home. She's meeting him.'

'He must still write to her then. They always were close that pair. It used to make Mrs Crainby and Eve Ware furious because she had a doctor for her boyfriend.' Milly was unaware she was twisting a knife in Andrew's heart. He mumbled a response and hurried away. Milly watched him thoughtfully. She liked Andrew.

The following Sunday Andrew made a point of cycling down to the kirk. Even seeing Victoria from a distance was better than not seeing her at all. She seemed pleased, almost relieved that he was there. After the service she ran after him instead of staying to talk to Mark. He was tempted to ignore her call and hurry on, but Victoria caught up with him.

'Andrew, please wait?' she gasped. 'I have a favour to ask you, a big favour.'

'Oh?' He frowned. 'What could you possible want from me?' he asked coolly and watched the light die out of her dark eyes.

'Dr and Mrs Grantly have invited me to dinner next Wednesday evening,' she said. 'Mrs Grantly says it is a special dinner. Dr Grantly has an announcement to make.' She gave a fleeting smile. 'I think I can guess what it is but it's supposed to be a secret.'

'What has that to do with me?' Andrew made to shrug off her hand.

'Oh Andrew, I know you're busy and tired, but please don't be cross with me. I need you to come. Mrs Grantly asked me to bring a friend.

316

Someone whose friendship I value.' She frowned. 'I can't imagine why she thinks I shall need anyone, but please come with me. You're my very best friend.'

'Am I?' Andrew said cynically. 'I think you're a bit mixed up, Victoria.'

'You mean, you're not my friend? You won't come?' Her voice trembled and her brown eyes were dark with distress. Andrew felt his heart would burst with love for her.

'Oh, all right. What time?' Her face was transformed like sunshine after rain.

'Oh thank you, Andrew!' She hugged his arm. He saw one or two elderly ladies raising their eyebrows disapprovingly and he disentangled himself from her grasp.

'What time, Victoria?'

'Seven thirty. It's to be a proper dinner, like at the castle.'

'I see. I'll call for you in the car then.' It gave him a good feeling to say that. He had barely used Mr Rennie's car since he died. He couldn't think of it as his own yet. Anyway it cost petrol to run it and it cost nothing to pedal a bicycle.

Victoria was wrong. None of the four young people who gathered at the doctor's house that evening could have guessed the news, or the effect it would have on them.

Andrew had arrived at his parents' cottage promptly. He looked young and handsome. Miss Traill had pressed his suit specially and starched the collar of his best white shirt. He was wearing the tie that Victoria had bought for him at

317

Christmas. He had vowed he would take Miss Traill's advice before the evening was over and ask Victoria if she loved Mark Jacobs. She was ready and waiting for him in the dress his mother had helped her make for the dance. He realized Victoria didn't have much money to spend on pretty dresses and he wished with all his heart he could afford to buy them for her. Maybe he should have struggled to get an education and a good job, like his young brother Josh.

Andrew's first shock of the evening came as he drew the car to a halt in the doctor's drive. Victoria turned to him with a conspiratorial smile.

'I've known about Catriona and Mark for ages and ages, but he made me promise to keep it a secret. He thought his aunt and uncle would disapprove of her father.' She climbed out of the car, adding: 'But instead they've invited her to come and stay. Isn't it exciting?'

Andrew stared at her dumfounded. 'But Victoria?'

'Ssh...' She put a finger to her lips, but her eyes were sparkling with anticipation. 'I think the dinner must be to announce their engagement,' she whispered.

'B-but I didn't know there was to be anyone else here...I...' Andrew was bewildered. He pulled at his tie nervously as Mrs Grantly opened the door, smiling warmly in welcome. There was no opportunity to ask Victoria the questions which were teeming in his mind.

Eighteen

Dr Grantly watched Mark introduce Victoria to Catriona McTeir. There was no doubt the girl had given Mark a new assurance, and it was a pleasure to see the happiness which radiated from him, but young love could be so fragile. He hoped his news would not shatter her illusions. They had agreed to wait until Mark had qualified before they married, but Mark felt they should get engaged.

'You see, Uncle Peter, Catriona seems so insecure, even though I have told her she is my first and only love.'

He understood what Mark meant when he saw Victoria was smiling warmly, clasping Catriona's hand in both of hers. Although Catriona smiled the warmth was not reciprocated. She seemed wary and uncertain and she withdrew her hand as soon as she could and turned to link her arm in Mark's, almost as though staking her claim. She was more at ease when introduced to Andrew.

'Dinner is ready now,' Mrs Grantly called. 'Will you come through.'

As they ate it occurred to Peter Grantly that Andrew eyed Mark in the same cautious manner as Catriona had greeted Victoria, but he joined in the conversation with ease, asking Catriona questions about her nursing, and seeking her opinion on the effects of mustard gas, which the Italians had used on the Abyssinians.

'And how do you feel about the Milk Marketing Board's scheme and the plan to pay extra for milk from dairy herds which have no tuberculosis, Andrew?' Dr Grantly asked.

'I read everything I can about it,' Andrew said eagerly. 'Mr Rennie was convinced the milk prices would improve if we got unity amongst producers. If I manage to keep the farm going this year, and if Mr Crainby will take me on as a tenant with a five-year lease, like the rest of the Darlonachie tenants, I could plan for the future. A penny a gallon extra would make all the difference, but a lot depends on how many cows fail the tuberculin test and have to be slaughtered. The whole herd must have three clear tests to gain accredited status and get the payment. If one animal fails we must start all over again. Also we would need a double fence between ourselves and neighbouring farms to avoid infection, and we cannot share drinking water in the fields. That would be a big expense. So you see, it will not be so easy as it sounds in the newspapers.'

'Wouldn't your landlord pay for fencing?' Catriona asked. 'It would be such a worthwhile scheme. Many of my father's patients die from tuberculosis.'

'Our landlord can barely afford to maintain the

present boundary fences,' Andrew said ruefully. 'Even though that is part of the tenancy agreement. Mr Rennie always maintained them himself so ours are in good order. I hope I can keep them that way.'

'After seeing the poverty in some parts of the city it makes me realize how lucky we are in the country, and what a very unfair world it is,' Mark said.

Eventually the dessert was finished and Mrs Grantly said she would serve the coffee in the front parlour.

'My husband has something to tell you.' She looked at Peter. He met her eyes. This was a task he had put off for years and he dreaded it still.

'You look dreadfully solemn, Uncle Peter. There's nothing wrong, is there?' Mark asked anxiously. 'Are you in good health?'

'Ah, Mark my boy, there speaks the doctor to the doctor. Yes, I'm well. Sit down, all of you. I hope you'll let me finish before you ask questions. What I have to say will be a shock, I know. I pray you, Victoria, and you, Mark, will find it in your hearts to forgive me if I acted wrongly.'

'Now we are curious...' Mark said.

Dr Peter Grantly began to tell them about the night he was called out to a young mother who was giving birth, about the complications which made it so difficult for the midwife to deliver the child.

'Truly there was nothing I could do to save the life of that young girl,' Peter Grantly said, and

321

his voice was gravelly with emotion. Victoria had gone very pale. She knew instinctively that he was talking about her own mother.

'My father would understand how you felt, Dr Grantly. He lost a young mother two months ago and he still can't put it out of his mind,' Catriona said sympathetically. Victoria was tense. She wished she would keep quiet, but Dr Grantly was nodding at her.

'Thank you. It is not something a doctor can forget. In this case the girl was very young. She had lost all her family in a tragic accident, all except her grandmother, who had raised her. No one knew the father of the child, not even her grandmother. I...we think she had been raped. Remember, she was young, she had led a sheltered existence. The shock of such a thing would be terrible, especially if it was someone she knew and trusted.' He paused, looking back down the years.

'I was first called to her nearly nine months before when she caught a severe chill. It developed into a raging fever. She recovered but her whole personality seemed to have changed. She rarely spoke. She refused to go out during the day. She never mentioned her ordeal.'

Victoria was twisting her hands in agitation. Why did Doctor Grantly want to talk about her family now, and in front of a stranger, she thought angrily. Her eyes burned but she would not cry. Andrew was sitting beside her. She felt him reach for her hand and she slipped hers into his comforting clasp. When she glanced at him she knew he had guessed too.

'When I went to the birth...' Doctor Grantly chewed hard on his lower lip. He frowned and looked across at his wife. She nodded encouragement. 'I realized, almost at once, there was not one baby but two.' Victoria gasped and clenched Andrew's hand tightly. 'The midwife was unaware this was the cause of the problems. She had been up most of the night before. She was very tired. I sent her home with a note, asking my wife to come.' He looked up and Anna smiled gently back at him. 'I needed her help and – and certain instruments...' Victoria shuddered. 'There was nothing nothing anyone could have done.' He rubbed a hand across his brow. 'The first child, a little girl, was born before midnight on the first of November. I knew then I could not save her mother. I'm convinced she had lost the will to live. The second child was lying in a breech position. Amazingly he was born alive ten minutes after midnight –' he looked across at Mark and held his eyes – 'on the second of November.'

'I – I don't understand...' Mark looked at his uncle, then at Victoria.

'Yes, Mark, you and Victoria are twins. May God forgive me for separating you, but believe me we all, all of us, thought it was for the best at the time. You needed great care...'

'I don't understand...'

'Mrs McCrady had already reared one grandchild, now she had two great-grandchildren. She needed to work to earn her living. Her home

323

depended on her continuing to cook at the castle – and remember she was not a young woman. We didn't expect you to live. You were small and delicate, both of you. Truly we did what we thought was best. My sister longed for children, but she had never been blessed with any of her own. We knew she would give a child every possible care. As a colonel in the army her husband was often away, but he had agreed to adopt a child. We didn't expect he would be killed two years later. They did love you dearly, Mark.'

'Yes,' Mark whispered hoarsely, 'I know. But...'

'When my sister died, I knew I had to bring you back to Darlonachie, where you belonged. Our own family were grown up. Anna and I decided we should bring you up and give you a good education, as my sister would have wished had she given birth to you herself. I confess Mrs McCrady wanted to tell both of you the truth. But you, Mark, had suffered enough traumas with the death of the person who had loved and cared for you as your mother. You had to move to a new area and a new school, and you were a bright intelligent boy who deserved an education.'

He looked at Victoria's white, set face. 'Remember, lassie, your grandmother was no longer young. She longed to have you both, living together as a family, but it costs money to feed and clothe two children, let alone give them an education. Do you understand, Victoria?' His eyes were pleading.

She was too bewildered, too choked to speak.

'Sir William Crainby had known sorrow himself. He allowed Victoria in the kitchens and in the nursery from the day she was born.'

'He has always been kind to me,' Victoria whispered hoarsely.

'But he may not have been so tolerant if there were two children running around the castle. We already regarded you as our nephew, Mark. We knew we should love you as our own son.'

'And we do,' Anna Grantly said tremulously. 'We shall always love you. Can you...can you forgive us for our deception?'

'So you are brother and sister!' Catriona exclaimed as the news finally sank in.

Doctor Grantly thought the news seemed a relief to her, rather than a matter for condemnation. She had been jealous of Mark's friendship with Victoria, he realized. Andrew sat silent, his eyes fixed on Victoria's face, his own almost as pale as hers.

'I can't believe it...I can't believe it...' she whispered brokenly. 'All these years I thought I had no one of my own.'

Andrew winced. He wanted to shout, You've always had me!

Mark was beginning to accept the news more readily, still incredulous, still only half believing – but thinking it through. 'It explains so many things.' He said half to himself. 'Almost from the beginning we were drawn together, as though by an invisible thread. We understood each other when no one else did, didn't we,

Victoria? Remember...' He broke off, noticing Victoria's stunned expression, her brown eyes like dark pools, swamping her white face.

'You didn't know Granny McCrady. Really know her,' she said brokenly. 'She never knew you.'

'She did know, Victoria,' Doctor Grantly said softly.

'No! How could she? I – I can't believe it. All these years when I felt so alone, so incomplete, I had a twin brother...' She wanted to weep for the years that were lost. 'Why didn't I guess? Why didn't Granny say she had...?' She couldn't go on. 'I – I think I'd like to go home now. Please...? Andrew?'

'But, Victoria! We have so much to talk about,' Mark began eagerly, but Victoria shook her head. She was having difficulty holding back the tears. Dr Grantly watched her anxiously but Anna understood.

'Come, Victoria, I'll get your coat,' she said quietly. 'There'll be plenty of other opportunities to talk. You have always been welcome here. Now you know how very welcome you will always be, my dear. Take care of her. Andrew,' she added softly, 'it has been a big shock.'

'I will,' he said gravely. He wanted to fold her in his arms and protect her from the whole world, but he knew this was not the time.

Andrew drove home slowly, understanding Victoria needed time to absorb and come to terms with the evening's revelations. Part of him rejoiced to know Mark Jacobs was her brother, but if she had thought herself in love with him as a man, her heartbreak would be worse than losing him through death. Yet she hadn't seemed upset by Catriona's presence; she had been forewarned. Had she put on an act?

His own thoughts revolved in circles. His concentration wavered. The car swerved violently, jerking him back to attention.

'What was that?' Victoria gasped, grabbing his sleeve.

'Sorry. The front wheel caught the grass verge. It was my fault.'

'Oh.' It was a small bereft sound.

'It will be light for a long time yet. Shall I stop for a while beside the wood, or do you want to go straight home?'

'Please, I – I need time...'

'Of course you do, my wee Victoria.' Andrew's voice was soft and gentle, just as he had talked to her when she was a child dreading going to school. He had comforted her then and she knew he would comfort her now, if that was what she wanted from him still.

He drew the car off the road beneath the trees. It was a calm, peaceful evening. The scent of wild honeysuckle wafted into the open window. Birds still darted hither and thither, feeding their last brood of the season, chirruping and calling to each other. Above them came the drowsy cooing of a wood pigeon and Andrew felt his own turbulent thoughts calming in response to the world around them.

'The evening is too beautiful to waste on regrets, Victoria,' he murmured gently.

'It isn't regret I feel.' She turned to him, her brown eyes shadowed. 'I feel...deceived. I feel cheated. Deprived. I – I ...Oh Andrew, I don't know what I feel...' The tears she had struggled to hold back poured down her cheeks. Andrew drew her into his arms, holding her gently, resting his chin on the softness of her hair. He let her weep, stroking her hair and whispering soothing sounds as he might have used to a child, but Victoria was not a child. Earlier he had loosened his tie and opened his jacket and waistcoat on account of the warm evening. He could feel the softness of her breasts pressed against the front of his shirt. Eventually her tears began to ease and she looked up at him, her lashes still spiked and damp. His heart ached with longing.

'Why didn't they tell us? Why wait so long? All these years, all wasted? So much time...Why didn't I guess?' A torrent of questions poured forth as she tried to sort out her pent-up emotions.

'Dear Victoria, of course you're upset, but surely the years have not been wasted. You and Mark have been close friends.'

'But I'd have had a brother, a family of my very own. I've only just discovered him and I'm going to lose him already.'

'I don't understand?' Andrew frowned. It was not like Victoria to be unreasonable. 'Why should you lose him?'

'Because he's going to marry Catriona as soon as he qualifies.'

'That doesn't mean you will lose him, unless...' Andrew drew in his breath sharply. He put a hand beneath Victoria's chin and turned her face up to his. He had to know. 'Victoria, will you tell me the truth? Did you regard Mark as more than a brother?'

'You know I did. We were friends. We spoke the same language, liked the same things...well mostly.'

'You – you hoped to marry him,' Andrew said dully.

'Marry Mark? Of course not. I could never have thought of him like – like that.'

'Like what, Victoria?' Andrew's voice sharpened.

'Well, I suppose, he was always like a brother to me. Oh Andrew, why didn't I guess? I should have known. There were so many things...'

'Did you feel the same way about Mark as you feel about Josh, about me?'

'Oh no! Not you, anyway. Like Josh maybe.' Her face softened. 'I always wanted Josh for my wee brother. There was always an empty space somehow.'

'So you didn't...you don't think of me as your brother?' Andrew asked carefully. Bright colour suffused Victoria's face and she tried to look away, but Andrew held her still, looking down into her eyes, searching their depths. Whatever the cost he had to know the truth.

'Victoria?'

'I – I used to think of you as a brother, I suppose, when I was a child.'

'And now?' Again she tried to look away. When she couldn't she lowered her eyelids and the dark fan of her lashes caressed her cheeks. Andrew bent his head and very gently brushed her lips with his.

'Could you ever learn to love me as a man, Victoria?' he asked softly.

Her eyes flew open, searching his face, her cheeks pink. 'You – you've guessed?' she asked in a horrified whisper and struggled to be free. He released her chin but his arms tightened around her, holding her against him.

'I've no right to say this to you, Victoria. Heaven knows, I've nothing to offer you and I've been so bloody jealous of Mark.'

'You were jealous of Mark, Andrew? But why?'

'I thought you loved him and he has so much. All I have to offer you is hard work and poverty – as a tenant farmer if I'm very lucky, as a farm worker if I'm not. But I love you to distraction, Victoria. I have done ever since you—'

'Andrew? You said you love me. Can it be true?' Her eyes were shining as brightly as the young moon which was beginning to peep by the edge of the wood.

'It's true all right. I've loved you ever since you moved into our house. You were only thirteen then, but you were so courageous, and stubborn and determined to work and be independent. I've loved you ever since and my

330

love has grown so much I can't contain it any longer...'

'Oh, Andrew...' Victoria's voice was husky with emotion. 'It feels as though I've loved you forever, but I always thought...I never dreamed...'

'Don't think...' His mouth sought hers.

It was a long time before they spoke again. Twilight was falling gently around them, the shadows lengthening.

'I can't believe all this is happening in one single evening,' Victoria whispered against his cheek. 'Kiss me again. Convince me it's true...'

'A-ah Victoria, you drive me to distraction...' But he didn't resist. 'Can't you feel what you are doing to me, you wicked woman,' he murmured as his lips moved to the hollow at her neck.

'There's so many things I still don't know, Andrew,' she said a little anxiously, 'and I do want to be a good wife to you.'

'That's all I ask, my love. All I want is you...' He kissed her again and again and Victoria felt the heat of desire filling and swelling in her.

It was Andrew who raised his head and brought them back to earth. 'It's getting late,' he whispered. 'I must take you home.'

'I know. I'm too excited to sleep though. Shall we tell your mother and father tonight.'

'Do you want to? Are you sure?'

'Can you doubt it, Andrew Pringle! If so then I must convince you.' She launched herself back into his arms and kissed his lips. It was a little while longer before he was free again. He

331

chuckled. 'What a brazen woman I'm getting for my wife!' he teased.

'I'm not brazen,' Victoria said indignantly. Then, uncertainly: 'Am I?'

Andrew laughed aloud and seized her again. 'Whatever you are, my dearest Victoria, I love you dearly and I don't ever want you to change. Now we'd better go and tell Ma and Pa. Are you prepared for the lectures and why we must wait to get married?'

'You think they will disapprove of you marrying me?' Victoria looked up at him in the remaining light.

'They love you dearly, Victoria, and Ma always wanted you for a daughter, and you will be when we get married. But I know they will say I should have a more secure future to offer you.'

Victoria snuggled against his chest. 'You've always looked after me, Andrew, for as long as I remember. All I want is for us to be together. I want to help you to be a success at Langmune and make your dreams come true. I don't want to be like the girls at the dance who only want a husband so he will keep them. You know I don't mind hard work. I'm used to it. If we can be together surely that's what matters.'

'It is to me, dearest, but I'm warning you Ma and Pa will probably want us to wait until you're twenty-one.'

'But that's far too long!'

'I agree, and believe me, I don't want to wait. I only want to do what's best for you.'

'We must convince them. I have plans. It is what I have dreamed of but I never thought you could love me, Andrew, as – as your wife. If I save up really hard I shall be able to carry out my plan soon, and I promise I shall not be a burden to you.'

'You'll never be a burden, Victoria. Never.'

Polly was sitting by the dying fire, awaiting Victoria's return but Joe was already snoring gently behind the curtains of the box bed. She raised her eyebrows when Andrew followed her into the house.

'You're a lot later than I expected. Is everything all right?' She moved to the centre of the room to turn up the lamp and moved round to face them. 'You look...You both look different,' she finished lamely. 'What happened? Did you enjoy dinner at the doctor's house?'

'I can't believe it!' Victoria gasped. 'I'd almost forgotten how the evening began...' She turned to Andrew. He couldn't control his wide smile.

Polly looked at her eldest son suspiciously. 'Something's pleasing you, or you've had too much of the doctor's good wine.'

'We've so much to tell you, Aunt Polly, I hardly know where to begin,' Victoria said breathlessly.

'The beginning's always a good place,' Joe's sleepy voice came from behind the curtains. They heard a scuffling sound and knew he was pulling his trousers back on to come and talk to them.

'We didn't mean to disturb you, Father.'

'So what's the news? Out with it, laddie, and then I can get back to sleep.' His eyes were twinkling.

Both Joe and Polly were flabbergasted when they heard Mark Jacobs was Victoria's twin brother. They showered questions until they had the full story.

'Well I never!' Polly said for the umpteenth time. 'That's the best kept secret the folks in Darlonachie will ever have heard.'

'Mark has a friend staying,' Victoria said. 'Her name is Catriona. I think they will be engaged now.'

'You think?' Polly was puzzled. 'Don't you know?'

'Victoria was a bit upset because they hadn't told her before,' Andrew explained. 'She wanted to come away.'

'Aye, lassie,' Joe said sympathetically, 'I can understand it would be a shock.'

'But where have ye been until this time o' night then?' Polly asked.

'Talking,' Andrew said briefly. 'We had a lot of things to sort out too. Sit down, Ma.'

'Sit down?' Polly frowned and went to sit beside Joe. 'There's nothing wrong?'

'We don't think so, not now anyway,' Andrew assured her. 'I've been a fool though. I thought Victoria loved Mark Jacobs. I was jealous of him, I admit it.'

'Well, I could have told ye Mark wasna the husband for Victoria,' Polly said robustly. 'Even

334

if he is going to be a doctor and all that, and the best friend a lassie ever had.'

'Well, I wish you'd told me that.'

'You wouldna have listened if I had. And if ye'd used your eyes...'

'Victoria is going to marry me,' Andrew said at last, his smile stretching from ear to ear as he put his arm around Victoria's shoulders and drew her closer.

'Well, I'm delighted to hear it,' Polly said smiling broadly. She came across and hugged Victoria, and kissed her warmly. 'Eh, lassie, I've always wanted ye for a daughter and now you will be a real one.'

'Aye, it's good news, and we're real pleased you'll be a member of the family at last, lassie,' Joe acknowledged cautiously, 'But it willna be for a while yet, eh? Ye'll wait until Victoria's twenty-one, son?'

'What difference will that make?' Andrew's arm tightened around Victoria.

'Well, it would give ye time to see how things go with the tenancy, get a bit money gathered up. You have to be able to keep a wife, and – and bairnies too when they come along. Victoria's young yet. I feel responsible for her. Marriage is a serious business. You both need to be sure...'

'But we are!' they said in unison and turned to smile at each other in delight.

'Aye,' Joe sighed heavily. 'So it seems, but I still think ye ought to wait a while. Enjoy your courting days.' He looked at Polly for support.

'They're the happiest days of your lives –

before ye settle down and raise a family and get worries with money and such like. Your father's right, Andrew. Give Victoria time.'

'A compromise then,' Andrew suggested. 'We'll wait until the New Year. If we get married then we'll be settled before lambing. That's nearly six months.'

Polly and Joe sighed. Andrew laughed.

'Well, I suppose it gives Victoria time to change her mind if she wants to,' Joe said.

'And if we don't all get to bed it will be morning before we know it,' Polly said. 'In fact, it is morning. See it's nearly one o'clock! Miss Traill will be thinking you've had an accident, Andrew.'

'Yes, I must be on my way.' He gave Victoria a chaste kiss on the cheek, but his eyes were full of love as they looked into hers.

The following morning Victoria overslept for the first time in her life. It had been after four o'clock before she fell asleep. She hurried into her clothes and gulped down a glass of water. She needed her job more than ever now if she and Andrew were to be married. As she ran along the path, then through the castle gardens to the rear entrance she was wishing Milly was still here. She was dying to tell someone her news.

Ware was waiting in a rage and Victoria could smell singed porridge.

'Where have you been? D'ye know what time it is? I shall tell Mrs Crainby you've been slacking. While she's in London you think you'll get away with your idle ways, sly little bitch that you are.'

'Gosh, I'd forgotten Mr and Mrs Crainby are away.' Victoria exclaimed and felt a surge of relief.

'Well, don't imagine she'll not hear of the time you came to work.'

'I'm sure you'll make certain she hears,' Victoria said wryly, but she couldn't help the lightness of her heart and it was reflected in her step and her smile. Ware eyed her suspiciously.

'Shall I make Sir William some fresh porridge? He hates the singed taste when you let it burn.'

'See to it.' Ware's tone was abrupt. She sensed Victoria was happy about something. All morning she niggled at her, finding fault where there was no fault to find. Then Stella came in to help peel the vegetables.

'Morning, Victoria. We thocht ye werena coming today. Did ye enjoy going out to dinner last night?'

'I did, Stella. Thank you for asking,' Victoria said gently. Stella was small and slow-witted and she often received a tongue lashing from Ware which invariably reduced her to tears.

'Ah yes,' Ware said. 'I'd forgotten you got off early last night. Give some folks an inch and they take a mile. I shall report this to Mrs Crainby.'

'So you keep saying,' Victoria sighed. 'I've apologized. What more do you want?'

'You can work on your day off for a start. That

337

should make up for neglecting your work.'

'No.' Victoria was longing to see Andrew again already. There was no way she would give up her day off to make up for an hour's delay this morning. 'I will work an extra hour the evening Mrs Crainby returns.'

'It isn't up to you to say what you'll do. Just because you had dinner at the doctor's you needn't think you are somebody, or that his nephew will marry a trollop like you.' Ware's sneer was worse than usual and Victoria was tired, physically tired because she had not slept much, and tired of Ware's constant carping. Before she could stop herself she turned to face Ware.

'I wouldn't want to marry Mark. I am going to marry Andrew Pringle. Mark is my brother, my very own twin brother.' Even as she said the words she felt the happiness return and her spirits soar again.

Ware was gaping at her, open mouthed. 'You're mad!' Ware yelled at last. 'You're completely mad.'

'Think that if you like,' Victoria said blithely, 'but it's true.'

'Even Sir William, daft old fool that he is, even he wouldn't believe that stupid tale.'

Victoria shrugged and got on with her work, a small smile lifting the corners of her mouth as her thoughts settled on Andrew, then flitted to Mark and Catriona. As soon as she could she must go and congratulate them, tell them her own news, and apologize to Mrs Grantly for leaving so abruptly. Ware had addressed her three times before she heard, so lost was she in her own thoughts.

She knew Ware was malicious, and Mrs Crainby spiteful, but nothing prepared her for their combined reaction, even less Mrs Crainby's vengeance.

Nineteen

Henrietta Crainby had persuaded her husband to make a trip to London on the pretext of seeing a well known doctor who specialized in complaints of the stomach. Luke Crainby had been reluctant to go. For one thing he had faith in Dr Grantly and secondly the thought of making a visit to the capital and staying in a hotel, of keeping appointments and being dragged to the theatre, exhausted him before the journey even commenced.

The truth was he had not been himself for months now. He had not even had the energy to visit his pretty widow as often as usual. He had always found Maggie Lennox's company relaxing or stimulating according to his mood and since she had given him a beautiful baby son his joy had been boundless. It was for Maggie Lennox and their child that he had decided to make the effort to seek the opinion of the

London doctors.

It was unlike Henrietta to be concerned for anyone except herself, but on this occasion she appeared to have his interests at heart. He soon discovered how mistaken he had been. Her main purpose in dragging him off to London was to see the latest fashions and buy everything which took her fancy while she had the opportunity. She had expected one brief appointment with the doctor would be all that was required. Instead he had ended up with several, including one of those new fangled photographs called an X-ray, and innumerable blood samples. It had all taken more time and energy than either of them had anticipated. It had also cost a great deal more than consultations with Doctor Grantly would have done. Consequently he had tried to curb Henrietta's spending.

'I don't see why you have to be so mean,' she complained angrily. 'My mother told me your aunt and Sir William often came to London when they were young and your family had a town house as well as a house by the sea.'

'I told you before we married, Henrietta, such things happened before the war. You know my eldest brother had just come into his inheritance when he went to France. There were death duties to pay. Father was forced to sell the house in London. Besides we hardly ever came down after my mother died. As I've explained often, there are many layers of gentry. The Crainbys are in the lower echelons.'

'I don't see why I should have to scrimp so

much when you have a country estate.'

'My dear Henrietta,' Luke Crainby sighed, controlling his impatience and irritation with an effort. 'The estate needs money to maintain it. The rents – even if they were all paid in full – are needed for repairs and the payment of estate workers and your maids. Soon there will be fees for Charlotte's education. The castle is old and constantly needing maintenance. Times are not good right now. Don't you ever read the newspapers? There is too much unemployment and unrest.'

'That's in the towns, with the miners and factory workers. I married a landowner with a castle. We have a position in society. We are expected to set an example.'

'Buying extravagant gowns is scarcely setting an example to the men and women who can't afford to feed their children.'

'Well, don't expect me to make sacrifices to please your tenants. You should choose men who do pay their rent in full. Evict the rest of them.'

'For God's sake, Henrietta! Don't you realize there are big landowners in the South East of England who can't even get tenants to farm their land, even for nothing? The fields are growing wild, hedges uncut, buildings derelict. Ambitious Scottish farmers are taking advantage and moving down there to the better land. The landlords welcome them with a year free of rent. Such farmers are used to milking cows instead of cropping and they work hard. Most of them will prosper when things improve. We're lucky to have tenants who are loyal.'

'Well, I refuse to lower my standards for them.'

'Your standards!' Normally Luke Crainby walked away from such disputes – to the library, the farm office, the garden, anywhere so long as he escaped a petty argument with Henrietta. Here he felt trapped and ill and the doctor's verdict had not offered any hope. His wife had not even asked. 'Your standards,' he repeated angrily. 'You were a squire's daughter, for goodness sake, little better than the tenant farmers on Darlonachie, the people you despise so much!'

Henrietta's face flushed an ugly red. 'You – you bastard! And what about you? Oh I've heard the servants talk about you visiting your strumpet up the glen. The only female tenant. And how does she pay her rent?' she sneered.

'That is enough.' His voice was low and steely, his face pale with anger. 'We leave for home today. I shall make arrangements.'

'No. We can't do that, Luke. Come back here.' It was a command, not a request.

Luke Crainby turned at the door. 'My dear Henrietta, it was so kind of you to enquire about my health and the doctor's verdict.' She looked up at the steely tone and saw his contempt. 'I had decided not to burden you with my problems, but we both know you only married me so that you could live in a castle and call yourself Lady one day.' His lip curled. 'You will be interested to hear the doctor thinks I may have six months to live – if I am lucky. You'll be lucky if you can keep Darlonachie Castle, or the life that goes with it.'

He closed the door with a final click. Henrietta stared at it in shock. She picked up a shoe and threw it in anger. Luke Crainby heard the clatter, and guessed his wife wished she had been quick enough to throw the missile at him. His smile was grim. He was seeing things with a new clarity and his chief regret was that he had so little time to enjoy Maggie Lennox's generous loving and share her delight in watching their son grow to manhood. He must put his affairs in order without delay.

His first priority must be his father. He was sixty-five and he had not expected to outlive his only surviving son. Henrietta didn't like her father-in-law. She would not take care of him if he grew old and infirm. She had a mean streak. His other concern must be to make sure Maggie Lennox had a secure tenancy and enough capital to run the little farm for as long as she wished to live there. In fact, he thought with rare malice, it would be safer to take the farm out of the estate and put the title deeds in Maggie's name. Henrietta would be powerless to evict her then, and he knew she would try. He had become well acquainted with her jealousy and spite.

Back at Darlonachie Victoria knew nothing of Henrietta Crainby's aggravations, or her determination to demonstrate how ruthless she could be at cutting expenses. Being so happy herself she was sure it was like something in the air and

343

everyone must share it. So it was a shock when Henrietta Crainby summoned her the day after her return.

'You are dismissed, Lachlan,' she said baldly, without any warning or explanation.

'B-but what have I done?' Victoria stared at her set face, the tight lips.

'You were insolent and arrogant during my absence. You arrived late, offered no apologies and refused to make up the time.'

'That's not true! I—'

'Don't argue with me. You've always been trouble. You were responsible for Milly leaving. You are a bad influence on Stella. You tell lies.'

'I never tell lies,' Victoria said indignant at the injustice.

'You invent ridiculous stories. We all know how you pursued the doctor's nephew, cheap strumpet as you are. Now that he's to marry someone else you pretend he is your brother. No one could believe such a tissue of lies.'

'It is true. Ask Dr Grantly if—'

'I shall do no such thing. Now go.' Victoria turned towards the door but before she had opened it Henrietta Crainby said icily, 'One more thing. Now that you are no longer employed by the estate everything must be removed from Burnside cottage. Immediately. Make sure it is scrubbed ready for the next tenant.' Victoria stared at her. Then she raised her head proudly, turned and left the room. She had to get out before she lost her temper. She did not see Dr Grantly entering the main hall as she hurried the

344

short distance to the stone steps which lead to the kitchen.

Henrietta Crainby sat back in her chair exultantly. She had dealt with three birds with but a single blow. She had always considered the girl was too favoured by the Crainbys and now she had got rid of her at last; she would enjoy telling Deborah Landour the chit had had to be dismissed for insolence and insubordination. As for the cottage, it was ridiculous to leave it empty in case Lachlan needed a home. Luke thought the castle couldn't function without her family. She would find a tenant herself and charge a good rent.

Victoria was furious. She found Ware smirking in the kitchen. She had nothing to lose now. It was almost a relief. Ever since the episode over Granny's recipe book she had struggled to hold her tongue and her temper. Now she had lost her position anyway. She stood squarely in front of Ware.

'You are the most vindictive person I ever hope to meet. You're lazy and sly and you don't know anything about cooking. I hope you're satisfied. You'll be on your own now and they will all know what a rotten cook you are. There'll be no one to blame, no one to rectify your stupid mistakes. I wish you luck. You'll need it.'

Ware stared at her, mouth open; her sallow face paled even more. She hadn't expected Mrs Crainby to dismiss Lachlan. She had looked forward to seeing her cowed after a tongue lashing, and to giving her extra work on her day off.

'Y-you're leaving?'

'What did you expect after the lies you've told her. She's a fool to believe you.' Victoria kept her head high as she walked out of the kitchen, up the stone stairs and out of the front door of the castle.

As she walked along the path her anger drained away. She was hurt that anyone should believe Ware's lies, but worse was a growing feeling of despair which was replacing her earlier anger. Without a job she would have no money to carry out her plans to help Andrew. She knew he was worried about making enough money to pay the rent. She knew Joe was right, it did cost money to feed and clothe a wife, even without babies. She had devised a plan in her head to add to Andrew's income, not add to his expenses. Now she didn't even have money for clothes or board and lodgings.

Polly was astonished to see her home in the middle of the morning.

'I've been dismissed because I overslept,' she said flatly. 'Ware told a lot of lies and Mrs Crainby believed her.' Victoria's face was pale. 'What shall I do, Aunt Polly? I had so many plans to help Andrew earn enough money to pay the rent.'

'Whisht lassie, dinna worry,' Polly said, but her mouth was set and angry. She hugged Victoria. 'So Ware and Mrs Crainby have got their way at last. Well, we can all manage without them. If half the rumours are true Ware could be looking for a job herself before long.'

'But I wanted to save up to buy two sows before we get married. I don't want to be a burden to anyone, least of all Andrew.'

'You'll never be a burden to Andrew, lassie. He loves you. And he needs you beside him. You do a full day's work up there every week already. It bothers him because he can't pay you, but he knows Miss Traill can't do it any more.'

'Do you think I could put a notice in Miss Phipp's window?' Victoria asked.

'You could,' Polly said doubtfully, 'but there's not many houses around here can afford a cook. Darlonachie Estate owns most of the cottages and farms. We could put one in the post office in Annan. I could go in on Friday on the bus. I enjoy a ride on Mackie's bus.'

'All right. I'll write it out, but it seems a long time until Friday.'

'I expect there's plenty to do up at Langmune. To tell the truth it troubles me that Miss Traill is keeping house and looking after Andrew at her age, and she refuses to take any money.'

'I know.' Victoria nodded, 'but however much I help at Langmune it doesn't bring in any more money unless I can buy more animals and look after them.'

'That sounds like Dr Grantly's car.' Polly glanced out of the window. 'It is.' She opened the door almost before the doctor had time to knock.

'Good morning, Mrs Pringle, Victoria,' Peter

Grantly said lightly. 'I was in at the castle and I heard a little of the trouble. I hoped to catch you, Victoria.'

'Come in, come in, doctor. Would you like a cup of tea?'

'Yes please, Mrs Pringle. Just what the doctor ordered!' He gave his attractive smile. 'I gather Mrs Crainby didn't believe Mark is your twin brother, Victoria? I'm pleased to say I was there when she informed Mr Crainby and I was able to correct her. Her face was a picture. Not a pretty one though.' His grin was almost boyish. 'Mr Crainby is furious because she dismissed you on some pretext that Miss Ware invented. He insisted you must have your job back. I'm afraid I took it upon myself to intervene. Working in such an atmosphere, with such malice, could sour the sweetest nature. Anyway there is a much better solution.'

'A better solution?' Victoria asked.

'Why yes. Surely you can bring forward the wedding. I know Andrew will be delighted to have you at Langmune all the time, and you're needed there. Miss Traill cannot cope any longer. I'm on my way up there now to deliver some pills for her.'

'But I need to earn some money before I can marry Andrew. He is worried about paying the rent so that he can be a proper tenant with a lease. If he has to keep me as well I would add to his burdens. I was saving up to buy two sows for when we marry, so that I can rear three times as many piglets and earn extra income.' She broke off, aware that both Polly and the doctor were staring in astonishment.

'Andrew loves you, Victoria. You will never be a burden to him,' Dr Grantly said with quiet conviction.

'Pigs!' Polly squealed. 'You wanted to buy pigs? And there was I, thinking you wanted to save up for your wedding dress and your bottom drawer.'

'I don't need a bottom drawer,' Victoria said. 'There are all Granny's blankets in her chest, and the china and pots and pans.' She clapped a hand to her mouth. 'I almost forgot. Mrs Crainby wants the cottage cleared and scrubbed immediately ready for a tenant who pays rent.'

'Scrubbed?' Polly bristled. 'She can scrub it herself then. We'll empty it all right. Every last stick. We'll ask Andrew to bring a horse and cart to take your things up to the farm. But there'll be no scrubbing!'

'I doubt if she'll find a tenant around here anyway,' Dr Grantly said, before he bit into one of Polly's freshly baked scones. 'It would be a good idea if you came up to Langmune with me now, Victoria. We could tie your bicycle on the back of my car for your return. Andrew should be told what's going on.'

'Aye, so he should. Joe and me, well, we thought Victoria should wait six months or a year before she rushed into marriage. She's so young, but now...I'm sure I can persuade Joe it's for the best.'

'They know each other well enough,' Dr

Grantly said. 'We have insisted Mark and Catriona must wait until he has qualified as a doctor and can keep a wife, but this is different and Victoria deserves some happiness.'

All the way to Langmune Victoria was quiet, her thoughts turning in circles. She had so badly wanted to buy the extra pigs and earn extra money.

Andrew came out of the house when he heard the car. His lean face was strained and anxious. 'Ah, Dr Grantly I'm relieved to see you. Miss Traill doesn't know I asked you to call. She's worse this morning...' He broke off as the other door opened and Victoria climbed out. 'Victoria.' His face lit up at the sight of her. 'Am I pleased to see you!' Ignoring Dr Grantly he strode round the car and hugged her joyously. 'Maybe you will be able to make Miss Traill rest a bit. But how did you manage to come today? This is only Tuesday...Did Dr...'

'No.' Victoria shook her head. 'Oh Andrew, I've been dismissed from the castle.'

'That's not strictly true,' Dr Grantly intervened, seeing the dismissal had been a bigger blow to Victoria's confidence than he had realized. 'Mrs Crainby's trip to London was not the pleasure she anticipated. She took her anger out on Victoria. Mr Crainby wants Victoria to go back but I'm afraid I interfered. Victoria has suffered too much malice at the hands of Ware and Mrs Crainby. Anyway it would be better for Miss Traill if you bring the wedding date forward, Andrew. Your mother agrees, but only you

350

two can decide that.'

'Mother agreed to that?' Andrew swung Victoria off her feet in his exuberance. 'And to think when I got up this morning the world seemed so black, and the next six months like an eternity. Please excuse us and go into the house, Doctor Grantly.' He grinned widely. Dr Grantly's eyes twinkled as he smiled at them both.

'I don't want to be another burden for you, Andrew,' Victoria said urgently as soon as they were alone. 'I want to be independent and I want to contribute too.' Her chin wobbled.

'Ah, my wee Vicky. You're bringing me the most precious thing in the world.' His voice was low and intense. 'We'll talk later, but I can't tell you how happy it would make me if we were together. I dream of wakening up with you beside me every morning, and lying beside me when I go to sleep at night.' He chuckled when Victoria blushed, then he added seriously, 'But I am worried about Miss Traill too. I think she will listen to you better than she does to me.'

'I'm not so sure about that, especially when she hears I've been sacked from my job. I – I feel so inadequate. I don't think I can marry you, Andrew.'

'What?' Andrew stared at Victoria. The colour drained from his face. 'You can't mean that, Victoria,' he whispered hoarsely.

'I can't get married just because I have nothing else to do. Don't you see? I'd be like the other girls, marrying you because I need kept. You must see...'

'No! I do not see. Dear God, Victoria!' He pushed a hand through his thick hair. 'We wanted to get married anyway. It was only my parents who insisted we wait.'

'They were right,' Victoria said stubbornly. 'I don't want to marry you, or anyone else, if I'm not capable of earning my living.'

'We'll talk about it later,' Andrew said shortly. 'Miss Traill needs us now.'

They found Dr Grantly bending over Miss Traill's leg. Victoria gasped when she saw how badly swollen it was.

'You've been overdoing things,' Dr Grantly was saying. 'You must keep it up on a stool, Miss Traill. I shall send you a liniment but meanwhile I have brought you some tablets for the pain and to reduce the inflammation.'

'Thank you, doctor,' Miss Traill said wearily. She looked up and saw Andrew and Victoria a step behind.

'Victoria? Oh, my dear. The angels must be looking down on me. You don't know how relieved I am to see you today. There's so much to do.'

'You see, Victoria,' Andrew said. 'We all need you. It's nonsense to imagine you should work somewhere else. I'm the one with a problem. We need your help so badly but I have no money to pay you a wage. You may as well say I want a slave bride.'

Victoria frowned, chewing her lip. It was clear Miss Traill needed to rest.

'If Mrs Crainby only knew it, she has done me

the best favour possible,' Andrew said. 'The harvest will soon be ready for the binder and every pair of hands will be needed to stook the sheaves.'

Victoria was silent. She would rather be at Langmune, and she did want to help Miss Traill. If only she could have done something to bring extra money to help pay the rent. Later she tried to explain this to him but he was adamant that one more mouth to feed would never be noticed.

'Even if you ate a mountain of food it would still be worth it to have your help, Victoria. It seems to me you were sent from heaven when we needed you.'

'All right then, I'll come up every day and help with the harvest, until Miss Traill has recovered.'

'We'll get married as soon as it can be arranged, then you'll not need to go home every night,' Andrew said with a sigh of satisfaction.

'I must earn more money first.'

'I've never known you so bothered about money.' Andrew frowned. 'You've always saved a bit each week, as we all did.'

Apart from needing money towards the rent Victoria couldn't explain that her dismissal made her feel a failure. Miss Traill said she had too much pride, and that was a sin.

'If Andrew is short of money, he knows I can give him a loan,' she said. 'All I want is to see you both happily married. Between us we shall see that he does not lose the tenancy of Langmune for the sake of the rent.'

Ten days later a letter arrived for Victoria from Lady Landour. It was late evening by the time Victoria got back to the cottage and opened it.

'She's offering me the job as Cook again,' she said, waving the letter jubilantly at Polly. 'She says the pay and everything else is the same as before. She doesn't believe a word of the character Mrs Crainby has written about me...' Victoria gasped and stared at Polly. 'Mrs Crainby must have written to tell her I had been dismissed.' The smile died from her eyes.

'That shows how spiteful Mrs Crainby is,' Joe Pringle muttered.

'She's a bitch,' George said through gritted teeth.

'Well, it doesn't matter anyway,' Polly declared. 'It's backfired. Lady Landour believes in Victoria. Now I hope that reassures you, lassie, and you can forget about needing a job and earning money before you can get married.'

'Lady Landour says she can easily believe Mark is my brother. She only saw us together once but she was struck by our resemblance. She thinks we have the same smile and the same big brown eyes and chestnut hair.'

'Aye, so you have, now she mentions it,' Polly said. 'It's strange how none of us noticed.'

'Josh noticed,' George said. 'He once remarked on the way they both looked but I told him he was talking daft.'

'Not so daft though, was he?' his father chuckled. 'Strangers and children often notice things that are right under our noses.'

'She seems to have written a friendly letter for a lady offering employment,' Polly remarked. 'But surely you'll tell her you're getting married?'

'I don't know...' Victoria said slowly. 'Before I do anything I must clear Granny's cottage. Andrew said he would bring down a horse and cart at the weekend.'

'I'll lend a hand,' George volunteered.

'And after that?' Polly persisted.

'I don't want to go away, but I did want to buy extra pigs so that I could look after them and earn more money for Andrew. Miss Traill isn't making a very quick recovery though. She tires easily.'

'Well, she is over seventy,' Joe reminded them. 'I get tired easier than I did when I was your age, young Victoria.' His eyes twinkled.

'It's a relief to know Lady Landour didn't believe all those nasty things.'

'Ach, lassie.' Polly came over and hugged her. 'You shouldn't take any notice of women like Mrs Crainby. They're only happy if they're criticising.'

'I dinna think Mrs Crainby is ever happy,' Joe grunted. 'Mr Luke has been away a lot in the car lately but he was walking through the gardens yesterday. He always stops for a chat. He looked real sad, I thought, and he doesn't seem in good health.'

'Maybe that's why Dr Grantly's car has been up at the castle so often lately,' Polly mused. She looked at Victoria and sighed. 'Is it only the money to buy silly old pigs that bothers ye, Victoria?'

'It is now.' Victoria nodded. She laughed aloud and twirled around the kitchen, waving the letter. 'I knew in my heart that I wasn't as wicked and useless as Mrs Crainby said, but now I feel a worthwhile person again.'

'Well, I'm jolly glad to hear it,' George grunted. 'You know, Victoria Lachlan, for a lassie who is supposed to be intelligent, you were a silly bugger for taking any notice o' such a besom.'

'George! You swore. Tell him off, Joe,' Polly urged.

'We-ell...' Joe winked at Victoria. 'I think maybe he's right for once.'

'Aye, so he is,' Polly agreed. 'So I'll tell you a wee secret I've been keeping as a surprise until you and Andrew got married, Victoria.'

'A secret?' Victoria asked intrigued. Polly was not known for being able to keep a secret.

'Aye. When you first came to live with us, and you started work in the castle kitchens, Sir William came to see Joe and me. He insisted on paying us for your board and lodging and he paid far more than he should have done. You ate most of your meals at the castle for one thing, and you insisted on buying your own clothes. Anyway Joe and me agreed we would use half the money and put the other half in the bank for you.'

'But that's your money, Aunt Polly. I can't...'

'Yes you can. That miserable woman never

did pay you what you were worth and I reckon Sir William guessed what she would be like once she married Mr Luke, so he set things up to compensate a wee bit. Anyway I always hoped ye'd marry one o' my laddies and be a proper daughter, and now you will be. So I'll get the money from the bank and if you want to use it to buy pigs instead of fancy clothes for your wedding you can, so long as Andrew agrees. That way maybe the money will benefit both o' ye and make ye happy together, and we shall be happy too.'

'Aye, Victoria, Polly is right,' Joe said. 'It's what we'd both like to see.'

'Oh, Aunt Polly! I don't know what to say, or how to thank you both.' She flung herself into Polly's arms.

Andrew arrived on Saturday morning with the horse and cart. As soon as she saw him Victoria ran to tell him of his mother's generosity and how she wanted to buy two sows if he agreed.

'So long as I have you, Victoria, I don't care about anything else,' Andrew assured her and stole a kiss before the rest of his family appeared. All of them had volunteered to help clear the cottage. Polly examined the blankets in the wooden blanket chest.

'They smell terrible, Mother.' Andrew held his nose and grinned.

'That's because we put so many camphor balls in to keep the moths away. They'll be fine when Victoria has given them a good wash and dried them in the sunshine. Have you got a good mangle up at Langmune for ringing the water out?'

'The rollers are a bit worn and getting too wide,' Victoria said. 'We'd better take Granny's. Be careful with the two boxes in the corner Andrew. They're full of Granny's best china.'

'Hey, Victoria,' George called from upstairs. 'There's a huge cupboard up here. It's solid as a rock.'

'We'll never shift it in one piece,' Willie said. They all trooped upstairs to inspect the little loft room where Victoria had slept.

'Granny McCrady said the estate joiner made it for my mother when she was twelve. It was always too heavy to move but Mrs Crainby said the cottage had to be completely emptied.'

'Don't worry,' Josh said grinning. 'It will be easy enough to take the doors off. Andrew can build you another cupboard and make use of them. We can chop up the rest of the frame for firewood. It seems to be fixed to the wall to prevent it toppling over but the back and shelves are made of good strong pine.'

The brothers worked together happily and Andrew stacked everything neatly in the cart, agreeing he would return for the mangle and the washtubs another day. Gradually the heavy cupboard was taken apart by Josh and Willie.

'Here's an old letter or something,' Josh said. 'It must have fallen down the gap between the cupboard and the wall.'

'It can't be important. Somebody screwed it up. Looks as though they tossed it in the air and it fell down the back,' Willie remarked.

'Let me see,' Victoria said with a smile. 'I wonder how old it is.'

'Good quality paper anyway,' Josh remarked casually. He threw the screw of paper across to her and went on dismantling the cupboard.

Victoria began to smooth it out. It had a crest on top, the crest of the Crainby family. She recognized it as the same sort of paper which was always left ready on Sir William's writing table in the library and in each of the guest bedrooms. Curiously she began to read. The black ink had faded a little but the writing was perfectly legible. The boys were too busy dismantling to notice the colour drain from her face, or to bother when she went stumbling blindly down the stairs.

'This letter, Andrew,' she gasped. 'It was written to my m-mother.'

'Victoria! You're white as a ghost. Whatever's the matter?' Andrew put an arm around her and led her to the grassy bank at the side of the cottage. They sat side by side. 'What does it say?'

'Read it. I think – I think I know...who my father w-was...'

Twenty

Andrew scanned the sheet of thick, yellowing paper. He drew in his breath and began to read again, more slowly. Could it mean what he thought it meant?

16th February 1917

My dearest little Friend,

It will be dawn soon but I cannot sleep. I fear I may never sleep again with easy conscience. In my head I hear you pleading. I hear your bewilderment. Why, oh why did I not listen to you in the cave, pleading to cease from my evil passion. Can you ever forgive me, Elizabeth? The darkest of devils had me in their possession. I had sought to drown my memories of hell and its horrors. Instead I drank the whisky and wine and became an animal, an animal deaf to your pleas. May God forgive, me for I cannot forgive myself.

Nothing, not even my fearful dread of returning to the trenches, with their stench of death and decay, can ever excuse the way I treated you, dearest Elizabeth. You of all people, friend of my childhood, with your merry laughter and kindly spirit.

I pray to God, that you, with your generosity, I pray you may forgive me. I need your pardon so very badly. I leave tomorrow for France. Please send me a token that you understand it was not I who attacked you so cruelly, but some demon in my fearful soul. My innocent little friend, without your forgiveness I shall have no reason to go on living.

You have my promise that I shall always treat you with honour and respect, Elizabeth. If, by the grace of God, I return from this evil that is war, I shall plead with you to become my wife.

Ever your faithful friend,
Rodderick Manton

PS I beg you to take this letter to my mother if you should find yourself in need of help, Elizabeth.

R.

Andrew looked up from the sheet of paper and met Victoria's eyes. She was shivering although the afternoon was warm. He folded the letter carefully and put his arm around her.

'I think you should show this to Dr Grantly. It may make sense to him. He brought you into the world and he has been more than generous to Mark. If it means what we think it means then he deserves to know.'

'Will you come with me? I need you so much, Andrew.'

'Of course I will, my love. I think we should keep it to ourselves for now. We could call on Dr Grantly after church tomorrow.'

'All right.' Victoria nodded. 'Can we leave now? The cart seems almost full.'

'Yes, we'll get away to Langmune and collect the few remaining things another day. You sit up front.' He lifted her as though she was a feather and seated her in the front of the cart where he had left a space for her. She gave him a wan smile of gratitude. 'I'll shout upstairs and tell them we're away,' he said.

Doctor Grantly was surprised to see Andrew and Victoria but he welcomed them warmly. Victoria handed him the letter. Puzzled by her strained face he began to read it. Like Andrew he had to read it twice to take it in.

'Well,' he said at last, expelling a long breath, 'this explains so many things.' His wife came through from the kitchen with a tray of tea and a plate of biscuits. 'Do you mind if my wife reads this?'

'No,' Victoria said as she shook her head, 'but we have not told anyone else yet.'

'I think you should go with Andrew and Victoria to the castle and show this to Sir William,' Anna Grantly said when she had finished reading the letter. 'I know he is getting old, but you did say his memory is excellent, didn't you, dear?'

'It is, but this may prove rather a shock,' Dr Grantly said doubtfully. 'Rodderick Manton was his nephew after all, his sister's only child.'

'I know, but he is the best person alive to remember that night. Didn't he mention more than once that Victoria reminded him of his sister when she was a child? According to this it is likely she was Victoria's grandmother. Maybe there was reason for his fancies.'

'Even so I wouldn't like to upset him, but...yes,' he said more decisively, 'we owe it to Victoria, and to Mark, to shed what light we can on this, and Sir William has come through more troubles than most in his lifetime, and now he seems likely to outlive his youngest son.'

Victoria gasped and stared at Dr Grantly.

'I apologize,' he said awkwardly. 'I should not have said that aloud. It's the shock. Normally I am very careful to keep a patient's confidence. Mr Crainby has a serious illness but I trust you will both keep that to yourselves.'

Andrew and Victoria nodded but Andrew felt his heart sink. If Mr Crainby were to die there was little hope of him being granted the tenancy if Mrs Crainby took over the estate. Was that why she wanted the cottage emptied all of a sudden? Was she preparing to make changes already?

Victoria knew she would never have been allowed into the castle through the front entrance if Dr Grantly had not been with them. They were shown into the library where Sir William had been dozing in front of the fire. He greeted them affably. After preliminary greetings Dr Grantly drew the sheet of paper from his pocket and slowly smoothed it out before placing it on the desk in front of Sir William.

'This may be a shock to you, Sir William, but we think this letter may have been written by your nephew. We would like your opinion.'

'My nephew...?' The old man drew the letter towards him and adjusted his spectacles. He read slowly and carefully. When he looked up a little of the colour seemed to have drained from his lined cheeks but he did not appear unduly shocked. 'Where did you get this?'

'It was behind the wardrobe in Granny's cottage,' Victoria explained. 'It had never been moved since the day it was built for my mother.'

'I see...' he said again and his eyes took on a faraway look. 'The date, you know, it was written the morning after Billy's coming of age. Roddy had been granted a short leave. He travelled to Scotland specially for the party but he tried to advise Billy not to enlist, I remember. Oh yes, I remember it all so clearly now. Billy laughed and told Roddy he wanted to keep all the adventures and medals to himself, but Roddy didn't laugh.'

'I saw a big change in the boy. We all did. He had spent a lot of time here, at the castle. He was a gentle laddie. He hated to see cruelty. He didn't like to watch the horses being broken for work even. He had become a man all of a sudden, a man with a grim set to his mouth and a dark brooding expression. I didn't like that. It troubled me. On the evening of the party he barely danced, yet he had always loved dancing.

He sat alone much of the time, drinking and brooding.' Sir William blinked and brought his mind back to the present. He looked at the three faces. He frowned and fixed his gaze on Andrew.

'And you are?'

'Andrew Pringle, Sir William. My father is your gardener. I am the tenant at Langmune, at least for now.'

'I see...Why are you here?'

'We're going to be married soon, Sir William,' Victoria said quickly and moved closer to Andrew.

'I see.' The old man nodded.

'Do you believe the letter was written by your nephew, Sir William?' Dr Grantly asked, recalling his attention to the business.

'Yes, I do. I have no doubts. I remember his mother thought he was too ill to return to France, although he had been pronounced physically fit for active service. Her mother's instinct was probably right. It was completely out of character for Roddy to have behaved as he did towards Elizabeth that night.' He tapped the letter with his finger and shook his head in distress. 'They all loved her. She was a good child. It was unforgivable under any circumstances. If only my sister had known...And you, Victoria, your birth would at least have given her a reason to live.

'Before she died she told me Roddy had done something of which he was bitterly ashamed, so wicked he could not tell her. She assumed it was the killing of his fellow men. He wept. She knew it was something he would never forget. Now we know he had good reason for his remorse. Your mother was a child, Victoria, a beautiful, happy child who had lost both her parents in my service. Oh yes, my dear, the Crainby family owe your family a debt which can never be repaid, so Roddy's behaviour was doubly wicked and unforgivable. I hear you have a twin brother too? Now that was a surprise, Doctor Grantly.'

'Yes, I'm sure it was, but at the time I thought I was acting for the best.'

'And no doubt you did. I understand the boy is intelligent and you have given him a good education.' He lifted his eyes to Victoria. 'I don't know how to begin to recompense you, dear child.'

'All I want is confirmation, sir. Now I know who I am at last. I feel...complete.' She beamed up at Andrew and he smiled back.

Sir William watched them and nodded. 'Thank you for bringing this to me, Dr Grantly.' He handed back the letter.

'Mark will be interested to read it too.'

Henrietta Crainby had asked one of the maids who was with Sir William. Curiously she made a point of being in the hall as they made their way to the door. She had been prepared for Dr Grantly but she was astonished and indignant when she saw not only Victoria, but the gardener's son too, walking to the front door no less.

'Lachlan! How dare you come here? And you...' She glared at Andrew but Dr Grantly interrupted calmly.

'We had a matter of great importance to discuss with Sir William, Mrs Crainby. Now if you will excuse us?' He took Victoria's arm and guided her to the entrance and down the steps. They all breathed deeply in the fresh cool air.

Then Andrew grinned. 'I'm glad you're finished at the castle, Victoria. I don't know how you survived so long.'

'Yes, it is a relief to be free. If only Mrs Crainby had not said those awful things.'

'When she learns the reason for our visit I suspect Mrs Crainby will get the biggest shock of all,' Dr Grantly mused. 'She will certainly have reason to eat her words. Very indigestible she will find them too, I imagine.'

In fact Henrietta Crainby lost no time in finding her husband. He was lying on the long window seat asleep. She did not pause to consider how thin his face had grown recently, or how sallow his skin looked. She shook him awake impatiently.

'Dr Grantly has been here. He brought Lachlan. The gardener's son was with them. He said they had business with your father. You are supposed to be the laird now. Find out what they wanted.'

Luke Crainby opened his eyes reluctantly. He slept badly most nights and he was grateful to snatch a few pain-free hours where and when he could. Twice recently he had spent the night at the little farm up the glen with Maggie and enjoyed a few hours of peaceful repose. He had been comforted by her soothing voice as they talked away the remainder of the night. He had no passion left now but Maggie's was a gentle, selfless companionship and he was eternally grateful to her. That he would be leaving her so soon was his only regret.

'Luke!' Henrietta's harsh voice shattered his reflections. Her bony fingers dug into his shoulder as she shook him. 'Did you hear what I said?'

'I heard. I'm sure Father will tell us at dinner, if Dr Grantly's business was any of our concern.'

'It is our concern. They showed him a letter.'

Luke slowly brought his feet to the floor and sat up. 'You wakened me for a letter?'

'It was from your cousin. An old letter...Or supposed to be!'

'And how could you know that, dear Henrietta?' His voice had a bitter twist. 'Listening at the door again, were you?'

'The door was open a little. I happened to be in the hall.'

'Whatever it was, my father will tell us if we need to know.'

'I'll tell you now, dear boy,' Sir William said from the doorway.

Henrietta spun around, guilt colouring her face. Sir William was leaning on his stick. How much had he overheard?

'Do you want me to come to the library,

Father?'

'No. Henrietta may as well listen openly.' He eased himself on to a hard, high-backed chair, leaning on his silver-topped cane, with one hand clasped on top of the other. Henrietta was in a ferment of impatience.

'Dr Grantly brought a letter for my opinion. I was able to confirm that it was written by your cousin Roddy. Without doubt Victoria, and her brother, are his children.'

'That's ridiculous!' Henrietta jumped to her feet. 'The letter must be a fake!'

'It was no fake. It was written from here, on paper with the Crainby crest.'

'Lachlan could easily have stolen the paper. She had plenty of opportunity. Oh, she's clever, that one. You taught her to write yourself.' She glared accusingly at her father-in-law.

'I doubt if such a thing would enter Victoria's head. Why should it? She wants nothing from me, nothing except to know who she is. The inheritance she should have had has already been squandered.' Sir William's eyes were cold and challenging. Henrietta was the first to look away.

Her stepfather, Sir Joshua Manton, had been killed after a fall from his horse soon after she married Luke. Her mother had never been able to manage money. Eighteen months ago she had died quietly in her sleep. Instead of grieving Henrietta had been furious when she discovered the small estate had been entailed. After the funeral expenses had been paid and the debts settled there had been little left of the fortune she had anticipated.

'I don't believe the letter was genuine,' Henrietta insisted. 'Maybe Dr Grantly put her up to it.'

'For the love of God, Henrietta, what will you think of next?' Luke exclaimed angrily. 'Where is the letter, Father? May I see it?'

'Dr Grantly took it away with him. He wanted to show it to the boy. It demonstrated Roddy's contrition for the way he had treated Elizabeth. It also showed something of his black and troubled thoughts. I believe he hated war.'

'But the men who returned, those from his battalion, all spoke so highly of his bravery.'

'It's possible it was a bravery borne of desperation...and remorse. Perhaps he felt he didn't deserve to survive. We shall never know.' Sir William sighed. 'We can only pray his soul now rests in peace.'

'Yes, I hope it does.'

'When was it written, this letter?' Henrietta demanded.

'It was written on the morning following the coming of age of my eldest son,' Sir William said, shaking his white head sadly as memories flitted through his mind.

'I remember Billy's party well,' Luke said. 'I was allowed to stay up late that night. I remember thinking there was a sort of false happiness in the air, as though everyone wanted to make the most of it, and yet...and yet...I didn't understand then of course that so many of them would 'never come back.'

'For goodness sake do you have to be so melancholy, Luke!' Henrietta snapped. 'If Lachlan didn't want anything, why did she bother coming? Why did they bring the letter? She must want something.'

'As I said, all she wanted was confirmation that it was written by the man who was her father,' Sir William said testily. He rose to his feet. 'We'll discuss this later.'

'Very well, Father. I will come to the library straight after breakfast in the morning. Dr Grantly will be calling to see me later on. I would like to hear the details before he arrives.'

Henrietta waited until Sir William left the room.

'I can't see what there is to discuss,' she said sharply.

'Can't you, Henrietta? Even you must realize those two children have been deprived of their inheritance.'

'I don't know what you're talking about,' Henrietta muttered sullenly.

'The girl you've been treating as a kitchen slave is my cousin's child. A child who would have inherited my aunt's money and her grandfather's property. I wonder if your mother would have been so keen to marry Uncle Josh if she had known he had two grandchildren?'

'They're illegitimate. They're bastards!'

'Their father was killed fighting for his country,' Luke spoke through gritted teeth, his face pale. How had he ever allowed himself to be

371

inveigled into marriage with such a shrew? He made towards the door.

'What are you going to do?'

'I shall consider what small recompense I can make.'

'It's not your responsibility! You can't deprive my daughter...'

'Our daughter,' he corrected. 'Charlotte will benefit from a good education, an opportunity Victoria has never had.' He opened the door and left abruptly, leaving Henrietta staring after him with narrowed eyes.

The following morning Luke went to the library. Sir William had gone over and over Roddy's letter in his mind and now he recounted the details.

'So there's no doubt in your mind about the authenticity of the letter, or that Victoria and her twin are Roddy's children?'

'I have no doubt at all. There were many small things about Victoria which used to remind me of my sister as a child. It is my greatest regret the truth has taken so long to come to light.'

'Yes, I can understand that, Father. If there is anything you want me to do I shall attend to it without delay. I think you know my time is limited.'

'So...it is as I feared, Luke?' Sir William rubbed his brow, a habit he had when worried or disturbed. 'Is there nothing Dr Grantly can do?'

'There's nothing anyone can do. The doctors in London confirmed his opinion.'

'I see...Are your own affairs in order?'

'I thought they were, but now I want to do something for Victoria. Her brother will make his own way in life. Dr Grantly has been generous. He has had a good education and will qualify as a doctor in a couple of years.'

'Have you any suggestions?'

'As you know there will be death duties to pay on Darlonachie again,' Luke sighed. 'This place takes too much in maintenance. I had hoped you would never have to leave it, Father, but...'

'Don't worry about me, Luke. My time is nearly over.'

'Sixty-five is not so very old. I want to be sure you are comfortable and content however long you live. The factor has been overseeing an extension to Home Farm. It looks good now it is almost finished. Would you like me to drive you over to see?'

'Yes, I would. You think I should move there?'

'You would be comfortable. It is smaller and easier to maintain. One room is particularly suited to a library. I should like to know you are...secure.' He couldn't tell his father he didn't trust his own wife. 'John Swift would like to remain as your farm manager. There will be a new factor. Forsythe intends to move on when my time comes, so I've removed Home Farm from the estate. It will be yours to do with as you wish.'

'I see. You think that is necessary, Luke?'

'Yes, I do. Shall we discuss other matters as we drive?' He was sure Henrietta was hovering in the hall again.

'Victoria is going to marry Andrew Pringle,' he said when his father was settled in the Bentley. 'He's a good man. Mr Rennie praised him highly. He would like a lease and a proper tenancy agreement for Langmune.'

'You think he'll manage to make a living? Farming is very depressed.'

'I believe he will do as well as, if not better than, the other tenants, but now I know Victoria is Roddy's daughter I have another suggestion and I would like your opinion, Father. I have little time to lose and Mr Jenkinson is going to London next week. I shall ask him to attend to my affairs as soon as he can fit them in.'

The following day Luke Crainby called at the Pringles' cottage in search of Victoria.

'She goes to Langmune every day now,' Polly told him. 'You'll find her there.'

Luke Crainby nodded. He was oblivious to the time these days. He had little appetite for food and Ware's abysmal efforts did nothing to tempt him. He arrived at Langmune as Victoria was dishing out bowls of chicken soup.

'That smells good,' he remarked involuntarily. 'We're missing your cooking at Darlonachie, Victoria.'

'Would you care to join us, Mr Crainby?' Miss Traill asked, seeing Victoria's uncertainty. She thought the poor man was in need of a good meal. She didn't know how ill he was.

'I would indeed, thank you. Perhaps we can discuss your lease for Langmune as we dine, Andrew?'

'If that is your wish, Mr Crainby,' Andrew agreed cautiously, joining them round the kitchen table.

Victoria was pink with embarrassment. The table was spotlessly clean but there was no table cloth on and it was too late to lay it as she would have done if she had known Mr Crainby was joining them for lunch. She began to apologize.

'Ah, Victoria, if you only knew,' Luke Crainby said with a sigh, 'some of my happiest memories were of following your grandmother down to the castle kitchens when I was a small boy. We ate at a table like this. Mrs McCrady always made favourite dishes for Billy and me when it was Nanny's day off, and later when I was on holiday from school. Don't you remember?'

'Yes, I remember.' Victoria smiled. She thought he would have forgotten the days which had seemed so carefree and so long ago. She was glad he hadn't.

'You have set your heart on farming then, Andrew, in spite of the hard work and poor returns?'

'It is what I have always wanted to do, sir. I – I...Victoria and I plan to get married soon though. I would like to feel I could offer her some security. If you could grant me a proper lease, even three years...?' He flushed and broke off, wondering if he was asking too much before he had proved himself.

'I have a better plan. You are certain farming is the future both of you want?'

'It is,' they said in unison and smiled shyly at

375

each other.

'And we would like to know Miss Traill could share our home without anxiety too,' Victoria said earnestly.

'I understand. This is what I propose to do then, but there are disadvantages to my proposition too.' They all waited tensely for him to explain.

'I propose to put the deeds for Langmune farm into your name, Victoria. It is small recompense for what you should have had if my cousin had lived to claim you as his daughter. Unfortunately, the past can never be undone but—'

'Oh, but I never wanted...I never expected...' Victoria broke off in confusion.

'Nevertheless it is what I intend to do. My father approves.' He didn't notice that Andrew had gone a shade paler, nor did he see the look of consternation in his blue eyes. He went on. 'You will both have some security. Even with a lease there are ways of evicting tenants. That is not a risk I intend to take. I regret the house is so poor, especially in comparison to the former dwelling. The disadvantage in being the owner means you have to pay for your own repairs.' He grimaced. 'I'm afraid Mr Rennie did that anyway. The estate is no more prosperous than its tenants at the present time. So what do you think, Andrew?'

'It means I shall be marrying my landlord,' he said promptly, his pride rising in revolt.

'It is a kind and generous offer,' Victoria said hurriedly, 'but it is Andrew who is the farmer.

Please don't think I am ungrateful, but could you put it in his name?'

'I could, or in joint names. At the end of the day it is only a piece of land.' He sighed wistfully. 'You two have the most precious gift of all, a selfless love for each other. If only you knew how precious that is. To have the one you love to share your life, to be your friend and your partner in all things. It seems to me you two have found that love in each other.'

A dull colour suffused Andrew's face and then it cleared. He looked Mr Crainby in the eye.

'You are right, sir. Victoria means more to me than anything in the world, even the farm. Would it be possible for Mr Jenkinson to make us partners together in everything, the stock as well as the land?'

'Indeed it would. What do you think, Victoria?'

'So long as we can be together I am happy.' Her cheeks were pink and she smiled shyly.

Miss Traill nodded in approval. 'That is a splendid solution. These two young people both have too much pride.'

'I shall instruct Mr Jenkinson without delay.' Luke Crainby smiled broadly. 'And may you always have a pretty wife who is so compliant with your wishes, Andrew.'

'I know Victoria has too much spirit for that,' he chuckled, 'but I think we shall do very well together.' His eyes were filled with love as they met Victoria's.

'I also intend to transfer the small cottage next

to the smithy into your brother's name, Victoria,' Luke Crainby went on. 'He will always have a home near to you if he wishes to return to Darlonachie. I hope it will strengthen your family ties.'

'Thank you. That is very thoughtful, and generous. I don't want to lose Mark now that we have found each other as brother and sister.'

'Perhaps we could call on Mr Jenkinson this afternoon, but not until I have finished Victoria's delicious caramel custard. It is one of my favourites.' Luke Crainby smiled, though Victoria thought it only accentuated the hollows and planes of his thin face and her heart ached for him.

He sat quietly by the fire as he waited for Andrew to wash and change. He closed his blue veined eyelids and Victoria saw how ill and gaunt he had become. When Andrew returned to the kitchen Luke Crainby looked up at him with a wan smile.

'I have a great favour I would ask of you, Andrew Pringle. If you refuse it will have no effect on what we are about to do, I promise.'

'If there is anything I can do for you, Mr Crainby, I shall be happy to oblige,' Andrew said, his blue eyes widening.

'When you are in the top fields of Langmune, if you look across the burn and up the glen you will see a small farm and a white house, nestling in the fold of the hill.'

'Yes, I know it. High Bowie Farm?'

'That's right. It has a large area of heather

covered hill land, but it has two hundred acres of good land and it is in excellent order. I advised Mrs Lennox on various strategies during her husband's illness. Since he died we have become friends, er...very close friends. She has a child. A little boy. We call him Billy. His full name is William Crainby Lennox.' He held Andrew's gaze steadily. 'When I am gone Maggie may need advice occasionally, maybe a little help even, though she has a good man who has served her family well. I would like to think there was someone trustworthy to whom she could turn if needed, or –' his gaze moved to Victoria – 'a friendly face now and then.' A faint flush stained his sallow skin.

'Please tell Mrs Lennox I shall be pleased to have her call at Langmune any time,' Victoria said sincerely. 'That is when I am living here.' She looked at Andrew but his smile was warm and reassuring as he nodded agreement.

'And the sooner that happens the better,' he grinned. 'If I can help Mrs Lennox with the farm I shall be happy to do so.'

'Thank you, both of you,' he said and there was no doubt he seemed relieved by their response. He knew in his heart that Henrietta would try every possible provocation to oust Maggie Lennox once he was gone. She would be furious when she discovered he had transferred the farm into her name, and the Home Farm back to his father. He had no idea how Andrew or Victoria might help but he was relieved to know they would do their best to befriend Maggie.

He had hesitated about introducing his mistress and her young son to his father, but time was running out. He wanted Billy to know his grandfather.

The meeting had gone better than he had dared to hope. He had taken his father to view the improvements to Home Farm, leaving him to wander around the rooms, deciding which furniture and books he wanted to bring from the castle. Only the large sitting room had been furnished and a fire burned cheerfully in the grate. It was a lovely room with a fine view. Luke collected Maggie and three-year-old Billy and drove them down to the house.

Maggie was wary, and diffident, but his father took her hand in his firm grip and assured her he was pleased to meet her. His shrewd blue eyes fixed on the small boy, then travelled swiftly to the single painting hanging on the wall. It was of his wife, with Billy, his eldest son at her side, and Felix on her knee. It had been painted before Luke was born. Sir William looked back again at the child standing quietly beside his mother, though his blue eyes were alight with curiosity.

'They are so alike...' Sir William said softly, looking again at the painting. He lifted his cane and pointed at the boy in the portrait. 'He was Billy too. He looks like you, young man.' He then said to Maggie, 'I hope you will bring him to see me often, Mrs Lennox. I shall be moved here within a week. Yes, call whenever you wish.'

Luke had felt his heart fill with love and pride for the three people smiling at each other. He was certain they were going to be friends.

Twenty-One

Ten days after Luke Crainby's visit to Langmune news of his death spread rapidly around the estate. The cancer had won. Two days earlier Andrew and Victoria had been summoned to Mr Jenkinson's office to sign the necessary documents which made them joint owners and farmers of Langmune Farm.

'I never expected Mr Crainby to give me anything,' Victoria told Miss Traill, 'but I am thankful he acted with such speed. I know Mrs Crainby would have made our life impossible. It would have ruined Andrew's dreams.'

'I think Mr Crainby understood that, but he seemed far too young to die,' she sighed. 'Poor man. Death does not distinguish between slave and master.'

Two weeks later Andrew and Victoria were married as they had planned in the little village church with their families and friends to wish them well. They had intended it to be a very quiet affair but Mrs Grantly had organized some of the ladies from the church to help her prepare a wedding breakfast. Miss Traill had secretly baked a large cake and Dr Grantly had taken it to one of his patients to be iced in white. Polly and Miss Phipps had sewn a white silk gown for Victoria, and with the addition of the veil Polly had worn, she looked ethereal. Polly shed a few tears.

'Why are you crying, Mother?' Andrew asked. 'I'm not going to ill-treat my beautiful bride, you know.'

'I know that, son. It's a mother's privilege...' She hugged Victoria tightly.

'I'll bet you don't cry when I get married,' George teased.

'Oh yes, I shall. They'll be tears of joy to pass you on to someone else,' Polly retorted, though everyone knew she loved all her boys and she was longing for them to provide her with grandchildren.

Victoria blushed when she heard these comments, but later that night when she and Andrew were alone at last in the narrow little house at Langmune, she discovered a joy far greater than anything she had dreamed of.

'If this is how babies are made I think we shall have a very large family, Andrew,' she said softly.

'You'll never know how often I have longed for this,' he murmured as his lips explored her silken skin one more time. All their fears and inhibitions had been swept away in the passion of their loving. Andrew had been gentle, concerned that Victoria might be alarmed by the depths of his feelings. He need not have worried. She was young but she loved him with an age-old passion and she was generous in her giving.

Andrew offered a silent prayer of thankfulness that he had been so truly blessed.

'You always were quick to learn,' he whispered against the softness of her breast and felt the desire swell within her at the touch of his lips.

'And you, dearest Andrew, were always the best teacher I ever had.'

'Then I hope you will never need another in these particular lessons,' he whispered huskily.

'Never. I've loved you for as long as I can remember, Andrew Pringle. I know our love will last until the end of time.'